"Intriguing, original." —*Kirkus Reviews*

"I found *A Coming of Age* a warm and sympathetic story. Enjoy." —*Analog*

SPINNERET

"Timothy Zahn's specialty is technological intrigue—international and interstellar . . . [A] convoluted high-tech thriller." —*The Christian Science Monitor*

"Timothy Zahn's latest novel is a fast-paced adventure yarn. He brings together exploration for new starts, racial tensions, Third World activism and a group of vanished aliens with a high-tech twist. The relative newcomer to the science fiction field continues his quick rise to the upper levels." —*United Press International*

"Brisk and entertaining." —*Publishers Weekly*

NIGHT TRAIN TO RIGEL

"Zahn's ingenuity, a steady resource during a writing career now a generation long, makes it easy for him to come up with reader-rewarding demonstrations of his characters' similar quality. A highly readable thriller in space-opera trappings. A great read." —*Booklist*

THE THIRD LYNX

"Good thriller, full of red herrings, blind alleys, and rising tension." —*Booklist*

ODD GIRL OUT

"Nonstop action keeps the reader turning the pages." —*SFRevu*

THE DOMINO PATTERN

"The plot grabs from the get-go, characters and style are well-wrought and complementary, so SF and thriller fans alike should be pleased."
—*Booklist*

JUDGMENT AT PROTEUS

"A blockbuster of a novel, showing Timothy Zahn at the top of his form."
—Mike Resnick,
Hugo and Nebula Award–winning author

PAWN'S GAMBIT

PAWN'S GAMBIT

AND OTHER STRATAGEMS

TIMOTHY ZAHN

OPEN ROAD

INTEGRATED MEDIA

NEW YORK

"The Price of Survival" first appeared in *Analog*, June 22, 1981.
"The Giftie Gie Us" first appeared in *Analog*, July 20, 1981.
"The Final Report on the Lifeline Experiment" first appeared in *Analog*, May 1983.
"Cascade Point" first appeared in *Analog*, December 1983.
"Music Hath Charms" first appeared in *Analog*, April 1985.
"The President's Doll" first appeared in *Analog*, July 1987.
"Clean Slate" first appeared in *Amazing Stories*, January 1989.
"Hitmen—See Murderers" first appeared in *Amazing Stories*, June 1991.
"Protocol" first appeared in *Analog*, September 2002.
"Old-Boy Network" first appeared in *Sol's Children*, August 2002.
"Proof" first appeared in *Amazing Stories*, September 2004.
"The Ring" first appeared in *Pandora's Closet*, DAW Books, August 2007.
"Trollbridge" first appeared in *Spells of the City*, DAW Books, December 2009.
"Chem Lab 301" first appeared in the FenCon program book, September 2014.
"Pawn's Gambit" first appeared in *Analog*, March 29, 1982.

Copyright © 2016 by Timothy Zahn

Cover design by Kat JK Lee

978-1-5040-1622-3

Published in 2016 by Open Road Integrated Media, Inc.
345 Hudson Street
New York, NY 10014
www.openroadmedia.com

CONTENTS

THE PRICE OF SURVIVAL

"That's it, Shipmaster," Pliij said from his helmboard with obvious relief. "Target star dead ahead; relative motion and atmospheric density established, and vector computed. Final course change in nine *aarns*."

Final course change. There were times in the long voyage, Shipmaster Orofan reflected, that he had thought he would never live to hear those words, that he would be called prematurely to sit among the ancestors and another would guide his beloved *Dawnsent* to her final resting place. But he knew now that he would live to see the new world that the Farseers back home had found for them. "Very good, Pilot," he responded formally to Pliij's announcement—and then both Sk'cee broke into huge, multi-tentacled grins.

"Almost there, Orofan," Pliij said, gazing out the forward viewport. "Almost there."

"Yes, my friend." Orofan touched the viewport gently with one of his two long tentacles, feeling the vibration of the fusion drive and a slight tingle from the huge magnetic scoop spread hundreds of *pha* ahead of them. Nothing was visible; the viewport was left uncovered only for tradition's sake. "Do you suppose the sleepers will believe us when we tell them we carried them hundreds of star-paths without seeing any stars?"

Pliij chuckled, his short tentacles rippling with the gesture. "The rainbow effect through the side viewports is nice, but I'm looking forward to seeing the sky go back to normal."

"Yes." Orofan gazed into the emptiness for a moment, then shook himself. Back to business. "So. The course change is programmed. Are the scoop and condensers prepared?"

"All set. Thistas is running a final check now."

"Good." Nine *aarns* to go. Six of those would make for a good rest. "I'll be in my quarters. Call me if I'm not back here two *aarns* before insertion."

"Right. Sleep well."

"I certainly will." Orofan smiled and left the bridge.

It was, General Sanford Carey thought, probably the first time in history that representatives from the Executor's office, the Solar Assembly, the Chiron Institute, and the Peacekeepers had ever met together on less than a week's notice. Even the Urgent-One order he'd called them with shouldn't have generated such a fast response, and he wondered privately how many of them had their own sources at the Peacekeeper field where the tachship had landed not three hours ago.

Across the room a Security lieutenant closed the door and activated the conference room's spy-seal. He nodded, and Carey stepped to the lectern to face his small audience.

"Ladies and gentlemen, thank you for coming here this afternoon," he said in a smooth, melodious voice—a voice, he'd been told, which contrasted violently with his craggy appearance. "Approximately three hours ago we learned that there is a large unidentified object rapidly approaching the solar system."

Only a third of the nine men and women present kept the impassive—if tense—expressions that betrayed prior knowledge. The rest displayed a kaleidoscope of shock, wonderment, and uneasiness as Carey's words sank in.

He continued before the murmurings had quite died down. "The object is traveling a hair below lightspeed, at about point nine nine nine cee, using an extremely hot fusion drive of some kind and what seems to be an electromagnetic ramscoop arrangement. He's about eight light-days out—under fourteen hundred A.U.—and while we haven't got his exact course down yet, he'll definitely pass through the System."

"'Through,' General?" asked Evelyn Woodcock, chief assistant to the Executor. "It's not going to stop here?"

"No, his drive's still pointing backwards," Carey told her. "Decelerating to a stop now would take hundreds of gees."

From their expressions it was clear they weren't sure whether to be relieved or insulted by the Intruder's disinterest. "Then why is it coming here?" Assembly-Prime Wu-sin asked.

"Reconnaissance, possibly, though that's unlikely. He's coming in at a steep angle to the ecliptic—a poor vector if he wants to see much of the System. He could also be trying for a slight course correction by passing close to the sun; we'll know that better when we get more accurate readings on him. It's even possible the Intruder doesn't yet know we're here. At the speed he's making, the sun's light is blue-shifted into the ultraviolet, and he might not have the proper instruments to detect it."

"Unlikely," Dr. Louis Du Bellay of the Chiron Institute murmured. "I would guess they've done this before."

"Agreed, Doctor," Carey nodded. "It's a very remote possibility. Well. The Intruder, then, is not likely to be of great danger to us, provided we keep local traffic out of his way. By the same token, he's not likely to advance our store of knowledge significantly, either. With one exception: we now know we're not alone in the universe. You'll appreciate, I'm sure, the importance of not springing this revelation on the System and colonies without some careful thought on the part of all of us. Thank you for coming here; we'll keep you informed."

Carey stepped from the lectern and headed toward the door as his audience came alive with a buzz of intense conversation. As Carey passed him, Dr. Du Bellay rose and fell into step. "Would you mind if I tagged along with you back to the Situation Room, General?" he asked. "I'd like to keep close tabs on this event."

Carey nodded. "I rather expected you'd want to. I've already had you cleared for entry." He raised his hand warningly as the Security man reached for the spy-seal control. "No talking about this, Doctor, until we're past the inner security shield."

It was only a short walk to the central section of Peacekeeper Headquarters, and the two men filled the time by discussing Du Bellay's latest trip to the ancient ruins at Van Maanen's Star. "I heard about that," Carey said. "I understand it was your first solo tachship run."

"Yes. The Directorate at Chiron's been encouraging everyone to learn to fly—it's cheaper than always having to hire a pilot along with a tachship. Fortunately, they haven't yet suggested I do all my own digging as well."

Carey chuckled. "That's what students are for. Are those ruins really as extensive as people say?"

"Even more so. We've barely scratched the surface, and there's at least one more civilization under the one we're working on."

They passed the security shield to the clickings of invisible security systems, and the topic abruptly changed. "How in blazes did a tachship stumble across something moving that fast?" Du Bellay asked.

"Pure dumb luck," Carey said. "A merchantman coming in from Alpha Centauri had dropped back into normal space to do a navigational check. They'd just finished when this thing went roaring past."

"They're lucky they weren't fried by the ramscoop fields," Du Bellay commented.

"They damn near were. A few million kilometers over and they probably would have been. Anyway, they recovered from the shock and got a preliminary reading on his course. Then they jumped ahead the shortest distance they could and waited the sixteen minutes it took the Intruder to catch up. They got another decimal in his course, confirmed he was heading toward Sol, and hightailed it here with the news."

"Hmm. Ironic, isn't it, that the great search for intelligent life should be ended by a puddle-jumping business whip whose navigator didn't trust his own computer. Well, what's next?"

"We've sent out a dozen tachships, strung along the Intruder's route, to get better data. They should be reporting in soon."

The Peacekeeper Situation Room was a vast maze of vision screens, holotanks, and computer terminals, presided over by a resident corps of officers and technicians. Halfway across the room was the main screen, currently showing a map of the entire solar system. From its lower right-hand corner a dotted red line speared into the inner system.

A young captain glanced up from a paper-strewn table as they approached. "Ah, General," he greeted Carey. "Just in time, sir: Chaser data's coming in."

"Let's see what you've got, Mahendra."

Mahendra handed him a computer-printed page. Carey scanned it, aware that Du Ballay was reading over his shoulder.

The Intruder was *big*. Compensating for relativistic effects and the difficulty of taking data at such speeds, the computer judged the alien craft at well over fifteen hundred meters long, two hundred meters in diameter, and massing near the two-hundred-million-ton mark. Its cone-shaped ramscoop fields spread out hundreds of kilometers in front of it. The drive spectrum showed mainly helium, but with a surprisingly high percentage of other elements.

Behind him, Du Bellay whistled softly. "Talk about your basic Juggernaut! Where'd it come from?"

"We've backtracked him to the 1228 Circini system," Mahendra said, referring to one of his sheets. "He didn't originate there, though—it's a dead system. We're trying to track him further back."

Carey looked up at the main screen. "Why isn't the Intruder's course projected beyond Sol?"

Mahendra frowned. "I don't know, sir." He swung a keyboard over and typed something. "The projection stopped when the course intersected the sun," he reported, frowning a bit harder.

"What?" Du Bellay said.

"Show us the inner system," Carey ordered.

Mahendra punched a key and the screen changed, now showing only out to Mars. Sure enough, the dotted line intersected the edge of the dime-sized image of the sun. Without being told to, Mahendra jumped the scale again, and the sun filled the screen.

Carey squinted at it. "Almost misses. How dense is the stuff he'll hit?"

"The computer says about ten to the minus seventh grams per cc. Not much by Earth standards, but that's almost a hundred trillion times anything in the interstellar medium. And he'll pass through several thousand kilometers of it."

"Like hell he will," Carey winced. "He'll burn to a crisp long before that. I was right after all, Doctor—he hasn't noticed the solar system's in his path."

He glanced at Du Bellay, then paused for a longer look. The archaeologist was frowning into space. "Doctor?"

"Captain, does that console have DatRetNet capability?" Du Bellay asked. "Please look up data on that star you mentioned—1228 Circini. Cross-reference with unusual stellar activity."

Mahendra nodded and turned to the console. "Something wrong?" Carey asked Du Bellay. The other's expression worried him.

"I don't know. I seem to remember hearing about that star a few years ago. . . ." He trailed off.

"Got it, Doctor," Mahendra spoke up.

Both Du Bellay and Carey leaned over to look at the console screen. "I was right," Du Bellay said in a graveyard voice, pointing at the third paragraph.

"'Planetary studies indicate a giant solar flare occurred approximately one hundred years ago, causing extensive melting patterns as far out as one point eight A.U.,'" Carey read aloud. "'Such behavior in a red dwarf is unexplainable by current theory.' I don't see the connec—" He broke off in mid-sentence.

Du Bellay nodded grimly. "1228 Circini is ninety-six light-years away. It's too close to be coincidence."

"Are you suggesting the Intruder *deliberately* rammed 1228 Circini? That's crazy!"

Du Bellay merely nodded at the main screen. Carey gazed up at the dotted line for a long minute. Then he tapped Mahendra's shoulder. "Captain, get me Executor Nordli. Priority Urgent-One."

Orofan woke to hear the last wisp of sound from his intercommunicator. He reached for the control, noting with some surprise that the shading of the muted wall light indicated half past *cin*—he'd been asleep less than an *aarn*.

"Yes?"

It was Pliij. "Shipmaster, we have a problem. You'd best come up immediately."

Was something wrong with his ship? "I'll be right there."

Pliij was not alone when Orofan arrived on the bridge. Lassarr was also there. "Greetings, Voyagemaster," Orofan said, giving the required salute even as his eyes darted around the room. No problem was registering on any of the displays.

"The trouble is not with the *Dawnsent*," Voyagemaster Lassarr said, interpreting Orofan's actions and expression with an ease the Shipmaster had never liked.

"Then what is it?"

"Here, Shipmaster." Pliij manipulated a control and an image, relativistically compensated, appeared on a screen. "This is the system we're approaching. Look closely here, and here, and here."

Tiny flecks of light, Orofan saw. The spectrometer read them as hot helium. . . .

Orofan felt suddenly cold all over. Fusion-drive spacecraft! "The system is inhabited!" he hissed.

"You understand our dilemma," Lassarr said heavily.

Orofan understood, all right. The *Dawnsent's* scooping procedure would unavoidably set up massive shock waves in the star's surface layers, sending flares of energy and radiation outward. . . .

"How is our fuel supply?" Lassarr asked.

Orofan knew, but let Pliij check anyway. "Down to point one-oh-four maximum," the Pilot said.

"We can't reach our new home with that," Lassarr murmured.

"Correction, Voyagemaster," Orofan said. "We can't reach it in the appointed time. But our normal scooping gives us sufficient fuel to finish the voyage."

"At greatly reduced speed," Lassarr pointed out. "How soon could we arrive?"

There was silence as Pliij did the calculation. "Several lifetimes," he said at last. "Five, perhaps six."

"So," Lassarr said, short tentacles set grimly. "I'm afraid that settles the matter."

"Settles it how?" Orofan asked suspiciously.

"It's unfortunate, but we cannot risk such a delay. The sleep tanks weren't designed to last that long."

"You're saying, then, that we continue our present course? Despite what that'll do to life in this system?"

Lassarr frowned at him. "I remind you, Shipmaster, that we carry a million of our fellow Sk'cee—"

"Whose lives are worth more than the billions of beings who may inhabit that system?"

"You have a curious philosophy, Shipmaster; a philosophy, I might add, that could be misunderstood. What would the ancestors say if you came among them after deliberately allowing a million Sk'cee to perish helplessly? What would those million themselves say?"

"What would they say," Orofan countered softly, "if they knew we'd bought their lives at such a cost to others? Is there honor in that, Voyagemaster?"

"Honor lies in the performance of one's duty. Mine is to deliver the colonists safely to their new world."

"I'm aware of that. But surely there's a higher responsibility here. And we don't *know* the sleep tanks won't survive the longer journey."

Lassarr considered him silently. "It's clear you feel strongly about this," he said finally. "I propose a compromise. You have one *aarn* to offer a reasonable alternative. If you can't we'll carry out our fuel scoop on schedule." He turned and strode out.

Pliij looked at Orofan. "What now?"

The Shipmaster sank into a seat, thinking furiously. "Get me all the information we have on this region of space. Our own sensor work, Farseer charts and data—everything. There *has* to be another way."

The group sitting around the table was small, highly select, and very powerful. And, Carey thought as he finished his explanation, considerably shaken. Executor Nordli took over even as the general was sitting down. "Obviously, our first order of business is to find out why our visitor is planning to dive into the sun. Suggestions?"

"Mr. Executor, I believe I have a logical explanation," an older man sitting next to Du Bellay spoke up. Dr. Horan Roth, Carey remembered: chief astrophysicist at the Chiron Institute.

"Go ahead, Dr. Roth," Nordli said.

Roth steepled his fingers. "The speed of a ramjet is limited not by relativity, but by friction with the interstellar medium. The mathematics are trivial; the bottom line is that the limiting speed is just that of the ship's exhaust. Now, if you use a magnetic scoop to take in hydrogen, fuse it to helium, and use the energy liberated to send this helium out your exhaust, it turns out that your velocity is only twelve percent light-speed."

"But the Intruder's moving considerably faster than that," Assembly-Prime Wu-sin objected.

"Exactly," Roth nodded. "They're apparently using an after-accelerator of some sort to boost their exhaust speed. But this takes energy, requiring extra fuel."

"I see," Nordli rumbled. "They have to carry extra hydrogen which can't be replaced in the interstellar medium. So they periodically dive into a star to replenish their tanks?"

"It would seem so."

"Dr. Du Bellay, you're an expert on alien cultures, correct?" Nordli asked.

"To some extent, sir," Du Bellay said, "bearing in mind we've so far studied only dead civilizations, and only a handful of those."

"Yes. In your opinion, what are the chances of communicating with these aliens? And what are the chances that would make any difference in their actions?"

Du Bellay frowned. "I'm afraid the answer to both questions is very poor," he said slowly. "It's true that various scientists have developed so-called 'first-contact primers' in case we ever came across a living intelligent species. But it's also true that teaching any of our language to an alien would take considerable time, and we haven't got that time. No ship ever built could match speeds with the Intruder, so we would have to give everything to them in short, high-density data bursts. And even assuming they were equipped to receive whichever wavelengths we use, they have only seven or eight hours—in their time frame—to decipher it."

"I have to concur with Dr. Du Bellay," Carey spoke up. "As a matter of fact, we've already sent out a series of tachships to try precisely what he suggested, but we don't expect anything to come of it."

"Perhaps we could signal our existence some other way," Evelyn Woodcock, Nordli's assistant, suggested. "Say, a fusion drive pointed at them, blinking off and on. They couldn't miss that."

"And then what?" Carey asked.

"Why—surely they'd change course."

"With their own mission at stake? If it's a colony ship of some kind, its supplies are likely very tightly figured. If they change course, they may die. At the speed they're making we sure as hell can't offer to refuel them."

"There's an even more disturbing possibility," Nordli said quietly. "This refueling technique may be *deliberately* designed to sterilize the system for future colonization."

"I think it's unfair to ascribe motives like that to them without proof," Du Bellay said. The words, Carey judged, were more reflex than true objection—the archaeologist looked as uneasy as everyone else.

"No?" Nordli shrugged. "It doesn't really matter. What matters is that the Intruder is threatening us with massive destruction. We must stop him."

Wu-sin stirred. "Executor Nordli, you're proposing what amounts to an act of war against another intelligent species. A decision of that magnitude must be approved by the full Solar Assembly at least; ideally by all the colonies as well."

"There's no time to consult the colonies," Nordli said. "As to the Assembly . . . you have two hours to get their approval."

"And if I can't?"

"I'll go ahead without it."

Wu-sin nodded grimly. "I needed to know where you stand. I'll get their approval." He rose, bowed, and left the room.

Nordli turned to Carey. "General, how do we proceed?"

Carey let his eyes sweep the others' faces as he thought. They were all on Nordli's side, he saw: Du Bellay, like himself, only because there was no other choice. How many lives were they planning to snuff out?—innocent lives, perhaps, who may not realize what they were doing? "The trouble, Mr. Executor, is that the Peacekeeper forces really aren't set up for this kind of threat."

"You've got nuclear missiles, don't you? And ships to deliver them?"

"There are two problems. First, hitting the Intruder would be extremely difficult. A shot from the side would probably miss, alerting them as to our intentions. A head-on shot would hit, all right, but the extremely high magnetic fields it would have to penetrate would almost certainly incapacitate any missile we've got. And second, there's no guarantee even a direct hit would do any good. Just because they don't have FTL drives doesn't mean they're primitives—only that their technology developed along different lines. And don't forget, that ship is designed to bore through the edge of a star at nearly lightspeed."

"There's one further problem," Dr. Roth spoke up. "Disabling or even disintegrating it at this point wouldn't help us any. The fragments would still hit the sun, with the same consequences."

There was a moment of silence. "Then we have to stop or deflect it." Evelyn suggested. "We have to put something massive in its path."

Nordli looked at Carey. "General?"

Carey was doing a quick calculation in his head. "Yes, either would work. Slowing it even slightly would send it through a less dense region of the photosphere. Assuming, of course, that he stays with his present course."

"What can we put in his path?" Nordli asked. "Could we tow an asteroid out there?"

Carey shook his head. "Impossible. As I pointed out, he's far off the ecliptic plane. Moving an asteroid there would take months." Even as he spoke he was mentally checking off possibilities. Tachships were far too small to be useful, and the only heavy Peacekeeper ships in the System were too far away from the Intruder's path. "The only chance I can see," he said slowly, "is if there's a big private or commercial ship close enough to intercept him a good distance from the sun. But we don't have authority to requisition nonmilitary spacecraft."

"You do now," Nordli said grimly. "The government also guarantees compensation."

"Thank you, sir." Carey touched an intercom button and gave Captain Mahendra the search order.

There was a lot of traffic in mankind's home system, but the Peace-keepers' duties included monitoring such activity, and it was only a few minutes before Mahendra was back on the intercom. "There's only one really good choice," he reported. "A big passenger liner, the *Origami*, almost a hundred thousand tons. She's between Titan and Ceres at present and has a eighty-four percent probability of making an intercept point on time; seventy-nine if she drops her passengers first. One other liner and three freighters of comparable size have probabilities of fifteen percent or lower."

"I see," Carey said through suddenly dry lips. "Thank you, Captain. Stand by."

Ne looked back up at Nordli. The Executor nodded. "No choice. Have that liner drop its passengers and get moving."

"Yes, sir." Turning to the intercom, Carey began to give the orders. He was vaguely surprised at the self-control in his voice.

"Well, Shipmaster?" Lassarr asked.

Orofan kept his expression neutral. "I have no suggestion other than the one I offered an *aarn* ago, Voyagemaster: that we change course and continue at reduced speed."

"For six lifetimes?" Lassarr snorted. "That's unacceptable."

"It won't be that bad." Orofan consulted his calculations. "We could penetrate the outer atmosphere of the star without causing significant damage to the system. We'd collect enough fuel that way to shorten the trip to barely two lifetimes."

"That's still not good enough. I have no wish to join the ancestors before our people are safely to their new home."

"That can be arranged," Orofan said stiffly. "You and any of the *Dawnsent's* crew who wished could be put in the spare sleep tanks. If necessary, I could run the ship alone."

For a moment Orofan thought Lassarr was going to take offense at his suggestion. But the Voyagemaster's expression changed and he merely shrugged. "Your offer is honorable, but impractical. The critical factor is still the durability of the sleep tanks, and that hasn't changed. However, I've come up with an alternative of my own." He paused. "We could make our new colony in *this* system."

"Impossible," Orofan said. "We don't have the fuel to stop."

"Certainly we do. A large proportion of this spacecraft's equipment could be done without for a short time. Converting all of that to fusion material and reaction mass would give us all that we need, even considering that we would overshoot and have to come back."

"No!" The exclamation burst involuntarily from Orofan. His beloved *Dawnsent* broken up haphazardly and fed to a fusion drive?

"Why not?"

His emotional response, Orofan knew, wouldn't impress the other, and he fumbled for logical reasons. "We don't know if there's a planet here we could live on, for one thing. Even if there is, the natives may already be living there. We are hardly in a position to bargain for territory."

"We are not entirely helpless, however," Lassarr said. "Our starshield's a formidable defense, and our meteor-destroyer could be adapted to offense. Our magnetic scoop itself is deadly to most known forms of life." His tentacles took on a sardonic expression. "And if they're too advanced to be subjugated, we'll simply ask for their help in rebuilding and refueling our ship and continue on our way."

Orofan could hardly believe what he was hearing. "Are you *serious*? You'd start a *war* for the sake of only a million Sk'cee—a *million,* out of our eight hundred billions?"

Suddenly, Lassarr looked very tired. "I'll say this one more time, Shipmaster. The voyage, and those million Sk'cee, are my prime responsibility. I don't have the luxury of taking a broader view. By both nature and training I am highly protective toward my charges—if I were otherwise I wouldn't have been made Voyagemaster. Racial selfishness is sometimes necessary for survival, a fact those who sent us knew well. This is one of those times. I will do what I must, and will face the ancestors without shame."

There was nothing Orofan could say—the struggle to follow the honorable path was vital to him as well. But what did honor demand here?

Lassarr gazed at the blackness outside the viewport. "You have one-half *aarn* to choose between our current course and ending the voyage here," he said. "If you won't choose, I'll do so for you."

Heart pounding painfully, Orofan signed assent. "Very well."

One of the nicest traditions still remaining from the days of the old seagoing luxury ships, Chandra Carey thought, was that of the officers eating dinner with their passengers. She delighted in choosing who would join her at the captain's table, always making certain someone interesting sat at her side. She was therefore annoyed when First Officer Goode interrupted a lively discussion on genetics with a call suggesting she join him on the bridge.

"Mechanical trouble?" she asked softly into the intercom. No sense alarming the passengers.

"No, Captain. But you'll want to get up here right away." Goode's voice was casual—far too casual.

Chandra's annoyance evaporated. "On my way."

She made her apologies and reached the bridge in ninety seconds. Goode was waiting, a message flimsy in his hand. "Get a grip on your guyline," he advised, handing her the paper.

A frown creased Chandra's forehead; it deepened as she read. "This is ridiculous. Drop my passengers and fireball it 'way the hell off the ecliptic? What for?"

"The explanation's still coming in—tight beam, with the line's own security code," Goode told her. "And it's under your father's name, no less." He took the flimsy back and headed toward the navigator.

"Dad?" Chandra stepped to the communications console and peered at the paper sliding slowly from the slot. Sure enough: PEACE-KEEPER HEADQUARTERS, EARTH — TO P.L. ORIGAMI: FROM GEN. SANFORD CAREY. Beneath the heading the message was nearly complete, and Chandra read it with a mixture of fascination and horror.

"Well?" Goode asked.

She tore off the paper and thrust it into his hands even as she groped for the main intercom board. For a moment she paused, organizing the thoughts that whirled like Martian winds through her mind. Then she stabbed the "general" button.

"Attention, attention," she said in her most authoritative voice. "This is Captain Carey. All passengers and nonessential crewmembers are to report to the lifeboats *immediately.* There is no immediate danger to the *Origami,* but this is *not* a drill. Repeating: all passengers and nonessential crew report immediately to lifeboats. This is *not* a drill."

The "abandon ship" alarm sounded even as she keyed a different circuit. "Bridge to Power. I want the drive up to full ergs in twenty minutes. Start tying in for full remote to the bridge, too." She waited for an acknowledgment and switched off. "Navigator!" she called across the bridge. "Get me a course to the vector on that paper—" She stabbed a finger at the flimsy Goode had shown her. "I want a minimum-time path to the earliest possible intercept point that leaves us stationary.

Any acceleration she can handle, and you can run the tanks. Everyone else: if you're not on flight prep, help get the passengers off. We fireball in twenty minutes. Move!"

The bridge erupted with activity. Chandra sank into her chair, rereading the message carefully. It was hard to believe that the long search was ending like this, with a kill-or-die confrontation that made less sense even than shooting a deadly snake. And yet, despite the danger and irony, she felt a small surge of excitement. The safety of the entire solar system had unexpectedly fallen into her hands—and her father himself was counting on her. She wouldn't let him down.

Glancing up at the chrono, she keyed the intercom. "Captain to lifeboat bays—status report?"

Lassarr returned to the bridge at precisely the appointed time. "The half-*aarn* is past, Shipmaster," he announced.

Orofan looked up from the sensor monitor he and Pliij were seated at. "One moment, Voyagemaster," he said distractedly. "A new factor has entered the situation."

"I have it now, Orofan," Pliij muttered, both long and short tentacles dancing over the instruments. "Medium-frequency electromagnetic radiation, with severe shifting and aberration. I have a recording."

"Good. Get to work on it at once. And keep the sensors watching for more." Orofan stood and went to where Lassarr waited.

"What is it?" the Voyagemaster asked.

"Signals of some sort, beamed at us every few *aarmis*. The natives are trying to communicate."

Lassarr frowned. "Interesting. Any known language?"

"Unfortunately, no. But there's a great deal of information in each pulse. We may have a preliminary translation in a few *aarns*."

"Good. That'll help us if we need to negotiate for the *Dawnsent's* repair."

Orofan blinked. "What do you mean? Whether or not we're stopping here is still *my* decision."

"Not any more. I've reconsidered and have decided this is our best course. Further planetary data is coming in, and it now seems likely that there are one or two planets here we could colonize."

Orofan forced calmness into his voice. "You can't do that, Lassarr. You can't commit us to an uncertain war; certainly not one of conquest.

Even if they were primitives—which they're clearly not—we would have no right to take their worlds. This is not honorable—"

"Peace, Shipmaster." Lassarr favored him with a hard, speculative glare. "You protest far too much. Tell me, if the *Dawnsent* didn't need to be cannibalized for the required fuel mass, would you be nearly as opposed to stopping here?"

"Your insinuations are slanderous," Orofan said stiffly. "The ship is my responsibility, yes, but I've not been blinded to all else. My overall duty is still to the Sk'cee in our sleep tanks."

"I'm sure you believe that," Lassarr said, more gently. "But *I* can't afford to. The very nature of your training makes your judgment suspect in a case like this. The decision has been made. I've instructed the library to catalog nonessential equipment; disassembly will begin in two *aarns*."

"You can't do this," Orofan whispered.

"I can," the Voyagemaster said calmly, "and I have."

Trembling with emotion, Orofan turned and fled from the bridge.

"That's the last of them," Goode reported from his position at the *Origami's* helm. He sounded tired.

Chandra nodded, several neck muscles twinging with the action. Two days of two-gee deceleration wasn't enough to incapacitate anyone, but it was more than enough to be a nuisance, and she was glad it was almost over. "That was what, the engineering crew?"

"Right—four lifeboats full. We're all alone, Captain."

She smiled tightly. "Fun, isn't it? Okay. Chaser Twelve just checked in; the Intruder's still on course. Our ETA on his path is four hours?"

"Just under. Three fifty-seven thirty."

She did a quick calculation. "Gives us a whole six minutes to spare. Tight."

Goode shrugged. "I would've been perfectly happy to take the whole trip at two gees and get here a day earlier. But creating fuel isn't one of my talents."

"I'll suggest a tachship tanker fleet to Dad when we get home," Chandra said dryly. "Okay. Number 81 should be our last boat. Fifteen minutes before we arrive I want you to go down and prep it. We'll want to cut out the minute the *Origami's* in position."

"Roger."

Conversation lapsed. It felt strange, Chandra thought, to be deliberately running towards a collision: strange and frightening; It brought her back to her first driving lessons, to her father's warnings that she was never, *never* to race a monorail to a crossing. He'd hammered the point home by showing her pictures of cars that had lost such contests, and even now she shuddered at the memory of those horrible tangles.

And it was her father himself who had authorized this. She wondered how he was feeling right now. Worse than she was, probably.

Strange how, in the pictures, the monorail never seemed particularly damaged. Would it be that way this time too? She had no desire to kill any of the aliens aboard that ship if it could be avoided. This mess wasn't really their fault.

Six minutes. . . . She hoped like hell the Intruder hadn't changed course.

Captain Mahendra's hands rested lightly on the Situation Room's communications board, showing no sign whatsoever of tension. General Carey watched those hands in fascination, wondering at the man's self-control. But, then, Mahendra didn't have a daughter out there racing the ultimate monorail to its mathematical crossing.

Mahendra turned from the board, taking off his headphone, and Carey shifted his gaze to the captain's face. "Well?"

"Chaser Six reports both the Intruder and the *Origami* still on course: Chasers Eight through Thirteen are still picking up lifeboats. Almost all the passengers are back; about three-quarters of the crew are still out there."

Carey nodded. "How long will the *Origami* have before impact?"

"From now, three hours twenty minutes. Once in place, about six minutes."

Carey hissed softly between his teeth. "Pretty slim margin."

Mahendra frowned. "Should be enough, General. Those boats can handle two gees for ten minutes or so before running their tanks. Even if you allow them three minutes for launching, they can get—oh, three hundred kilometers out before impact. That should be a relatively safe distance."

"I suppose so."

"You seem doubtful," a new voice cut in from behind him. Carey turned to discover Du Ballay had come up, unnoticed, and was standing at his shoulder.

"I'm concerned about those still aboard that ship," the general growled. "They're civilians and shouldn't have to go through this."

"I agree." Du Bellay paused. "I, uh, looked up the *Origami's* registry data. The captain is listed as a Chandra Carey."

He stopped without asking the obvious question. Carey answered it anyway. "She's my daughter."

"Your daughter, sir?" Mahendra asked, eyes widening momentarily. "I'm sorry; I didn't know." His fingers danced over keys; numbers appeared on his screen. "Sir, we *could* pull a tachship off of the Intruder's path and have it waiting to pick up Captain Carey when the *Origami* reaches position."

"No. We've only got three tachships left on chaser duty and I'd rather leave them there. Chandra's good, and I know she thinks highly of her crew. The best thing we can do for them is to keep feeding them good data on the Intruder's course."

"What about sending one of the tachships that's on lifeboat-pickup duty?" Du Bellay suggested.

"Those boats don't carry all that much food and air," Carey said, shaking his head. "The *Origami* dropped a lot of boats, and some of them are getting close to the wire. Tachships can't carry more than a single lifeboat at a time, and with all civilian craft officially barred from the area we're going to have enough trouble picking up everyone as it is." Both men still looked disturbed, so Carey flashed what he hoped was a reassuring smile. "Don't worry, Chandra can take care of herself. Captain, what's the status of our attempts at communication?"

Du Bellay drifted off as, almost reluctantly, Mahendra turned back to his board. His hands, Carey noted, didn't look nearly as relaxed as before.

The door opened, and Orofan paused on the threshold for a moment before stepping onto the bridge. Lassarr glanced up from the console where he and Pliij were working. "Yes, what is it?" the Voyagemaster growled.

"I'm asking you once more to reconsider," Orofan said. His voice was firm, devoid of all emotion.

Lassarr evidently missed the implications of that. "It's too late. Disassembly has begun; our new course is plotted."

"But not yet executed," Orofan pointed out. "And equipment can be reassembled. This path is not honorable, Voyagemaster."

Deliberately, Lassarr turned his back on the Shipmaster. "Prepare to execute the course change," he instructed Pliij.

"You leave me no alternative," Orofan sighed.

Lassarr spun around—and froze, holding very tightly to the console, his eyes goggling at the assault gun nestled in Orofan's tentacle. "Have you gone insane, Shipmaster?"

"Perhaps," Orofan said. "But I will not face the ancestors having stood by while war was made against a race which has offered no provocation."

"Indeed?" Lassarr's voice dripped with the sarcasm of fear and anger combined. "And destroying them outright, without warning, is more honorable? A few *aarns* ago you didn't think so. Or do you intend instead to condemn a million Sk'cee to death?"

"I don't know," Orofan said, gazing at the screen that showed the approaching star. "There is still time to decide which path to take."

Lassarr was aghast. "You're going to leave this decision to a last-*aarmi* impulse?"

"Orofan, there's barely a tenth of an *aarn* left," Pliij said, his voice strained.

"I know." Orofan focused on Lassarr. "But the *Dawnsent* is mine, and with that power goes responsibility for its actions. It is not honorable to relinquish that load."

Slowly, as if finally understanding, Lassarr signed agreement. "But the burden may be transferred to one who is willing," he said quietly.

"And what then of my honor?" Orofan asked, tentacles rippling with half-bitter amusement. "No. Your honor is safe, Voyagemaster—you were prevented only by force from following the path you deemed right. You may face the ancestors without fear." He hefted the assault gun. "The final choice is now mine. *My* honor, alone, stands in the dock."

And that was as it should be, Orofan knew. In the silence he stared at the screen and made his decision.

Ten minutes till cutoff. Alone on the bridge, Chandra tried to watch every read-out at once, looking for deviations from their calculated course. The *Origami's* navigational computer was as good as anything on the market, but for extremely fine positioning it usually had the aid of beacons and maser tracking. Out here in the middle of nowhere, six A.U. from the sun, the computer had to rely on inertial guidance and star positions, and Chandra wasn't sure it could handle the job alone.

She reached for the intercom, changed her mind and instead switched on the radio. The lifeboat bay intercoms were situated a good distance from the boats themselves, and Goode would have a better chance of hearing her over the boat's radio. "Goode? How's it going?" she called.

Her answer was a faint grunt of painful exertion. "Goode?" she asked sharply.

"Trouble, Captain," his voice came faintly, as if from outside the boat. Chandra boosted both power and gain, and Goode's next words were clearer. "One of the lines of the boat's cradle is jammed—something's dug into the mesh where I can't get at it. I'll need a laser torch to cut it."

"Damn. The nearest one's probably in the forward hobby room." Chandra briefly considered dropping back to one gee while Goode was traveling, but immediately abandoned the idea. At this late stage that would force extra high-gee deceleration to still get to the rendezvous position on time, and there was no guarantee they had the fuel for that.

Goode read her mind, long-distance. "Don't worry, I can make it. What's the latest on the Intruder?"

"As of four minutes ago, holding steady. At a light-minute to the nearest tachship, though, that could be a little old."

"I get the point. On my way."

The minutes crawled by. Eyes still on the read-outs, Chandra mentally traced out Goode's path: out the bay, turn right, elevator or stairway down two decks, along a long corridor, into the Number Two hobby and craft shop; secure a torch from the locked cabinet and return. Even with twice-normal weight she thought she was giving him plenty of time, but she was halfway through her third tracing when the drive abruptly cut off.

The sudden silence and weightlessness caught her by surprise, and she wasted two or three seconds fumbling at the radio switch. "Goode!" she shouted. "Where the hell *are* you?"

There was no reply. She waited, scanning the final location figures. Sure enough, the *Origami* had overshot the proper position by nearly eighty meters. She was just reaching for her power controls when the radio boomed.

"I'm back," Goode said, panting heavily. "I didn't trust the elevator—didn't realize how hard the trip back would be. Sorry."

"Never mind; just get to work. Is there anything you can hang onto? I've got to run the nose jets."

"Go ahead. But, damn, this torch is a genuine *toy*. I don't know how long it'll take to cut the boat loose."

A chill ran down Chandra's spine, and it was all she could do to keep from hitting the main drive and getting them the hell out of there. "Better not be long, partner. It's just you and me and a runaway monorail out here."

"Yeah. Hey—couldn't you call for a tachship to come and get us?"

"I already thought of that. But the nearest tachship is only a light-minute out, way too close to get here in one jump. He'd have to jump out a minimum of two A.U., then jump back here. Calculating the direction and timing for two jumps that fine-tuned would take almost twenty minutes, total."

"Damn. I didn't know that—I've never trained for tachships." A short pause. "The first three strands are cut; seven to go. Minute and a half, I'd guess."

"Okay." Chandra was watching the read-outs closely. "We're almost back in position; I'll be down there before you're done. The boat ready otherwise?"

"Ready, waiting, and eager."

"Not nearly as eager as I am." A squirt of the main drive to kill their velocity as the nose jets fell silent; one more careful scan of the read-outs—"I'm done. See you below."

Goode was on the second to the last of the cable strands when she arrived. "Get in and strap down," he told her, not looking up.

She did, wriggling into the pilot's couch, and was ready by the time he scrambled in the opposite side. Without waiting for him to strap down, she hit the "release" button.

They were under two gees again practically before clearing the hull. Holding the throttle as high as it would go, Chandra confirmed that they were moving at right angles to the Intruder's path. Only then did she glance at the chrono.

Ninety seconds to impact.

Next to her, Goode sighed. "I don't think we're going to make it, Chandra," he said, his voice more wistful than afraid.

Chandra opened her mouth to say something reassuring—but it was the radio that spoke. "Avis T-466 to *Origami* lifeboat; come in?"

A civilian tachship? "Lifeboat; Captain Carey here. Listen, you'd better get the hell out of—"

"I know," the voice interrupted. "I eavesdropped a bit on your problems via radio. You're running late, but I'm right behind you. Kill your drive; I think I've got time to grapple onto you."

Chandra hadn't bothered to look at the 'scope yet, but even as she killed the drive Goode was pointing at it. "There he is. Coplanar course, intercept vector, two-five gee. . . ." The blip changed direction slightly, and Chandra realized suddenly that an amateur was at the controls.

Goode realized it, too. Muttering something, he jabbed at the computer keyboard, kicking in the drive again. "Tachship, we're shifting speed and vector to match yours at intercept; just hold your course," he called. "You've got standard magnetic grapples?"

"Yes, and they're all set. Sit tight; here I come."

The seconds ticked by. The blip on the scope was coming up fast . . . and then it was on top of them, and the lifeboat lurched hard as the grapples caught. "Gotcha!" the radio shouted. "Hang on!"

And with seconds to spare—

The universe vanished. Blackness filled the viewports, spilled like a physical thing into the lifeboat. For five long seconds—

And the sun exploded directly in front of them, brighter than Chandra had seen it for weeks. A dozen blips crawled across the 'scope, and the lifeboat's beacon-reader abruptly came to life, informing them they were six thousand kilometers north-west-zenith of Earth's Number Twelve navigational beacon.

Beside her, Chandra felt Goode go limp with released tension. "Still with me?" the radio asked.

"Sure are," Chandra said, wiping the sweat off her palms. "I don't know how to thank you, Mr.—?"

"Dr. Louis Du Bellay," the voice identified himself. "And don't thank me yet. If what you did out there didn't work, there's a worse death coming for all of us."

Chandra had almost forgotten about that. The thought sobered her rising spirits considerably. "You're right. Can you get us into contact with Peacekeeper HQ? We need to report in."

"I can maybe do better than that. Come aboard and we'll find out."

They were given special priority to land, and a car was standing by for them at the field.

General Carey was waiting outside the Situation Room. "I ought to pull your pilot's license for going out there against specific Peacekeeper orders," he told Du Bellay half-seriously, even as he gave his daughter a bear hug. "If Mahendra hadn't confessed to helping you get hold of that tachship I probably would. But he's too good a man to lose to a court-martial. Let's get inside; the Chasers have been reporting in for nearly twenty minutes."

Mahendra looked up as the group approached. "Captain Carey and Officer Goode? Congratulations; it looks like you've done it."

Chandra felt a lump the thickness of ion shielding in her throat. "We slowed him?"

"No, but you deflected him a couple hundredths of a second in the right direction."

"Confirmed?" General Carey asked sharply, as if not daring to believe it.

"Confirmed, sir," Mahendra nodded. "He'll be passing through the upper solar chromosphere instead of deep into the photosphere. We'll get some good flares and a significant radiation increase for a few weeks, but nothing much worse than that."

"And the Intruder hasn't tried to correct his course?" Du Bellay asked quietly.

Mahendra's expression was both sad and grim. "No, Doctor."

Puzzled, Chandra glanced between her father, Mahendra, and Du Bellay, all of whom wore the same look. Even Goode's face was starting to change . . . and suddenly she understood. "You mean . . . the impact killed *all* of them?"

Carey put his arm around her shoulders. "We had no choice, Chandra. It was a matter of survival. You understand, don't you?"

She sighed and, reluctantly, nodded. Goode took her arm and led her to a nearby chair. Sitting there, holding tightly to his hand, she watched with the rest of the Situation Room as the computer plot of the Intruder's position skimmed the sun's surface and shot out once more toward deep space. What had they been like, she wondered numbly . . . and how many of them had she killed so that Earth could live?

She knew she would never know.

Behind the *Dawnsent,* the star receded toward negative infinity, its light red-shifted to invisibility. With mixed feelings Orofan watched its shrinking image on the screen. Beside him, Pliij looked up from the helmboard. "We're all set, Shipmaster. The deviation's been calculated; we can correct course anytime in the next hundred *aarns.*" He paused, and in a more personal tone said, "You did what was necessary, Orofan. Your honor is unblemished."

Orofan signed agreement, but it was an automatic gesture. The assault gun, he noticed, was still in his tentacle, and he slipped it back into its sheath.

A tentacle touched his. "Pliij is right," Lassarr said gently. "Whatever craft that was, its inhabitants had almost certainly been killed by our scoop before we detected it. You could have done nothing to help them. Refusing to accept the ship's mass at that point would have been dishonorable. You did well; your decisions and judgments have been proved correct."

"I know," Orofan sighed. It *was* true; fate had combined with his decisions to save the system from destruction without adding appreciable time to the *Dawnsent's* own journey. He should be satisfied.

And yet . . . the analyzers reported significant numbers of silicon, carbon, oxygen, hydrogen, and nitrogen atoms among the metals of the spacecraft the *Dawnsent* had unintentionally run down. Which of those atoms had once belonged to living creatures? . . . And how many of those beings had died so that the Sk'cee might reach their new home?

He knew he would never know.

THE GIFTIE GIE US

The sun was barely up as I left the cabin that morning, but it was already promising to be a beautiful day. Some freak of nature had blown away the usual cloud cover and was treating the world—or at least the middle Appalachians—to an absolutely clear blue sky, the first I'd seen in months. I admired the sky and the budding April greenery around me as I made my way down the wooded slope, long practice enabling me to avoid trees and other obstructions with minimal effort. It was finally spring, I decided, smiling my half-smile at the blazing sun which was already starting to drive the chill from the morning air. Had it not been for the oppressive silence in the forest, it would almost be possible to convince myself that the Last War had been only a bad dream. But the absence of birds, which for some reason had been particularly hard hit by the Soviet nuke bac barrage, was a continual reminder to me. I had hoped that, by now, nearly five years after the holocaust, they would have made a comeback. Clearly, they had not, and I could only hope that enough had survived the missiles to eventually repopulate the continent. Somehow, it seemed the height of injustice for birds to die in a war over oil.

I had reached the weed-overgrown gravel road that lay southwest of my cabin and had started to cross it when a bit of color caught my eye. About fifty yards down the road, off to the side, was something that looked like a pile of old laundry. But I knew better; no one threw away clothes these days. Almost undoubtedly it was a body.

I regarded it, feeling my jaw tightening. I'd looked at far too many bodies in my lifetime, and my natural impulse was to continue across the road and forget what I'd seen. But someone had to check this out—find out whether it was a stranger or someone local, find out whether it had been a natural death or otherwise—and that someone might just as well be me. Aside from anything else, if there was a murderer running around loose, I wanted to know about it. I took a step toward the form, and as I did so my foot hit a small pile of gravel, scattering it noisily.

The "body" twitched and sat up abruptly, and I suddenly found myself looking at a strikingly lovely woman wrapped up to her chin in a blanket. "Who's there?" she called timidly, staring in my direction.

I froze in panic, waiting for her inevitable reaction to my face, and silently cursed myself for being so careless. It was far too late to run or even turn my head; she was looking straight at me.

But the expected look of horror never materialized. "Who's there?" she repeated, and only then did I notice that her gaze was actually a little to my right. Then I understood.

She was blind.

It says a lot for my sense of priorities that my first reaction was one of relief that she couldn't see me. Only then did it occur to me how cruelly rough postwar life must be for her with such a handicap. "It's all right," I called out, starting forward again. "I won't hurt you."

She turned slightly so that she was facing me—keying on my voice and footsteps, I presume—and waited until I had reached her before speaking again. "Can you tell me where I am? I'm trying to find a town called Hemlock."

"You've got another five miles to go," I told her. Up close, she wasn't as beautiful as I'd first thought. Her nose was a little too long and her face too angular; her figure—what I could see of it beneath the blanket and mismatched clothing—was thin instead of slender. But she was still nice-looking, and I felt emotions stirring within me which I thought had died years ago.

"Are there any doctors there?"

"Only a vet, but he does reasonably well with people, too." I frowned, studying the fatigue in her face, something I'd assumed was just from her journey. Now I wasn't so sure. "Do you feel sick?"

"A little, maybe. But I mostly need the doctor for a friend who's up the road a few miles. We were traveling from Chilhowie and he came down with something." A chill shook her body and she tightened her grip on the blanket.

I touched her forehead. She felt a little warm. "What were his symptoms?"

"Headache, fever, and a little nausea at first. That lasted about a day. Then his muscles started to hurt and he began to get dizzy spells. It wasn't more than an hour before he couldn't even stand up anymore. He told me to keep on going and see if I could find a doctor in Hemlock."

"When did you leave him?"

"Yesterday afternoon. I walked most of the night, I think."

I nodded grimly. "I'm afraid your friend is probably dead by now. I'm sorry."

She looked stricken. "How do you know?"

"It sounds like a variant of one of the bacterial diseases the Russians hit us with in the war. It's kind of rare now, but it's still possible to catch it. And it works fast."

Her whole body seemed to sag, and she closed her eyes. "I have to be sure. You might be wrong."

"I'll go and check on him after we get you settled," I assured her. "Come on."

She let me help her to her feet, draping the blanket sari-style around her head and torso and retrieving the small satchel that seemed to be her only luggage. "Where are you taking me?"

That was a very good question, come to think of it. She wasn't going to make it to Hemlock without a lot more rest, and I sure wasn't going to carry her there. Besides, if she was carrying a Russian bug, I didn't want her going into the town anyway. Theoretically, she could wipe the place out. That left me exactly one alternative. "My cabin."

"I see."

I had never realized that two words, spoken in such a neutral tone, could hold that much information. "It's not what you think," I assured her hastily, feeling an irrational urge to explain my motives. "If you're contagious, I can't let you go into town."

"What about you?"

"I've already been exposed to you, so I've got nothing to lose. But I'm probably not in danger anyway—I've been immunized against a lot of these diseases."

"Very handy. How'd you manage it?"

"I was in the second wave into Iran," I explained, gently pulling her toward the slope leading to my cabin. She came passively. "They had us pretty well doped up against the stuff the Russians had hit the first wave with."

We reached the edge of the road and started up. "Is it uphill all the way?" she asked tiredly.

"It's only a quarter mile," I told her. "You can make it."

We did, but just barely, and I had to half-carry her the last few yards. I put her on the old couch in the living room and then went and got the medical kit I'd taken when I cleared out of Atlanta just hours before the missiles started falling. She had a slight fever and a rapid pulse, but I couldn't tell whether or not that was from our climb. But if she'd really been exposed to one of those Sidewinder strains, I couldn't take any chances, so I gave her one of my last few broad-spectrum pills and told her to get some rest. She was obviously more fatigued than I'd realized, and was asleep almost before the pill reached her stomach.

I covered her with her blanket and then stood there looking at her for a moment, wondering why I was doing all this. I had long ago made the decision to isolate myself as much as possible from what was left of humanity, and up till now I'd done a pretty good job of it. I wasn't about to change that policy, either. This was only a temporary aberration, I told myself firmly; get her well and then send her to Hemlock where she could get a job. Picking up the medical kit, I went quietly out.

It was late afternoon when I returned with the single rabbit my assorted snares had caught. The girl was still asleep, but as I passed her on my way to the kitchen she stirred. "Hello?"

"It's just me," I called back to her. I tossed the rabbit on the kitchen counter and returned through the swinging door to the living room. "How do you feel?"

"Very tired," she said. "I woke up a couple of times while you were gone, but fell asleep again."

"Any muscle aches or dizziness?"

"My leg muscles hurt some, but that's not surprising. Nothing else feels bad." She sat up and shook her head experimentally. "I'm not dizzy, either."

"Good. The tiredness is just a side effect of the medicine I gave you." I sat down next to her, glad to get off my feet. "I think that you're going to be all right."

She inhaled sharply. "Don! I almost forgot—did you get to him in time?"

I shook my head, forgetting how useless that gesture was. "I'm sorry. He was already dead when I found him. I buried him at the side of the road."

Her sightless eyes closed, and a tear welled up under each eyelid. I wanted to put my arm around her and comfort her, but a part of me was still too nervous to try that. So I contented myself with resting my hand gently on her arm. "Was he your husband?" I asked after a moment.

She sniffed and shook her head. "He'd been my friend for the last three years. Sort of a protector and employer. I'll miss him." She swallowed and took a deep, shuddering breath. "I'll be okay. Can I help you with anything?"

"No. All I want you to do right now is rest. I'll get dinner ready—I hope you like rabbit. Uh, by the way, my name's Neil Cameron."

"I'm Heather Davis."

"Nice to meet you. Look, why don't you lie down again. I'll call you when dinner's ready."

Supper was a short, quiet affair. Heather was too groggy and depressed to say or eat much, and I was far too out of practice at dinner conversation to make up for it. So we ate roast rabbit and a couple of carrots from last summer's crop, and then, as the sun disappeared behind the Appalachians, I led her to my bedroom. She sat on the edge of the bed, a puzzled and wary look on her face, as I rummaged in my footlocker for another blanket. "You'll be more comfortable here," I told her.

"I don't mind the couch," she murmured in that neutral tone she'd used on me before.

"I insist." I found the blanket and turned to face her. She was still sitting on the bed, her hands exploring the size and feel of the queen-size mattress. There was plenty of room there for two, and for a moment I was tempted. Instead, I took a step toward the door. "I've got another hour's worth of work to do," I said. "Uh, the bathroom's out the door to the left—the faucets and toilet work, but easy on the water and don't flush unless it's necessary. If you need me tonight, just call. I'll be on the couch."

Her face was lifted toward mine, and for a second I had the weird feeling she was studying my face. An illusion, of course. But whatever she heard in my voice apparently satisfied her, because she nodded wearily and climbed under the blanket.

Leaving the bedroom door open so I could hear her, I headed for the kitchen, tossing my blanket onto the couch as I passed it. I lit a candle against the growing darkness and, using the water from the solar-heated tank sparingly, I began to clean up the dinner dishes. And as I worked, not surprisingly, I thought about Heather Davis.

All the standard questions went through my mind—who was she, where did she come from, how had she survived for five years—but none of them was really uppermost in my mind. Five years of primitive hardship and self-imposed solitude should have pretty well wiped out my sex urge, or so I would have thought. But it was all coming back in a rush, and as my lust grew my thoughts became increasingly turbulent. I knew she would accept me into her bed—if not willingly, at least passively. In her position, she couldn't risk refusing me. Besides, I'd given her food and shelter and maybe saved her life. She owed me.

And then I glanced up, and all the passion left me like someone had pulled a plug. Reflecting dimly back at me from the kitchen window, framed by the bars I'd installed for security, was my face. I'd lived with it for over five years now, ever since the Soviet nerve gas barrage near Abadan that had somehow seeped through my mask, but it still made me shudder. The reactions of other people were even worse, ranging from wide-eyed stares to gasps of horror, the latter especially common among women and children. Frozen by some trick of the gas into a tortured grimace, the left side of my face looked more like a fright mask than like anything human; the right side, normal except for three parallel scars from a mortar fragment, only made the other half look worse. My hair and beard followed the same pattern: a normal chestnut brown on the right, pure white on the left. And if all that weren't enough, there was my left eye; mobile and still with perfect vision, it had turned from brown to a pale yellow, and sometimes seemed to glow in the dark.

I stared at my reflection for a long minute before returning to my work. No, I couldn't take advantage of Heather's blindness that way. It would be unfair of me to go to bed with her when she couldn't tell how horrible I looked. Somewhere in the back of my mind, I was aware that this was the same argument, in reverse, that I used to avoid approaching any of the sighted girls in Hemlock, but that was irrelevant. The discussion was closed.

I finished the dishes in a subdued frame of mind and then headed toward the front door. As I reached it, I heard a muffled sound from the bedroom and tiptoed in to investigate.

Curled into a fetal position under the blanket, her back to the door, Heather was crying. I stood irresolutely for a moment, then went in and sat down by her on the bed. She flinched as I touched her shoulder. "It's all right," I whispered to her. "You're safe now. It's all right. I won't hurt you."

Eventually, the sobs ceased and the tenseness went out of her body, and a few minutes later the rhythm of her breathing changed as she fell asleep. Careful not to wake her, I got up and went back to the doorway. There I stopped and looked at her for a moment, ashamed of my earlier thoughts. Heather wasn't just a warm female body put here for my amusement. She was another human being, and whether she stayed here an hour or a week she was entitled to courtesy and respect. It was the least I could do for her in the face of the barbarism out there. For that matter, it was the least I could do for *me*. There were enough savages in the world today; I had no desire to add to their number.

I closed the bedroom door halfway as a gesture to her privacy and went to finish my chores.

I stayed close to the cabin for the next couple of days, tending my garden and doing needed repairs and odd jobs. Heather's fever disappeared, and she recovered quickly from the effects of her journey and the medicine I'd given her. By the third morning after her arrival, I felt it was safe to leave her and go check on my snares. They were empty; but after a few hours of hunting with my bow and arrows I bagged a small squirrel, so at least we wouldn't go hungry. I swung by my "refrigerator" to pick up some vegetables and then returned to the cabin. Once there, I went straight to the bedroom to check on Heather.

She was gone.

I stood there for a moment, dumbfounded. The damn girl had cleared out, sure enough—and probably helped herself to everything she could get her hands on. I'd been a naïve fool to leave her here alone. "Heather!" I barked, the name tasting like a curse.

"I'm back here," a voice called faintly.

I started, and after a second I went outside and made my way to the rear of the cabin. Sleeves rolled up, Heather was standing by the hand pump that brought water from the nearby stream and sent it into the storage tank on the roof. She smiled in the direction of my footsteps, her face glistening with sweat. "Hi," she said. "I was just taking a break. How was the hunting?"

"Fair; we've got squirrel for supper," I told her, trying to keep my voice casual—hard to do when you're feeling like a jerk. "Also brought some corn. Why aren't you in bed?"

She shrugged. "I've never liked being a professional freeloader. Besides, you forgot to pump any water last night."

I hadn't forgotten—I'd just been too lazy—but I hadn't expected her to notice. The tank usually held enough water for three or four days, though I tried to keep it full. "Well, thanks very much. I appreciate it."

"No charge. You said you had some corn? Where did you get that?"

I started to point north, remembered in time the gesture would be wasted. "About a mile upstream there's a hollow right behind a small waterfall. The creek comes from underground at that point and stays pretty cold even in the summer. I use the hollow as my refrigerator. In winter, of course, it's more like a freezer."

"That's a good idea," Heather nodded, "although it's kind of far to go for a midnight snack. I'll bet it's fun keeping the animals out, too."

"It was, but I've pretty well got that problem solved." I suddenly realized I was still holding the squirrel and corn. "Come on, let's go inside. You look tired."

"Okay." She seemed to hesitate just a second, then stepped up to me and took my arm, letting me lead her back into the cabin.

Another surprise awaited me in the living room. Heather had neatly folded my blanket and laid it at one end of the couch; her satchel, some of its contents strewn around it, sat at the other end. In the middle lay a shirt I'd torn just that morning, neatly mended.

"I'll be darned," I exclaimed in delight, unaware of the pun until after I'd said it. "How did you know that shirt needed sewing?"

She shrugged. "I heard you getting dressed this morning, and right in the middle of it I heard something tear. You muttered under your breath and threw whatever it was onto the couch. When I got up I found the shirt and used a needle and thread from my sewing kit to mend it. I hope the thread doesn't look too bad there—I had no idea what colors I was working with."

I opened my mouth, but closed it again and instead reached for the shirt, my cheerful mood suddenly overshadowed by an uncomfortable feeling creeping up my backbone. Dimly, I remembered the sequence of events Heather had described, but it seemed too incredible that she should have pieced such subtle clues together that easily. Was it possible she wasn't quite blind?

There was a way to check. Still holding the shirt, I walked over to the window, loosening my belt with one hand until the big brass army buckle was free. The sun had come out from behind the clouds and light was streaming brightly through the glass. I turned slightly so that I was facing Heather and twisted my buckle, sending a healthy chuck of that sunlight straight at her eyes.

Nothing. She didn't flinch or even blink. Feeling a little silly, I let the loosened buckle flop back down against my leg and held up the shirt for a close examination, trying to pretend that that had been my reason for moving into the light in the first place. The seam was strong and reasonably straight, though the material bunched a little in places and the white thread was in sharp contrast with the brown plaid. "It looks fine," I told Heather. "Its exactly what I needed. Thank you for doing it for me."

Her face, which had been looking a little apprehensive, broke into a tentative smile. "I'm glad it's all right," she said, and I wondered that I had ever doubted her handicap. Only a blind woman could ever face me and still smile like that. And even though I knew how undeserved that smile was, I rather liked it.

I cleared my throat. "I guess I'd better go skin the squirrel and start cooking it."

"Okay. First, though, come on back and show me how to tell when the water tank's full. I want to finish that pumping before dinner."

It was pretty clear that Heather was completely healed from whatever she had caught, but I decided to keep her at the cabin for a few more days anyway. My official reason was that it would be best to keep her under observation for a bit longer, but this was at least eighty percent rationalization, if not outright lie: the simple fact was that I found her very nice to have around. I had never before had the chance to find out how much easier primitive life could be with an extra pair of hands to help with the work. Despite her blindness, Heather pitched in with skill and determination, and if I somehow failed to give her enough to do she would seek out work on her own. One morning, for example, as I was weeding the garden, she came to me with a pile of dirty clothes and insisted that I lead her down to the stream and find a place where she could wash them.

But most of all, I enjoyed just being able to relax in the company of another human being. That sounds almost trite, I suppose, but it was something I hadn't been able to do for five years. And, while I'd buried my need for companionship as deeply as I could, I hadn't killed it, a fact my infrequent trips to Hemlock usually only emphasized. The people of that tiny community were helpful enough—their assistance and willingness to teach me the necessary backwoods survival skills had probably saved my life the first year after the war—but I couldn't relax in their presence, any more than they could in mine. My face was a barrier as strong as the Berlin Wall.

But with Heather the problem didn't exist. We talked a great deal together, usually as we worked, our conversation ranging from trivia to philosophy to the practical details of postwar life. Heather's knowledge of music, literature, and household tasks was far superior to mine, while I held an edge in politics, hunting, and trapping. Her sense of humor, while a little dry, meshed well with mine, and a lot of our moral values were similar. Under different circumstances I would have been happy to keep her here just as long as I possibly could. But I knew that wouldn't be fair to her.

My conscience finally caught up with me late one evening after dinner as we sat together on the couch. Heather was continuing her assault on the pile of mending I'd accumulated over the years; I was trying to carve a new ax handle. My heart wasn't really in it, though, and my thoughts and gaze kept drifting to Heather. Her sewing skill had increased since that first shirt she'd mended for me; her fingers moved swiftly, surely, and the seam was straight and clean. Bathed in the soft light of a nearby candle, the warmth of which she enjoyed, she was a pleasure to watch. I wondered how I was going to broach the subject.

She gave me the opening herself. "You're very quiet tonight, Neil," she said after a particularly long lull in the conversation. "What are you thinking about?"

I gritted my teeth and plunged in. "I've been thinking it's about time to take you to Hemlock, introduce you around, and see if we can get you a job or something with one of the families there."

The nimble fingers faltered for a moment. "I see," she said at last. "Are you sure I'm not contagious anymore? I wouldn't want to get anyone sick."

"No, I'm certain you're completely recovered. I'm not even sure you had a deadly bug, anyway."

"Okay. But I wonder if it might be better if I stick around for another week or two, until the garden's going a little better and you don't have to spend so much time on it."

I frowned. This was going all wrong—she was supposed to be jumping at the chance to get back to humanity again, not making excuses to stay here. "Thanks for the offer, but I can manage. You've been a lot of help, though, and I wish I could repay you more than . . ." I let the sentence trail off. Heather's face and body had gone rigid, and she was no longer sewing. "What's the matter? Would you rather go somewhere else instead of Hemlock? I'll help you get to anywhere you want."

Heather shook her head and sighed. "No, its not that. I just . . . don't want to leave you."

I stared at her, feeling sandbagged. "Why?"

"I like being here. I like working with you. You don't—you don't care that I'm blind. You accept me as a person."

There was a whole truckload of irony in there somewhere but I couldn't be bothered with it at the moment. "Listen, Heather, don't get the idea I'm all noble or anything, because I'm not. If you knew more about me you'd realize that."

"Perhaps." Her tone said she didn't believe it.

There was no way out of it. Up till now I'd been pretty successful at keeping my appearance a secret from her, but I couldn't hide the truth any longer. I would have to tell her about my face. "If you weren't blind, Heather, you wouldn't have wanted to stay here ten minutes. I'm . . . my face is pretty badly disfigured."

She nodded casual acceptance of the information. Maybe she didn't believe it, either. "How did it happen?"

"I was a captain in the army during the Iranian segment of the Last War; you know, the Soviet drive toward the oil fields. They were using lots of elaborate nerve gases on us, and one of them found its way into the left side of my gas mask." I kept my voice even; I was just reciting facts. "None of it got into the nosepiece or respirator, so it didn't kill me, but it left one side of my face paralyzed. I won't trouble you with any details, but the net effect is pretty hideous."

"I thought something must have happened to you in the war," she murmured. "You never speak of your life during that time. . . . Is that why you were here when the missiles came?"

"Yes. I was in a hospital in Atlanta, undergoing tests to see if my condition could be reversed. They hadn't made any progress when I saw the handwriting on the wall and decided it was time to pull out. A friend of mine had told me about his cabin in the Appalachians, so

I loaded some supplies in a Jeep and came here. I beat the missiles by about three hours."

"Oh, so this place wasn't originally yours. And I'd been thinking all along how terribly clever and foresighted you'd been to have built a cabin out here in case the world blew itself up."

"Sorry. Major Frank Matheson was the one with all the foresight. He was also one of the best friends I ever had." That sounded too much like an epitaph for my taste; I was still hoping he'd show up here some-day. But he and his wife had been in Washington when the missiles started falling. . . . I shook my head to clear it. "Anyway, we're getting off the subject. The point is that I'm taking advantage of you by keeping you here. I think you'd be better off living in a community with other people."

"Yes, I suppose you would think that." Heather's lip curled, and for the first time since I'd met her I heard bitterness in her voice. "You prob-ably think it's been beer and skittles for me. Well, it hasn't." She glowered at some unknown memory; but even as I groped for something to say, her anger turned to sadness, and when she spoke again her voice was quiet. "I went blind almost a year before the war; two weeks after my eighteenth birthday. I had a small brain tumor in the back of my head and was taking an experimental interferon derivative. Somehow, some-thing went wrong with the batch they were giving me, and at about the same time I caught some kind of viral infection. The combination nearly killed me—they told me afterwards that I had delirium, high fever, and an absolutely crazy EEG trace for nearly forty hours. When I recovered, the tumor was shrinking and I was blind. That first morning, when I woke up . . . I thought I was either dead or insane." Her eyes closed, and she shivered violently. After a moment she continued. "People hate me, Neil. Either hate me or are afraid of me, especially now that civilization's becoming a thing of the past."

"Why would people hate you?" I asked. "I mean, that's a pretty dras-tic reaction."

She hesitated, and a series of unreadable expressions flashed across her face. The moment passed, and she shrugged. "I guess its because I'm blind. It makes me an oddball and—well, something of a parasite."

I snorted. "You're no parasite."

"You're very kind, Neil. But I know better."

I shook my head, thinking of all the work she did around here. To me it was perfectly obvious that she was pulling her own weight, if not a little more. I wondered why she couldn't see that; and, in response, a fragment from a half-forgotten poem swam up from my subconscious. "'O wad some Pow'r the giftie gie us / To see oursels as others see us . . .'" I murmured, trailing off as the rest of the piece drifted from my grasp.

Surprisingly, Heather picked up where I'd left off: "'It wad frae mony a blunder free us.

"'And foolish notion:

"'What airs in dress an' gait wad lea'e us,

"'And ev'n devotion!'"

She paused for a moment, as if listening to the last echoes from her words. "I've always liked Robert Burns," she said quietly.

"That's the only thing of his I know," I confessed. "My father used to quote it at us whenever our views of life were at odds with his. Despite your own estimation, Heather, the fact is that you're a very talented and hardworking woman and no one in his right mind is going to care whether you're blind or not. People won't think any less of you because of that."

A wry smile touched her lips. "You're not being consistent, Neil dear. That's exactly what you seem to think people are doing to you. If they can judge you by your face, why can't they judge me by my blindness?"

She had me there. I wanted to tell her that was different, but it was obvious she wouldn't buy any explanation like that—her blindness made it impossible for her to realize just how strongly my appearance affected everyone who saw it. I tried to think up some other reasoning I could use . . . and suddenly it dawned on me what I was doing. Here I was, sitting next to a lovely woman who was very possibly the last person on Earth who could endure my company—and I was trying to send her away from me!

Insanity has never run in my family, unless you count our military traditions. I'd tried being noble and honest, and my conscience was clear. If she wanted to think I was doing her a favor, that was up to her. "All right, Heather. If you're really sure you want to stay, I'll be more than happy to have you here. I have to admit that the thought of you leaving was pretty hard. But I had to—you know."

She reached over and touched my arm. "Yes. Thank you for being honest. And for letting me stay."

"Sure. Look, it's getting late, and we've got to get up by dawn. Let's get some rest."

"Okay." She paused. "Neil, were you ever married?"

I blinked at the abrupt change of subject. "Once, for a couple of years, when I was twenty-one. It ended in divorce. Why?"

She turned her head half away from me as if she didn't want me to see her face. "I was just wondering why you were still . . . sleeping on the couch instead of . . . with me."

The evening was rapidly taking on a feeling of unreality for me. I hadn't felt this strangely nervous since my first date in high school, and I opened my mouth twice before I got any words to come out. "I didn't want to impose on you." Damn, that sounded stupid! I tried again. "I mean, it wouldn't be fair for me to take advantage of you like that. You might just do it because you felt you owed it to me. I don't want it that way. I figured that if you ever wanted me like that you'd let me know somehow."

She nodded, her face still averted, and swallowed. "Neil . . . will you come to bed with me?"

I looked at her, my eyes sweeping her body, and for the first time I noticed that her hands were trembling. And suddenly I realized that she was not just offering an altruistic favor to a lonely hermit. In many ways Heather was an outcast, too, and she needed this as much as I did.

Never having been the romantic type, I didn't know the right words to say. So, instead, I blew out the candles, took Heather by the arm, and led her to the bedroom.

Afterwards she fell asleep next to me, one arm across my chest with her hand resting against my good right cheek. I watched the moonlight throwing shadows on the bedroom wall for a few minutes longer before drifting off myself, and I slept more restfully that night than I had in months.

The weeks went by, spring turning into summer with astonishing speed. Heather continued to take on a good deal of the day-to-day work of running our cabin, leaving me free to hunt, trap, and carry out repairs and maintenance that I'd been putting off for lack of time. We had our share of disagreements and misunderstandings, but as we got to know each other's moods and thoughts we began to mesh together, to the point where it sometimes seemed to me that we were becoming two parts of a single, well-oiled machine. Within the first four months I felt I knew this woman better than I'd known anyone else in my entire life. And, although I refused to use the word even to myself, I was quickly learning to love her.

And yet, there was something about Heather that bothered me, something so subtle that it was a long time before I could even put my finger on it. It wasn't anything big, and it didn't happen with any regularity, but sometimes Heather just seemed to know too much about what was going on around her.

I brooded about it off and on for several weeks, trying to remember everything Heather had ever said about her blindness. From her explanation I assumed her eyes and optic nerves were still healthy, that only the sight center of her brain had been affected, and for a while I wondered if her blindness was either incomplete or possibly intermittent. But neither explanation was satisfactory: if she was blind enough that she couldn't make out my face, she was too blind for any practical purpose; and if she occasionally regained her vision, her first reaction to my appearance would have been impossible for me to miss. Besides, there was no reason why she would keep such a thing secret, especially since she was so open about every other aspect of her life.

Eventually I gave up thinking about it and chalked up her abilities to the enhanced senses blind people are reputed to have. It really wasn't important, after all, and Heather and I had come too far for me to start wondering if she was hiding something from me. Having overcome the problems of my face and her blindness, I wasn't about to let a figment of my imagination become a barrier between us.

So we worked and sweated, laughed and occasionally loafed, and generally got by pretty well. As the crops in our garden grew large enough that Heather could take over some of the weeding duties, I began to expand the network of handmade traps and snares that I had set up in the wooded hills around our cabin. I took the job seriously—I was after enough meat and furs for two people this year—and I ranged farther than usual in search of good sites.

It was on one of these trips that I stumbled across the freshly killed man.

I stood—or, rather, crouched—by the still form lying face downwards in the rotting leaves, my bow and arrow half-drawn and ready as my eyes raked the woods for signs of a possible attacker. Nothing moved, and after a moment I put down the bow and began to examine the body. He was a middle-aged man whom I vaguely remembered as living in a shack some six miles west of Hemlock and a couple of miles southwest of my cabin. He seemed to have run and crawled here under his own steam before dying, probably no more than a few hours ago. The cause of death was obvious; a homemade knife hilt still protruded from his back just above the right kidney.

I rose slowly to my feet. The dead man couldn't have made it all the way here from his shack with that wound. He must have been either in the woods or on the road, which was only a quarter mile or so away from here, when he ran into . . . who? Who would murder a harmless old man like this? On a hunch, I knelt down and checked the pockets in the faded overalls. Empty. No pocketknife, snare wire, fishhooks, or any of the other things he was likely to have been carrying. So the crime had probably started out as a robbery, perhaps turning into murder when the victim tried to escape. Not a local, I decided; more likely a wandering vagrant, who was probably long gone by now. Unless, of course, he'd gone down into Hemlock.

Or had found my cabin.

My heart skipped a beat, and before my fears were even completely formed I was racing through the woods as fast as I dared, heading for home. The cabin was not easy to see, even from higher spots on the surrounding hills, but it wasn't invisible, and there'd been only so much I'd been able to do to disguise the old drive leading up to it from the road. If anything happened to Heather . . . I refused to think about it, forcing myself instead to greater speed. Maybe I could beat him there.

I was too late. Out of breath, I had slowed to a walk as I approached the cabin, and as I started the last hundred yards I heard male voices. Cursing inwardly, I nocked an arrow and made my way silently forward.

There were six young men standing casually around the front of our cabin, chatting more or less amicably with Heather, who was leaning back against the closed front door. The visitors were all of the same type: thin and hungry-looking, with hard-bitten faces that had long ago forgotten about compassion or comfort. Their transport—six well-worn bicycles—stood a little further from the cabin. In another age the men would have fit easily into any motorcycle gang in the country; the image of them pedaling along on bicycles was faintly ludicrous. But there was nothing funny about the sheath knives they were wearing.

I raised my bow and started to draw it, aiming for the man nearest Heather . . . and hesitated. I had no proof that they had killed the man I'd found, and until I did I couldn't shoot them down in cold blood. Besides, there were too many of them. I couldn't get all six before one of them got to Heather and used her as a shield.

Lowering the bow again, I tried to think. The smart thing to do would be to triple-time it down to Hemlock and recruit some help. But I didn't dare leave Heather alone. From the bits of conversation I could hear I gathered that Heather had told them I would be returning soon, and it was clear that they had decided to behave themselves until I showed up. But they wouldn't wait forever, and if they came to the conclusion she was lying things could turn ugly very quickly.

There were really no choices left to me. I would have to go on in and confront them, playing things by ear. If I bluffed well, or played stupid enough, there was a chance that they would take whatever food we offered them and leave without causing trouble. Even at six-to-one odds murder could be a tricky business; hopefully, I could convince them we weren't worth the risk.

One thing I was *not* going to do, though, was provide them with more weapons. Backing a few yards further into the woods, I found a pile of leaves and hid my bow and quiver beneath it. My big bowie knife went into concealment in my right boot. I then made a wide quarter-circle around the cabin so as to approach from a different direction. Taking a deep breath, I strode forward.

I deliberately made no attempt to be quiet, with the result that, as I broke from the woods, all eyes were turned in my direction. I hesitated just an instant, as if startled by their presence, and then walked calmly up to them.

Heather must have recognized my footsteps. "Is that you, Neil? Hello, dear—we have some visitors."

"I see that," I replied. I'd been wondering how I could tip Heather off that there could be trouble here, but I saw now that that wouldn't be necessary. Her voice was cheery enough, but her smile was too brittle and there were lines in her face that I knew didn't belong there. She already knew something was wrong. "Welcome, gentlemen; it isn't often that we get this much company."

Their apparent leader—who looked to be all of twenty-five—recovered first from the shock of my face. "Uh, howdy," he said. "My name's Duke. We were wondering if maybe you could spare some food."

"We haven't got much ourselves, but I guess we've got a little extra," I told him, studying the six as unobtrusively as possible. They were all younger than I was, by twenty years in some cases, which probably gave them a slight edge in speed and maybe stamina. All were armed with knives, and two of them also sported club-sized lengths of metal pipe.

On the plus side, I was much better fed than they were and had had a good deal of combat training and experience. If I'd been alone with them, I would have judged the odds as roughly equal. But Heather's presence put me at a dangerous disadvantage.

I would have to remedy that, and while I still had the initiative was the best time to try. "Heather," I said, turning to face her, "why don't you see how much rabbit meat is left from last night."

"Okay," she breathed and started to open the door behind her.

But Duke was smarter than I thought. "Colby" he called to one of the boys nearest Heather, "go with her and give her a hand."

"That's not necessary," I said, as Heather hesitated and Colby moved to her side. "She's perfectly capable."

"Sure, man, but she *is* blind," Duke soothed. "Hey, Colby won't take nothing."

"Yeah," Colby agreed. "C'mon, kid, let's go in."

"No!" I barked, taking a step toward him. I knew instantly that I had overreacted, but I couldn't help it. Attached to Colby's belt were two sheaths, one of which was empty. From the other protruded a hilt whose workmanship I recognized.

Perhaps Colby saw me looking at his empty sheath, or maybe it was something in my voice that tipped him off. Whichever, when I raised my eyes to his face I found him staring at me with a mixture of anger and fear. "He knows!" he croaked, and reached for his remaining knife.

He never got a chance to use it. Even before the words were out of his mouth I had taken the single long stride that put me within range; and as the knifetip cleared the sheath, I snapped a savage kick to his belly. He doubled over, and I had barely enough time to regain my balance and turn around before I found myself surrounded. Out of the corner of my eye I saw Heather disappear into the cabin, one of the boys in hot pursuit, but I had no chance to go to her aid. Knives glinting, they moved in.

I didn't wait for them to get within range, but charged the closest one. He probably hadn't been attacked by an unarmed man in years, and the shock seemed to throw his timing off. I deflected his knife hand easily and gave him an elbow across the face as I passed him. The others, yelling obscenities, ran forward, trying to encircle me again. One came too close and got his knife kicked from his hand. He backpedaled fast enough to avoid my next kick and drew the metal pipe from his belt.

Clearly surprised by my unexpected resistance, my attackers hesitated, and I used the breathing space to pull my bowie knife from my boot.

For a second we stood facing each other. "All right," I said in the deadliest voice I could manage, "I'll give you punks just one chance. Drop your weapons or I'll carve you into fertilizer."

I'd never fought with a knife in actual combat, but the training was there, and it must have showed in my stance and grip. "Duke . . . ?" the boy I'd elbowed began.

"Shut up, Al," Duke said, but without too much conviction.

A sound from the cabin door caught my attention. Heather, struggling against an arm across her throat, was being forced outside by the punk who'd been chasing her earlier. "Not so fast, you son of a bitch," he called at me, panting slightly.

"Attaboy, Jackson," Duke crowed. He turned back to me, eyes smoldering. "Now you drop *your* knife, pal. Or else your broad gets it."

"Don't listen to him, Neil!" Heather shouted, her sentence ending with a little gasp of pain.

"Leave her alone!" I took a half step toward the door—and heard the faint sound of cloth against skin behind me.

Heather shrieked even as I started to turn, my left arm rising to block. But I was too late. The whistling iron pipe, intended for my head, landed across my shoulder instead, still hard enough to stun. I felt my legs turn to rubber, and as I hit the ground the world exploded in front of me and then went black.

I must have been out only a few seconds, because when my head cleared I was lying on my back with Duke and two of his pack standing over me. I wondered what they were waiting for, and gradually realized Heather was shouting at them. "Don't kill him! I'll make a deal with you!"

"You don't have nothing to offer that we can't take by ourselves," Duke said flatly, his glare still on me.

"That's not strictly true," Heather shot back, her voice tinted with both horror and determination. "Rape isn't nearly as enjoyable as sex with a willing woman. But I'm not talking about that. I can tell you where there's a big cache of food and furs."

That got Duke's attention, but good. He looked up at her, eyes narrowed. "Where?"

"It's well hidden. You'll never find it if you hurt either of us."

"Willy! Zac! What've we got?" Duke called.

I turned my head slowly toward the cabin as two of the boys came out the door. Heather, I saw, was no longer being held, though Jackson stood close by her with his knife drawn.

"Not too much in here," one of the two called back. "A couple days' worth of food, maybe, and some other stuff we can use."

Duke looked back down at me. "Okay, lady, it's a deal. Zac, go see if you can find some rope."

"You gonna tie him up out here?" Al asked. "Someone might find him."

"Naw, we're gonna take them inside. But I want his hands tied before he gets up." Duke grinned down at me. "You've got a good place here to hole up. We almost missed it."

I didn't bother to reply. A moment later Zac brought out most of my last coil of nylon rope, and in two minutes my hands were tied tightly behind my back. I was then dragged to my feet and marched at knifepoint into the cabin. Heather was already inside, her hands similarly tied.

"Let's put 'em in the kitchen," Willy suggested. "We can tie 'em to chairs there."

We were taken in and made to sit down, but they ran short of rope and only I was actually tied to my chair. Al suggested instead that Heather and I be roped to each other, but Duke decided against it. "She can't get into any trouble," he scoffed. Stepping over to me, he inspected my ropes and then drew his knife, resting its tip against my Adam's apple. "Okay, girl, I got my knife at your friend's throat. Give."

She gave them directions to my upstream "refrigerator" hollow. "You'll probably need to walk—there's too much undergrowth for bikes," she concluded.

"Okay, we'll go take a look." Duke sheathed his knife and glanced at the others. "Jackson, you and Colby stay here and keep an eye on things. And keep your paws off the food—hear?"

"Gotcha," Jackson said. Colby, mobile but still hunched over from my kick, nodded weakly.

Willy caught Duke's eye, glanced meaningfully in my direction. "Why bother with guards?"

"'Cause if she's lying we want him in good shape, so we can take him apart for her," he said calmly. "Let's get started."

They left. Jackson and Colby hung around a little longer, until the sounds of conversation from the others faded into the distance, and then went into the living room where they'd be more comfortable. The swinging door closed behind them and we were alone.

I looked at Heather, wishing I had something encouraging to say. "Did they hurt you?" I whispered instead.

"No." She paused. "They're going to kill us, aren't they?"

There was no point in lying to her. "Probably. I blew it, Heather." The words made my throat ache.

"Maybe not. They took the four kitchen knives out of the drawers earlier. But they didn't find your bayonet."

I stared at her, hope and surprise fighting for supremacy in my mind. I'd long ago told Heather of the weapon and its hiding place, of course: it had been put on top of the wall cabinet over the kitchen sink precisely for a circumstance like this. There was only a three-inch-high gap between the cabinet and ceiling, an easy spot to overlook in a quick search. But how did Heather know Duke's punks had missed it?

For the moment, though, the answer was unimportant. Carefully, I tested the ropes that held me to the chair. It was a complete waste of time—the boys hadn't taken any chances. "There's no way for me to get over to it," I admitted to Heather at last.

"I know." Her face was very pale, but her mouth was set in grim lines. Swaying slightly, she stood up from her chair. Her feet were tied at the ankles, but by swiveling alternately on heels and toes she was able to inch across the floor. Turning her back to the counter that adjoined the sink, she used her tied hands to help push herself into a sitting position on top of it. The counter was, for a change, clear of dishes and other obstacles, and by twisting around Heather was able to rise into a kneeling posture. Positioning herself carefully, she bowed forward at the waist and stretched her hands upwards toward the bayonet.

She couldn't reach it.

"Damn, damn, damn," she whispered bitterly. She tried again, straining an inch or two higher this time, but she was still nearly a foot too short. Standing up would help, but there was no way, tied as she was, for her to get the needed leverage to manage such a move.

She seemed to realize that, and for a moment she knelt motionlessly. I could see tears of frustration in her eyes. "It's all right, Heather—" I began.

"Shut up, Neil." She thought for another minute and I could see her come to some decision. Moving cautiously, she turned so that she was leaning over the sink in a precarious-looking position. Then, taking a deep breath, she hit the window sharply with her elbow. It shattered with a loud crash.

I bit back my involuntary exclamation. Jackson and Colby stormed in, knives at the ready. "What the hell's goin' on?" Jackson demanded. He glanced at me to confirm that my ropes were still intact, then strode to the counter and roughly hauled Heather down. "What the hell were you trying to pull, bitch?"

She shook her head defiantly. He slapped her, hard, and turned to me. "What was she tryin' to do?"

A damn good question, especially as I hadn't the slightest idea. "She didn't say, but I think she was trying to get out," I said, hoping I was way off the mark. "I guess she forgot about the security bars."

He looked back at Heather, who was now looking sullen. From the doorway, Colby spoke up. "I'll bet she was looking for something. Let's check those cupboards."

Jackson dragged Heather back to her chair and then returned to the cabinet. I watched in helpless silence as he searched all the cabinet shelves and then, almost as an afterthought, climbed onto the counter and looked on top of it. With a triumphant war whoop, he pulled out the bayonet. "Trying to get out, huh?" he sneered at me. "Hot damn! Wait'll Duke sees this."

"Jackson," Heather said, speaking to him for the first time, "won't you let us go? Please? We can't hurt you anymore—you'll all be long gone before we could do anything."

"Screw you, sister." He looked at her a moment, as if wondering whether she should be punished for her escape attempt, then apparently decided against it. Swinging the bayonet idly, he nodded at Colby. "Let's get back to the cards. I don't think we'll have any more trouble from these two."

I squeezed my eyes shut, feeling crushed. The bayonet had been, at best, a very long shot, but somehow it had helped just to know it was there if I was ever able to get to it. Now that last chance was gone; and all because I hadn't had a convincing lie ready when it had been needed. I'd blown it for us twice.

A faint scraping sound made me open my eyes. Heather had stood up again and was once more inching her way toward the sink. "Heather—?"

"Shh!" she hissed. Her face held concentration, and not even a touch of the despair I was feeling. What was she up to?

I soon found out. Again she hoisted herself to a sitting position, on the edge of the sink itself this time. Instead of getting up on her knees, though, she extended her hands back toward the jagged spikes of glass in the broken window. Without hesitation—and without touching anything else—her fingers zeroed in on a particularly loose fragment. She tugged, breaking it free with only the slightest *snap,* and I finally realized what her plan had been. Hopping down with her prize, she started back toward me.

But we were still a long way from freedom. We now had something to cut the ropes with, but with my hands half-numbed from loss of circulation I knew I could never cut Heather's bonds without severing a vein in the process. Her hands were probably in the same condition, and even with her enhanced sense of touch she wouldn't do much better on my ropes. Still, it was our only hope.

Heather, however, seemed to have an entirely different idea. "Open your legs an inch," she whispered as she reached me. I started to object, but she seemed to know what she was doing, so I shut up and did as I was told. Turning so that her back was to me, she stooped down and placed the piece of glass directly between my knees. "Close 'em," she said.

"Wait a second, Heather, this is too dangerous," I objected, suddenly realizing what she had in mind. "Why don't you go around and cut my ropes instead?"

She ignored the suggestion. "Close your knees and hold it tight," she hissed furiously.

I did so. I was terrified for her hands, and my stomach was knotted at the thought of what was probably going to happen, but we were running out of time. If we did nothing before Duke returned, we were dead. Heather crouched a bit more, placed one of her bonds gingerly against the glass, and began to rub.

After all my fears it was like watching a minor miracle happen. Quickly, accurately, and with no wasted motion, Heather attacked the ropes around her wrists. Even with her hands undoubtedly numb she always seemed to know exactly where the ropes and glass were relative to her skin, almost as if she had eyes in the back of her head. Only once did she so much as scratch herself, and that was due to a momentary loss of balance that made her sway a little.

Seconds later her hands were free. Sitting down on the floor, she took the glass from between my knees and set to work on her ankle ropes. They were off almost immediately. For another few seconds she remained where she was, grimacing as the blood flowed back into her hands and feet. Then she stood up and walked around behind me, and I felt her fingers tugging and probing at the ropes on my wrists. "Come on, hurry up," I muttered impatiently.

"Just a minute," she whispered back, her voice strangely tense. Her examination finally over, she began to cut my ropes, moving much more slowly than she had earlier. Despite her caution, though, she nicked me twice and once even managed to cut her own finger. However she had worked her earlier miracle, things unfortunately seemed to be back to normal now.

But finally I was free, and as I rubbed life back into my tingling hands Heather cut the ropes on my feet and those tying me to the chair. Standing up carefully, I tiptoed over to the cupboard and utensil drawers to arm myself. A large pan lid and carving fork went into my left hand, the fork extending a couple of inches past the lid's rim; a one-piece wooden rolling pin, the housewife's traditional weapon, went into my right. I handed Heather a small metal frying pan and positioned her by the swinging door. "I'll announce myself before I come back in," I told her. "If anyone else comes through, clobber him."

"All right." She paused. "They're both still sitting on the couch playing cards. The bayonet is on the floor in front of Jackson."

I nodded. I still didn't understand Heather's strangely capricious radar, but for the moment the *how* and *why* were irrelevant. She seemed to know how it worked and when it could be trusted, and that was what mattered right now. "Good. This should only take a minute."

"Be careful, Neil," she said, moving next to me for a quick hug.

I kissed her. "You bet, honey." Facing the door, I settled my nerves for combat. I'd nearly blown it for us twice now. This time was going to be different.

And it was.

The rest of the incident, though not without some danger, was straight-forward and almost not worth mentioning. Jackson and Colby, taken completely by surprise, were easy to overpower and tie up. By the time Duke and the others came trooping back, Heather and the two prisoners were safely locked in the cabin and I was outside with my bow and arrows and lots of cover. The boys put up some resistance, but they had no real chance, and after two of them collected arrows in the shoulder they finally gave up. I marched the whole group to Hemlock, confirming my story by taking the town leaders to the body in the woods. Frontier justice being what it is, the boys were found guilty of murder and hanged that evening.

The stars were shining through gaps in the cloud cover when I returned to the cabin. Heather had left a candle burning in the window and was waiting for me on the couch. "How did it go?" she asked quietly.

"They were convicted. I'm giving their bikes to the town; some of the men will come by tomorrow to pick them up."

She nodded. "I'm almost sorry for them . . . but I don't suppose we could have let them go."

"No. If it bothers you too much, try thinking about their victim." I sat down next to her. "Heather, we have to talk. I need to know how you were able to do the things you did today. I think you know what I mean."

"Yes." Her smile was bittersweet, with traces of fear and weariness, and I suddenly realized this wasn't the first time she'd had this discussion. "You're wondering if I'm really blind or somehow faking it." She nodded heavily. "Yes, I am completely and totally blind. My eyes are useless. But the . . . disease, accident, whatever . . . that blinded me did something strange to my brain's optic center. Somehow, I'm able to pick up the images that all nearby people are getting. In other words, I *can* see—sort of—but only through other people's eyes."

I nodded slowly as all sorts of pieces finally fell into place. "That was one possibility that never occurred to me," I said. "A lot of things make sense now, though. What sort of range do you have?"

"Oh, thirty or forty feet." She sounded vaguely surprised. I wondered why, and then realized that the usual reaction was probably one of shock or revulsion. I wasn't following the pattern.

"It must have been rough for you," I said gently, taking her hand in mine.

She shrugged, too casually. "A little. I haven't told very many people. They usually . . . aren't sympathetic."

"I can imagine. I'm glad you told me, though."

"I couldn't hardly keep it a secret after all that stuff with the ropes," she smiled faintly. Then she turned serious again, and when she spoke her voice was low and just a little apprehensive. "Do you want me to leave?"

"Don't be silly. My gosh, Heather, is that why you held out on me this long? You thought I would toss you out?"

"Well . . ." She squeezed my hand. "No, not really; not after the first two months. By then I knew you cared for me and wouldn't treat me like a freak or something worse. But . . ." Her voice trailed off.

But she couldn't override her own defenses, I decided. Not really surprising—a good set of defenses would be vital to protect her from both external and internal assaults. I thought of what it must have been like, waking up that first time to see your body from someone else's point of view. No wonder she'd almost gone insane.

And a horrible thought hit me like a sledgehammer.

Heather must have sensed my tension, for she gripped my hand tightly. "Neil! What is it?"

It took me two tries to get the words out through my suddenly dry mouth. "Those hoodlums. If you could see through them . . . you saw my face."

She sighed. "Neil, I've known what you look like since the first night you brought me here. I saw your reflection in the kitchen window while you were washing the dinner dishes."

I stared at her, my head spinning. No wonder she'd cried herself to sleep that night! "But if you knew—?"

"Then why did I stay? I explained that to you months ago. Because you're a warm, generous man and I like being with you."

"But my face—"

"Damn your face!" she flared. "That thing has become an obsession with you!" She closed her eyes, and after a moment the anger drained from her expression, leaving weariness in its place. "Neil," she said, her quiet voice brimming with emotion, "I've wanted to tell you about my . . . ability . . . for a long, long time. But I couldn't, because I was afraid that you'd never believe I could care for you if I knew what you looked like. I was afraid you'd make me leave you."

Letting go of Heather's hand, I put my arm around her and held her close. All around me, I could feel reality going *tilt*. "I get the distinct feeling I've been acting like a jerk," I told her humbly. "I'm a little old to start changing all of my preconceived ideas around, though. I'll probably need a lot of help. You'll stick around and give me a hand, won't you?"

She took my free hand in both of hers and rested her head on my shoulder. "I'll stay as long as you want me here."

"I'm glad." I paused. "Heather, I think I love you."

Eyes glistening with tears, she treated me to the happiest smile I'd ever seen. Then she chuckled. "You mean you're just finding that out? My darling Neil, sometimes I think you're blinder than I am."

I denied that, of course. But now, after fifteen years with her, I sometimes wonder if she was right.

THE FINAL REPORT ON THE LIFELINE EXPERIMENT

It has been less than a month now since the sealed personal files of the late Daniel Staley have been opened, but already the rumors are beginning to be heard: rumors that explosive new information concerning the Lifeline Experiment has been uncovered. Though these rumors contain a grain of truth, they are for the most part the products of prejudice and hysteria, and it is in an effort to separate the truth from the lies that I have consented to write this report. Since, too, I find that even after twenty years a great number of popular misconceptions still surround the experiment itself, I feel it is necessary for me to begin with a full recounting of those controversial events of 1994.

I suppose I should first say a word about my credentials. I became Dr. Staley's private secretary in 1989 and continued in this role full-time until his tragic death. My usefulness to him stemmed from my eidetic memory which, especially when coupled with his telepathic abilities, made me a sort of walking information retrieval system for him. It is also the reason I can claim perfect accuracy for my memories of the events and conversations I am about to describe.

The popular press usually credits Dr. Staley with coming up with the Lifeline Experiment idea on his own, but the original suggestion actually came from the Reverend Ron Brady in mid-January of 1994. Brady, a good friend of Dan's, was driving us back to San Francisco from a seminar on bioethics at USC and the conversation, almost inevitably, turned to the subject of abortion.

"You realize last week's decision makes the third time the Supreme Court's reversed itself in the last twenty years," Brady commented. "I think that must be some kind of record."

"I wasn't keeping score, myself," Dan replied, stretching his legs as far as the seat permitted. It had been a hard weekend for him, I knew; though it had been over two years at that point since the National Academy of Sciences had officially certified his telepathic ability, there were still a few die-hard skeptics around determined to prove he was a fraud. From the number of handshakes I'd seen him wince over I gathered most of the doubters must have converged on USC for the weekend, and he was only now beginning to relax.

"It's crazy." Brady shook his head. "The legality of something like that shouldn't change every time a new administration sets up shop in Washington. It makes for emotional and legal chaos all around and gives the impression that there are no absolute standards of morality at all."

Dan shrugged. "You know me, Ron. I believe in letting people do what they like in this life, on the theory that whatever they do wrong will catch up with them in the next."

Brady smiled lopsidedly. "The laissez-faire moralist. But don't we have an obligation to help our fellow men minimize the problems they'll have in the next life? That seems to me a perfectly good rationale for the inclusion of morality in law."

Dan reached a hand back over the seat toward me. "Iris: a devastating quotation to put this fellow in his place, if you please."

I made no move to take his hand. "I'm sorry, Dr. Staley," I said primly, "but it would be unethical for me to help you in your arguments. Especially against a man of the cloth."

He chuckled, threw me a wink, and withdrew his hand. "Seriously, though, I don't see how you can expect anything but political flip-flopping when you have an issue that's so long on emotion and so short on real scientific fact. A human fetus is alive, certainly; but so are mosquitoes and inflamed tonsils. *When* a fetus becomes a human being and entitled to society's protection is something we may never know."

"True." Brady glanced at Dan. "Maybe you ought to try contacting a fetus telepathically someday; see if *you* can figure it out."

"Sure," Dan deadpanned. "I could go in claiming to be womb service or something."

Brady came back with a pun of his own, and the conversation shifted to the topic of microcurrent therapy for certain brain disorders, where it remained for the rest of the drive. But even though Dan didn't say anything about it for four months, it is clear in retrospect that Brady's not-quite-serious comment had taken root in his imagination. Even for somebody as phlegmatic as Dan, the possibility that he could take a swing at such a persistent controversy must have been an intriguing idea, especially after the weekend he'd just gone through. Unfortunately, it also is abundantly clear that he started things in motion without any real understanding of what he was getting himself into.

It was just before five o'clock on May 23, and I was preparing to go home when Dan called me into his office. "Iris, didn't I meet a couple of professors in the Child Development Department of Cal State Hayward down at USC last January? What were their names?"

"Dr. Eliot Jordan and Dr. Pamela Halladay," I supplied promptly. "Do you want the conversation, too?"

He pursed his lips, then nodded. "I'd better. I'm pretty foggy on what they were like."

I sat down next to him and took his hand in mine. Even now there are many people who don't realize that Dan's telepathy required some form of physical contact with his subject. They envision him tapping into the secrets of government or industry from his San Mateo home. In reality a moderately thick shirt would block his reception completely.

The conversation hadn't been very long to begin with, and playing it back took only a few seconds. When I'd finished, Dan let go and frowned off into space for a moment, while I played the conversation back again for myself, wondering what he was looking for. "They both seemed pretty reasonable people to you, didn't they?" he asked, breaking into my thoughts. "Competent scientists, honest, no particular axes at the grindstone?"

"I suppose so." I shrugged. "It might help if you told me what you had in mind."

He grinned. "I'll show you. What's the phone number over there?"

I gave him the college's number, and within a few minutes he'd been routed to the proper department. "Of course I remember you, Dr. Staley," Dr. Jordan said after Dan had identified himself and mentioned their brief USC meeting. Even coming out of a tiny phone speaker grille, his voice sounded as full and hearty as it had in person. "It would be very hard to forget meeting such a distinguished person as yourself. What can I do for you?"

"How would you like to help me with an experiment that might possibly put the lid on the abortion debate once and for all?"

There was a long moment of silence. "That sounds very interesting," Jordan said, somewhat cautiously. "Would you care to explain?"

Dan leaned his chair back a notch and began to stroke his cheek idly with the end of his pencil. "It seems to me, Doctor, that the issue boils down to the question of when, exactly, the fetus becomes a human being. I believe that, with a little bit of practice, I might be able to telepathically follow a fetus through its entire development. With luck, I may be able to pin down that magic moment. At worst, I may be able to show that a fetus *isn't* human during the entire first month or trimester or whatever. Either way, an experiment like that should inject some new scientific facts into the issue."

"Yes," Jordan said slowly, "depending on whether your findings would be considered 'scientific' by any given group, of course." He paused. "I agree that its at least worth some discussion. Can you come to Hayward any time this week to talk about it?"

"How about tomorrow afternoon?"

"Tomorrow's Tuesday . . . yes, my last class is over at two."

"Good. I'll see you about two, then. Good-bye."

"Good-bye."

Dan hung up the phone and looked at me. "Does that answer your question?"

It took me a moment to find my voice. "Dan, you're crazy. How exactly do you propose to read a fetus's mind without climbing into the embryonic sac with it?"

"Via the mother's nervous system, of course. There must be neural pathways through the placenta and umbilical cord I can use to reach the fetus's brain."

"With the mother blasting away and drowning out whatever the fetus may be putting out?"

"Well, yes, I suppose that might be a problem," he admitted.

"*And,* even if you do manage to touch the baby's mind, are you even going to know it?" I persisted. "This isn't going to be like the colic studies you did with Sam Sheeler, you know—those babies were at least being exposed to a normal range of stimuli. What on Earth has a fetus got to think about?"

He grinned suddenly. "I *said* it might take some practice." He stood up. "Look, there's no sense dithering over these questions now. We'll go see Jordan tomorrow and hash it all out then. Okay?"

"All right," I said. "After all, if it doesn't work out, no one will ever have to know we came up with such a crazy idea."

"That's what I like about you, Iris: your confidence in me. See you tomorrow."

We arrived on the Hayward campus at two o'clock sharp the next day—and it took only ten minutes for my hopes of keeping this idea under wraps to be completely destroyed.

They were waiting for us outside the door to Jordan's office: a man and woman, both dressed in conservative business suits. I recognized them from TV news shorts of the previous year, but before I could clue Dan in they had stepped forward to intercept us. "Dr. Staley?" the man said. "My name's John Cooper; this is Helen Reese. I wonder if we might have a word with you?" He gestured down the hall to where the door of a small lounge was visible.

"We have an appointment with Dr. Jordan," I put in.

"He's not back from class yet," Mrs. Reese said. "This will only take a few minutes, if you don't mind."

Dan shrugged. "All right," he said agreeably.

The others remained silent until we were seated in a small circle in a corner of the otherwise deserted lounge. "Dr. Staley, we understand you're planning some sort of experiment with Dr. Jordan to determine when life begins," Cooper said, leaning forward slightly in his chair. "We'd like to ask you a few questions about this, if we may."

Dan cocked an eyebrow. "I fail, first of all, to see how you learned about my private conversation with Dr. Jordan," he said calmly, "and, secondly, to understand what business it is of yours."

"Mr. Cooper is the Bay Area president of the Family Alliance," I told him. "Mrs. Reese is their chief antiabortion advocate."

They both looked at me with surprise. "I see," Dan nodded. "Well, that explains the second part of my question. You folks want to take a crack at the first part now?"

"How we heard about it is unimportant," Mrs. Reese said. "What *is* important is that we find out how you stand on the abortion issue."

Dan blinked. "Why?"

"Surely, Doctor, you understand the highly subjective nature of the experiment you're planning," she said. "Naturally, we need to know what your own beliefs are concerning when life arises."

"My telepathic ability is *not* subjective," Dan said, a bit stiffly. "It's as scientific and accurate as anything you'd care to name. Whatever my beliefs happen to be, I can assure you they do *not* interfere with either my perception or interpretation."

"Beliefs *always* affect interpretation, to one degree or another," Cooper said. "Now, you yourself said you could prove the fetus wasn't human until the second trimester of pregnancy. It seems to us that, with such an attitude, you would be very likely to interpret any brain activity before that point as 'nonhuman,' whether it is or not."

Dan looked at me. "Iris?" he invited.

I nodded. "The exact quote, Dr. Cooper, was as follows: 'At worst, I may be able to show that a fetus *isn't* human during the entire first month or trimester or whatever.' End quote. Dr. Staley made no assumptions in that statement. I suggest you ask your spies to be more accurate in the future."

Reese bristled. "We weren't spying on anyone, Miss Marx; the information relayed to us was obtained quite legitimately."

"I'm sure it was," Dan said, getting to his feet. "Now if you'll excuse us, Dr. Jordan is expecting us."

The rest of us stood, as well. "We haven't finished our conversation, though—" Cooper began.

"Yes, we have," Dan interrupted him. "If—*if*, mind you—I do this experiment it'll be because I'm convinced it can be done objectively and accurately. If you have any suggestions or comments you're welcome to write them up and send them to my office. Good day."

Threading between them, we left the lounge.

Jordan and Dr. Pamela Halladay were waiting for us when we arrived back at Jordan's office. "Sorry we're late," Dan told them after quick handshakes all around, "but we ran into the local ethics committee. Any idea how the Family Alliance might have overheard our conversation, Dr. Jordan?"

The two of them exchanged glances, then Jordan grimaced. "My secretary, probably," he said. "I called Pam right after I talked to you, and the door to her office was open. I'm sorry; it never occurred to me that she'd go off and tell anyone."

"No harm done," Dan shrugged. "Let's forget it and get down to business, shall we?"

"Your idea sounds very interesting, Dr. Staley," Halladay said, "but I think there are one or two technical points that need clearing up. First of all, would you be following a single fetus from conception to term, or would you try to reach a group of fetuses at various stages of growth?"

"I hadn't really thought that much about it," Dan said slowly. "I suppose the second method would be faster."

"It would give better statistics, too," Jordan said. "What do you think, Pam—would a hundred be enough?"

"A hundred subjects?" Dan said, looking a little taken aback.

"Well, sure. If you want this to have scientific validity you'll need a reasonable sample. Why?—did you have a smaller number in mind?"

"Yeah. About ten." Dan frowned. "Maybe we could compromise at twenty-five or so."

"You cut the sample too small and it won't be scientific enough to satisfy the skeptics," Jordan warned.

"Whether it'll be scientific enough anyway was my second question," Halladay put in.

We all looked at her. "What do you mean?" Jordan asked.

"Oh, come on now, Eliot—the heart of the scientific method is the reproducibility of an experiment. With only one proven telepath on Earth, this one is inherently unrepeatable. Whatever Dr. Staley concludes we'll have to take on faith."

"Are you suggesting I might lie?" Dan asked quietly.

"No—I'm suggesting you might misinterpret what you hear. How are you going to know, say, whether the differences you see are human versus nonhuman or simply four months versus two months?"

Dan nodded. "I see. I wondered why you hadn't told Dr. Jordan you'd seen Cooper and Mrs. Reese loitering out in the hall earlier. You called them down on us, didn't you?"

Halladay's face reddened. "No, I . . . uh . . . look, I didn't expect anyone to come out here and ambush you like that. I just wanted to know whether you were pro- or anti-abortion; if you'd ever taken a public stand on the issue. I mean, they keep files on that sort of thing."

Jordan was looking at his co-worker as if she'd just shown a KGB membership card. "Pam! What on *earth*—"

"It's all right, Dr. Jordan. As I said before, no harm done." Dan turned to Halladay, and there was a glint in his eye I didn't often see. "I'll tell you what I told your friends: I'm not doing this to push anyone's opinions, and that includes any *I* might have. If you have to pigeonhole me anywhere, put me down as 'protruth.' I won't wear any other labels, understand?"

"Yes. I'm sorry, Doctor." She smiled wanly. "I guess I'm not immune to the emotions the whole subject generates. I'll keep my feelings to myself from now on—I promise."

"Will you prove your sincerity?" Dan leaned forward and offered his hand.

She frowned at it for a second before understanding flickered across her face. Then, visibly steeling herself, she reached out and gingerly took his hand. They held the position for nearly twenty seconds before Dan released his grip and sat back. "Thank you," he said. "I'm sure you'll be a great help to us." Turning to Jordan, he nodded. "Now then, are we ready to begin working out some of the details?"

The discussion took nearly an hour, and the experimental design arrived at was essentially the one that was actually used later that year. Several important problems still remained, however, notably the question of masking the mother's thoughts while Dan tried to touch those of the fetus. From past experience we knew that a deep, sedative-induced sleep would probably do the trick, but Jordan was understandably opposed to giving large dosages of such drugs to pregnant women. The question of whether or not Dan could recognize humanness in a fetal mind at all also remained unanswered.

During the drive back to San Francisco, I asked Dan if Halladay could be trusted.

"I think so," he said. "I didn't see any evidence of duplicity when I touched her. And she *was* genuinely upset to find the Family Alliance people lying in wait for us."

"What about them? Do you think they'll make trouble?"

"How could they? Denouncing the experiment before it even takes place would make them look silly—especially since a check with Halladay will show them that the design still has some pretty basic problems. Saying this far in advance that they reject the results will leave them wide open to a charge that they're afraid of the truth."

Something in his voice caught my attention. "You sound less optimistic than you did yesterday," I said. "You thinking of calling it off?"

He was silent a long moment. "No, not really. It's just that the whole thing is getting more complicated than I'd envisioned it."

I shrugged. "True—but don't forget that it's *your* experiment. If you don't want to do things Jordan's way, all you have to do is say so."

"I know. But he's unfortunately got a good point: that if we don't at least take a stab at doing things rigorously, all we're going to do is throw more gasoline at the emotional bonfire." He paused. "Tell me, do you have any relatives or close friends who are pregnant?"

I blinked at the abrupt change of subject. "Yes—four to nine, depending on how close a friend you need."

"Let me have a fast rundown, will you?"

I drove one-handed for a while as I gave him a brief personality sketch of each of the nine women. Afterward he sat silently for several minutes, digesting it all. "What do you think Kathy would say if I asked to be present at her delivery?" he said at last.

"I don't know," I said. "But I know the right person to ask."

We called Kathy as soon as we got back to Dan's office. Though clearly surprised by the request, she agreed to act as Dan's guinea pig, provided her husband didn't object. I got the most recent estimate of her due date—another month—and extracted a promise of secrecy before hanging up. "You going to tell Jordan and Halladay about this?" I asked Dan.

He shook his head. "No, I don't think so. A slip of the tongue could have the entire Fresno chapter of the Family Alliance descending on Kathy's birthing room, and I have no intention of putting the Ausberrys through that."

"Besides which, if you find you can't even read the mind of a baby that's only hours from birth, you don't want anyone to know?" I hazarded.

His slightly pained smile was my only answer.

But the Family Alliance was subtler than we'd expected, and neither of us was prepared for the page-twenty story in the *Chronicle* the next morning.

"I don't *believe* this," I fumed, stomping around Dan's office with a copy of the paper gripped tightly in my hand. "How can they print something like this without at least contacting you first?"

"'The Lifeline Experiment,'" Dan quoted, reading at his desk. "Gack. Why do newspeople always have to come up with cutesy titles for everything? Contact me? Of course they should have. Obviously, some fine upstanding citizen or group of same convinced them that the story didn't need checking."

"Someone like our Family Alliance friends?"

"Undoubtedly. You'll notice they don't include any of the details we discussed yesterday, which implies Halladay has dried up as an information source for them. I guess that's something."

"*How* can you sit there and take it so calmly?" I snapped, slapping my newspaper down on the desktop for emphasis. "Look: there it is for the whole damn world to see."

He looked up at me. "Simmer down, Iris—the first client's due in ten minutes and the last thing he'll want is to have his head taken off by my secretary. I'm mad, too, but there's nothing we can do now except make sure the experiment comes off as planned."

I was only listening with half an ear. "But *why*? What did they expect to gain by leaking the story? It's not even particularly slanted."

"Sure it is," Dan contradicted me. "Sixth paragraph, fourth and fifth sentences."

"'In addition to his private psychiatric practice, Staley does volunteer counseling once a week at the Rappaport Mental Health Clinic of San Mateo County, which he helped found. He also works frequently with the public defender's office and has worked with the Greenpeace Save-the-Whales Project.'" I rattled off. "So?"

"So someone realized that this was going to be a very difficult experiment to do. So difficult, in fact, that we conceivably might have to give it up—and that someone wanted to make sure I was established in the public mind as a liberal right from the start. A liberal and, by implication, pro-abortion."

"I still don't see—oh. Sure. If the experiment turns out to be unworkable they'll claim you learned something in the initial stages that clashed with your liberal views on the issue, won't they, and that you backed out because of it."

"Bull's-eye. Or so I'm guessing."

I sat down, my anger replaced by a sudden chill. "Who exactly are we up against here—the Family Alliance or the CIA covert operations group?"

"We're up against people who've been up to their necks in politics for at least a decade," he told me, laying his own paper on top of mine. "Along the way they've probably picked up all the standard political tricks one can employ against an opponent—which is almost funny, since the experiment has just as much chance of supporting their point of view as it has of opposing it."

"One would think they haven't much faith in their beliefs, wouldn't one?" I suggested.

"I think that's a self-contradictory sentence, but you've got the right idea," Dan said, smiling. "And you might remember that any group that size is a mixed bag. Some of the members would probably be madder than you are if they knew what was being tried here." He tapped the newspaper.

Just then there was a knock on the outer office door. "Mr. Raymond's early," I commented, heading out to unlock it.

"No problem," Dan called after me. "You can send him right in."

But it wasn't Raymond, or any of Dan's other clients. It was, instead, a committee of four people.

"We'd like to see Dr. Staley for a moment, if he isn't too busy," their spokeswoman, a young woman with a recognizable face, said briskly. Without waiting for a reply she started forward.

Out in Hayward I'd been taken by surprise, but here in my own office I had better control of things. I remained standing in the doorway, and the woman had to pull up sharply to keep from running into me. "I'm sorry, Ms. McClain, but Dr. Staley is expecting a client," I said firmly. "If you'd like to make an appointment he has an hour available a week from Friday."

It was abundantly clear from her expression that she hadn't expected to be put off like that, but she recovered quickly. "Perhaps Dr. Staley will be able to squeeze us in between appointments later this morning," she said. "Would you tell him Jackie McClain and other representatives of the National Institute for Freedom and Equality are here? We'll wait until he's free."

I couldn't legitimately deny them waiting-room space, so I let them in, hoping that what I knew would be a long wait would discourage them. Three of them did eventually get up and leave, the last one about one o'clock, with whispered apologies to their leader. But McClain stayed all the way until Dan's last client left at five-thirty, a persistence I had to admire. I consulted briefly with Dan and he agreed to see her.

"I'm sorry you had to wait so long, Ms. McClain," he said as we all sat down in his office. "But, as Iris said, this was a particularly long day."

"She's a very efficient secretary," McClain said ambiguously. "I'll get right to the point, Dr. Staley: this so-called Lifeline Experiment. We'd like to know exactly what it is you intend to prove."

Dan frowned. "I'm not out to *prove* anything, really. I'm simply trying to find where in its development a fetus becomes a human being."

"In what sense? Medical, moral, legal—there are several ways to define *human,* and they don't necessarily correspond."

"I'm not sure I understand the question," Dan said, frowning a bit.

"Suppose you discover that, in your opinion, human life begins during the third month of pregnancy," McClain said. "The Supreme Court earlier this year stated that abortions through the sixth month are legal, which implies that a fetus is not *legally* human through that point."

"In that case the law would have to be changed, obviously," I told her.

"Obviously, you've never been pregnant with a child you didn't want," she said, a bit tartly. "A law like that would condemn thousands of women to either the trauma of an unwanted pregnancy and labor or to the danger of an illegal abortion. It would necessarily put the rights of a fetus over those of her mother—a mother whose rights, I'll point out, *are* clearly and definitely guaranteed by the Constitution."

"I understand all that," Dan said, "but I don't really know what to do about it. I'm not trying to make a legal or political statement with this, though I'm sure others will probably do so. But, then again, shouldn't the law reflect medical realities wherever possible?"

"Yes—but you're talking metaphysics, not medicine," McClain returned. "And as far as the law goes, what right do you or any other man have to tell women what we can or cannot do with our own bodies?"

"Just a second," I put in before Dan could reply. "Aren't we jumping the gun just a little bit here? Dr. Staley hasn't even *done* the experiment yet and already you're complaining about the results. It's entirely possible that the whole thing will be a boost to your point of view."

"You're right, of course," McClain admitted, cooling down a bit. "I'm sorry, Doctor; I guess I forgot that working with Pamela Halladay didn't automatically mean you were against us."

Dan waved a hand. "That's all right," he said, clearly thankful the argument had been temporarily defused. "I was unaware when we started that Dr. Halladay had strong feelings on the subject, but I'm convinced she'll be able to keep her feelings under wraps."

"I hope so." McClain paused. "I wonder, Doctor, if you would consider allowing a member of NIFE to participate in the planning of your experiment. We have quite a few doctors and other bioscience people who would be qualified to understand and assist in your work."

"Actually, I don't think we really need any help at the moment," Dan said slowly. "There are only a couple of problems to be dealt with, and I'm sure we can find solutions reasonably quickly. If not, I'll keep NIFE in mind."

"Will we at least be permitted to have an observer present during the main part of the experiment?" McClain persisted.

"If it'll make you feel better, sure," Dan said tiredly. "Give Iris your phone number and we'll do our best to keep you informed."

She gave me the number and then stood up, her expression that of someone who's gotten more or less what she hoped for. "Thank you for your time, Doctor. I hope this Lifeline Experiment of yours will prove to be something we can wholeheartedly support."

I saw her out and returned to Dan's office. "Is it my imagination," I asked, "or is this project starting to get just a little out of hand?"

He shook his head. "I can't believe it. First the Family Alliance and now NIFE—people are practically standing in line for a chance to complain about the experiment. Is the opportunity to find out the truth really so frightening?"

"I thought all psychologists were cynics," I said. "Of *course* nobody wants to hear facts that'll contradict their long-held beliefs. And organizations are even worse than individuals."

"*I'd* rather know what the truth is," he countered. "So would you. Are we the only intellectually honest people around?" He held up a hand. "Skip it. I'm just tired. Let's go somewhere quiet where we won't run into a hit squad from the PTA and get some dinner."

Sometime that evening both the wire services and the major networks picked up on the story, and by the next morning the entire country was hearing about the Lifeline Experiment—the name, unfortunately, having been picked up as well. Commentaries, both pro and con, appeared soon after. Though the publicity was stifling to Dan's everyday work, I think he found a grim sort of amusement in watching the creative ways various organizations phrased their statements so as to condemn the experiment without actually saying they would reject its results. Only the most fanatical were willing—or clumsy enough—to burn such a potentially useful bridge behind them.

The reporters who began hanging around Dan's home and office were more of a nuisance, but Dan had years ago mastered the art of giving newspeople enough to keep them satisfied without unduly encouraging them to keep coming. Fortunately, though, as the initial excitement passed and the experiment itself still seemed far in the nebulous future, the media's interest waned, and within ten days of the story's initial release the reporters' physical presence was replaced by periodic phone calls asking if anything was new. I, at least, was relieved by this procedural change; my friend Kathy would be calling any day now, and I preferred sneaking away from telephones than from people.

Late one evening in the last week of June the call came, and Dan and I drove down to Fresno for the birth of Kathy's third daughter.

It was the first birth I'd ever seen, but even so I gave the main operation scant attention; I was far more interested in what Dan was doing. The obstetrician, a close family friend, had been clued in, but I could still sense his professional uneasiness each time Dan's ungloved hand probed gently into the birth canal. What was visible of Dan's expression above his mask indicated a frown of intense concentration that remained even when his hand had been withdrawn, a look that silenced the questions I was dying to ask. He reached into the canal four times during the labor, and in addition had a hand on the baby's head from its first appearance to the moment when the crying child was laid across her mother's breast.

"What did you find out?" I asked him a few minutes later, after our tactful withdrawal from the birthing room. "Can you reach the baby through its mother's nervous system?"

"Yes," he said, absently picking at a bloodstain he hadn't quite managed to get off his finger. "Once I knew what I was looking for I could find it even with the loud interference from Kathy's mind. I wouldn't want to try it with a baby much farther from term, though—we're still going to have to find a safe way to knock out the mothers."

I nodded. "How about . . . humanness?"

"No doubt," he said promptly. "Those people who want to believe the first breath is the dividing line are fooling themselves. Elizabeth Anne's mind was as human as ours in there."

"'Elizabeth Anne'?"

He smiled sheepishly. "Well, that's the name they were planning for a girl. I sort of picked that up along the way." The smile vanished. "Picked it up through a *lot* of real trauma. I don't think I ever realized before how much it *hurts* to have a baby—I'm exhausted, and I only got it secondhand."

"Why do you think they call it labor?" I asked, only half humorously. He grimaced, and I quickly changed the subject. "So what does a baby think about in there? I mean, she couldn't have all that much sensory experience to draw on and certainly wouldn't have what we'd consider abstract thoughts."

"Oh, there really was a fair amount of sensory input—tactile and auditory mostly, but taste and even vision also got used some." He shook his head thoughtfully, his forehead corrugated with concentration. "But it wasn't the use of her senses, or even the way that such information was processed that made her a human being. It was—oh, I don't know: a feeling of *kinship,* I guess I'd have to say. Something familiar in the mental patterns, though I'll be damned if I can describe it."

"Whatever it was didn't change at the actual birth?"

"Not really. There was a sudden sensory overload, of course, but if anything it heightened the feeling . . ." He trailed off, then abruptly snapped his fingers. "*That's* what it was. On some very deep level the baby felt herself to be an *individual,* distinct in some way from the rest of the universe."

"I didn't think even young children understood that," I said.

"On a conscious level, no—but that part of the mind seems to be the last to develop, long after the more instinctive levels are firmly in place. Now that I think about it, I've picked up this sense of distinctness in babies before—even in the Kilogram Kids I worked with at Stanford last year—but just never bothered to put a label on it."

I pondered that for a moment. "Is that the yardstick you're going to use, then?"

He shrugged uncomfortably. "Unless I can come up with something better, I guess I'll have to. I know it sounds like pretty flimsy evidence, but it really seems to be an easy characteristic to pick up. And I'm sure I've never felt it in any of the other mammals I've touched."

"Um. It still sounds awfully mystical for an experiment that purports to be scientific."

"I'm sorry," he said with a touch of asperity. "It's the best I can do. If you don't think it's worth anything we can quit right now."

I took his arm, realizing for the first time how heavily the national controversy was weighing on him. "It'll be all right," I soothed him. "As long as people know exactly what you're testing for, no one will be able to claim you misrepresented either yourself or the experiment."

"Yeah." He sighed and looked at his watch. "Two-thirty. No wonder I'm dead tired. Come on, Iris; let's go say goodbye to your friends and get out of here."

For a wonder, the news of our unofficial test run didn't leak to the media at that time, and so Dan was spared the extra attention such a revelation would have generated. As it was, public interest—which had remained at a low level for the past two or three weeks—began to rise again as the procedural problems began to be worked out and Jordan announced a tentative date of July 25 for the experiment to take place.

In light of the recently discovered papers, there is one conversation from that period that I feel must be included in this report.

It took place on the evening of July 12 at the home of Ron Brady and his wife Susan. It had been only the previous day that Halladay's idea of using electrical sleep stimulation had been proved adequate for Dan's needs, removing the final obstacle still holding things up.

"So the Lifeline Experiment's going to come off after all," Ron said after the dinner dishes had been cleared and the four of us had settled down in the living room.

Dan nodded. "Looks that way. Eliot and Pam are lining up volunteers now; they expect to have that finished in ten days at the most." He cocked an eyebrow. "You seem disapproving, somehow."

Ron and his wife exchanged glances. "It's not disapproval, exactly," Ron said hesitantly, "and it's certainly not aimed at you. But we *are* a little worried about the potential influence this one experiment is going to have on the way people think about abortion and human life in general, both here and in other countries."

Dan shrugged. "I'm just trying to inject some facts into the situation. Is influencing people to use rational thought instead of emotion a bad thing?"

"No, of course not," Susan said. "But what you're doing and what the public *perceives* you as doing are not necessarily the same. You're searching for the place where a fetus's mind becomes human; but a person is more than just his mind. Will the Lifeline Experiment show where the child's soul and spirit enter him? I'm not at all sure it will."

"That almost sounds like quibbling," I pointed out. "If Dan can detect a unique humanness in the mind, isn't that basically the same thing as the soul?"

"I don't know," Susan said frankly. "What's more, I haven't the foggiest idea of how you'd even begin to test that kind of assumption. It's just the fact that the assumption *is* being made that concerns me."

"The problem we see," Ron put in, "is that the media isn't bothering with this—to us, at least—very important point, but is preparing the public to expect a clear-cut answer to come out of the experiment. What's worse, every organized group that sees support for their point of view will immediately jump on the bandwagon, reinforcing the media's oversimplification. Do you see what I'm getting at?"

"Yes." Dan pulled at his lower lip. "Iris, have I been clear enough with the media as to exactly what the Lifeline Experiment will and won't show?"

Dan had talked to reporters over a hundred times since the story's first appearance; quickly, I played back the relevant parts. "I think so," I said slowly. "Especially since our trip to Fresno."

"The media's not picking up on it," Ron insisted.

I nodded. "He's right, Dan. I haven't seen any major newspaper or TV report even mention questions like Susan's, let alone seriously discuss them."

Dan pondered a moment. "Well, what do you think I should do about it? I could yell a little louder, I suppose, but evidence to date indicates that won't do a lot of good."

"I tend to agree," Ron said. "You've been something of a folk hero since you fought the National Academy of Sciences and won, but the extremists—on both sides—have louder voices. I'm afraid yours would probably get lost amid the postexperiment gloatings and denunciations."

"Do you think I should cancel the whole thing, then?" Dan asked bluntly.

For a moment there was silence. Then Susan shook her head. "I almost wish you could, or at least that you could postpone it for a while. But at this late date canceling would probably just start fresh rumors, with each faction trying to persuade people that you'd quit because you'd learned something that supported their particular point of view and conflicted with your own."

Dan's own words the morning the story appeared in the *Chronicle* came back to me; from the look on his face I knew he was remembering them, too. "Yeah," he said slowly. "Yeah, I guess you're right."

I think we all heard the pain in his voice. Susan was the first one to respond to it. "I'm sorry, Dan—we didn't mean to add to the pressure. We're not blaming you for what other people are doing with your words."

"I know," Dan said. "Don't worry about it—the pressure was there long before tonight." He sighed. "I really wasn't expecting it to be so intense, somehow. It wasn't nearly this bad when I was trying to prove my telepathic ability, not even when they were calling me a criminal fraud on network TV. I must be getting soft in my old age."

"I doubt it," Ron said. "The problem is more likely that last time *you* were the only one under the hatchet, so to speak, whereas this time your actions are going to be affecting the lives of others. You're suffering because, whatever happens, the Lifeline Experiment is likely to hurt some group of people. That's an infinitely heavier burden for someone like you than watching your own name dragged through the mud."

Dan nodded. "I wish I'd thought about that two months ago. If I'd known how I'd react, I'd never have started this whole thing in motion."

"Well, if it makes you feel any better," Susan said gently, "it's only *because* you're so sensitive that Ron and I aren't more worried about the experiment. We can trust you, at least, to be as honest and fair-minded in what you report as is humanly possible."

"Thanks." Dan took a deep breath, let it out slowly. "Let's change the subject, shall we?"

There are films of the Lifeline Experiment itself, of course, films that have been shown endless times over the past twenty years. I have seen them all and do not deny that they adequately portray the physical events that took place on July 25, 1994. But there was more than just a scientific test taking place that day. There was a battle taking place in Dan's own mind, a battle between what his senses told him and what his reason could accept; and it was this unresolved conflict, I know now, that ultimately led to the secret study whose results have only now come to light.

Dan and I arrived at the small lecture room where the experiment was to take place just before one o'clock. The TV and film cameras had long since been set up, and the spectators' gallery was crammed with nearly fifty reporters and representatives of interested groups. I glimpsed Eve Unger, NIFE's handpicked representative, and John Cooper of the Family Alliance sitting several rows apart. Near the front, in seats Dan had had reserved for them, were Ron and Susan Brady.

The front of the room looked uncomfortably like a morgue. Laid out in neat rows were thirty waist-high gurneys, each bearing the form of a sleeping woman. From the neck down each was covered by a pup-tent sort of arrangement designed to give Dan limited access to the area near the uterus while minimizing physical cues that might otherwise influence him. A number was sewn onto each tent, corresponding to a numbered envelope containing the woman's name and length of time she'd been pregnant. At a raised table at one end of the floor sat Jordan, Halladay, and John Cottingham of the Associated Press, who held the stack of envelopes.

"We're all set here, Dan," Jordan said as we reached the table. "You can begin whenever you want."

Dan nodded, and as I slid into my own front-row seat he stepped to the nearest gurney. With a single glance at the cameras, he reached into the tent's access tunnel. Almost immediately he withdrew his hand and silently picked up the number card lying on the gurney beside her. Marking one of the squares on the card, he stepped carefully over the sleep-stimulator wires and walked to the table, placing the card face down in front of Cottingham so that only its number showed. "Is it a boy or a girl, Dr. Staley?" the reporter quipped, sliding the card to one side without turning it over.

"I'm not even going to try to guess, Mr. Cottingham," Dan said. A slightly nervous chuckle rippled through the spectators; but I could see that Dan hadn't meant the comment to be funny. Not even a hint of a smile made it to his face as he walked back to the next gurney. He held the contact a little longer this time, but there was no hesitation I could detect as he picked up her card and marked it. Cottingham didn't try any jokes this time, and Dan went on to the third woman.

All the reports I've ever seen refer to the tension in the room that afternoon; what they don't usually mention is the strangely uneven quality the experimental setup imposed on it. Dan had expected—correctly, as it turned out—that the younger the fetus, the harder it would be to make both the initial contact and the determination of its human-ness. But with the random order and the camouflaging tents it was impossible for anyone watching to tell how far along a given mother was. With some, the spectators would barely have settled into a watch-ful silence before Dan was walking away with the card; but with others, he would stand motionlessly for minutes at a time as the tension slowly grew more and more oppressive. At those times, his movement toward the card was like a lifting of Medusa's curse, and there would be a brief flurry of noise as people shifted in their seats and whispered comments to each other. The reprieve would last until Dan started his next contact, and the tension would then begin its slow rise again.

The first forty-five minutes went smoothly enough, both Dan and the spectators quickly growing more or less accustomed to the emotional roller coaster ride we were on. Dan made decisions on seventeen fetuses during that time, and while he was clearly not having fun up there, I could tell from his face that he was holding up reasonably well against the pressure.

The eighteenth subject changed all that.

Dan stood by her for nearly five minutes, his face rigid with concentration and something else. Finally, leaving her card untouched on the gurney, he stepped over to the table. "There's something wrong," he said, his voice low but audible from where I was sitting. "I can't find any life at all in there. I think the fetus must be dead. I . . . please don't release the moth—the woman's name. It's going to be hard enough on her as it is."

Jordan tapped Cottingham's arm and muttered something. The reporter grimaced slightly, but gamely shuffled out the proper envelope and opened it. His frown vanished as he read the contents and he smiled wryly. "Number twenty-eight. Linda Smith; not pregnant. Control."

There was a collective sigh of released tension. An unreadable expression flickered across Dan's face as he glanced at Jordan and Halladay. Then, clamping his jaw tightly, he walked back to the gurneys. To others in the room he may have simply looked determined—but I knew better. He was flustered, and flustered badly. He'd counseled several women in the past who'd given birth to stillborn children, and dropping the memory of that trauma into the middle of an already emotional experience must have been like a kick in the head. The fact that he obviously hadn't even considered the possibility of a control was clear evidence of his overwrought state. I wondered briefly if he would call for a break, but I already knew that he wouldn't permit himself that luxury. He had fought hard these past few weeks to portray himself as a calm, dispassionate scientist who could make the Lifeline Experiment a genuinely impartial search for truth, and he would turn his stomach into a massive ulcer before he would undermine that effort with even a suggestion of weakness.

From that point on, Dan's face was a granite mask, and for the next forty minutes I sat helplessly by, grinding my fingernails into my palms.

The silence in the room as Dan handed Cottingham the last card was so complete that I could clearly hear the ticking of Jordan's antique wristwatch. Picking up the first of his envelopes, Cottingham opened it. "Number twenty-three," he read into the microphone, enunciating his words carefully. "Alice Grant; nine months pregnant." Reaching to the line of cards in front of him, he turned the corresponding one over. "Human," he read. Card and envelope went to one side, and as he opened the second envelope I shifted my attention to Dan. He had stepped back among the gurneys and was watching Cottingham, his expression calm but with a strange, brittle quality to it that sent a sudden shiver up my back. "Number one. Vicki Thuma; eight and a half months pregnant," Cottingham read. Pause. "Human."

One by one he worked his way down the stack, finishing with the third-trimester mothers and starting on those in their second three months . . . and as each card he picked up identified the child as fully human, the silence began to give way to a buzz of unsure conversation. Cottingham read on; and as he reached the first-trimester women the buzz took on edges of both triumphant and angry disbelief. No one, I sensed, had really expected the result that was unfolding.

He reached the last envelope, and as he tore it open the room suddenly became quiet again. "Number fourteen. Barbara Remington: five weeks pregnant." His hand was trembling just slightly as he turned over the final card. "Human. Human," he repeated, as if not quite believing it.

"That's impossible!" Eve Unger's clear voice cut through the silence, a fraction of a second before the whole room exploded into pandemonium. "A fetus's brain has hardly *started* development at five weeks," she shouted over the din. "It's a fraud—Staley's been bought by the Family Alliance!"

Dan didn't reply, though anything he said would have been inaudible anyway through the accusations, claims, and counterclaims filling the air like opposing mortar barrages. He just stood there, looking up at the NIFE representative, his expression still calm. He knew what he'd seen and would not be moved from his testimony. And yet, as I look back on his face now, I can see the faintest hint of the uneasiness—the knowledge that what she said made sense—that I now know must have haunted the last fifteen years of his life.

Of the aftermath there is little that isn't common knowledge. Though the Lifeline Experiment carried no legal weight whatsoever, it was very clearly the rallying point for the final successful drive that established the Fetal Rights Amendment in the Constitution. But the bitter struggle that surrounded the issue made it a Pyrrhic victory at best, threatening at times to tear the country apart as had no issue since the Vietnam War. It was too much for Dan to bear at close range, and for eight years after the experiment he remained outside the country, living in self-imposed seclusion in Australia. I think that the only thing that got him through that period was the knowledge that he *had* seen humanity in those tiny bits of new life, and that whatever the cost he had done the right thing. Eventually things settled down, the pro-abortion forces gradually losing strength as grudging acceptance of the new law grew, until they became the vocal but powerless minority of the present day. And I wish with all my heart the controversy could be left alone to continue its slow death.

But it can't.

I enclose the following excerpt from Dan's papers with a feeling of dread, remembering the agony of the past two decades as few others remember it and knowing that my action is likely to rekindle the fires again. But above all other things Dan prized his reputation for honesty, and it is solely because of this that I quote here the last entry from his private journal, made just two days before the car accident that took his life. I believe that, given the time, he would have come to the same conclusion.

> **October 18, 2009:** I have been sitting here since the sky first began to show the colors of sunset, wondering how to write this. The stars now shine brightly where I watched the sun go down, and I am no nearer to finding a way to ease the shock of what my seven-year study has shown me . . . to finding a less brutal way to confess what I have unwittingly done to all the people who trusted me.
>
> There can be no further doubt as to what I have done. Linda Grant, whose mother was nine months pregnant at the experiment, shows virtually none of the traits I myself showed as a teenager; at the other end of the scale Tom Remington, whose mother was only five weeks along, is so like me it is agonizing to watch him. Only today I learned that, while he has my passionate love of basketball, he does not intend to try out for the school team, despite his skill and height. There is no reason why he would not do well at

the game . . . except that I was a mere five foot six at his age and convinced I could never play. All the rest of them fall somewhere between these two extremes, their individual degrees of mimicry directly correlated with their ages at the experiment . . . and for what I've done to these children alone I owe a debt I'll never be able to repay. What I've done to the country and the millions of women whose lives my naïveté had changed—I can't even comprehend the enormity of my crime.

My crime. The word is harsh, unforgiving. But I can't justify it as anything else. In my foolish arrogance I assumed the universe was simple, that its secrets were absolute and could be had for the asking. Worse yet, I assumed it would bend its own rules just for my convenience.

The experimenter influences his experiment. How long has that truth been known? Close to a hundred years, I'm sure, at least since the earliest beginnings of quantum mechanics. Such a simple thing . . . and yet neither I nor any of those I worked with ever even bothered to consider what it might mean to us.

The Lifeline Experiment was doomed from the very beginning. Young minds, their development barely started—how could they fail to be overwhelmed as I touched them with what must have been the delicacy of an elephant? That flicker of humanness I saw in each fetus—how much of that was innate and how much merely my own imposed reflection? I'll never know. No one ever will. My very presence obliterated the line I was trying to find.

And in the meantime I have helped to force what is essentially an arbitrary decision on the country. What should I do with this knowledge? Do I keep it to myself and allow the lie to continue, or do I speak out and risk tearing the society apart once again?

I wish I knew the answer.

CASCADE POINT

In retrospect, I suppose I should have realized my number had come up on the universe's list right from the very start, right from the moment it became clear that I was going to be stuck with the job of welcoming the *Aura Dancer's* latest batch of passengers aboard. Still, I suppose it's just as well it was me and not Tobbar who let Rik Bradley and his psychiatrist onto my ship. There are some things that a captain should have no one to blame for but himself, and this was definitely in that category.

Right away I suppose that generates a lot of false impressions. A star liner captain, resplendent in white and gold, smiling toothily at elegantly dressed men and women as the ramp carries them through the polished entry portal—forget all of that. A tramp starmer isn't polished anywhere it doesn't absolutely have to be, the captain is lucky if he's got a clean jumpsuit—let alone some pseudo-military Christmas tree frippery—and the passengers we get are the steerage of the star-traveling community. And look it.

Don't get me wrong; I have nothing against passengers aboard my ship. As a matter of fact, putting extra cabins in the *Dancer* had been my idea to start with, and they'd all too often made the difference between profit and loss in our always marginal business. But one of the reasons I had gone into space in the first place was to avoid having to make small talk with strangers, and I would rather solo through four cascade points in a row than spend those agonizing minutes at the entry portal. In this case, though, I had no choice. Tobbar, our master of drivel—and thus the man unofficially in charge of civilian small talk—was up to his elbows in grease and balky hydraulics; and my second choice, Alana Keal, had finally gotten through to an equally balky tower controller who wanted to bump us ten ships back in the lift pattern. Which left exactly one person—me—because there was no one else I'd trust with giving a good first impression of my ship to paying customers. And so I was the one standing on the ramp when Bradley and his eleven fellow passengers hoved into sight.

They ranged from semiscruffy to respectable-but-not-rich—about par for the *Dancer*—but even in such a diverse group Bradley stood out like a red light on the status board. He was reasonably good-looking, reasonably average in height and build; but there was something in the way he walked that immediately caught my attention. Sort of a cross between nervous fear and something I couldn't help but identify as swagger. The mix was so good that it was several seconds before it occurred to me how mutually contradictory the two impressions were, and the realization left me feeling more uncomfortable than I already did.

Bradley was eighth in line, with the result that my first seven greetings were carried out without a lot of attention from my conscious mind—which I'm sure only helped. Even standing still, I quickly discovered, Bradley's strangeness made itself apparent, both in his posture and also in his face and eyes. Especially his eyes.

Finally it was his turn at the head of the line. "Good morning, sir," I said, shaking his hand. "I'm Captain Pall Durriken. Welcome aboard."

"Thank you." His voice was bravely uncertain, the sort my mother used to describe as mousy. His eyes flicked the length of the *Dancer*, darted once into the portal, and returned to my face. "How often do ships like this crash?" he asked.

I hadn't expected any questions quite so blunt, but the fact that it was outside the realm of small talk made it easy to handle. "Hardly ever," I told him. "The last published figures showed a death rate of less than one per million passengers. You're more likely to be hit by a chunk of roof tile off the tower over there."

He actually cringed, turning halfway around to look at the tower. I hadn't dreamed he would take my comment so seriously, but before I could get my mouth working the man behind Bradley clapped a reassuring hand on his shoulder. "It's all right, Rik—nothing's going to hurt you. Really. This is a good ship, and we're going to be perfectly safe aboard her."

Bradley slowly straightened, and the other man shifted his attention to me. "I'm Dr. Hammerfeld Lanton, Captain," he said, extending his hand. "This is Rik Bradley. We're traveling in adjoining cabins."

"Of course," I said, nodding as if I'd already known that. In reality I hadn't had time to check out the passenger lists and assignments, but I could trust Leeds to have set things up properly. "Are you a doctor of medicine, sir?"

"In a way," Lanton said. "I'm a psychiatrist."

"Ah," I said, and managed two or three equally brilliant conversational gems before the two of them moved on. The last three passengers I dispatched with similar polish, and when everyone was inside I sealed the portal and headed for the bridge.

Alana had finished dickering with the tower and was running the prelift computer check when I arrived. "What's the verdict?" I asked as I slid into my chair and keyed for helm check.

"We've still got our lift slot," she said. "That's conditional on Matope getting the elevon system working within the next half hour, of course."

"Idiots," I muttered. The elevons wouldn't be needed until we arrived at Taimyr some six weeks from now, and Matope could practically rebuild them from scratch in that amount of time. To insist they be in prime condition before we could lift was unreasonable even for bureaucrats.

"Oh, there's no problem—Tobbar reported they were closing things up a few minutes ago. They'll put it through its paces, it'll work perfectly, they'll transmit the readout, and that'll be that." She cleared her throat. "Incidentally . . . are you aware we've got a skull-diver and his patient aboard?"

"Yes; I met—*patient*?" I interrupted myself as the last part of her sentence registered. "Who?"

"Name's Bradley," she said. "No further data on him, but apparently he and this Lanton character had a fair amount of electronic and medical stuff delivered to their cabins."

A small shiver ran up my back as I remembered Bradley's face. No wonder he'd struck me as strange. "No mention at all of what's wrong—of why Bradley needs a psychiatrist?"

"Nothing. But it can't be anything serious." The test board bleeped, and Alana paused to peer at the results. Apparently satisfied, she keyed in the next test on the check list. "The Swedish Psychiatric Institute seems to be funding the trip, and they presumably know the regulations about notifying us of potential health risks."

"Um." On the other hand, a small voice whispered in my ear, if there was some problem with Bradley that made him marginal for space certification, they were more likely to get away with slipping him aboard a tramp than on a liner. "Maybe I should give them a call, anyway. Unless you'd like to?"

I glanced over in time to see her face go stony. "No, thank you," she said firmly.

"Right." I felt ashamed of the comment, not really having meant it the way it had come out. All of us had our own reasons for being where we were; Alana's was an overdose of third-degree emotional burns. She was the type who'd seemingly been born to nurse broken wings and bruised souls, the type who by necessity kept her own heart in full view of both friends and passersby. Eventually, I gathered, one too many of her mended souls had torn out the emotional IVs she'd set up and flown off without so much as a backward glance, and she had renounced the whole business and run off to space. Ice to Europa, I'd thought once; there were enough broken wings out here for a whole shipload of Florence Nightingales. But what I'd expected to be a short vacation for her had become four years' worth of armor plate over her emotions, until I wasn't sure she even knew anymore how to care for people. The last thing in the universe she would be interested in doing would be getting involved in any way with Bradley's problems. "Is all the cargo aboard now?" I asked, to change the subject.

"Yes, and Wilkinson certifies it's properly stowed."

"Good." I got to my feet. "I guess I'll make a quick spot survey of the ship, if you can handle things here."

"Go ahead," she said, not bothering to look up. Nodding anyway, I left.

I stopped first at the service shafts where Matope and Tobbar were just starting their elevon tests, staying long enough to satisfy myself the resulting data were adequate to please even the tower's bit-pickers. Then it was to each of the cargo holds to double-check Wilkinson's stowing arrangement, to the passenger area to make sure all their luggage had been properly brought on board, to the computer room to look into a reported malfunction—a false alarm, fortunately—and finally back to the bridge for the lift itself. Somehow, in all the running around, I never got around to calling Sweden. Not, as I found out later, that it would have done me any good.

We lifted right on schedule, shifting from the launch field's grav booster to ramjet at ten kilometers and kicking in the fusion drive as soon as it was legal to do so. Six hours later we were past Luna's orbit and ready for the first cascade maneuver.

Leeds checked in first, reporting officially that the proper number of dosages had been drawn from the sleeper cabinet and were being distributed to the passengers. Pascal gave the okay from the computer room, Matope from the engine room, and Sarojis from the small chamber housing the field generator itself. I had just pulled a hard copy of the computer's course instructions when Leeds called back. "Captain, I'm in Dr. Lanton's cabin," he said without preamble. "Both he and Mr. Bradley refuse to take their sleepers."

Alana turned at that, and I could read my own thought in her face: Lanton and Bradley had to be nuts. "Has Dr. Epstein explained the reasons behind the procedure?" I asked carefully, mindful of both my responsibilities and my limits here.

"Yes, I have," Kate Epstein's clear soprano came. "Dr. Lanton says that his work requires both of them to stay awake through the cascade point."

"Work? What sort of work?"

A pause, and Lanton's voice replaced Kate's. "Captain, this is Dr. Lanton. Rik and I are involved in an experimental type of therapy here. The personal details are confidential, but I assure you that it presents no danger either to us or to you."

Therapy. Great. I could feel anger starting to churn in my gut at Lanton's casual arrogance in neglecting to inform me ahead of time that he had more than transport in mind for my ship. By all rights I should freeze the countdown and sit Lanton down in a corner somewhere until *I* was convinced everything was as safe as he said. But time was money in this business; and if Lanton was glossing things over he could probably do so in finer detail than I could catch him on, anyway. "Mr. Bradley?" I called. "You agree to pass up your sleeper, as well?"

"Yes, sir," came the mousy voice.

"All right. Dr. Epstein, you and Mr. Leeds can go ahead and finish your rounds."

"Well," Alana said as I flipped off the intercom, "at least if something goes wrong the record will clear us of any fault at the inquest."

"You're a genuine ray of sunshine," I told her sourly. "What else could I have done?"

"Raked Lanton over the coals for some information. We're at least entitled to know what's going on."

"Oh, we'll find out, all right. As soon as we're through the point I'm going to haul Lanton up here for a long, cozy chat." I checked the read-outs, cascade point in seventeen minutes. "Look, you might as well go to your cabin and hit the sack. I know it's your turn, but you were up late with that spare parts delivery and you're due some downtime."

She hesitated; wanting to accept, no doubt, but slowed by consider-ations of duty. "Well . . . all right. I'm taking the next one, then. I don't know, though; maybe you shouldn't be up here alone. In case Lanton's miscalculated."

"You mean if Bradley goes berserk or something?" That thought had been lurking in my mind, too, though it sounded rather ridiculous when spoken out loud. Still . . . "I can lower the pressure in the passen-ger deck corridor to half an atmosphere. That'll be enough to lock the doors without triggering any vacuum alarms."

"Leaves Lanton on his own in case of trouble . . . but I suppose that's okay."

"He's the one who's so sure it's safe. Go on, now—get out of here."

She nodded and headed for the door. She paused there, though, her hand resting on the release. "Don't just haul Lanton away from Bradley when you want to talk to him," she called back over her shoulder. "Try to run into him in the lounge or somewhere instead when he's already alone. It might be hard on Bradley to know you two were off somewhere together talking about him." She slapped the release, almost viciously, and was gone.

I stared after her for a long minute, wondering if I'd actually seen a crack in that heavy armor plate. The bleep of the intercom brought me back to the task at hand, Kate telling me the passengers were all down and that she, Leeds, and Wilkinson had taken their own sleepers. One by one the other six crewers also checked in. Within ten minutes they would be asleep, and I would be in sole charge of my ship.

Twelve minutes to go. Even with the *Dancer's* old manual setup there was little that needed to be done. I laid the hard copy of the computer's instructions where it would be legible but not in the way, shut down all the external sensors and control surfaces, and put the computer and other electronic equipment into neutral/standby mode. The artificial gravity I left on; I'd tried a cascade point without it once and would never do so again. Then I waited, trying not to think of what was coming . . . and at the appropriate time I lifted the safety cover and twisted the field generator control knob.

And suddenly there were five of us in the room.

I will never understand how the first person to test the Colloton Drive ever made it past this point. The images silently surrounding me a bare arm's length away were life-size, lifelike, and—at first glance, anyway—as solid as the panels and chairs they seemed to have displaced. It took a careful look to realize they were actually slightly transparent, like some kind of colored glass, and a little experimentation at that point would show they had less substance than air. They were nothing but ghosts, specters straight out of childhood's scariest stories. Which merely added to the discomfort . . . because all of them were me.

Five seconds later the second set of images appeared, perfectly aligned with the first. After that they came more and more quickly, as the spacing between them similarly decreased, forming an ever-expanding horizontal cross with me at the center. I watched—forced myself to watch—knew I *had* to watch—as the lines continued to lengthen, watched until they were so long that I could no longer discern whether any more were being added.

I took a long, shuddering breath—peripherally aware that the images nearest me were doing the same—and wiped a shaking hand across my forehead. *You don't have to look,* I told myself, eyes rigidly fixed on the back of the image in front of me. *You've seen it all before. What's the point?* But I'd fought this fight before, and I knew in advance I would lose. There was indeed no more point to it than there was to pressing a bruise, but it held an equal degree of compulsion. Bracing myself, I turned my head and gazed down the line of images strung out to my left.

The armchair philosophers may still quibble over what the cascade point images "really" are, but those of us who fly the small ships figured it out long ago. The Colloton field puts us into a different type of space, possibly an entire universe worth of it—that much is established fact. Somehow this space links us into a set of alternate realities, universes that might have been if things had gone differently . . . and what I was therefore seeing around me were images of what I would be doing in each of those universes.

Sure, the theory has problems. Obviously, I should generate a separate pseudoreality every time I choose ham instead of turkey for lunch, and just as obviously such trivial changes don't make it into the pattern. Only the four images closest to me are ever exactly my doubles; even the next ones in line are noticeably if subtly different. But it's not a matter of subconscious suggestion, either. Too many of the images are . . . unexpected . . . for that.

It was no great feat to locate the images I particularly needed to see: the white-and-gold liner captain's uniforms stood out brilliantly among the more dingy jumpsuits and coveralls on either side. Liner captain. In charge of a fully equipped, fully modernized ship; treated with the respect and admiration such a position brought. It could have been— *should* have been. And to make things worse, I knew the precise decision that had lost it to me.

It had been eight years now since the uniforms had appeared among my cascade images; ten since the day I'd thrown Lord Hendrik's son off the bridge of the training ship and simultaneously guaranteed myself a blackballing with every major company in the business. Could I have handled the situation differently? Probably. Should I have? Given the state of the art then, no. A man who, after three training missions, still went borderline claustrophobic every time he had to stay awake through a cascade point had no business aboard a ship, let alone on its bridge. Hendrik might have forgiven me once he thought things through. The kid, who was forced into a ground position with the firm, never did. Eventually, of course, he took over the business.

I had no way of knowing that four years later the Aker-Ming Autotorque would eliminate the need for *anyone* to stay awake through cascade maneuvers. I doubt seriously the kid appreciated the irony of it all.

In the eight years since the liner captain uniforms had appeared they had been gradually moving away from me along all four arms of the cross. Five more years, I estimated, and they would be far enough down the line to disappear into the mass of images crowded together out there. Whether my reaction to that event would be relief or sadness I didn't yet know, but there was no doubt in my mind that it would in some way be the end of a chapter in my life. I gazed at the figures for another minute . . . and then, with my ritual squeezing of the bruise accomplished, I let my eyes drift up and down the rest of the line.

They were unremarkable, for the most part: minor variations in my appearance or clothing. The handful that had once showed me in some nonspacing job had long since vanished toward infinity; I'd been out here a long time. Perhaps too long . . . a thought the half-dozen or so gaps in each arm of the pattern underlined with unnecessary force. I'd told Bradley that ships like the *Dancer* rarely crashed, a perfectly true statement; but what I hadn't mentioned was that the chances of simply disappearing en route were something rather higher. None of us liked to think about that, especially during critical operations like cascade point maneuvers. But the gaps in the image pattern were a continual reminder that people still died in space. In six possible realities, apparently, I'd made a decision that killed me.

Taking another deep breath, I forced all of that as far from my mind as I could and activated the *Dancer's* flywheel.

Even on the bridge the hum was audible as the massive chunk of metal began to spin. A minute later it had reached its top speed . . . and the entire ship's counterrotation began to register on the gyroscope set behind glass in the ceiling above my head. The device looked out of place, a decided anachronism among the modern instruments, control circuits, and readouts filling the bridge. But using it was the only way a ship our size could find its way safely through a cascade point. The enhanced electron tunneling effect that fouled up electronic instrument performance was well understood; what was still needed was a way to predict the precise effect a given cascade point rotation would generate. Without such predictability, readings couldn't even be given adjustment factors. Cascade navigation thus had to fall back on gross electrical and purely mechanical systems: flywheel, physical gyroscope, simple on-off controls, and a nonelectronic decision maker. Me.

Slowly, the long needle above me crept around its dial. I watched its reflection carefully in the magnifying mirror, a system that allowed me to see the indicator without having to break my neck looking up over my shoulder. Around me, the cascade images did their own slow dance, a strange kaleidoscopic thing that moved the images and gaps around within each branch of the cross, while the branches themselves remained stationary relative to me. The effect was unexplained; but then, Colloton field theory left a lot of things unexplained. Mathematically, the basic idea was relatively straightforward: the space we were in right now could be described by a type of bilinear conformal mapping—specifically, a conjugate inversion that maps lines into circles. From that point it was all downhill, the details tangling into a soup of singularities, branch points, and confluent Riemann surfaces; but what it all eventually boiled down to was that a yaw rotation of the ship here would become a linear translation when I shut down the field generator and we reentered normal space. The *Dancer's* rotation was coming up on two degrees now, which for the particular configuration we were in meant we were already about half a light-year closer to our destination. Another—I checked the printout—one point three six and I would shut down the flywheel, letting the *Dancer's* momentum carry her an extra point two degree for a grand total of eight light-years.

The needle crept to the mark, and I threw the flywheel switch, simultaneously giving my full attention over to the gyro. Theoretically, over- or undershooting the mark could be corrected during the next cascade point—or by fiddling the flywheel back and forth now—but it was simpler not to have to correct at all. The need to make sure we were stationary was another matter entirely; if the *Dancer* were still rotating when I threw the field switch we would wind up strung out along a million kilometers or more of space. I thought of the gaps in my cascade image pattern and shivered.

But that was all the closer death was going to get to me, at least this time. The delicately balanced spin lock worked exactly as it was supposed to, freezing the field switch in place until the ship's rotation was as close to zero as made no difference. I shut off the field and watched my duplicates disappear in reverse order, waiting until the last four vanished before confirming the stars were once again visible through the bridge's tiny viewport. I sighed; and fighting the black depression that always seized me at this point, I turned the *Dancer's* systems back on and set the computer to figuring our exact position. Someday, I thought, I'd be able to afford to buy Aker-Ming Autotorques and never, *never* have to go through this again.

And someday I'd swim the Pacific Ocean, too.

Slumping back in my chair, I waited for the computer to finish its job and allowed the tears to flow.

Crying, for me, has always been the simplest and fastest way of draining off tension, and I've always felt a little sorry for men who weren't able to appreciate its advantages. This time was no exception, and I was feeling almost back to normal by the time the computer produced its location figures. I was still poring over them twenty minutes later when Alana returned to the bridge. "Another cascade point successfully hurdled, I see," she commented tiredly. "Hurray for our side."

"I thought you were supposed to be taking a real nap, not just a sleeper's worth," I growled at her over my shoulder.

"I woke up and decided to take a walk," she answered, her voice suddenly businesslike. "What's wrong?"

I handed her a printout, pointed to the underlined numbers. "The gyroscope reading says we're theoretically dead on position. The stars say we're short."

"Wumph!" Frowning intently at the paper, she kicked around the other chair and sat down. "Twenty light-days. That's what, twice the expected error for this point? Great. You double-checked everything, of course?"

"Triple-checked. The computer confirmed the gyro reading, and the astrogate programs got positive ident on twenty stars. Margin of error's no greater than ten light-minutes on either of those."

"Yeah." She eyed me over the pages. "Anything funny in the cargo?"

I gestured to the manifest in front of me. "We've got three boxes of technical equipment that include Ming metal," I said. "All three are in the shield. I checked that before we lifted."

"Maybe the shields sprung a leak," she suggested doubtfully.

"It's supposed to take a hell of a break before the stuff inside can affect cascade point configuration."

"I can go check if you'd like."

"No, don't bother. There's no rush now, and Wilkinson's had more experience with shield boxes. He can take a look when he wakes up. I'd rather you stay here and help me do a complete programming check. Unless you'd like to obey orders and go back to bed."

She smiled faintly. "No, thanks; I'll stay. Um . . . I could even start things alone if you'd like to go to the lounge for a while."

"I'm fine," I growled, irritated by the suggestion.

"I know," she said. "But Lanton was down there alone when I passed by on my way here."

I'd completely forgotten about Lanton and Bradley, and it took a couple of beats for me to catch on. Cross-examining a man in the middle of cascade depression wasn't a terrifically nice thing to do, but I wasn't feeling terrifically nice at the moment. "Start with the astrogate program," I told Alana, getting to my feet. "Give me a shout if you find anything."

Lanton was still alone in the lounge when I arrived. "Doctor," I nodded to him as I sat down in the chair across from his. "How are you feeling?" The question was more for politeness than information; the four empty glasses on the end table beside him and the half-full one in his hand showed how he'd chosen to deal with his depression. I'd learned long ago that crying was easier on the liver.

He managed a weak smile. "Better, Captain; much better. I was starting to think I was the only one left on the ship."

"You're not even the only one awake," I said. "The other passengers will be wandering in shortly—you people get a higher-dose sleeper than the crew takes."

He shook his head. "Lord, but that was weird. No wonder you want everyone to sleep through it. I can't remember the last time I felt this rotten."

"It'll pass," I assured him. "How did Mr. Bradley take it?"

"Oh, fine. Much better than I did, though he fell apart just as badly when it was over. I gave him a sedative—the coward's way out, but I wasn't up to more demanding therapy at the moment."

So Bradley wasn't going to be walking in on us any time soon. Good. "Speaking of therapy, Doctor, I think you owe me a little more information about what you're doing."

He nodded and took a swallow from his glass. "Beginning, I suppose, with what exactly Rik is suffering from?"

"That would be nice," I said, vaguely surprised at how civil I was being. Somehow, the sight of Lanton huddled miserably with his liquor had taken all the starch out of my fire-and-brimstone mood. Alana was clearly having a bad effect on me.

"Okay. Well, first and foremost, he is *not* in any way dangerous, either to himself or other people. He has no tendencies even remotely suicidal or homicidal. He's simply . . . permanently disoriented, I suppose, is one way to think of it. His personality seems to slide around in strange ways, generating odd fluctuations in behavior and perception."

Explaining psychiatric concepts in layman's terms obviously wasn't Lanton's forte. "You mean he's schizophrenic? Or paranoid?" I added, remembering our launch-field conversation.

"Yes and no. He shows some of the symptoms of both—along with those of five or six other maladies—but he doesn't demonstrate the proper biochemical syndrome for any known mental disease. He's a fascinating, scientifically annoying anomaly. I've got whole bubble-packs of data on him, taken over the past five years, and I'm convinced I'm teetering on the edge of a breakthrough. But I've already exhausted all the standard ways of probing a patient's subconscious, and I had to come up with something new." He gestured around him. "This is it."

"This is what? A new form of shock therapy?"

"No, no—you're missing the point. I'm studying Rik's cascade images."

I stared at him for a long moment. Then, getting to my feet, I went to the autobar and drew myself a lager. "With all due respect," I said as I sat down again, "I think you're out of your mind. First of all, the images aren't a product of the deep subconscious or whatever; they're reflections of universes that might have been."

"Perhaps. There *is* some argument about that." He held up a hand as I started to object. "But either way, you have to admit that your conscious or unconscious mind *must* have an influence on them. Invariably, the images that appear show the results of *major* decisions or events in one's life; never the plethora of insignificant choices we all make. Whether the subconscious is choosing among actual images or generating them by itself, it *is* involved with them and therefore can be studied through them."

He seemed to settle slightly in his chair, and I got the feeling this wasn't the first time he'd made that speech. "Even if I grant you all that," I said, "which I'm not sure I do, I think you're running an incredibly stupid risk that the cascade point effects will give Bradley a shove right over the edge. They're hard enough on those of us who *haven't* got psychological problems—what am I telling you this for? *You* saw what it was like, damn it. The last thing I want on my ship is someone who's going to need either complete sedation or a restraint couch all the way to Taimyr!"

I stopped short, suddenly aware that my volume had been steadily increasing. "Sorry," I muttered, draining half of my lager. "Like I said, cascade points are hard on all of us."

He frowned. "What do you mean? You were asleep with everyone else, weren't you?"

"Somebody's got to be awake to handle the maneuver," I said.

"But . . . I thought there were autopilots for cascade points now."

"Sure—the Aker-Ming Autotorque. But they cost nearly twenty-two thousand apiece and have to be replaced every hundred cascade points or so. The big liners and freighters can afford luxuries like that; tramp starmers can't."

"I'm sorry—I didn't know." His expression suggested he was also sorry he hadn't investigated the matter more thoroughly before booking aboard the *Dancer*.

I'd seen that look on people before, and I always hated it. "Don't worry; you're perfectly safe. The manual method's been used for nearly two centuries, and my crew and I know what we're doing."

His mind was obviously still a half kilometer back. "But how can it be that expensive? I mean, Ming metal's an exotic alloy, sure, but it's only selenium with a little bit of rhenium, after all. You can buy psy-test equipment with Ming-metal parts for a fraction of the cost you quoted."

"And we've got an entire box made of the stuff in our number one cargo hold," I countered. "But making a consistent-property rotation gauge is a good deal harder than rolling sheets or whatever. Anyway, you're evading my question. What are you going to do if Bradley can't take the strain?"

He shrugged, but I could see he didn't take the possibility seriously. "If worst comes to worst, I suppose I could let him sleep while I stayed awake to observe his images. They *do* show up even in your sleep, don't they?"

"So I've heard." I didn't add that I'd feel like a voyeur doing something like that. Psychiatrists, accustomed to poking into other people's minds, clearly had different standards than I did.

"Good. Though that would add another variable," he added thoughtfully. "Well . . . I think Rik can handle it. We'll do it conscious as long as we can."

"And what's going to be your clue that he's *not* handling it? The first time he tries to strangle one of his images? Or maybe when he goes catatonic?"

He gave me an irritated look. "Captain, I *am* a psychiatrist. I'm perfectly capable of reading my patient and picking up any signs of trouble before they become serious. Rik is going to be all right; let's just leave it at that."

I had no intention of leaving it at that; but just then two more of the passengers wandered into the lounge, so I nodded to Lanton and left. We had five days before the next cascade point, and there would be other opportunities in that time to discuss the issue. If necessary, I would manufacture them.

Alana had only negatives for me when I got back to the bridge. "The astrogate's clean," she told me. "I've pulled a hard copy of the program to check, but the odds that a glitch developed that just happened to look reasonable enough to fool the diagnostic are essentially nil." She waved at the long gyroscope needle above us. "Computer further says the vacuum in the gyro chamber stayed hard throughout the maneuver and that there was no malfunction of the mag-bearing fields."

So the gyroscope hadn't been jinxed by friction into giving a false reading. Combined with the results on the astrogate program, that left damn few places to look. "Has Wilkinson checked in?"

"Yes, and I've got him testing the shield for breaks."

"Good. I'll go down and give him a hand. Have you had time to check out our current course?"

"Not in detail, but the settings look all right to me."

"They did to me, too, but if there's any chance the computer's developed problems we can't take anything for granted. I don't want to be in the wrong position when it's time for the next point."

"Yeah. Well, Pascal's due up here in ten minutes. I guess the astrogate deep-check can wait until then. What did you find out from Lanton?"

With an effort I switched gears. "According to him, Bradley's not going to be any trouble. He sounds more neurotic than psychotic, from Lanton's description, at least at the moment. Unfortunately, Lanton's got this great plan to use cascade images as a research tool, and intends to keep Bradley awake through every point between here and Taimyr."

"He *what*? I don't suppose he's bothered to consider what that might do to Bradley's problems?"

"That's what *I* wanted to know. I never did get an acceptable answer." I moved to the bridge door, poked the release. "Don't worry, we'll pound some sense into him before the next point. See you later."

Wilkinson and Sarojis were both in the number one hold when I arrived, Sarojis offering minor assistance and lots of suggestions as Wilkinson crawled over the shimmery metal box that took up the forward third of the narrow space. Looking down at me as I threaded my way between the other boxes cramming the hold, he shook his head.

"Nothing wrong here, Cap'n," he said. "The shield's structurally sound; there's no way the Ming metal inside could affect our configuration."

"No chance of hairline cracks?" I asked.

He held up the detector he'd been using. "I'm checking, but nothing that small would do anything."

I nodded acknowledgement and spent a moment frowning at the box. Ming metal had a number of unique properties inside cascade points, properties that made it both a blessing and a curse to those of us who had to fly with it. Its unique blessing, of course, was that its electrical, magnetic, and thermodynamic properties were affected only by the absolute angle the ship rotated through, and not by any of the hundred or so other variables in a given cascade maneuver. It was this predictability that finally had made it possible for a cascade point auto-drive mechanism to be developed. Of more concern to smaller ships like mine, though, was that Ming metal drastically changed a ship's "configuration"—the size, shape, velocity profile, and so on from which the relation between rotation angle and distance traveled on a given maneuver could be computed. Fortunately, the effect was somewhat analogous to air resistance, in that if one piece of Ming metal were completely enclosed in another, only the outer container's shape, size, and mass would affect the configuration. Hence, the shield. But if it hadn't been breached, then the cargo inside it couldn't have fouled us up. . . . "What are the chances," I asked Wilkinson, "that one of these other boxes contains Ming metal?"

"Without listing it on the manifest?" Sarojis piped up indignantly. He was a dark, intense little man who always seemed loudly astonished whenever anyone did anything either unjust or stupid. Most everyone on the *Dancer* OD'd periodically on his chatter and spent every third day or so avoiding him. Alana and Wilkinson were the only exceptions I knew of, and even Alana got tired of him every so often. "They couldn't do that," Sarojis continued before I could respond. "We could sue them into bankruptcy."

"Only if we make it to Taimyr," I said briefly, my eyes on Wilkinson.

"One way to find out," he returned. Dropping lightly off the shield, he replaced his detector in the open tool box lying on the deck and withdrew a wandlike gadget.

It took two hours to run the wand over every crate in the *Dancer's* three holds, and we came up with precisely nothing. "Maybe one of the passengers brought some aboard," Sarojis suggested.

"You've got to be richer than any of *our* customers to buy cases with Ming-metal buckles." Wilkinson shook his head. "Cap'n, it's got to be a computer fault, or else something in the gyro."

"Um," I said noncommittally. I hadn't yet told them that I'd checked with Alana midway through all the cargo testing and that she and Pascal had found nothing wrong in their deep-checks of both systems. There was no point in worrying them more than necessary.

I returned to the bridge to find Pascal there alone, slouching in the helm chair and gazing at the displays with a dreamy sort of expression on his face. "Where's Alana?" I asked him, dropping into the other chair and eyeing the pile of diagnostic printouts they'd thoughtfully left for me. "Finally gone to bed?"

"She said she was going to stop by the dining room first and have some dinner," Pascal said, the dreamy expression fading somewhat. "Something about meeting the passengers."

I glanced at my watch, realizing with a start that it was indeed dinnertime. "Maybe I'll go on down, too. Any problems here, first?"

He shook his head. "I have a theory about the cascade point error," he said, lowering his voice conspiratorially. "I'd rather not say what it is, though, until I've had more time to think about it."

"Sure," I said, and left. Pascal fancied himself a great scientific detective and was always coming up with complex and wholly unrealistic theories in areas far outside his field, with predictable results. Still, nothing he'd ever come up with had been actually dangerous, and there was always the chance he would someday hit on something useful. I hoped this would be the day.

The *Dancer's* compact dining room was surprisingly crowded for so soon after the first cascade point, but a quick scan of the faces showed me why. Only nine of our twelve passengers had made it out of bed after their first experience with sleepers, but their absence was more than made up for by the six crewers who had opted to eat here tonight instead of in the duty mess. The entire off-duty contingent . . . and it wasn't hard to figure out why.

Bradley, seated between Lanton and Tobbar at one of the two tables, was speaking earnestly as I slipped through the door. ". . . less symbolic than it was an attempt to portray the world from a truly alien viewpoint, a viewpoint he would change every few years. Thus *A Midsummer Wedding* has both the slight fish-eye distortion *and* the color shifts you might get from a water-dwelling creature; also the subtleties of posture and expression that such an alien wouldn't understand and might therefore not get right."

"But isn't strange sensory expression one of the basic foundations of art?" That was Tobbar—so glib on any topic that you were never quite sure whether he actually knew anything about it or not. "Drawing both eyes on one side of the head, putting nudes at otherwise normal picnics—that sort of thing."

"True, but you mustn't confuse weirdness for its own sake with the consistent, scientifically accurate variations Meyerhäus used."

There was more, but just then Alana caught my eye from her place at the other table and indicated the empty seat next to her. I went over and sat down, losing the train of Bradley's monologue in the process. "Anything?" she whispered to me.

"A very flat zero," I told her.

She nodded once but didn't say anything, and I noticed her gaze drift back to Bradley. "Knows a lot about art, I see," I commented, oddly irritated by her shift in attention.

"You missed his talk on history," she said. "He got quite a discussion going over there—that mathematician, Dr. Chileogu, also seems to be a history buff. First time I've ever seen Tobbar completely frozen out of a discussion. He certainly seems normal enough."

"Tobbar?"

"Bradley."

"Oh." I looked over at Bradley, who was now listening intently to someone holding forth from the other end of his table. *Permanently disoriented,* Lanton had described him. Was he envisioning himself a professor of art or something right now? Or were his delusions that complete? I didn't know; and at the moment I didn't care. "Well, good for him. Now if you'd care to bring your mind back to ship's business, we still have a problem on our hands."

Alana turned back to me, a slight furrow across her forehead. "I'm open to suggestions," she said. "I was under the impression that we were stuck for the moment."

I clenched my jaw tightly over the retort that wanted to come out. We *were* stuck; and until someone else came up with an idea there really wasn't any reason why Alana shouldn't be down here relaxing. "Yeah," I growled, getting to my feet. "Well, keep thinking about it."

"Aren't you going to eat?"

"I'll get something later in the duty mess," I said.

I paused at the door and glanced back. Already her attention was back on Bradley. Heading back upstairs to the duty mess, I programmed myself an unimaginative meal that went down like so much wet cardboard. Afterwards, I went back to my cabin and pulled a tape on cascade point theory.

I was still paging through it two hours later when I fell asleep.

I tried several times in the next five days to run into Lanton on his own, but it seemed that every time I saw him Bradley was tagging along like a well-behaved cocker spaniel. Eventually, I was forced to accept Alana's suggestion that she and Tobbar offer Bradley a tour of the ship, giving me a chance to waylay Lanton in the corridor outside his cabin. The psychiatrist seemed preoccupied and a little annoyed at being so accosted, but I didn't let it bother me.

"No, of course there's no progress yet," he said in response to my question. "I also didn't expect any. The first cascade point observations were my baseline. I'll be asking questions during the next one, and after that I'll start introducing various treatment techniques and observing Rik's reactions to them."

He started to slide past me, but I moved to block him. "Treatment? You never said anything about treatment."

"I didn't think I had to. I *am* legally authorized to administer drugs and such, after all."

"Maybe on the ground," I told him stiffly. "But out here the ship's doctor is the final medical authority. You will *not* give Bradley any drugs or electronic treatment without first clearing it with Dr. Epstein." Something tugged at my mind, but I couldn't be bothered with tracking it down. "As a matter of fact, I want you to give her a complete list of all the drugs you've brought aboard before the next cascade point. Anything addictive or potentially dangerous is to be turned over to her for storage in the sleeper cabinet. Understand?"

Lanton's expression stuck somewhere between irritated and stunned. "Oh, come on, Captain, be reasonable—practically every medicine in the book can be dangerous if taken in excessive doses." His face seemed to recover, settling into a bland sort of neutral as his voice similarly adjusted to match it. "Why do you object so strongly to what I'm trying to do for Rik?"

"I'd hurry with that list, Doctor—the next point's scheduled for tomorrow. Good day." Spinning on my heel, I turned and stalked away.

I called back Kate Epstein as soon as I reached my cabin and told her about the list Lanton would be delivering to her. I got the impression that she, too, thought I was overreacting, but she nevertheless agreed to cooperate. I extracted a promise to keep me informed on what Lanton's work involved, then signed off and returned once more to the Colloton theory tapes that had occupied the bulk of my time the past four days.

But despite the urgency I was feeling—we had less than twenty hours to the next cascade point—the words on my reader screen refused to coalesce into anything that made sense. I gritted my teeth and kept at it until I discovered myself reading the same paragraph for the fourth time and still not getting a word of it. Snapping off my reader in disgust, I stretched out on my bed and tried to track down the source of my distraction.

Obviously, my irritation at Lanton was a good fraction of it. Along with the high-handed way he treated the whole business of Bradley, he'd now added the insult of talking to me in a tone of voice that implied I needed his professional services—and for nothing worse than insisting on my rights as captain of the *Dancer*. I wished to hell I'd paid more attention to the passenger manifest before I'd let the two of them aboard. Next time I'd know better.

Still . . . I had to admit that maybe I *had* overreacted a bit. But it wasn't as if I was being short-tempered without reason. I had plenty of reasons to be worried; Lanton's game of cascade-image tag and its possible effects on Bradley, the still-unexplained discrepancy in the last point's maneuvers, the changes I was seeing in Alana—

Alana. Up until that moment I hadn't consciously admitted to myself that she was behaving any differently than usual. But I hadn't flown with her for four years without knowing all of her moods and tendencies, and it was abundantly clear to me that she was slowly getting involved with Bradley.

My anger over such an unexpected turn of events was not in any way motivated by jealousy. Alana was her own woman, and any part of her life not directly related to her duties was none of my business. But I knew that, in this case, her involvement was more than likely her old affinity for broken wings, rising like the phoenix—except that the burning would come afterwards instead of beforehand. I didn't want to see Alana go through that again, especially with someone whose presence I felt responsible for. There was, of course, little I could do directly without risking Alana's notice and probable anger; but I could let Lanton know how I felt by continuing to make things as difficult as possible. And I would.

And with that settled, I managed to push it aside and return to my studies. It is, I suppose, revealing that it never occurred to me at the time how inconsistent my conclusion and proposed course of action really were. After all, the faster Lanton cured Bradley, the faster the broken-wing attraction would disappear and—presumably—the easier Alana would be able to extricate herself. Perhaps, even then, I was secretly starting to wonder if her attraction to him was something more than altruistic.

"Two minutes," Alana said crisply from my right, her tone almost but not quite covering the tension I knew she must be feeling. "Gyro checks out perfectly."

I made a minor adjustment in my mirror, confirmed that the long needle was set dead on zero. Behind the mirror, the displays stared blankly at me from the control board, their systems having long since been shut down. I looked at the computer's printout, the field generator control cover, my own hands—anything to keep from looking at Alana. Like me, she was unaccustomed to company during a cascade point, and I was determined to give her what little privacy I could.

"One minute," she said. "You sure we made up enough distance for this to be safe?"

"Positive. The only possible trouble could have come from Epsilon Eridani, and we've, made up enough lateral distance to put it the requisite six degrees off our path."

"Do you suppose that could have been the trouble last time? Could we have come too close to something—a black dwarf, maybe, that drifted into our corridor?"

I shrugged, eyes on the clock. "Not according to the charts. Ships have been going to Taimyr a long time, you know, and the whole route's been pretty thoroughly checked out. Even black dwarfs have to come *from* somewhere." Gritting my teeth, I flipped the cover off the knob. "Brace yourself; here we go."

Doing a cascade point alone invites introspection, memories of times long past, and melancholy. Doing it with someone else adds instant vertigo and claustrophobia to the list. Alana's images and mine still appeared in the usual horizontal cross shape, but since we weren't seated facing exactly the same direction, they didn't overlap. The result was a suffocatingly crowded bridge—crowded, to make things worse, with images that were no longer tied to your own motions, but would twitch and jerk apparently on their own.

For me, the disadvantages far outweighed the single benefit of having someone there to talk to, but in this case I had had little choice. Alana had steadfastly refused to let me take over from her on two points in a row, and I'd been equally insistent on being awake to watch the proceedings. It was a lousy compromise, but I'd known better than to order Alana off the bridge. She had her pride too.

"Activating flywheel."

Alana's voice brought my mind back to business. I checked the printout one last time, then turned my full attention to the gyro needle. A moment later it began its slow creep, and the dual set of cascade images started into their own convoluted dances. Swallowing hard, I gave my stomach stern orders and held on.

It seemed at times to be lasting forever, but finally it was over. The *Dancer* had been rotated, had been brought to a stop, and had successfully made the transition to real space. I slumped in my seat, feeling a mixture of cascade depression and only marginally decreased tension. The astrogate program's verdict, after all, was still to come.

But I was spared the ordeal of waiting with twiddled thumbs for the computer. Alana had barely gotten the ship's systems going again when the intercom bleeped at me. "Bridge," I answered.

"This is Dr. Lanton," the tight response came. "There's something very wrong with the power supply to my cabin—one of my instruments just burned out on me."

"Is it on fire?" I asked sharply, eyes flicking to the status display. Nothing there indicated any problem.

"Oh, no—there was just a little smoke and that's gone now. But the thing's ruined."

"Well, I'm sorry, Doctor," I said, trying to sound like I meant it. "But I can't be responsible for damage to electronics that are left running through a cascade point. Even something as simple as an AC power line can show small voltage fluc—*oh, damn it!*"

Alana jerked at my exclamation. "What—"

"Lanton!" I snapped, already halfway out of my seat. "Stay put and *don't touch anything.* I'm coming down."

His reply was more question than acknowledgment, but I ignored it.

"Alana," I called to her, "call Wilkinson and have him meet me at Lanton's cabin—and tell him to bring a Ming-metal detector."

I caught just a glimpse of her suddenly horrified expression before the door slid shut and I went running down the corridor. There was no reason to run, but I did so anyway.

It was there, of course: a nice, neat Ming-metal dual crossover coil, smack in the center of the ruined neural tracer. At least it *had* been neat; now it was stained with a sticky goo that had dripped onto it from the blackened circuit board above. "Make sure none of it melted off onto something else," I told Wilkinson as he carefully removed the coil. "If it has we'll either have to gut the machine or find a way to squeeze it inside the shield." He nodded and I stepped over to where Lanton was sitting, the white-hot anger inside me completely overriding my usual depression. "What the *hell* did you think you were doing, bringing that damn thing aboard?" I thundered, dimly aware that the freshly sedated Bradley might hear me from the next cabin but not giving a damn.

His voice, when he answered, was low and artificially calm—whether in stunned reaction to my rage or simply a reflexive habit I didn't know. "I'm very sorry, Captain, but I swear I didn't know the tracer had any Ming metal in it."

"Why not? You told me yourself you could buy things with Ming-metal parts." And I'd let that fact sail blithely by me, a blunder on my part that was probably fueling ninety percent of my anger.

"But I never see the manufacturing specs on anything I use," he said. "It all comes through the Institute's receiving department, and all I get are the operating manuals and such." His eyes flicked to his machine as if he were going to object to Wilkinson's manhandling of it. "I guess they must have removed any identification tags, as well."

"I guess they must have," I ground out. Wilkinson had the coil out now, and I watched as he laid it aside and picked up the detector wand again. A minute later he shook his head.

"Clean, Cap'n," he told me, picking up the coil again. "I'll take this one to One Hold and put it away."

I nodded and he left. Gesturing to the other gadgets spread around the room, I asked, "Is this all you've got, or is there more in Bradley's cabin?"

"No, this is it," Lanton assured me.

"What about your stereovision camera? I know some of those have Ming metal in them."

He frowned. "I don't have any cameras. Who told you I did?"

"I—" I frowned in turn. "You said you were studying Bradley's cascade images."

"Yes, but you can't take pictures of them. They don't register on any kind of film."

I opened my mouth, closed it again. I was sure I'd known that once, but after years of watching the images I'd apparently clean forgotten it. They were so lifelike . . . and I was perhaps getting old. "I assumed someone had come up with a technique that worked," I said stiffly, acutely aware that my attempt to save face wasn't fooling either of us. "How *do* you do it, then?"

"I memorize all of it, of course. Psychiatrists have to have good memories, you know, and there are several drugs that can enhance one's basic abilities."

I'd heard of mnemonic drugs. They were safe, extremely effective, and cost a small fortune. "Do you have any of them with you? If so, I'm going to insist they be locked away."

He shook his head. "I was given a six-month treatment at the Institute before we left. That's the main reason we're on your ship, by the way, instead of something specially chartered. Mnemonic drugs play havoc with otherwise reasonable budgets."

He was making a joke, of course, but it was an exceedingly tasteless one, and the anger that had been draining out of me reversed its flow. No one needed to remind me that the *Dancer* wasn't up to the Cunard lines standards. "My sympathies to your budget," I said briefly. Turning away, I strode to the door.

"Wait a minute," he called after me. "What are my chances of getting that neural tracer fixed?"

I glanced back over my shoulder. "That probably depends on how good you are with a screwdriver and solder gun," I said, and left.

Alana was over her own cascade depression by the time I returned to the bridge. "I was right," I said as I dropped into my seat. "One of the damned black boxes had a Ming-metal coil."

"I know; Wilkinson called from One Hold." She glanced sideways at me. "I hope you didn't chew Lanton out in front of Bradley."

"Why not?"

"Did you?"

"As it happens, no. Lanton sedated him right after the point again. Why does it matter?"

"Well . . ." She seemed embarrassed. "It might . . . upset him to see you angry. You see, he sort of looks up to you—captain of a star ship and all—"

"Captain of a struggling tramp," I corrected her more harshly than was necessary. "Or didn't you bother to tell him that we're the absolute bottom of the line?"

"I told him," she said steadily. "But he doesn't see things that way. Even in five days aboard he's had a glimpse of how demanding this kind of life is. He's never been able to hold down a good job himself for very long, and that adds to the awe he feels for all of us."

"I can tell he's got a lot to learn about the universe," I snorted. For some reason the conversation was making me nervous, and I hurried to bring it back to safer regions. "Did your concern for Bradley's idealism leave you enough time to run the astrogate?"

She actually blushed, the first time in years I'd seen her do that. "Yes," she said stiffly. "We're about thirty-two light-days short this time."

"Damn." I hammered the edge of the control board once with my clenched fist, and then began punching computer keys.

"I've already checked that," Alana spoke up. "We'll dig pretty deep into our fuel reserve if we try to make it up through normal space."

I nodded, my fingers coming to a halt. My insistence on maintaining a high fuel reserve was one of the last remnants of Lord Hendrik's training that I still held onto, and despite occasional ribbing from other freighter captains I felt it was a safety precaution worth taking. The alternative to using it, though, wasn't especially pleasant. "All right," I sighed. "Let's clear out enough room for the computer to refigure our course profile. If possible, I'd like to tack the extra fifty light-days onto one of the existing points instead of adding a new one."

She nodded and started typing away at her console as I called down to the engine room to alert Matope. It was a semimajor pain, but the *Dancer's* computer didn't have enough memory space to handle the horribly complex Colloton calculations we needed while all the standard operations programming was in place. We would need to shift all but the most critical functions to Matope's manual control, replacing the erased programs later from Pascal's set of master tapes.

It took nearly an hour to get the results, but they turned out to be worth the wait. Not only could we make up our shortfall without an extra point, but with the slightly different stellar configuration we faced now it was going to be possible to actually shorten the duration of one of the points further down the line. That was good news from both practical and psychological considerations. Though I've never been able to prove it, I've long believed that the deepest depressions follow the longest points.

I didn't see any more of Lanton that day, though I heard later that he and Bradley had mingled with the passengers as they always did, Lanton behaving as if nothing at all had happened. Though I knew my crew wasn't likely to go around blabbing about Lanton's Ming-metal blunder, I issued an order anyway to keep the whole matter quiet. It wasn't to save Lanton any embarrassment—that much I was certain of—but beyond that my motives became uncomfortably fuzzy. I finally decided I was doing it for Alana, to keep her from having to explain to Bradley what an idiot his therapist was.

The next point, six days later, went flawlessly, and life aboard ship finally settled into the usual deep-space routine. Alana, Pascal, and I each took eight-hour shifts on the bridge; Matope, Tobbar, and Sarojis did the same back in the engine room; and Kate Epstein, Leeds, and Wilkinson took turns catering to the occasional whims of our passengers. Off duty, most of the crewers also made an effort to spend at least a little time in the passenger lounge, recognizing the need to be friendly in the part of our business that was mainly word of mouth. Since that first night, though, the exaggerated interest in Bradley the Mental Patient had pretty well evaporated, leaving him as just another passenger in nearly everyone's eyes.

The exception, of course, was Alana.

In some ways, watching her during those weeks was roughly akin to watching a baby bird hacking its way out of its shell. Alana's bridge shift followed mine, and I was often more or less forced to hang around for an hour or so listening to her talk about her day. *Forced* is perhaps the wrong word; obviously, no one was nailing me to my chair. And yet, in another sense, I really *did* have no choice. To the best of my knowledge, I was Alana's only real confidant aboard the *Dancer,* and to have refused to listen would have deprived her of her only verbal sounding board. And the more I listened, the more I realized how vital my participation really was . . . because along with the usual rolls, pitches, and yaws of every embryo relationship, this one had an extra complication: Bradley's personality was beginning to change.

Lanton had said he was on the verge of a breakthrough, but it had never occurred to me that he might be able to begin genuine treatment aboard ship, let alone that any of its effects would show up en route. But even to me, who saw Bradley for maybe ten minutes at a time three times a week, the changes were obvious. All the conflicting signals in posture and expression that had bothered me so much at our first meeting diminished steadily until they were virtually gone, showing up only on brief occasions. At the same time, his self-confidence began to increase, and a heretofore unnoticed—by me, at least—sense of humor began to manifest itself. The latter effect bothered me, until Alana explained that a proper sense of humor required both a sense of dignity and an ability to take oneself less than seriously, neither of which Bradley had ever had before. I was duly pleased for her at the progress this showed; privately, I sought out Lanton to find out exactly what he was doing to his patient and the possible hazards thereof. The interview was easy to obtain—Bradley was soloing quite a bit these days—but relatively uninformative. Lanton tossed around a lot of stuff about synaptic fixing and duplicate messenger chemistry, but with visions of a Nobel Prize almost visibly orbiting his head he was in no mood to worry about dangerous side effects. He assured me that nothing he was using was in the slightest way experimental, and that I should go back to flying the *Dancer* and let him worry about Bradley. Or words to that effect.

I really *was* happy for Bradley, of course, but the fact remained that his rapid improvement was playing havoc with Alana's feelings. After years away from the wing-mending business she felt herself painfully rusty at it; and as Bradley continued to get better despite that, she began to wonder out loud whether she was doing any good, and if not, what right she had to continue hanging around him. At first I thought this was just an effort to hide the growth of other feelings from me, but gradually I began to realize that she was as confused as she sounded about what was happening. Never before in her life, I gathered, had romantic feelings come to her without the framework of a broken-wing operation to both build on and help disguise, and with that scaffolding falling apart around her she was either unable or unwilling to admit to herself what was really going on.

I felt pretty rotten having to sit around watching her flounder, but until she was able to recognize for herself what was happening there wasn't much I could do except listen. I wasn't about to offer any suggestions, especially since I didn't believe in love at first sight in the first place. My only consolation was that Bradley and Lanton were riding round trip with us, which meant that Alana wouldn't have to deal with any sort of separation crisis until we were back on Earth. I'd never had much sympathy for people who expected time to solve all their problems for them, but in this case I couldn't think of anything better to do.

And so matters stood as we went through our eighth and final point and emerged barely eight hundred thousand kilometers from the thriving colony world Taimyr . . . and found it deserted.

"Still nothing," Alana said tightly, her voice reflecting both the remnants of cascade depression and the shock of our impossible discovery. "No response to our call; nothing on any frequency I can pick up. I can't even find the comm satellites' lock signal."

I nodded, my eyes on the scope screen as the *Dancer's* telescope slowly scanned Taimyr's dark side. No lights showed anywhere. Shifting the aim, I began searching for the nine comm and nav satellites that should be circling the planet. "Alana, call up the astrogate again and find out what it's giving as position uncertainty."

"If you're thinking we're in the wrong system, forget it," she said as she tapped keys.

"Just checking all possibilities," I muttered. The satellites, too, were gone. I leaned back in my seat and bit at my lip.

"Yeah. Well, from eighteen positively identified stars we've got an error of no more than half a light-hour." She swiveled to face me and I saw the fear starting to grow behind her eyes. "Pall, what is going *on* here? Two hundred million people can't just disappear without a trace."

I shrugged helplessly. "A nuclear war could do it, I suppose, and might account for the satellites being gone as well. But there's no reason why anyone on Taimyr should *have* any nuclear weapons." Leaning forward again, I activated the helm. "A better view might help. If there's been some kind of war the major cities should now be big craters surrounded by rubble. I'm going to take us in and see what the day side looks like from high orbit."

"Do you think that's safe? I mean—" She hesitated. "Suppose the attack came from outside Taimyr?"

"What, you mean like an invasion?" I shook my head. "Even if there are alien intelligences somewhere who would want to invade us, we stand just as good a chance of getting away from orbit as we do from here."

"All right," she sighed. "But I'm setting up a cascade point maneuver, just in case. Do you think we should alert everybody yet?"

"Crewers, yes; passengers, no. I don't want any silly questions until I'm ready to answer them."

We took our time approaching Taimyr, but caution turned out to be unnecessary. No ships, human or otherwise, waited in orbit for us; no one hailed or shot at us; and as I turned the telescope planetward I saw no signs of warfare.

Nor did I see any cities, farmland, factories, or vehicles. It was as if Taimyr the colony had never existed.

"It doesn't make any sense," Matope said after I'd explained things over the crew intercom hookup. "How could a whole colony disappear?"

"I've looked up the records we've got on Taimyr," Pascal spoke up. "Some of the tropical vegetation is pretty fierce in the growth department. If everyone down there was killed by a plague or something, it's possible the plants have overgrown everything."

"Except that most of the cities are in temperate regions," I said shortly, "and two are smack in the middle of deserts. I can't find any of those, either."

"Hmm," Pascal said and fell silent, probably already hard at work on a new theory.

"Captain, you don't intend to land, do you?" Sarojis asked. "If launch facilities are gone and not merely covered over we'd be unable to lift again to orbit."

"I'm aware of that, and I have no intention of landing," I assured him. "But something's happened down there, and I'd like to get back to Earth with at least *some* idea of what."

"Maybe nothing's happened to the colony," Wilkinson said slowly. "Maybe something's happened to *us*."

"Such as?"

"Well . . . this may sound strange, but suppose we've somehow gone back in time, back to before the colony was started."

"That's crazy," Sarojis scoffed before I could say anything. "How could we possibly do something like that?"

"Malfunction of the field generator, maybe?" Wilkinson suggested. "There's a lot we don't know about Colloton space."

"It *doesn't* send ships back in—"

"All right, ease up," I told Sarojis. Beside me Alana snorted suddenly and reached for her keyboard. "I agree the idea sounds crazy, but whole cities don't just walk off, either," I continued. "It's not like there's a calendar we can look at out here, either. If we *were* a hundred years in the past, how would we know it?"

"Check the star positions," Matope offered.

"No good; the astrogate program would have noticed if anything was too far out of place. But I expect that still leaves us a possible century or more to rattle around in."

"No, it doesn't." Alana turned back to me with a grimly satisfied look on her face. "I've just taken signals from three pulsars. Compensating for our distance from Earth gives the proper rates for all three."

"Any comments on that?" I asked, not expecting any. Pulsar signals occasionally break their normal pattern and suddenly increase their pulse frequency, but it was unlikely to have happened in three of the beasts simultaneously; and in the absence of such a glitch the steady decrease in frequency was as good a calendar as we could expect to find.

There was a short pause; then Tobbar spoke up. "Captain, I think maybe its time to bring the passengers in on this. We can't hide the fact that we're in Taimyr system, so they're bound to figure out sooner or later that something's wrong. And I think they'll be more cooperative if we volunteer the information rather than making them demand it."

"What do we need *their* cooperation for?" Sarojis snorted.

"If you bothered to listen as much as you talked," Tobbar returned, a bit tartly, "you'd know that Chuck Raines is an advanced student in astrophysics and Dr. Chileogu has done a fair amount of work on Colloton field mathematics. I'd say chances are good that we're going to need help from one or both of them before this is all over."

I looked at Alana, raised my eyebrows questioningly. She hesitated, then nodded. "All right," I said. "Matope, you'll stay on duty down there; Alana will be in command here. Everyone else will assemble in the dining room. The meeting will begin in ten minutes."

I waited for their acknowledgments and then flipped off the intercom. "I'd like to be there," Alana said.

"I know," I said, raising my palms helplessly. "But I *have* to be there, and someone's got to keep an eye on things outside."

"Pascal or Sarojis could do it."

"True—and under normal circumstances I'd let them. But we're facing an unknown and potentially dangerous situation, and I need someone here whose judgment I trust."

She took a deep breath, exhaled loudly. "Yeah. Well . . . at least let me listen in by intercom, okay?"

"I'd planned to," I nodded. Reaching over, I touched her shoulder. "Don't worry; Bradley can handle the news."

"I know," she said, with a vehemence that told me she wasn't anywhere near that certain.

Sighing, I flipped the PA switch and made the announcement.

They took the news considerably better than I'd expected them to—possibly, I suspected, because the emotional kick hadn't hit them yet.

"But this is absolutely unbelievable, Captain Durriken," Lissa Steadman said when I'd finished. She was a rising young business-administration type who I half-expected to call for a committee to study the problem. "How could a whole colony simply vanish?"

"My question exactly," I told her. "We don't know yet, but we're going to try and find out before we head back to Earth."

"We're just going to leave?" Mr. Eklund asked timidly from the far end of the table. His hand, on top of the table, gripped his wife's tightly, and I belatedly remembered they'd been going to Taimyr to see a daughter who'd emigrated some thirty years earlier. Of all aboard, they had lost the most when the colony vanished.

"I'm sorry," I told him, "but there's no way we could land and take off again, not if we want to make Earth again on the fuel we have left."

Eklund nodded silently. Beside them, Chuck Raines cleared his throat. "Has anybody considered the possibility that *we're* the ones something has happened to? After all, it's the *Aura Dancer,* not Taimyr, that's been dipping in and out of normal space for the last six weeks. Maybe during all that activity something went wrong."

"The floor is open for suggestions," I said.

"Well . . . I presume you've confirmed we *are* in the Taimyr system. Could we be—oh—out of phase or something with the real universe?"

"Highly poetic," Tobbar spoke up from his corner. "But what does *out of phase* physically mean in this case?"

"Something like a parallel universe, or maybe an alternate time line," Raines suggested. "Some replica of our universe where humans never colonized Taimyr. After all, cascade images are supposed to be views of alternate universes, aren't they? Maybe cascade points are somehow where all the possible paths intersect."

"You've been reading too much science fiction," I told him. "Cascade images are at least partly psychological, and they certainly have no visible substance. Besides, if you had to trace the proper path through a hundred universes every time you went through a cascade point, you'd lose ninety-nine ships out of every hundred that tried it."

"Actually, Mr. Raines is not being all *that* far out," Dr. Chileogu put in quietly. "It's occasionally been speculated that the branch cuts and Riemann surfaces that show up in Colloton theory represent distinct universes. If so, it would be theoretically possible to cross between them." He smiled slightly. "But it's extremely unlikely that a responsible captain would put his ship through the sort of maneuver that would be necessary to do such a thing."

"What sort of maneuver would it take?" I asked.

"Basically, a large-angle rotation within the cascade point. Say, eight degrees or more."

I shook my head, feeling relieved and at the same time vaguely disappointed that a possible lead had evaporated. "Our largest angle was just under four point five degrees."

He shrugged. "As I said."

I glanced around the table, wondering what avenue to try next. But Wilkinson wasn't ready to abandon this one yet. "I don't understand what the ship's rotation has to do with it, Dr. Chileogu," he said. "I thought the farther you rotated, the farther you went in real space, and that was all."

"Well . . . it would be easier if I could show you the curves involved. Basically, you're right about the distance-angle relation as long as you stay below that eight degrees I mentioned. But above that point there's a discontinuity, similar to what you get in the curve of the ordinary tangent function at ninety degrees; though unlike the tangent the next arm doesn't start at minus infinity." Chileogu glanced around the room, and I could see him revising the level of his explanation downward. "Anyway, the point is that the first arm of the curve—real rotations of zero to eight point six degrees—gives the complete range of translation distance from zero to infinity, and so that's all a star ship ever uses. If the ship rotates *past* that discontinuity, mathematical theory would say it had gone off the edge of the universe and started over again on a different Riemann surface. What that means physically I don't think anyone knows; but as Captain Durriken pointed out, all our real rotations have been well below the discontinuity."

Wilkinson nodded, apparently satisfied; but the term "real rotation" had now set off a warning bell deep in my own mind. It was an expression I hadn't heard—much less thought about—in years, but I vaguely remembered now that it had concealed a seven-liter can of worms. "Doctor, when you speak of a 'real' rotation, you're referring to a mathematical entity, as opposed to an actual, physical one," I said slowly. "Correct?"

He shrugged. "Correct, but with a ship such as this one the two are for all practical purposes identical. The *Aura Dancer* is a long, perfectly symmetrical craft, with both the Colloton-field generator and Ming-metal cargo shield along the center line. It's only when you start working with the fancier liners, with their towers and blister lounges and all, that you get a serious divergence."

I nodded carefully and looked around the room. Pascal had already gotten it, from the expression on his face; Wilkinson and Tobbar were starting to. "Could an extra piece of Ming metal, placed several meters off the ship's center line, cause such a divergence?" I asked Chileogu.

"Possibly." He frowned. "Very possibly."

I shifted my gaze to Lanton. His face had gone white. "I think," I said, "I've located the problem."

Seated at the main terminal in Pascal's cramped computer room, Chileogu turned the Ming-metal coil over in his hands and shook his head. "I'm sorry, Captain, but it simply can't be done. A dual crossover winding is one of the most complex shapes in existence, and there's no way I can calculate its effect with a computer this small."

I glanced over his head at Pascal and Lanton, the latter having tagged along after I cut short the meeting and hustled the mathematician down here. "Can't you even get us an estimate?" I asked.

"Certainly. But the estimate could be anywhere up to a factor of three off, which would be worse than useless to you."

I nodded, pursing my lips tightly. "Well, then, how about going on from here? With that coil back in the shield, the real and physical rotations coincide again. Is there some way we can get back to our universe; say, by taking a long step out from Taimyr and two short ones back?"

Chileogu pondered that one for a long minute. "I would say that it depends on how many universes we're actually dealing with," he said at last. "If there are just two—ours and this one—then rotating past any one discontinuity should do it. But if there are more than two, you'd wind up just going one deeper into the stack if you crossed the wrong line."

"Ouch," Pascal murmured. "And if there are an infinite number, I presume, we'd never get back out?"

The mathematician shrugged uncomfortably. "Very likely."

"But don't the mathematics show how many universes there are?" Lanton spoke up.

"They show how many Riemann surfaces there are," Chileogu corrected. "But physical reality is never obliged to correspond with our theories and constructs. Experimental checks are always required, and to the best of my knowledge no one has ever tried this one."

I thought of all the ships that had simply disappeared, and shivered slightly. "In other words, trying to find the Taimyr colony is out. All right, then. What about the principle of reversibility? Will that let us go back the way we came?"

"Back to Earth?" Chileogu hesitated. "Ye-e-s, I think that would apply here. But to go back don't you need to know . . . ?"

"The real rotations we used to get here," I nodded heavily. "Yeah." We looked at each other, and I saw that he, too, recognized the implications of that requirement.

Lanton, though, was still light-years behind us. "You act like there's still a problem," he said, looking back and forth between us. "Don't you have records of the rotations we made at each point?"

I was suddenly tired of the psychiatrist. "Pascal, would you explain things to Dr. Lanton—on your way back to the passenger area?"

"Sure." Pascal stepped to Lanton's side and took his arm. "This way, Doctor."

"But—" Lanton's protests were cut off by the closing door.

I sat down carefully on a corner of the console, staring back at the Korusyn 630 that took up most of the room's space. "I take it," Chileogu said quietly, "that you can't get the return-trip parameters?"

"We can get all but the last two points we'd need," I told him. "The ship's basic configuration was normal for all of those, and the Korusyn there can handle them." I shook my head. "But even for those the parameters will be totally different—a two-degree rotation one way might become a one or three on the return trip. It depends on our relation to the galactic magnetic field and angular momentum vectors, closest-approach distance to large masses, and a half-dozen other parameters. Even if we *had* a mathematical expression for the influence Lanton's damn coil had on our first two points, I wouldn't know how to reprogram the machine to take that into account."

Chileogu was silent for a moment. Then, straightening up in his seat, he flexed his fingers. "Well, I suppose we have to start somewhere. Can you clear me a section of memory?"

"Easily. What are you going to do?"

He picked up the coil again. "I can't do a complete calculation, but there are several approximation methods that occasionally work pretty well; they're scattered throughout my technical tapes if your library doesn't have a list. If they give widely varying results—as they probably will, I'm afraid—then we're back where we started. But if they happen to show a close agreement, we can probably use the result with reasonable confidence." He smiled slightly. "*Then* we get to worry about programming it in."

"Yeah. Well, first things first. Alana, have you been listening in?"

"Yes," her voice came promptly through the intercom. "I'm clearing the computer now."

Chileogu left a moment later to fetch his tapes. Pascal returned while he was gone, and I filled him in on what we were going to try. Together, he and Alana had the computer ready by the time Chileogu returned. I considered staying to watch, but common sense told me I would just be in the way, so instead I went up to the bridge and relieved Alana. It wasn't really my shift, but I didn't feel like mixing with the passengers, and I could think and brood as well on the bridge as I could in my cabin. Besides, I had a feeling Alana would like to check up on Bradley.

I'd been sitting there staring at Taimyr for about an hour when the intercom bleeped. "Captain," Alana's voice said, "can you come down to the dining room right away? Dr. Lanton's come up with an idea I think you'll want to hear."

I resisted my reflexive urge to tell her what Lanton could do with his ideas; her use of my title meant she wasn't alone. "All right," I sighed. "I'll get Sarojis to take over here and be down in a few minutes."

"I think Dr. Chileogu and Pascal should be here, too."

Something frosty went skittering down my back. Alana knew the importance of what those two were doing. Whatever Lanton's brainstorm was, she must genuinely think it worth listening to. "All right. We'll be there shortly."

They were all waiting quietly around one of the tables when I arrived. Bradley, not surprisingly, was there too, seated next to Alana and across from Lanton. Only the six of us were present; the other passengers, I guessed, were keeping the autobar in the lounge busy. "Okay, let's have it," I said without preamble as I sat down.

"Yes, sir," Lanton said, throwing a quick glance in Pascal's direction. "If I understood Mr. Pascal's earlier explanation correctly, we're basically stuck because there's no way to calibrate the *Aura Dancer's* instruments to take the, uh, extra Ming metal into account."

"Close enough," I grunted. "So?"

"So, it occurred to me that this 'real' rotation you were talking about ought to have some external manifestations, the same way a gyro needle shows the ship's physical rotation."

"You mean like something outside the viewports?" I frowned.

"No; something inside. I'm referring to the cascade images."

I opened my mouth, closed it again. My first thought was that it was the world's dumbest idea, but my second was *why not*? "You're saying, what, that the image-shuffling that occurs while we rotate is tied to the real rotation, each shift being a hundredth of a radian or something?"

"Right"—he nodded—"although I don't know whether that kind of calibration would be possible."

I looked at Chileogu. "Doctor?"

The mathematician brought his gaze back from infinity. "I'm not sure what to say. The basic idea is actually not new—Colloton himself showed such a manifestation ought to be present, and several others have suggested the cascade images were it. But I've never heard of any actual test being made of the hypothesis; and from what I've heard of the images, I suspect there are grave practical problems besides. The pattern doesn't change in any mathematically predictable way, so I don't know how you would keep track of the shifts."

"I wouldn't have to," Lanton said. "I've been observing Rik's cascade images throughout the trip. I remember what the pattern looked like at both the beginning and ending of each rotation."

I looked at Bradley, suddenly understanding. His eyes met mine and he nodded fractionally.

"The only problem," Lanton continued, "is that I'm not sure we could set up at either end to do the reverse rotation."

"Chances are good we can," I said absently, my eyes still on Bradley. His expression was strangely hard for someone who was supposedly seeing the way out of permanent exile. Alana, if possible, looked even less happy. "All rotations are supposed to begin at zero, and since we always go 'forward' we always rotate the same direction."

I glanced back at Lanton to see his eyes go flat, as if he were watching a private movie. "You're right; it *is* the same starting pattern each time. I hadn't really noticed that before, with the changes and all."

"It should be easy enough to check, Captain," Pascal spoke up. "We can compute the physical rotations for the first six points we'll be going through. The real rotations should be the same as on the outbound leg, though, so if Dr. Lanton's right the images will wind up in the same pattern they did before."

"But how—?" Chileogu broke off suddenly. "Ah. You've had a mnemonic treatment?"

Lanton nodded and then looked at me. "I think Mr. Pascal's idea is a good one, Captain, and I don't see any purpose in hanging around here any longer than necessary. Whenever you want to start back—"

"I have a few questions to ask first," I interrupted mildly. I glanced at Bradley, decided to tackle the easier ones first. "Dr. Chileogu, what's the status of your project?"

"The approximations? We've just finished programming the first one; it'll take another hour or so to collect enough data for a plot. I agree with Dr. Lanton, though—we can do the calculations between cascade points as easily as we can do them in orbit here."

"Thank you. Dr. Lanton, you mentioned something about *changes* a minute ago. What exactly did you mean?"

Lanton's eyes flicked to Bradley for an instant. "Well . . . as I told you several weeks ago, a person's mind has a certain effect on the cascade image pattern. Some of the medicines Rik's been taking have slightly altered the—oh, I guess you could call it the *texture* of the pattern."

"Altered it how much?"

"In some cases, fairly extensively." He hesitated, just a bit too long. "But nothing I've done is absolutely irreversible. I should be able to re-create the original conditions before each cascade point."

Deliberately, I leaned back in my chair. "All right. Now let's hear what the problem is."

"I beg your pardon?"

"You heard me." I waved at Bradley and Alana. "Your patient and my first officer look like they're about to leave for a funeral. I want to know why."

Lanton's cheek twitched. "I don't think this is the time or the place to discuss—"

"The problem, Captain," Bradley interrupted quietly, "is that the reversing of the treatments may turn out to be permanent."

It took a moment for that to sink in. When it did I turned my eyes back on Lanton. "Explain."

The psychiatrist took a deep breath. "The day after the second point I used ultrasound to perform a type of minor neurosurgery called synapse fixing. It applies heat to selected regions of the brain to correct a tendency of the nerves to misfire. The effects *can* be reversed . . . but the procedure's been done only, rarely, and usually involves unavoidable peripheral damage."

I felt my gaze hardening into an icy stare. "In other words," I bit out, "not only will the progress he's made lately be reversed, but he'll likely wind up worse off than he started. Is that it?"

Lanton squirmed uncomfortably, avoiding my eyes. "I don't *know* that he will. Now that I've found a treatment—"

"You're about to give him a brand-new disorder," I snapped. "*Damn* it all, Lanton, you are the most coldblooded—"

"Captain."

Bradley's single word cut off my flow of invective faster than anything but hard vacuum could have. "What?" I said.

"Captain, I understand how you feel." His voice was quiet but firm; and though the tightness remained in his expression, it had been joined by an odd sort of determination. "But Dr. Lanton wasn't really trying to maneuver you into supporting something unethical. For the record, I've already agreed to work with him on this; I'll put that on tape if you'd like." He smiled slightly. "And before you bring it up, I *am* recognized as legally responsible for my actions, so as long as Dr. Lanton and I agree on a course of treatment your agreement is not required."

"That's not entirely true," I ground out. "As a ship's captain in deep space, I have full legal power here. If I say he can't do something to you, he can't. Period."

Bradley's face never changed. "Perhaps. But unless you can find another way to get us back to Earth, I don't see that you have any other choice."

I stared into those eyes for a couple of heartbeats. Then, slowly, my gaze swept the table, touching in turn all the others as they sat watching me, awaiting my decision. The thought of deliberately sending Bradley back to his permanent disorientation—*really* permanent, this time— left a taste in my mouth that was practically gagging in its intensity. But Bradley was right . . . and at the moment I didn't have any better ideas.

"Pascal," I said, "you and Dr. Chileogu will first of all get some output on that program of yours. Alana, as soon as they're finished you'll take the computer back and calculate the parameters for our first point. *You* two"—I glared in turn at Bradley and Lanton—"will be ready to test this image theory of yours. You'll do the observations in your cabin as usual, and tell me afterwards whether we duplicated the rotation exactly or came out short or long. Questions? All right; dismissed."

After all, I thought amid the general scraping of chairs, *for the first six points all Bradley will need to do is cut back on medicines. That means twenty-eight days or so before any irreversible surgery is done.*

I had just that long to come up with another answer.

We left orbit three hours later, pushing outward on low drive to conserve fuel. That plus the course I'd chosen meant another ten hours until we were in position for the first point, but none of that time was wasted. Pascal and Chileogu were able to program and run two more approximation schemes; the results, unfortunately, were not encouraging. Any two of the three plots had a fair chance of agreeing over ranges of half a degree or so, but there was no consistency at all over the larger angles we would need to use. Chileogu refused to throw in the towel, pointing out that he had another six methods to try and making vague noises about statistical curve-fitting schemes. I promised him all the computer time he needed between point maneuvers, but privately I conceded defeat. Lanton's method now seemed our only chance . . . if it worked.

I handled the first point myself, double-checking all parameters beforehand and taking special pains to run the gyro needle as close to the proper angle as I could. As with any such hand operation, of course, perfection was not quite possible, and I ran the *Dancer* something under a hundredth of a degree long. I'm not sure what I was expecting from this first test, but I *was* more than a little surprised when Lanton accurately reported that we'd slightly overshot the mark.

"It looks like it'll work," Alana commented from her cabin when I relayed the news. She didn't sound too enthusiastic.

"Maybe," I said, feeling somehow the need to be as skeptical as possible. "We'll see what happens when he starts taking Bradley off the drugs. I find it hard to believe that the man's mental state can be played like a yo-yo, and if it can't be we'll have to go with whatever statistical magic Chileogu can put together."

Alana gave a little snort that she'd probably meant to be a laugh. "Hard to know which way to hope, isn't it?"

"Yeah." I hesitated for a second, running the duty arrangements over in my mind. "Look, why don't you take the next few days off, at least until the next point. Sarojis can take your shift up here."

"That's all right," she sighed. "I—if it's all the same with you, I'd rather save any offtime until later. Rik will . . . need my help more then."

"Okay," I told her. "Just let me know when you want it and the time's yours."

We continued on our slow way, and with each cascade point I became more and more convinced that Lanton really would be able to guide us through those last two critical points. His accuracy for the first four maneuvers was a solid hundred percent, and on the fifth maneuver we got to within point zero two percent of the computer's previous reading by deliberately jockeying the *Dancer* back and forth until Bradley's image pattern was exactly as Lanton remembered it. After that even Matope was willing to be cautiously optimistic; and if it hadn't been for one small cloud hanging over my head I probably would have been as happy as the rest of the passengers had become.

The cloud, of course, being Bradley.

I'd been wrong about how much his improvement had been due to the drugs Lanton had been giving him, and every time I saw him that ill-considered line about playing his mind like a yo-yo came back to haunt me. Slowly, but very steadily, Bradley was regressing toward his original mental state. His face went first, his expressions beginning to crowd each other again as if he were unable to decide which of several moods should be expressed at any given moment. His eyes took on that shining, nervous look I hated so much: just occasionally at first, but gradually becoming more and more frequent, until it seemed to be almost his norm. And yet, even though he certainly saw what was happening to him, not once did I hear him say anything that could be taken as resentment or complaint. It was as if the chance to save twenty other lives was so important to him that it was worth any sacrifice. I thought occasionally about Alana's comment that he'd never before had a sense of dignity, and wondered if he would lose it again to his illness. But I didn't wonder about it all that much; I was too busy worrying about Alana.

I hadn't expected her to take Bradley's regression well, of course—to someone with Alana's wing-mending instincts a backsliding patient would be both insult *and* injury. What I wasn't prepared for was her abrupt withdrawal into a shell of silence on the issue which no amount of gentle probing could crack open. I tried to be patient with her, figuring that eventually the need to talk would overcome her reticence; but as the day for what Lanton described as "minor surgery" approached, I finally decided I couldn't wait any longer. On the day after our sixth cascade point, I quit being subtle and forced the issue.

"Whatever I'm feeling, it isn't any concern of yours," she said, her fingers playing across the bridge controls as she prepared to take over from me. Her hands belied the calmness in her voice: I knew her usual checkout routine as well as my own, and she lost the sequence no fewer than three times while I watched.

"I think it is," I told her. "Aside from questions of friendship, you're a member of my crew, and anything that might interfere with your efficiency is my concern."

She snorted. "I've been under worse strains than this without falling apart."

"I know. But you've never buried yourself this deeply before, and it worries me."

"I know. I'm . . . sorry. If I could put it into words—" She shrugged helplessly.

"Are you worried about Bradley?" I prompted. "Don't forget that, whatever Lanton has to do here, he'll have all the resources of the Swedish Psychiatric Institute available to undo it."

"I know. But . . . he's going to come out of it a different person. Even Lanton has to admit that."

"Well . . . maybe it'll wind up being a change for the better."

It was a stupid remark, and her scornful look didn't make me feel any better about having made it. "Oh, come *on*. Have you *ever* heard of an injury that did any real good? Because that's what it's going to be—an injury."

And suddenly I understood. "You're afraid you won't like him afterwards, aren't you? At least not the way you do now?"

"Why should that be so unreasonable?" she snapped. "I'm a damn fussy person, you know—I don't like an awful lot of people. I can't afford to . . . to lose any of them." She turned her back on me abruptly, and I saw her shoulders shake once.

I waited a decent interval before speaking. "Look, Alana, you're not in any shape to stay up here alone. Why don't you go down to your cabin and pull yourself together, and then go and spend some time with Bradley."

"I'm all right," she mumbled. "I can take my shift."

"I know. But . . . at the moment I imagine Rik needs you more than I do. Go on, get below."

She resisted for a few more minutes, but eventually I bent her sense of duty far enough and she left. For a long time afterwards I just sat and stared at the stars, my thoughts whistling around my head in tight orbit. What *would* the effect of the new Bradley be on Alana? She'd been right—whatever happened, it wasn't likely to be an improvement. If her interest was really only in wing-mending, Lanton's work would provide her with a brand-new challenge. But I didn't think even Alana was able to fool herself like that anymore. She cared about him, for sure, and if he changed too much that feeling might well die.

And I wouldn't lose her when we landed.

I thought about it long and hard, examining it and the rest of our situation from several angles. Finally, I leaned forward and keyed the intercom. Wilkinson was off duty in his cabin; from the time it took him to answer he must have been asleep as well. "Wilkinson, you got a good look at the damage in Lanton's neural whatsis machine. How hard would it be to fix?"

"Uh . . . well, that's hard to say. The thing that spit goop all over the Ming-metal coil was a standard voltage regulator board—we're bound to have spares aboard. But there may be other damage, too. I'd have to run an analyzer over it to find out if anything else is dead. Whether we would have replacements is another question."

"Okay. Starting right now, you're relieved of all other duty until you've got that thing running again. Use anything you need from ship's spares—" I hesitated—"and you can even pirate from our cargo if necessary."

"Yes, sir." He was wide awake now. "I gather there's a deadline?"

"Lanton's going to be doing some ultrasound work on Bradley in fifty-eight hours. You need to be done before that. Oh, and you'll need to work in Lanton's cabin—I don't want the machine moved at all."

"Got it. If you'll clear it with Lanton, I can be up there in twenty minutes."

Lanton wasn't all that enthusiastic about letting Wilkinson set up shop in his cabin, especially when I wouldn't explain my reasons to him, but eventually he gave in. I alerted Kate Epstein that she would have to do without Wilkinson for a while, and then called Matope to confirm the project's access to tools and spares.

And then, for the time being, it was all over but the waiting. I resumed my examination of the viewport, wondering if I were being smart or just pipe-dreaming.

Two days later—barely eight hours before Bradley's operation was due to begin—Wilkinson finally reported that the neural tracer was once again operational.

"This better be important," Lanton fumed as he took his place at the dining-room table. "I'm already behind schedule in my equipment setup as it is."

I glanced around at the others before replying. Pascal and Chileogu, fresh from their latest attempt at making sense from their assortment of plots, seemed tired and irritated by this interruption. Bradley and Alana, holding hands tightly under the table, looked more resigned than anything else. Everyone seemed a little gaunt, but that was probably my imagination—certainly we weren't on anything approaching starvation rations yet. "Actually, Doctor," I said, looking back at Lanton, "you're not in nearly the hurry you think. There's not going to be any operation."

That got everyone's full attention. "You've found another way?" Alana breathed, a hint of life touching her eyes for the first time in days.

"I think so. Dr. Chileogu, I need to know first whether a current running through Ming metal would change its effect on the ship's real rotation."

He frowned, then shrugged. "Probably. I have no idea how, though."

A good thing I'd had the gadget fixed, then. "Doesn't matter. Dr. Lanton, can you tell me approximately when in the cascade point your neural tracer burned out?"

"I can tell you exactly. It was just as the images started disappearing, right at the end."

I nodded; I'd hoped it was either the turning on or off of the field generator that had done it. That would make the logistics a whole lot easier. "Good. Then we're all set. What we're going to do, you see, is reenact that particular maneuver."

"What good will *that* do?" Lanton asked, his tone more puzzled than belligerent.

"It should get us home." I waved toward the outer hull. "For the past two days we've been moving toward a position where the galactic field and other parameters are almost exactly the same as we had when we went through that point—providing your neural tracer is on and we're heading back toward Taimyr. In another two days we'll turn around and get our velocity vector lined up correctly. Then, with your tracer running, we're going to fire up the generator and rotate the same amount—by gyro reading—as we did then. *You*"—I leveled a finger at Lanton—"will be on the bridge during that operation, and you will note the exact configuration of your cascade images at that moment. Then, *without shutting off the generator,* we'll rotate *back* to zero; zero as defined by your cascade pattern, since it may be different from gyro zero. At that time, I'll take the Ming metal from your tracer, walk it to the number one hold, and stuff it into the cargo shield; and we'll rotate the ship again until we reach your memorized cascade pattern. Since the physical and real rotations are identical in that configuration, that'll give us the real angle we rotated through the last time—"

"And from *that* we can figure the angle we'll need to make going the other direction!" Alana all but shouted.

I nodded. "Once we've rotated back to zero to regain our starting point, of course." I looked around at them again. Lanton and Bradley still seemed confused, though the latter was starting to catch Alana's enthusiasm. Chileogu was scribbling on a notepad, and Pascal just sat there with his mouth slightly open. Probably astonished that he hadn't come up with such a crazy idea himself. "That's all I have to say," I told them. "If you have any comments later—"

"I have one now, Captain."

I looked at Bradley in some surprise. "Yes?"

He swallowed visibly. "It seems to me, sir, that what you're going to need is a set of cascade images that vary a lot, so that the pattern you're looking for is a distinctive one. I don't think Dr. Lanton's are suitable for that."

"I see." Of course; while Lanton had been studying Bradley's images, Bradley couldn't help but see his, as well. "Lanton? How about it?"

The psychiatrist shrugged. "I admit they're a little bland—I haven't had a very exciting life. But they'll do."

"I doubt it." Bradley looked back at me. "Captain, I'd like to volunteer."

"You don't know what you're saying," I told him. "Each rotation will take twice as long as the ones you've already been through. *And* there'll be two of them back to back; *and* the field won't be shut down between them, because I want to know if the images drift while I'm moving the coil around the ship. Multiply by about five what you've felt afterwards and you'll get some idea what it'll be like." I shook my head. "I'm grateful for your offer, but I can't let more people than necessary go through that."

"I appreciate that. But I'm still going to do it."

We locked eyes for a long moment . . . and the word *dignity* flashed through my mind. "In that case, I accept," I said. "Other questions? Thank you for stopping by."

They got the message and began standing up . . . all except Alana. Bradley whispered something to her, but she shook her head and whispered back. Reluctantly, he let go of her hand and followed the others out of the room.

"Question?" I asked Alana when we were alone, bracing for an argument over the role I was letting Bradley take.

"You're right about the extra stress staying in Colloton space that long will create," she said. "That probably goes double for anyone running around in it. I'd expect a lot more vertigo, for starters, and that could make movement dangerous."

"Would you rather Bradley had his brain scorched?"

She flinched, but stood her ground. "My objection isn't with the method—it's with who's going to be bouncing off the *Dancer's* walls."

"Oh. Well, before you get the idea you're being left out of things, let me point out that *you're* going to be handling bridge duties for the maneuver."

"Fine; but since I'm going to be up anyway I want the job of running the Ming metal back and forth instead."

I shook my head. "No. You're right about the unknowns involved with this, which is why *I'm* going to do it."

"I'm five years younger than you are," she said, ticking off fingers. "I also have a higher stress index, better balance, and I'm in better physical condition." She hesitated. "And I'm not haunted by white uniforms in my cascade images," she added gently.

Coming from anyone else, that last would have been like a knife in the gut. But from Alana, it somehow didn't even sting. "The assignments are nonnegotiable," I said, getting to my feet. "Now if you'll excuse me, I have to catch a little sleep before my next shift."

She didn't respond. When I left she was still sitting there, staring through the shiny surface of the table.

"Here we go. Good Luck," were the last words I heard Alana say before the intercom was shut down and I was alone in Lanton's cabin. Alone, but not for long: a moment later my first doubles appeared. Raising my wrist, I keyed my chrono to stopwatch mode and waited, ears tingling with the faint ululation of the Colloton field generator. The sound, inaudible from the bridge, reminded me of my trainee days, before the *Dancer* . . . before Lord Hendrik and his fool-headed kid. . . . Shaking my head sharply, I focused on the images, waiting for them to begin their one-dimensional allemande.

They did, and I started my timer. With the lines to the bridge dead I was going to have to rely on the image movements to let me know when the first part of the maneuver was over; moving the Ming metal around the ship while we were at the wrong end of our rotation or—worse— while we were still moving would probably end our chances of getting back for good. Mindful of the pranks cascade points could play on a person's time sense, I'd had Pascal calculate the approximate times each rotation would take. Depending on how accurate they turned out to be, they might simply let me limit how soon I started worrying.

It wasn't a pleasant wait. On the bridge, I had various duties to perform; here, I didn't have even that much distraction from the ghosts surrounding me. Sitting next to the humming neural tracer, I watched the images flicker in and out, white uniforms dos-à-dosing with the coveralls and the gaps.

Ghosts. *Haunted*. I'd never seriously thought of them like that before, but now I found I couldn't see them in any other way. I imagined I could see knowing smiles on the liner captains' faces, or feel a coldness from the gaps where I'd died. Pure autosuggestion, of course . . . and yet, it forced me for probably the first time to consider what exactly the images were doing to me.

They were making me chronically discontented with my life.

My first reaction to such an idea was to immediately justify my resentment. I'd been cheated out of the chance to be a success in my field; trapped at the bottom of the heap by idiots who ranked political weaselcraft higher than flying skill. I had a *right* to feel dumped on.

And yet . . .

My watch clicked at me: the first rotation should be about over. I reset it and waited, watching the images. With agonizing slowness they came to a stop . . . and then started moving again in what I could persuade myself was the opposite direction. I started my watch again and let my eyes defocus a bit. The next time the dance stopped, it would be time to move Lanton's damn coil to the hold and bring my ship back to normal.

My ship. I listened to the way the words echoed around my brain. *My ship.* No liner captain owned his own ship. He was an employee, like any other in the company; forever under the basilisk eye of those self-same idiots who'd fired me once for doing my job. The space junk being sparser and all that aside, would I *really* have been happier in a job like that? Would I have enjoyed being caught between management on one hand and upper-crusty passengers on the other? Enjoyed, hell—would I have *survived* it? For the first time in ten years I began to wonder if perhaps Lord Hendrik had known what he was doing when he booted me out of his company.

Deliberately, I searched out the white uniforms far off to my left and watched as they popped in and out of different slots in the long line. Perhaps that was why there were so few of them, I thought suddenly; perhaps, even while I was pretending otherwise, I'd been smart enough to make decisions that had kept me out of the running for that particular treadmill. The picture that created made me smile: my subconscious chasing around with secret memos, hiding basic policy matters from my righteously indignant conscious mind.

The click of my watch made me jump. Taking a deep breath, I picked up a screwdriver from the tool pouch laid out beside the neural tracer and gave my full attention to the images. Slow . . . slower . . . stopped. I waited a full two minutes to make sure, then flipped off the tracer and got to work.

I'd had plenty of practice in the past two days, but it still took me nearly five minutes to extricate the coil from the maze of equipment surrounding it. That was no particular problem—we'd allowed seven minutes for the disassembly—but I was still starting to sweat as I got to my feet and headed for the door.

And promptly fell on my face.

Alana's reference to enhanced vertigo apart, I hadn't expected anything that strong quite so soon. Swallowing hard, I tried to ignore the feeling of lying on a steep hill and crawled toward the nearest wall. Using it as a support, I got to my feet, waited for the cabin to stop spinning, and shuffled over to the door. Fortunately, all the doors between me and One Hold had been locked open, so I didn't have to worry about getting to the release. Still shuffling, I maneuvered through the opening and started down the corridor, moving as quickly as I could. The trip—fifteen meters of corridor, a circular stairway down, five more meters of corridor, and squeezing through One Hold's cargo to get to the shield—normally took less than three minutes. We'd allowed ten; but already I could see that was going to be tight I kept my eyes on the wall beside me and concentrated on moving my feet . . . which was probably why I was nearly to the stairway before I noticed the kaleidoscope dance my cascade images were doing.

While the ship was at rest.

I stopped short, the pattern shifts ceasing as I did so. The thing I had feared most about this whole trick was happening: moving the Ming metal was changing our real angle in Colloton space.

I don't know how long I leaned there with the sweat trickling down my forehead, but it was probably no more than a minute before I forced myself to get moving again. There were now exactly two responses Alana could make: go on to the endpoint Lanton had just memorized, or try and compensate somehow for the shift I was causing. The former course felt intuitively wrong, but the latter might well be impossible to do—and neither had any particular mathematical backing that Chileogu had been able to find. For me, the worst part of it was the fact that I was now completely out of the decision process. No matter how fast I got the coil locked away, there was no way I was going to make it back up two flights of stairs to the bridge. Like everyone else on board, I was just going to have to trust Alana's judgment.

I slammed into the edge of the stairway opening, nearly starting my downward trip headfirst before I got a grip on the railing. The coil, jarred from my sweaty hand, went on ahead of me, clanging like a muffled bell as it bounced to the deck below. I followed a good deal more slowly, the writhing images around me adding to my vertigo. By now, the rest of my body was also starting to react to the stress, and I had to stop every few steps as a wave of nausea or fatigue washed over me. It seemed forever before I finally reached the bottom of the stairs. The coil had rolled to the middle of the corridor; retrieving it on hands and knees, I got back to the wall and hauled myself to my feet. I didn't dare look at my watch.

The cargo hold was the worst part yet. The floor was swaying freely by then, like an ocean vessel in heavy seas, and through the reddish haze surrounding me, the stacks of boxes I staggered between seemed ready to hurl themselves down upon my head. I don't remember how many times I shied back from what appeared to be a breaking wave of crates, only to slam into the stack behind me. Finally, though, I made it to the open area in front of the shield door. I was halfway across the gap, moving again on hands and knees, when my watch sounded the one-minute warning. With a desperate lunge, I pushed myself up and forward, running full tilt into the Ming-metal wall. More from good luck than anything else, my free hand caught the handle; and as I fell backwards the door swung open. For a moment I hung there, trying to get my trembling muscles to respond. Then, slowly, I got my feet under me and stood up. Reaching through the opening, I let go of the coil and watched it drop into the gap between two boxes. The hold was swaying more and more violently now; timing my move carefully, I shoved on the handle and collapsed to the deck. The door slammed shut with a thunderclap that tried to take the top of my head with it. I hung on just long enough to see that the door was indeed closed, and then gave in to the darkness.

I'm told they found me sleeping with my back against the shield door, making sure it couldn't accidentally come open.

I was lying on my back when I came to, and the first thing I saw when I opened my eyes was Kate Epstein's face. "How do you feel?" she asked.

"Fine," I told her, frowning as I glanced around. This wasn't my cabin. . . . With a start I recognized the humming in my ear. "What the hell am I doing in Lanton's cabin?" I growled.

Kate shrugged and reached over my shoulder, shutting off the neural tracer. "We needed Dr. Lanton's neural equipment, and the tracer wasn't supposed to be moved. A variant of the mountain/Mohammed problem, I guess you could say."

I grunted. "How'd the point maneuver go? Was Alana able to figure out a correction factor?"

"It went perfectly well," Alana's voice came from my right. I turned my head, to find her sitting next to the door. "I think we're out of the woods now, Pall—that four-point-four physical rotation turned out to be more like nine point one once the coil was out of the way. If Chileogu's right about reversibility applying here, we should be back in our own universe now. I guess we won't know for sure until we go through the next point and reach Earth."

"Is that nine point one with or without a correction factor?" I asked, my stomach tightening in anticipation. We might not be out of the woods quite yet.

"No correction needed," she said. "The images on the bridge stayed rock-steady the whole time."

"But . . . I saw them shifting."

"Yes, you told us that. Our best guess—excuse me; *Pascal's* best guess—is that you were getting that because you were moving relative to the field generator, that if you'd made a complete loop around it you would've come back to the original cascade pattern again. Chileogu's trying to prove that mathematically, but I doubt he'll be able to until he gets to better facilities."

"Uh-huh." Something wasn't quite right here. "You say I *told* you about the images? When?"

Alana hesitated, looked at Kate. "Actually, Captain," the doctor said gently, "you've been conscious quite a bit during the past four days. The reason you don't remember any of it is that the connection between your short-term and long-term memories got a little scrambled—probably another effect of your jaunt across all those field lines. It looks like that part's healed itself, though, so you shouldn't have any more memory problems."

"Oh, great. What sort of problems *will* I have more of?"

"Nothing major. You might have balance difficulties for a while, and you'll likely have a mild migraine or two within the next couple of weeks. But indications are that all of it is very temporary."

I looked back at Alana. "Four days. We'll need to set up our last calibration run soon."

"All taken care of," she assured me. "We're turning around later today to get our velocity vector pointing back toward Taimyr again, and we'll be able to do the run tomorrow."

"Who's going to handle it?"

"Who do you think?" she snorted. "Rik, Lanton, and me, with maybe some help from Pascal."

I'd known that answer was coming, but it still made my mouth go dry. "No way," I told her, struggling to sit up. "You aren't going to go through this hell. I can manage—"

"Ease up, Pall," Alana interrupted me. "Weren't you paying attention? The real angle doesn't drift when the Ming metal is moved, and that means we can shut down the field generator while I'm taking the coil from here to One Hold again."

I sank back onto the bed, feeling foolish. "Oh. Right."

Getting to her feet, Alana came over to me and patted my shoulder. "Don't worry," she said in a kinder tone. "We've got things under control. You've done the hard part; just relax and let us do the rest."

"Okay," I agreed, trying to hide my misgivings.

It was just as well that I did. Thirty-eight hours later Alana used our last gram of fuel in a flawless bit of flying that put us into a deep Earth orbit. The patrol boats that had responded to her emergency signal were waiting there, loaded with the fuel we would need to land.

Six hours after that, we were home.

They checked me into a hospital, just to be on the safe side, and the next four days were filled with a flurry of tests, medical interviews, and bumpy wheelchair rides. Surprisingly—to me, anyway—I was also nailed by two media types who wanted the more traditional type of interview. Apparently, the *Dancer's* trip to elsewhere and back was getting a fair amount of publicity. Just how widespread the coverage was, though, I didn't realize until my last day there, when an official-looking CompNote was delivered to my room.

It was from Lord Hendrik.

I snapped the sealer and unfolded the paper. The first couple of paragraphs—the greetings, congratulations on my safe return, and such—I skipped over quickly, my eyes zeroing in on the business portion of the letter:

As you may or may not know, I have recently come out of semiretirement to serve on the Board of Directors of TranStar Enterprises, headquartered here in Nairobi. With excellent contacts both in Africa and in the so-called Black Colony chain, our passenger load is expanding rapidly, and we are constantly on the search for experienced and resourceful pilots we can entrust them to. The news reports of your recent close call brought you to my mind again after all these years, and I thought you might be interested in discussing—

A knock on the door interrupted my reading. "Come in," I called, looking up.

It was Alana. "Hi, Pall, how are you doing?" she asked, walking over to the bed and giving me a brief once-over. In one hand she carried a slender plastic portfolio.

"Bored silly," I told her. "I think I'm about ready to check out—they've finished all the standard tests without finding anything, and I'm tired of lying around while they dream up new ones."

"What a shame," she said with mock sorrow. "And after I brought you all this reading material, too." She hefted the portfolio.

"What is it, your resignation?" I asked, trying to keep my voice light. There was no point making this any more painful for either of us than necessary.

But she just frowned. "Don't be silly. It's a whole batch of new contracts I've picked up for us in the past few days. Some really good ones, too, from name corporations. I think people are starting to see what a really good carrier we are."

I snorted. "Aside from the thirty-six or whatever penalty clauses we invoked on this trip?"

"Oh, that's all in here too. The Swedish Institute's not even going to put up a fight—they're paying off everything, including your hospital bills and the patrol's rescue fee. Probably figured Lanton's glitch was going to make them look bad enough without them trying to chisel us out of damages too." She hesitated, and an odd expression flickered across her face. "Were you really expecting me to jump ship?"

"I was about eighty percent sure," I said, fudging my estimate down about nineteen points. "After all, this is where Rik Bradley's going to be, and you . . . rather like him. Don't you?"

She shrugged. "I don't know *what* I feel for him, to be perfectly honest. I like him, sure—like him a lot. But my life's out there"—she gestured skyward—"and I don't think I can give that up for anyone. At least, not for him."

"You could take a leave of absence," I told her, feeling like a prize fool but determined to give her every possible option. "Maybe once you spend some real time on a planet, you'd find you like it."

"And maybe I wouldn't," she countered. "And when I decided I'd had enough, where would the *Dancer* be? Probably nowhere I'd ever be able to get to you." She looked me straight in the eye and all traces of levity vanished from her voice. "Like I told you once before, Pall, I can't afford to lose *any* of my friends."

I took a deep breath and carefully let it out. "Well. I guess that's all settled. Good. Now, if you'll be kind enough to tell the nurse out by the monitor station that I'm signing out, I'll get dressed and we'll get back to the ship."

"Great. It'll be good to have you back." Smiling, she disappeared out into the corridor.

Carefully, I got my clothes out of the closet and began putting them on, an odd mixture of victory and defeat settling into my stomach. Alana was staying with the *Dancer*, which was certainly what I'd wanted . . . and yet, I couldn't help but feel that in some ways her decision was more a default than a real, active choice. Was she coming back because she wanted to, or merely because we were a safer course than the set of unknowns that Bradley offered? If the latter, it was clear that her old burns weren't entirely healed; that she still had a ways—maybe a long ways—to go. But that was all right. I may not have the talent she did for healing bruised souls, but if time and distance were what she needed, the *Dancer* and I could supply her with both.

I was just sealing my boots when Alana returned. "Finished? Good. They're getting your release ready, so let's go. Don't forget your letter," she added, pointing at Lord Hendrik's CompNote.

"This? It's nothing," I told her, crumpling it up and tossing it toward the wastebasket. "Just some junk mail from an old admirer."

Six months later, on our third point out from Prima, a new image of myself in liner captain's white appeared in my cascade pattern. I looked at it long and hard . . . and then did something I'd never done before for such an image.

I wished it lots of luck.

MUSIC HATH CHARMS

"Oh, look, Jaivy! Spars and his Demonflute are on the news!"

I sighed and poked one eye over my filmreader. Eleni, almost bouncing in her excitement, was pointing at the screen. Sure enough, there was Spars, dressed to the hilt in the standard colander haircut, body paint, and idiot grin of a Thwokerjag performer—a look, I'd often thought, probably attained by dressing quickly in a dark swamp. Clutched in his hand was that monstrosity of an instrument he'd dug out of some ruins on Algol VI a month ago. "I still say it looks more like a clarinet," I commented, focusing on the Demonflute as the more photogenic of the two. A clarinet, that is, with a lopsided bulge in the middle, a strangely shaped and oversized flare at the end, a truly terrifying key arrangement—well, anyway, it looked even less like a flute.

"No one *cares* what it looks like," Eleni chided, her eyes still glued to the screen. "It's the neat *sound* that's gonna start Thwokerjag zooming again."

"You've *heard* it?" I asked, ignoring for the moment the musical tragedy that a Thwokerjag renaissance would signify.

"Sure—he was practicing downstairs when I went over to see Ryla yesterday. It sounds kind of like a chirper, only shriller. I'll bet it'll really knurl the neurons when he plays it with the amp tonight at Moiy's. I still think you could've gotten us tickets if you'd tried."

"Starguard preserve us," I muttered. "A shrill chirper and some idiot sold him an amplifier to go with it? Aren't there laws against abetting physical assault?"

"The amplifier's built in," she said, ignoring the dig. "It's in that bulge in the middle—that's what makes it so heavy. You don't have to plug it in, either—Ryla said it pulls energy from cosmic radiation or somewhere. Neat, huh?"

"Very." My half-formed fantasy of protecting the city by knocking out its power stations slid off into oblivion.

Spars had been replaced on the screen by someone else, and Eleni turned the full force of her Patient But Annoyed expression on me. "Y'know, I really don't understand how you could have spent your whole life here without at least being willing to give Thwokerjag a try. I mean, it all *started* here."

It had indeed; and it had singlehandedly raised Haruspex from total obscurity to a status of genuine distaste among music lovers throughout the galaxy. From here Thwokerjag had swept outward to the other worlds of the Great Republic, inciting whole teenage populations as no other movement before it. For a while it had looked like it might bury even Neodisco beneath its onslaught . . . but even as sheer size slowed its momentum an unexpected resurgence of Classical Impressionistic Rock dealt it a blow that had ultimately proved its undoing. Now, only on Haruspex was Thwokerjag the dominant musical force, and even here a more classically oriented person like myself could find concerts and records that suited my taste.

One eventually got used to feeling like a fifth columnist.

"I appreciate your patience with me," I told Eleni, hoping the implication that I might convert someday would sidetrack the otherwise inevitable argument-*cum*-recruitment pitch. "If you're finished with the news, why don't we grab the trans and go downtown for dinner?"

"Sure. Let's eat at Moiy's."

"You don't give up, do you? Anyway, I told you before that I couldn't get tickets." I passed up the obvious comment that if she were as well glommed onto the fringes of Spar's group as she thought she was, a brace of free tickets ought to have been forthcoming.

She sighed theatrically and got her coat, and a few minutes later we were on the inbound trans. As we sat there I found my mind drifting toward the Demonflute. The name itself, I guessed, was a product of Algol's "Demon Star" nickname and Spars's limited imagination. As far as I knew it was the first musical instrument of alien design ever found, and while I deplored the use it was about to be put to, that was hardly its fault. "Ele, you didn't by any chance get to see the Demonflute up close, did you?"

Eleni turned from her contemplation of the holo-ad drifting past our noses. "Sure. Spars let me hold it, even."

So she was deeper into Spars's friendstack than I'd thought. My opinion of the group went down one more notch: no free tickets for anyone, apparently, when a concert looked to turn a profit. "Can you describe it for me?"

"It's about yi by yi," she said, indicating sizes with her hands, "with a sort of flat mouthpiece and eighteen separate keys. The end—the far end, I mean—swivels a little, probably so you can change how you're holding it and still point the music at the audience. Um . . . it's made of a coppery sort of metal with some neat curlicue engraving down one side. Spars says it's at least three hundred years old, and that it says a lot about Algolite technology that the amp is still working."

And the fact that they'd made a gadget that sounded like a shrill chirper said a lot about their musical tastes, too, I told myself silently. No wonder the race had died off.

But I didn't care nearly as much about the late denizens of Algol VI as I did about what the Demonflute was going to do for Thwokerjag. I wasn't all that well-versed in musicology, but I *did* know that new instruments had often revitalized movements that were supposedly on the decline. Until Classical Rock or Canton-Nadir could adapt the Demonflute to their own music, Thwokerjag would have the edge in impressing the pocket change out of the billions of novelty-seekers out there. Of course, if someone started duplicating Demonflutes fast enough the power balance would remain essentially unchanged—

That is, if anyone *could* duplicate the thing. For all I knew, the Demonflute could have a tone/texture mix that even the best synthesizer couldn't handle.

A unique instrument in the hands of Spars and Thwokerjag. It gave me cold chills just to think of it.

The passageway door ahead opened and one of the security guards strolled through, eyes alert for trouble. I winced slightly as he passed me and the flared nozzle of the Peacekeeper in his belt almost brushed my ear. Call me paranoid, but I've never liked the idea of some overeager junior lawman being able to turn my legs to putty with instant subliminals. Sure it's humane, but I prefer to *know* when someone's telling me to stop or—

My trans of thought froze on its rail. Turning quickly, I got one more look at the guard before he left the car. There was no mistake: the nozzle of his Peacekeeper looked exactly like the flared end of the Demonflute.

Eleni was looking at me questioningly. "Ele," I said, choosing my words carefully, "why did Spars conclude the Demonflute was a musical instrument?"

Her eyebrows lifted a fraction. "Because when you blow into it music comes out?" she suggested, obviously waiting for a punchline.

I shook my head. "Not necessarily. *Sound* comes out, all right. But sound comes out of lots of things."

She rolled her eyes skyward. "I hate it when you get all abstruse like this. What, in plain English, are you driving at?"

"Could the Demonflute be the Algolite version of a Peacekeeper?"

She looked at me as if I'd sheared a pin. "You mean with all that subliminal suggestive stuff? Don't be silly. The group's been practicing with it for a month now. Nobody's gone frizz-brained yet."

"Has Spars tried it with the amp?"

"No-o-o," she said slowly. "They've checked to make sure the amp works, but I think that was all done electronically. I don't think he actually played it during the tests."

"Who would build a musical instrument with a built-in, self-contained amplifier?" I continued. "And you said yourself it sounded like a shrill chirper. A chirper alone is already playing close to the uppersonic frequencies a Peacekeeper's message comes in on."

"Wow," she breathed. "You mean the whole audience at Moiy's is going to be wide open to suggestion tonight? Thwokerjag really *will* be on the way back up."

"Maybe," I said, suppressing a shudder at that idea. "But only if the uppersonic carrier is the only part still working."

"There'll be interstellar tours again—what? What do you mean?"

"A Peacekeeper doesn't just set up a suggestive state, you know. It beams in a prerecorded capitulation message."

Eleni could be as dense as hullmetal when she wanted to be, but I could see by the look on her face that she'd picked up on this one fast enough. "But the Demonflute would have an Algolite message in it. What would it do to humans?"

"I don't know, but I'm not sure I'd like to find out first-hand."

"We've got to call the cops," she said, fumbling for her phone. "Or try to talk to Spars or—"

I stopped her. "We haven't got even a shred of evidence," I pointed out. "Until we do no one's going to waste ten seconds listening to us."

"What kind of evidence can we possibly get?"

"Well . . . you said there was some engraving on the Demonflute, right? Could it be some sort of writing?"

"I suppose so. But I can't even remember what it looked like."

"You won't have to." The trans was slowing down, and I took a quick look out the window to see where we were. "Come on," I said, grabbing Eleni and hauling her all but bodily out the door.

"This is where we get off for Moiy's," she said, looking around her as she rubbed her arm. "I thought you said we couldn't tell Spars yet."

"We're not going to. This way; come on."

The library was only two blocks from the trans station. Once inside, I pulled a copy of the newstape Eleni had been watching earlier and we ran it through a filmreader to the spot where Spars had been showing off the Demonflute. Moving the tape frame by frame, I finally found a shot that Eleni said was at the right angle to see the engraving. Jiggling the controls to keep the Demonflute centered on the screen, I ran the enlarger to its limit.

"There," Eleni said, pointing. "His hand's covering about half of it, but you can see the last few squiggles."

"Okay. Go find us a computer terminal while I get a hard copy of this picture."

It took a few minutes for me to get my photo and join Eleni at a terminal. We then spent the better part of an hour programming the machine to scan the engraving in the picture and compare it to any previous data on Algol VI languages. I wasn't sure any such information even existed, But it seemed unlikely that anyone would have let Spars poke around those ruins unless the archeologists had already been there and gone. The computer seemed to agree with my logic, informing us there would be a short wait while the proper files were located.

I leaned back in my chair and tried to relax. It was already seven fifty-eight, my watch told me, which meant Spars was due on stage in two minutes.

"Don't worry," Eleni said as I muttered something evil under my breath. "No Thwokerjag performer ever goes out on time."

"I hope they goof up his body paint and have to do the whole thing over," I growled. "No telling how long this is going to take."

"Jaivy," Eleni said after a moment, "if the Demonflute really is some sort of Peacekeeper, why did Customs let Spars bring it here?"

I shrugged. "Customs is so overworked these days that about all they can look for are drug smugglers and tariff jumpers. Spars probably just walked in, waved the thing under their noses, and walked back out again. He'd never get away with that on Earth or Vega, but out here in the boons everything's a lot slacker."

"Yeah." Abruptly, she stood up. "I'm going to go talk to the librarian, see if he can speed things up any."

I gazed at the viewscreen for a long minute after she left as new and unpleasant possibilities began to multiply in the back of my mind. What if it *hadn't* been simple incompetence that had turned the Demonflute loose on Haruspex? Could Customs have learned of its function while examining it and deliberately let it through? It seemed crazy . . . but there were a lot of people who missed the days when Haruspian Thwokerjag dominated music in the Great Republic . . . people who might be willing to do anything to see that power regained. If Eleni was right—if it turned out that only the uppersonic carrier remained of the Demonflute's original programming—then the hardcore fans at Moiy's tonight would leave there with Thwokerjag just a bit more firmly a part of their psyches. A few more profit-making concerts—some publicity—revived curiosity—and Thwokerjag would indeed be on its way back to the top.

And if some of the recorded Algolite messages *did* remain, the whole audience could wind up the evening by painting each other's feet orange.

Which, for all I knew, might add that much more to Thwokerjag's appeal.

Abruptly, the *standby* symbol vanished from the screen. I glanced around quickly without spotting Eleni, then hunched forward to read. The Algolite language, I was informed, wasn't completely deciphered yet; but the probability was greater than ninety-five percent that the word on the Demonflute was *ezt'ghic*, a verb-adjective form meaning—

Maker/causer of death.

I stared at those four words, listening to my heart thump and my theories crumble into kitty-litter. This was no simple opinion swayer—Spars had dug up a bona fide lethal *weapon*.

And brought it to the stronghold of Thwokerjag.

To play in front of Thwokerjag's most ardent followers.

My suspicions about official collusion did a fast and frightening backflip. Far from secretly supporting a Thwokerjag revival, could someone in power have decided to end it once and for all? And if so, what would happen to me if I got involved any deeper than I already was?

For that matter, where did my own sympathies lie? Didn't I, too, want to see Thwokerjag wiped out?

And then Eleni appeared around the corner a few booths away. "Anything yet?" she stage-whispered, hurrying toward me.

My finger was bare centimeters away from the *erase* button. The screen could be blank before Eleni was close enough to see. . . .

"It's even worse than we thought," I told her. "Take a look."

She did, and her jaw dropped. "Maker of *death*? Jaivy—does that mean what I think it does?"

"Yeah," I said, snapping off the terminal. "And we've got to stop Spars before he wipes out Moiy's whole place. Do you have the number for anyone in his group?"

She was already punching phone buttons. "I'll try Ryla. . . . Come, on; come *on* . . . They must already be on stage, Jaive. We'll have to call the cops."

Practicalities—and lingering questions about official involvement—forced my decision. "No. We can be at Moiy's faster than we could explain this mess over the phone. Come on."

We ran the entire five blocks and arrived at Moiy's gasping for breath. One of the least seamy of the cheap-food-ditto-entertainment type of places favored by Thwokerjag adherents, Moiy's covered nearly half a block and I had to pause just inside the foyer to orient myself. Spars would be performing in the main dining room, just ahead of us. One of the side doors might get me to the stage without having to run the entire maze of tables. Eleni beside me, I headed toward a likely-looking corridor.

"Tickets?" Like magic the ticket taker appeared in our path. From his size, I guessed he also doubled as a bouncer.

There was no time to explain, even if I'd had the breath to do so. "Gotta stop Spars," I gasped; and as he frowned, I ducked under his arm and tore down the hall. Reaching my target door several steps ahead of him, I yanked it open and dived into the cacophony of Thwokerjag at its worst.

And found I'd miscalculated. The door I'd come through was still ten meters from the stage, with several tables between Spars and me.

But even as I started to thread my way through the screaming fans, I saw I was too late. The back-up men on chirper, Omni-Chord, and xyloplane had brought the music to a fever pitch and Spars was raising the Demonflute to his lips.

There was no way I could get back out of the room in time. I froze in place, my eyes riveted to that swivel flare—adjusted, I saw, to sweep the audience at eye-level—and with a sick feeling in my stomach watched Spars start to play.

It was the most hideous sound I'd ever heard. Eleni had called the Demonflute a shrill chirper, but she'd been entirely too charitable—the damn thing sounded more like a banshee in heat running cats through a paper shredder. Spars played over a whole unearthly scale, hitting notes that must've grounded every bat for fifty kilometers. The noise went on and on . . . and suddenly I noticed I was still alive.

I looked around the room, dumfounded. Everywhere the Thwoker-jag fans were swaying and clapping with the beat, just as they always did. Unless the Demonflute killed by inducing St. Vitus's dance it didn't seem to have any effect on them at all.

I was still standing there like an idiot when the bouncer finally caught up and carried me unceremoniously from the room.

The bouncer was pretty casual about the whole thing, and once he learned that Eleni was an acquaintance of Spars's he even let us wait in the foyer for the end of the concert.

"I just don't understand," Eleni complained as we collapsed into chairs. "Did the computer goof?"

"I doubt it." I felt like a ribbon-winning moron. "The engraving was probably a pet name the original owner had for it—you know, like the way you call your cycle the Boneshaker."

"Or a model name, like the Nissan-Lockheed *Sunjammer*." She giggled with released tension. "Imagine some alien trying to make sense out of *that*."

"Uh-huh." But the issue wasn't settled yet, I knew; not by a long shot. If the Demonflute wasn't a killing weapon, then maybe we were back to the Peacekeeper idea—and if that blipped out, it would just mean looking somewhere else for the answer. Because the Demonflute *wasn't* just a musical instrument, and I knew I wouldn't rest until I found out what else it really was.

Eleni broke into my musings. "You could've gotten killed in there," she said quietly, taking my hand. "You risked your life to try and save people whose music you don't even like."

I shrugged, feeling a little uncomfortable in the role of hero. "People are people, no matter what their tastes are."

"Hard to argue with that," she conceded.

A motion off to the side caught my eye, and I looked up to see old man Moiy himself wander into the foyer. He was bent over strangely, his eyes on the floor, and for a moment I wondered if he was sick. But just then he noticed us and bounded over, beaming happily.

"Good evening," he said. "I trust you're enjoying the show?"

From his words and attitude it was obvious he'd mistaken us for paying customers who were taking a breather. Eleni apparently shared my thought that there was no point in disillusioning him. "Uh, the Demonflute's an unusual instrument, isn't it?" she said.

Moiy nodded vigorously. "A remarkable sound; just remarkable. That boy is welcome back any time he wishes. Remarkable!"

"You mean you *like* that racket?" I blurted without thinking.

"Just between us, the music makes my teeth hurt," he confided, winking. "But who cares? The kid and his whasis have done something me and City Health have been trying to do for years."

"Oh? What?"

"Why, look around," Moiy said, waving toward the corners of the foyer.

Where he pointed, I noticed for the first time, were some black spots scattered on the floor. With a strange feeling in my stomach, I looked back at Moiy.

Still beaming, he nodded. "Greatest little exterminator I've ever seen. Killed every single cockroach in the place."

THE PRESIDENT'S DOLL

It started—or at least *my* involvement in the case started—as a brief but nasty behind-the-scenes battle between the Washington Police and the Secret Service over jurisdiction. The brief part I was witness to: I was at my desk, attention split between lunch and a jewelry recovery report, when Agent William Maxwell went into Captain Forsythe's office; and I was still on the same report when they came out. The nasty part I didn't actually see, but the all-too-familiar glint in Forsythe's eyes was only just beginning to fade as he and Maxwell left the office and started across the crowded squad room. I noted the glint, and Maxwell's set jaw, and said a brief prayer for whoever the poor sucker was who would have to follow Forsythe's act.

So of course they came straight over to me.

"Detective Harland; Secret Service Agent Maxwell," Forsythe introduced us with his customary eloquence. "You're assigned as of right now to a burglary case; Maxwell will give you the details." And with that, he turned on his heel and strode back to his office.

For a second Maxwell and I eyed each other in somewhat awkward silence. "Burglary?" I prompted at last, expecting him to pick up on the part of the question I wasn't asking.

He did, and his tight lips compressed a fraction more. "A very special burglary. Something belonging to President Thompson. All I really need from you is access to the police files on—"

"Stolen from the White House?" I asked, feeling my eyebrows rise.

"No, the doll was—" He broke off, glancing around at the desks crowding around us. None of the officers there were paying the least bit of attention to us, but I guess Maxwell didn't know that. Or else mild paranoia just naturally came with his job. "Is there some place a little more private where we can go and talk?" he asked.

"Sure," I said, getting to my feet and snaring my coat from the chair back as I took a last bite from my sandwich. "My car. We can talk on the way to the scene of the crime."

I was very restrained. I got us downstairs, into the car, and out into Washington traffic before I finally broke down. "Did you refer to this burglared item as a 'doll'?" I asked.

Maxwell sighed. "Yes, I did," he admitted. "But it's not what you're thinking. The President's doll is—" He broke off, swearing under his breath. "You weren't supposed to know about this, Harland—none of you were. There's no reason for you to be in on this at all; it's a Secret Service matter, pure and simple. Left at the next light."

"Apparently Captain Forsythe thought differently. He gets like that sometimes—very insistent on having a hand in everything that happens in this town." I reached the intersection and made the turn.

"Yeah, well, this one is none of his business, and I'd have taken him right down on the mat if time wasn't so damn critical." Maxwell hissed through his teeth.

"So what files do you need?" I asked after a minute. "Professional burglars or safecrackers?"

He glanced over at me. "Nice guess," he conceded. "Probably both. We've checked over security at the—office—and it took a real expert to get in the way he did."

"Whose office?"

"Pak and Christophe. Doctors Sam and Pierre, respectively."

"Medical doctors?"

"They say yes. I say—" Maxwell shook his head. "Look, do me a favor; hold off on any more questions until we get there, okay? They're the only ones who can explain their setup. Or at least the only ones who can explain it so that you might actually believe it."

I blinked. "Uh . . ."

"Right at the next light."

Gritting my teeth, I sat on my curiosity and concentrated on my driving.

Dr. Sam Pak was a short, intense second generation Chinese-American. Dr. Pierre Christophe was a tall, equally intense first generation Haitian.

Pak's specialty was obvious; the lettering on their office door proclaimed it to be the Pak-Christophe Acupuncture Clinic. It wasn't until the two doctors led us to the back room and opened the walk-in vault there that I found out just what it was Christophe supplied to the partnership.

Believing it was another matter entirely.

"I don't believe it," I said, staring at the dozen or so row planters lining the shelves of the vault. Stuck knee deep into the planters' dirt were rows of the ugliest wax figures I'd ever seen. Figurines with bits of hair and fingernail stuck on and into them . . . "I don't believe it," I repeated, "*Voodoo acupuncture?*"

"It is not that difficult to understand," Christophe said in the careful tones and faint accent of one who'd learned English as a second language. "I might even say it is a natural outgrowth of the science of acupuncture. If—"

"Pierre," Pak interrupted him. "I don't think Detective Harland came here to hear about medical philosophy."

"Forgive me," Christophe said, ducking his head. "I am very serious about my work here—"

"Pierre," Pak said. Christophe ducked his head again and shut up.

I sighed. "Okay, I'll bite. Just how is this supposed to work?"

"You're probably familiar with at least the basics of acupuncture," Pak said, reaching into the vault to pluck out one of the wax dolls from its dirt footbath. "Thin needles placed into various nerve centers can heal a vast number of diseases and alleviate the pain from others." His face cracked in a tight smile. "From your reaction, I'd guess you also know a little about voodoo."

"Just what I've seen in bad movies," I told him. "The dead chickens were always my favorite part." Christophe made some sort of disgusted noise in the back of his throat; I ignored him. "Let me guess: instead of sticking the acupuncture needles into the patient himself, you just poke them into his or her doll?"

"Exactly." Pak indicated the hair and fingernail clippings on the doll he was holding. "Despite the impression Hollywood probably gave you, there *does* seem to be a science behind voodoo. It's just that most of the practitioners never bother to learn it."

I looked over at Maxwell, who was looking simultaneously worried, tense, and embarrassed. "And you're telling me the President of the United States is involved in something this nutzoid?"

He pursed his lips. "He has some pains on occasion, especially when he's under abnormal stress. Normal acupuncture was effective in controlling that pain, but it was proving something of a hassle to keep sneaking Dr. Pak into the White House."

"'Sneaking'?"

He reddened. "Come on, Harland—you watch the news. Half of Danzing's jibes are aimed at the state of the President's health."

And whether or not he was really up to a second term. Senator Danzing had played that tune almost constantly since the campaign started, and would almost certainly be playing it again at their first official debate tonight in Baltimore. And with the election itself only two months away . . . "So when the possibility opened up of getting his treatments by remote control, he jumped at it with both feet, huh?" I commented. "I can just see what Danzing would do with something like this."

"He couldn't do a thing," Maxwell growled. "What's he going to do, go on TV and accuse the President of dealing in voodoo? Face it—he'd be laughed right off the stage, probably lose every scrap of credibility he has right then and there. Even if he got the media interested enough to dig out the facts, he'd almost certainly still wind up hurting himself more than he would the President."

"He could still make Thompson look pretty gullible, though," I said bluntly. "Not to mention reckless."

"This wasn't exactly done on a whim," Maxwell said stiffly. "Drs. Pak and Christophe have been working on this technique for several years—these dolls right here represent their sixth testing phase over a period of at least eighteen months."

I looked at the dolls in their planters. "I can hardly wait to see the ads when they have their grand opening."

Maxwell ignored the comment. "The point is that they've been successful in ninety-five-plus percent of the cases where plain acupuncture was already working—those figures courtesy of the FBI and FDA people we had quietly check this out. Whatever else you might think of the whole thing, the President didn't go into it without our okay."

I glanced at the tight muscles in his cheek. "Your okay, but not your enthusiasm?" I ventured.

He gritted his teeth. "The President wanted to do it," he growled. "*We* obey *his* orders, not the other way around. Besides, the general consensus was that, crazy or not, if the treatment didn't help him it also probably wouldn't hurt him."

I looked at Pak and Christophe, standing quietly by trying not to look offended. "*Did* it help?"

"Of course it did," Christophe said, sounding a little hurt. "The technique itself is perfectly straightforward—"

"Yeah. Right." I turned back to Maxwell. "So what's the problem? Either Dr. Pak moves into the White House until after the dust of the election has settled, or else Dr. Christophe goes ahead and makes Thompson a new doll. Surely he can spare another set of fingernail clippings—he can probably even afford to give up the extra hair."

"You miss the point," Maxwell grated. "It's not the President's pain treatments we're worried about."

"Then what—?"

"You mean you have forgotten," Christophe put in, "how voodoo dolls were originally used?"

I looked at the doll still in Pak's hand. "Oh, hell," I said quietly.

"Our theory is that it is the protein signature in the hair and nail clippings that, so to speak, forms the connection between the doll and the subject," Christophe said, gesturing broadly at the dolls in the vault. "Once that connection is made, what happens to the doll is duplicated in what happens to the subject."

I gnawed at my lip. "Well . . . these dolls were made specifically for medical purposes, right? Is there anything about their design that would make it impossible to use them for attack purposes? Or even to limit the amount of damage they could do?"

Christophe's brow furrowed. "It is an interesting question. There was certainly no malice involved in their creation, which may be a factor. But whether some other person could so bend them to that purpose—"

"If you don't know," I interrupted brusquely, "just say so."

"I do not know," he said, looking a little hurt.

"What's all this dirt for?" Maxwell asked, poking a finger experimentally into one of the row planters.

"Ah!" Christophe said, perking up. "That is our true crowning achievement, Mr. Maxwell—the discovery that it is the soil of Haiti that is the true source of voodoo power."

"You're kidding," I said.

"No, it's true," Pak put in. "A doll that's taken away from Haiti soon loses its potency. Having them in Haitian soil seems to keep them working indefinitely."

"Or in other words, the doll they stole will eventually run out of steam," I nodded. "How soon before that happens? A few hours? Days?"

"I expect it'd be measured in terms of a few weeks, maybe longer. I don't think we've ever gotten around to properly experimenting with—"

"If you don't know," I growled, "just say so."

"I don't know."

I looked at Maxwell. "Well, that's something, anyway. If it takes our thief long enough to figure out what he's got, it won't do him any good."

"Oh, he knows what he's got, all right," Maxwell said grimly. "Unless you really think he just grabbed that one by accident?"

"I suppose not," I sighed, glancing back at the rows of figurines. None of the others showed evidence of even having been touched, let alone considered for theft. "Dr. Christophe . . . is there anything like a—well, a *range* for this . . . effect of yours? In other words, does the President have to be within five miles, say, of the doll before anything will happen?"

Christophe and Pak exchanged looks. "We've treated patients who were as far as a hundred miles away," Pak said. "In fact—yes. I believe President Thompson himself was on a campaign trip in Omaha two months ago when we treated a stomach cramp."

Omaha. Great. If this nonsensical, unreal effect could reach a thousand miles across country, the thief could be anywhere.

Maxwell apparently followed my train of thought. "Looks like I was right—our best bet is to try and narrow down the possibilities."

I nodded, eyeing the vault door. This wasn't some cheap chain lock substitute Pak and Christophe had here—only a genuine professional would have the know-how to get into it. "Alarm systems?" I asked.

"I've got the parameters," Maxwell said before either of the others could speak. "You think I've proved sufficient urgency now for us to head back and dig into your files?"

The President's life, threatened by the melding of two pseudosciences that no one in his right mind could possibly believe in . . . except maybe that the combination happened to work. "Yeah, I think you've got a case," I admitted. "How's the President taking it?"

Maxwell hesitated a fraction too long. "He's doing fine," he said.

I cocked my eyebrow at him. "Really?" I asked pointedly.

His jaw clenched momentarily. "Actually . . . I'm not sure he's been told yet. There's nothing he can do, and we don't want to . . . you know."

Stir up psychosomatic trouble, I finished silently for him. Made as much sense as any of the rest of it, I supposed—

"Wait a second," I interrupted my own thought. "I remember reading once that for acupuncture to work the subject has to believe in it, at least a little. Doesn't the same apply to voodoo?"

Christophe drew himself up to his full height. "Mr. Harland," he said stiffly, "we are not dealing with fantasies and legends here. Our method is a fully medical, fully *scientific* treatment of the patient, and whatever he believes or does not believe matters but little."

Maxwell looked at Pak. "You agree with that, Doctor?"

Pak pursed his lips. "There's some element of belief in it, sure," he conceded. "But what area of medicine doesn't have that? The whole double-blind/placebo approach to drug testing shows—"

"Fine, fine," Maxwell cut him off. "I suppose it doesn't matter, anyway. If the President has enough belief to get benefit out of it, he probably has enough to get hurt, too."

Pak swallowed visibly. "Mr. Maxwell . . . look, we're really sorry about all this. Is there anything at all we can do to help?"

Maxwell glanced at me. "You think of anything?"

I looked past him at the rows of dolls. There was still a heavy aura of unreality hanging over this whole thing. . . . With an effort I forced myself back to business. "I presume your people already checked for fingerprints?"

"In the entryway, on the windows, on the vault itself, and also on the file cabinet where the records are kept. We're assuming that's how the thief knew which doll was the President's."

"In that case—" I shrugged. "I guess it's time to get back to the station and warm up the computer. So unless you two know of a antidote to—"

I broke off as, for some reason, a train of thought I'd been sidetracked from earlier suddenly reappeared. "Something?" Maxwell prompted.

"Dr. Christophe," I said slowly, "what would happen if a given patient had *two* dolls linked to him? And different things were done to each one?"

Christophe nodded eagerly. "Yes—I had the exact same thought myself. If Sam's acupuncture can counteract any damage done through the stolen doll—" He looked at Pak. "Certainly you can do it?"

Pak's forehead creased in a frown. "It's a nice thought, Pierre, but

I'm not at all sure I can do it. If the dolls are both running the same strength—"

"But they won't be," Maxwell interrupted him. "The Haitian dirt, remember? You can keep yours stuck up to its knees in the stuff, while theirs will gradually be losing power." He shook his head abruptly. "I can't *believe* I'm actually talking like this," he muttered. "Anyway, it's our best shot until we get the first doll back. I'm going to phone for a car— have all the stuff you'll need ready in fifteen minutes, okay?"

"Wait a second," Pak objected. "Where are we going?"

"The White House, of course," Maxwell told him. "Well, Baltimore, actually—the President's there right now getting ready for the debate tonight. I want you to be right there with him in case an attack is made."

"But the doll will work—"

"I'm not talking about the damn doll—I'm talking about the problem of communications lag. If the President has to tell someone where it hurts and then they have to call you from Baltimore or the White House and then *you* have to get the doll out and treat it and ask over the phone whether it's doing any good—" He broke off. "What am I explaining all of this for? You're going to be with the President for the next few days and that's that. As material witnesses, if nothing else."

He hadn't a hope of getting that one to stick, and he and I both knew it. But Pak and Christophe apparently didn't. Or else they were feeling responsible enough that they weren't in any mood to be awkward. Whichever, by the time Maxwell got his connection through to the White House they'd both headed off to collect their materials and equipment, and by the time the car arrived ten minutes later they were ready to go. Maxwell gave the driver directions, and as they drove off he and I got back in my car and returned to the station.

"Well, there you have it," I sighed, leaning back in my chair and waving at the printout. "Your likeliest suspects. Take your pick."

Maxwell said a particularly obscene word and hefted the stack of paper. "I don't suppose there's a chance we missed any helpful criteria, is there?"

I shrugged. "You sat there and watched me feed it all in. Expert safecracker, equally proficient with fancy vaults and fancy electronic alarm systems, not dead, not in jail, et cetera, et cetera."

He shook his head. "It'll take *days* to sort through these."

"Longer than that to track all of them down," I agreed. "Any ideas you've got, I'll take them."

He gnawed at the end of a pencil. "What about cross-referencing with our hate mail file? Surely no ordinary thief would have any interest in killing President Thompson."

"Fine—but most of your hate-mail people aren't going to know about the President's doll in the first place. We'd do better to try and find a leak from either the White House or Pak and Christophe's place."

"We're already doing that," he said grimly. "Also checking with the CIA regarding foreign intelligence services and terrorist organizations. These guys"—he tapped the printout—"were more of a long shot, but we couldn't afford to pass it up."

"Nice to occasionally be included in what's going on," I murmured. "How's the President?"

"As of ten minutes ago he was fine." Maxwell had been calling at roughly fifteen minute intervals, despite the fact that the Baltimore Secret Service contingent had my phone number and had promised to let us know immediately if anything happened.

"Well, that's something, anyway." I glanced at my watch. It was nearly four o'clock; two and a half hours since we'd left the voodoo acupuncture clinic and maybe as many as sixteen since the doll had been stolen.

And something here was not quite right. "Maxwell, don't take this the wrong way . . . but what the hell is he waiting for?"

"Who, the thief?"

"Yeah." I chewed at my lip. "Think about it a minute. We assume he knows what he has and that that he went in deliberately looking for it. So why wait to use it?"

"Establishing an alibi?" Maxwell suggested slowly.

"For murder with a *voodoo doll*?"

"Yeah, I suppose that doesn't make any sense," he admitted. "Well . . . maybe he's not planning to use it himself. Maybe he's going to send out feelers and sell the doll to the highest bidder."

"Maybe," I nodded. "On the other hand, who would believe him?"

"Holding it for ransom, then?"

"He's had sixteen hours to cut out newspaper letters and paste up a ransom note. Anything like that shown up?"

He shook his head. "I'm sure I'd have been told if it had. Okay, I'll bite: what *is* taking him so long?"

"I don't know, but whatever he's planning he's up against at least two time limits. One: the longer he holds it, the better the chance that we'll catch up with him. And two: the longer he waits, the less power the doll's going to have."

"Unless he knows about the Haitian soil connection . . . no. If he'd known he should have helped himself to some when he took the doll."

"Though he *could* have a private source of the stuff," I agreed. "It's still a fair assumption, though. Could he have expected us to have Pak standing by waiting to counteract whatever he does? He might be holding off then until Pak relaxes his guard some."

"The theft went undiscovered for at least a couple of hours," Maxwell pointed out. "He could have killed the President in his sleep. For that matter, he could have done it right there in the vault and never needed to take the doll at all."

"Point," I conceded. "So simple murder isn't what he's looking for—complicated murder, maybe, but not simple murder."

"Oh, my God," Maxwell whispered suddenly, his face going pale. "The debate. He's going to do it at the *debate*."

For a long second we stared at each other. Then, simultaneously, we grabbed our jackets and bolted for the door.

It was something like forty miles to Baltimore; an hour's trip under normal conditions. Maxwell insisted on driving and made it in a shade over forty-five minutes. In rush hour traffic, yet.

We arrived at the Hyatt and found the President's suite . . . and discovered that all our haste had been for nothing.

"What do you mean, they won't cancel?" Maxwell growled to VanderSluis, the Secret Service man who met us just inside the door.

"Who's this 'they' you're talking about?" the other growled back. "It's the *President* who won't cancel."

"Didn't you tell him—?"

"We gave him everything you radioed in," VanderSluis sighed. "Didn't do a bit of good. He says canceling at the last minute like this without a good reason would be playing right into Danzing's rhetoric."

"Has he been told . . . ?"

"About the doll? Yeah, but it didn't help. Probably hurt, actually—he rightly pointed out that if someone's going to attack him using the doll, hiding won't do him a damn bit of good."

Maxwell glanced at me, frustration etched across his face. "What about Pak and Christophe?" he asked VanderSluis. "They here?"

"Sure—down the hall in seventeen."

"Down the *hall*? I thought I told them to stick by the President."

"They're as close now as they're likely to get," VanderSluis said grimly. "The President said he didn't want them underfoot while he was getting ready for the debate."

Or roughly translated, he didn't want any of the media bloodhounds nosing about to get a sniff of them and start asking awkward questions. "At least they're not back in Washington," I murmured as Maxwell opened his mouth.

Maxwell closed his mouth again, clenched his teeth momentarily. "I suppose so," he said reluctantly. "Well . . . come on, Harland, let's go talk to them. Maybe they'll have some ideas."

We found them in the room, lounging on the two double beds watching television. On the floor between the beds, the room's coffee table had been set up like a miniature surgical tray, with Pak's acupuncture needles laid out around a flower pot containing Christophe's replacement doll. It looked as hideous as the ones back in their Washington vault. "Anything?" Maxwell asked as the doctors looked up at us.

"Ah—Mr. Maxwell," Christophe said, tapping the remote to turn off the TV. "You will be pleased to hear that President Thompson is in perfect health—"

"He had some stomach trouble an hour ago." Pak put in, "but I don't think it had anything to do with the doll. Just predebate tension, probably. Anyway, I got rid of it with the new doll."

Maxwell nodded impatiently. "Yeah, well, the lull's about to end. We think that the main attack's going to come sometime during the debate."

Both men's eyes widened momentarily, and Christophe muttered something French under his breath. Pak recovered first. "Of course. Obvious, in a way. What can we do?"

"The same thing you were brought here for in the first place: counteract the effects of the old doll with the new one. Unfortunately, we're now back to our original problem."

"Communications?" I asked.

He nodded. "How are we going to know—fast—what's happening out there on the stage?"

I found myself gazing at the now-dark TV. "Dr. Pak . . . how are you at reading a man's physical condition from his expression and body language?"

"You mean can I sit here and tell how President Thompson is feeling by watching the debate on TV?" Pak shook his head. "No chance. Even if the camera was on him the whole time, which of course it won't be."

"Maybe a signal board," Maxwell suggested, a tone of excitement creeping into his voice. "With individual buttons for each likely target—joints, stomach, back, and all."

"And he does, what, pushes a button whenever he hurts somewhere?" I scoffed.

"It doesn't have to be that obvious," Maxwell said, reaching past Christophe to snare the bedside phone. "We can make it out of tiny piezo crystals—it doesn't take more than a touch to trigger those things. And they're small enough that a whole boardful of them could fit on the lectern behind his notes—Larry?" he interrupted himself into the phone. "Bill Maxwell. Listen, do we have any of those single-crystal piezo pressure gadgets we use for signaling and spot security? . . . Yeah, short range would be fine—we'd just need a booster somewhere backstage . . . Oh, great . . . Well, as many as you've got . . . Great—I'll be right down."

He tossed the phone back into it cradle and headed for the door. "We're in," he announced over his shoulder. "They've got over a hundred of the things. I'll be right back." Scooping up a room key from a low table beside the door, he left.

I looked at my watch. Five-fifteen, with the debate set to begin at nine. Not much time for the kind of wiring Maxwell was talking about. "You think it'll work?" I asked Pak.

He shrugged uncomfortably. "I suppose so. The bad part is that it means I'll be relying on diagnostics from someone who is essentially an amateur."

"It's *his* body, isn't it?"

Pak shrugged again, and for a few minutes the three of us sat together in silence. Which made it even more of a heart-stopping jolt then the phone suddenly rang.

Reflexively, I scooped it up. "Yes?"

"Who is this?" a suspicious voice asked.

"Cal Harland—Washington Police."

"Oh, yeah—you came with Maxwell. Has he gotten back with those piezos yet?"

I began to breathe again. Whatever was up, at least it wasn't a medical emergency. "No, not yet. Can I take a message?"

"Yeah," the other sighed, "but he's not going to like it. This is Vander-

Sluis. Tell him I called and that I just took his suggestion in to the President. And that he scotched the whole idea."

My mouth went dry all at once. "He *what*?"

"Shot it down. Said in no uncertain terms that he can't handle a debate and a damn push-button switchboard at the same time. Unquote."

"Did you remind him that it could be his *life* at stake here?" I snapped. "Or even fight dirty and suggest it could cost him the election?"

"Just give Maxwell the message, will you?" the other said coldly. "Leave the snide comments to Senator Danzing."

"Sorry," I muttered. But I was talking to a dead phone. Slowly, I replaced the handset and looked up to meet Pak's and Christophe's gazes. "What is the matter?" Christophe asked.

"Thompson's not going for it," I sighed. "Says the signal board would be too much trouble."

"But—" Pak broke off as the door opened and Maxwell strode into the room, his arms laden with boxes of equipment.

"Hell," he growled when I'd delivered VanderSluis's message. "Hell and *hell*. What's a little trouble matter when it could save his life?"

"I doubt that's his only consideration," Pak shook his head. "Politics, again, Mr. Maxwell—politics and appearances. If any of the press should notice the board, there are any number of conclusions they could come to."

"None of them good." I took a deep breath. "But damn it all, what does he want you to do?—defend him without his cooperation?"

"Probably," Maxwell said heavily. "There's a long tradition of that in the Secret Service." He took a deep breath. "Well, gentlemen, we've still got three and a half hours to come up with something. Suggestions?"

"Can you find the robber and get the doll back?" Christophe asked.

"Probably not," Maxwell shook his head. "Too many potential suspects, not enough time to sort through all of them."

"A shame the thief didn't leave any hair at the scene of the crime," I commented, only half humorously. "If he had, we could make a doll and take him out whether we knew who he was or not."

Maxwell cocked an eye at Christophe. "Anything you can do without something from his body?"

Christophe shook his head. "Only a little bit is required, Mr. Maxwell, but that little bit is absolutely essential."

Maxwell swore and said something else to Christophe . . . but I wasn't really listening. A crazy sort of idea had just popped into my head . . . "Dr. Christophe," I said slowly, "what about the doll itself? You made the thing—presumably you know everything about its makeup and design. Would there be any way to make a—I don't know, a counteracting doll that you could use to destroy the original?"

Christophe blinked. "To tell the honest truth, I do not know. I have never heard of such a thing being done. Still . . . from what I have learned of the science of voodoo, I believe I would still need to have something of the stolen doll here to create the necessary link."

"Wait a minute, though," Pak spoke up. "It's all the same wax that you use, isn't it? That strange translucent goop that's so pressure-sensitive that it bruises if you even look at it wrong."

"It is hardly that delicate," Christophe said with an air of wounded pride. "And it is that very responsiveness that makes it so useful—"

"I know, I know," Pak interrupted him. "What I meant was, would it be possible to link up with the stolen doll since you know what it's made of?"

"I do not think so," Christophe shook his head. "Voodoo is not a shotgun, but a very precise rifle. When a link is created between doll and subject it is a *very* specific one."

"And does that link work both ways?" Maxwell asked suddenly.

There was something odd in his voice, something that made me turn to look at him. The expression on his face was even odder. "Something?" I asked.

"Maybe. Dr. Christophe?"

"Uh . . ." Christophe floundered a second as he backtracked to the question Maxwell had asked. "Well, certainly the link works both ways. How could it be otherwise?"

For a moment Maxwell didn't say anything, but continued gazing off into space. Then, slowly, a grim smile worked itself onto his face. "Then it might work. It might just work. And the President should even go for it—yeah, I'm sure he will." Abruptly, he looked down at his watch. "Three and a quarter hours to go," he said, all business again. "We'd better get busy."

"Doing what?" Pak asked, clearly bewildered.

Maxwell told us.

The Hyatt ballroom was stuffed to the gills with people long before President Thompson and Senator Danzing came around the curtains, shook hands, and took their places at the twin lecterns. Sitting on the end of the bed, I studied Thompson's television image closely, wishing we'd been allowed to set up somewhere a little closer to the action. TV screens being what they were, it was going to be pretty hard for me to gauge how the President was feeling.

The moderator went through a short welcoming routine and then nodded to Thompson. "Mr. President, the first opening statement will be yours," he said. The camera shifted to a mid-closeup and Thompson began to speak—"

"Stomach," Maxwell said tersely from behind me.

"I see it," Pak answered in a much calmer voice. ". . . This should do it."

I kept my own eyes on the President's face. A brief flicker of almost-pain came and went. "He's looking okay now," I announced.

"Unfortunately, we can't tell if the treatment is working," Pak commented. "Only where the attack is directed—"

"Right elbow," Maxwell cut him off.

"Got it."

"Thank you, Mr. President," the moderator cut smoothly into Thompsons's speech. "Senator Danzing: your opening statement, sir."

The camera shifted to Danzing and I took a deep breath and relaxed a bit. Only for a second, though, as an angled side camera was brought into play and Thompson appeared in the foreground. "Watch it," I warned the other. "He's on camera again."

"Uh-huh," Maxwell grunted. "—stomach again."

"Got it," Pak assured him. "Whoever our thief is, he isn't very imaginative."

"Not terribly dangerous, either, at least so far," I put in. "Though I suppose we should be grateful for small favors."

"Or for small minds," Maxwell said dryly. "It's starting to look more and more like murder wasn't the original object at all."

"I do not understand," Christophe spoke up.

Maxwell snorted. "Haven't you ever heard of political dirty tricks?"

The camera was full on Danzing again, and I risked a glance around at the others hunched over the table set up between the two hotel beds. "You mean . . . all of this just to make Thompson look wracked by aches and pains on camera?"

"Why not?" Maxwell said, glancing briefly up at me. "Stupider things have been done. Effectively, I might add."

"I suppose." But probably, I added to myself, none stranger than this one. My eyes flicked to the table and to two wax figures standing up in flower pots of Haitian soil there: one with a half dozen acupuncture needles already sticking out of it, the other much larger one looking more like a pincushion than a doll.

But those weren't pins sticking into it. Rather, they were a hundred thin wires leading *out* of it. Out, and into a board with an equal number of neatly spaced and labeled lights set into it . . . and even as I watched, one of the tiny piezo crystals Christophe had so carefully embedded into his creation reacted to the subtle change in pressure of the wax and the corresponding light blinked on—

"Right wrist," Maxwell snapped.

"Got it," Pak said. Belatedly, I turned back to my station at the TV, just in time to see the President's arm wave in one of his trademark wide-open gestures. The arm swung forward, hand cupped slightly toward the camera . . . and as it paused there my eyes focused on that hand, and despite the limitations of the screen I could almost imagine I saw the slight discolorations under his neatly manicured fingernails. Would any of the reporters in the ballroom be close enough to see that? Probably not. And even if they did, they almost certainly wouldn't recognize Christophe's oddly translucent wax for what it really was.

Or believe it if they did. Doll-to-person voodoo was ridiculous enough; running the process in reverse, person-to-doll, was even harder to swallow.

The picture shifted to Danzing. "He's off-camera again," I announced, getting my mind back on my job.

The battles raged for just over an hour—the President's and Senator's verbal battle, and our quieter, behind-the-scenes one. And when it was over, the two men on the stage shook hands and headed backstage . . . and because I knew to look for it, I noticed the slight limp to the President's walk. Hardly surprising, really—though I've never tried it, I'm sure it's very difficult to walk properly when your socks are full of Haitian dirt.

The Secret Service dropped me out of the investigation after that, so I don't know whether or not they ever actually recovered the doll. But at this point it hardly matters. The President's clearly still alive, and by now the stolen doll is almost certainly inert. I haven't seen Pak or Christophe since the debate, either, but from the excited way they were talking afterwards I'd guess that by now they've probably worked most of the bugs out of the new voodoo diagnostic technique that Maxwell came up with that night. And I suppose I have to accept that all medical advances, whether they make me uncomfortable or not, are ultimately a good thing.

And actually, the whole experience has wound up saving me a fair amount of money, too. Instead of shelling out fifteen dollars for a haircut once a month, I've learned to do the job myself, at home.

I collect and destroy my fingernail clippings, too. Not paranoid, you understand; just cautious.

CLEAN SLATE

●

There were a hundred small towns and villages along the road to Abron Mysti, and at each one they warned Saladar that his trip was going to be wasted, that Gyran Pass had been forcibly closed. Those whose advice he ignored clearly labeled him a fool; those to whom he tried explaining just as clearly labeled him an arrogant fool. Eventually, he gave up explaining, and merely set his face toward the gray-green peaks of the Bartop Mountains and kept walking.

The last few leagues were the hardest. The towns and their well-meaning residents petered out as the road began to slope upward toward the mountains, and he quickly discovered why most travelers chose to make this trip on beastback. But he hardly noticed the effort. He was almost there, and it was looking more and more like he was going to be the first to arrive . . . and for the opportunity that lay ahead he would gladly have given years of his life.

As he had, of course, already done.

Whether by deliberate design or simple accident of landscape, the final approach to Abron Mysti was an impressive one. With the foothills of the Bartop Mountains rising up around him, Saladar topped a slight swell in the road itself; and suddenly the town was there, spread at his feet between the straight-walled gap leading into the mountains behind it and a narrow white-water river before it. The houses and trade buildings making up the town were clean and attractive; the lack of activity around them, highly abnormal.

Which meant he'd indeed made it in time. Travel through Gyran

Pass was still halted. Taking a deep breath, he straightened his cloak and started down toward the town.

The road ended at a drawbridge spanning the river, a posted sign nearby proclaiming the toll to be four *dan*. Two small cottages flanked the road on the far side of the bridge, but there was no sign of any bridge keeper. "Hello?" he called. "Is anyone there?"

For a minute the roaring of the river beneath the bridge was the only sound. Then the door of the cottage on the right opened, and a young woman peered out. "What is it?" she called.

Saladar gestured to the sign. "Are you the bridge keeper?" he shouted.

An odd look flicked across her face, but it passed and she gestured him forward. He crossed and stepped up to her. "Are you the bridge keeper?" he repeated.

She shook her head, lips compressing briefly. "The bridge keeper's in town. Probably getting drunk."

Saladar's gaze slipped to her neck, to the widow's white scarf knotted there. "Do you accept fees in his absence?" he asked.

Her eyes showed she was tempted . . . but those eyes held pride, too. "No," she said. "Forget the toll—if he's not here to collect, the city just loses out. A few *dan* aren't going to make any difference, anyway."

"No," he agreed. "Thank you. Do you serve the bridge in any capacity, then?"

"My husband was bridge keeper once," the woman said shortly. "He's dead now. I had nowhere else to go, so they allowed me to stay here. Is there anything else?"

Saladar inclined his head slightly. "I'm sorry; I didn't mean to pry. If I may ask one more favor, though, would you be kind enough to direct me to your ruler?"

She frowned. "Why?"

In answer, he reached down into his tunic and withdrew the blood-red heartstone on its chain. "My name is Saladar," he told her. "I've come to help you."

For a long moment the woman stared at the gently throbbing heartstone, a look of disgust and hatred distorting her features. Then without a word, she disappeared back inside, slamming the door behind her.

For a moment Saladar just stood there, staring at the spot where she'd been, his head spinning with the sheer unexpectedness of it. Throughout his lifetime he'd been greeted with everything from lavish adoration to utter indifference . . . but never by such complete revulsion.

But it didn't really matter. The wizard's oath he'd taken all those years ago had spoken of service to those in need. It had made no mention of serving only those who fed his pride.

And with the chance to fulfill that oath finally within his grasp, it would take a lot more than simple hatred to stop him. A *lot* more.

Abruptly, he realized he was still holding the heartstone out on its chain. Taking a calming breath, he slipped it back into his tunic, feeling the warmth as it settled again into the accustomed spot next to his heart. Stepping back from the cottage, he headed down toward the center of Abron Mysti.

Cyng Borthnin was a big, almost brutish-looking man—a living example, Saladar thought, of the small-village belief that equated physical stature and power with the ability to rule.

"A wizard, huh?" Borthnin grunted as Saladar slid the heartstone back into his tunic. "Took your time getting here, didn't you? It's been almost two months."

"I came as soon as word reached me, my lord Cyng," Saladar said evenly. "The world is a very large place, hardly something easily filled by a handful of wizards."

Borthnin made a face. "Oh, certainly," he said, a touch of bitterness in his voice. "Yes, we of Abron Mysti know very well just how few of you there are." He eyed Saladar with undisguised suspicion. "So. You're here to open Gyran Pass again, are you? How much do you plan to charge for this favor?"

Saladar frowned. "Nothing, my lord Cyng," he told the other. "Merely my room and board while I study the problem—"

One of the small group of men seated to either side of Borthnin muttered something under his breath. Saladar shifted his gaze to the man, and the other fell reluctantly silent. "My room and board while I study the problem," he repeated. "And that for no more than a week. Probably less."

Borthnin nodded. "So. A week's room and board. And when you've found how to vanquish the beast?"

"I charge no fee, if that's what you mean," Saladar said, anger beginning to stir within him. "If you'll forgive me, my lord Cyng, you don't talk like the ruler of a town whose sole means of livelihood has been snatched away from it. I'd think you'd be willing to pay practically any price to have Gyran Pass open again."

A growling rumble from Borthnin's counselors broke off at a wave of the Cyng's hand. "You think that, do you?" Borthnin said darkly. "Well, perhaps you also think we're more gullible than in truth we are."

"And you think I'm going to try to cheat you—?"

"Listen, wizard, we know just how close and exclusive your group is," Borthnin cut him off angrily. "One of our own tried to join, and they killed him for his effort." He stopped, visibly gathering his control about him again. "No, wizard. If it's some beast or natural creature in the Lighttower, it'll eventually leave of its own accord. And if it's some wizard's trick being played against Abron Mysti, we aren't going to come fawning to another of that same group to rescue us."

"Then your city may die," Saladar warned him.

"So be it," Borthnin shot back. "At least we'll die as men."

For a handful of heartbeats Saladar gazed into Borthnin's face. Then, without a word, he turned and left the council house.

Outside, he paused, letting his anger at such stupidity cool while he considered what to do next. It had taken longer to locate the Cyng than he'd expected, and the sun was dipping toward the horizon. Too late now to go up into Gyran Pass and get back before dark—and whatever it was that travelers were unable or unwilling to face by day he had no desire to encounter by night.

Which likewise left out the possibility of camping at the entrance to the pass. He could find a room in Abron Mysti, of course, staying at his own expense . . . but he had a measure of pride, too, and after that confrontation he would shrivel up and die before he would give Borthnin the satisfaction. Turning his back to the mountains, he retraced his steps back toward the river.

The bridge was still in place—the bridge keeper, no doubt, still drowning his sorrows in town. He was about to cross when a voice from his left stopped him. "You leaving?"

He turned. The woman he'd spoken to earlier had emerged from her cottage, a hoe in her hand. "Only for the night," he told her. "I'll be back in the morning to take a look at the pass."

Her lips compressed. "Is our hospitality that lacking that you prefer sleeping outside?"

"I wouldn't know. Cyng Borthnin decided the town isn't willing to provide me a bed for the night."

The sour look on her face flickered out, to be replaced by surprise. "He—? What did you say to him?"

"Only the truth. That I came to try to help Abron Mysti get rid of whatever was blocking Gyran Pass." He eyed the woman, a sudden suspicion dawning on him. "He mentioned that a local resident had tried to become a wizard. Your husband?"

Her face hardened, and for a moment he thought she would slam the door on him again . . . and then her whole body seemed to slump. "Yes," she said softly, her voice barely audible over the roar of the river.

Saladar felt an echo of pain in his own heart. "I'm sorry," he said quietly.

Slowly, her eyes came back up to his face. "Why did you come here?"

"I already told you. To try to help."

"And you're staying? Even after . . . everything?"

He nodded. "I have to."

"Why?"

He hesitated. *Because this may be the only chance I ever have to be a wizard,* the thought whispered through his mind. "Because it's my job," he said aloud. "Because it's what I'm called to do."

For a long moment she just stared at him. "My name is Marja," she said at last. "I . . ." She took a deep breath. "I have a spare room."

Her husband's name, Saladar learned two hours later, had been Nunisjan.

"He left three years ago this autumn," Marja told him, the soft candlelight bathing her face with gentle radiance as she collected the dishes from their evening meal. "Travel through the mountains slackens with the first snowfall of winter, you know, and for those months a bridge keeper has little to do. He'd always felt that Abron Mysti was important enough to have its own resident wizard, and so he . . . left . . . to try to become one."

"And never returned?" Saladar asked quietly.

She turned her back to him, busying herself with the dishes. "A dove arrived here a year later," she said over her shoulder, her voice wavering slightly. "It carried a message for me from his mentor. Word of his death."

Saladar sighed soundlessly. "I'm sorry."

She didn't reply, and for a few minutes the room was silent except for the clinking of dishware. "How did it happen?" he asked at last.

"The message didn't say." She paused. "I was hoping . . . you might be able to tell me."

Saladar shook his head. "I'm sorry. There are any number of dangerous spells a wizard has to learn. A mistake with any one of them—"

"Brings on the Wizard's Curse?"

He winced. "You've heard of the Wizard's Curse?"

"Hasn't everybody?" she retorted. "Though most people around here think it's nothing but a rumor started by the wizards to keep other people from seeking the Power for themselves."

"Yes, I got that impression from Cyng Borthnin earlier," Saladar said heavily. "I've heard that said before, too, in other places. But it isn't true. The number of wizards is limited solely by the number of heartstones available."

"You really need those things? I always thought they were just for impressing the peasants."

"No, they're absolutely vital. Without a heartstone to strengthen and guide the Power, none of the truly potent spells will work."

She seemed to consider that. "Then what's the Wizard's Curse?"

Saladar grimaced. "Perhaps by tomorrow I'll be able to tell you."

Marja turned from her work to frown at him. "What do you mean?"

He hesitated, his first instinct to deflect the question. But it had lain hidden in his heart for so long . . . and anyway, with this trouble facing her town perhaps she had a right to know. "No one's ever told me what the Wizard's Curse was," he said in a low voice. "It's the price a wizard must pay for the privilege of using the Power—that's all my mentor would ever tell me. He wouldn't say anything more."

"Yes, but you've been a wizard yourself for—surely for many years."

"Fifteen." He turned away from her eyes, to the small window and the still-lighted tips of the mountains beyond. "I've been a wizard for fifteen years. Or at least that's how long I've had my heartstone. But in all that time I've never had the chance to use the Power."

He could feel her eyes on him. "I don't understand."

"What's there not to understand?" he lashed out, fifteen years' worth of accumulated frustration welling from him like brackish water. "I'm never at the right place at the right time, that's all. I hear of some catastrophe—something where the wizard's Power is needed—and I go to try to help. But by the time I can get there and get ready, it's . . . it's too late. Someone else always manages to get there ahead of me and deal with the problem."

For a long moment she didn't speak. "Well," she said at last, her voice uncertain. "At least that means you . . . well, you've got a clean slate to work from, anyway. I mean, even if you haven't . . . done much, you haven't fouled anything up, either. Like some wizards I've heard stories of . . ."

She trailed off, and Saladar blinked against tears of shame and anger. *A clean slate.* The sheer lameness of the phrase fairly dripped with scorn and pity. "Would *you* be content with such a life?" he snarled.

"I *have* such a life," she whispered.

Saladar sighed. "I'm sorry," he said, ashamed of himself. His long bitterness was no excuse to stir up similar feelings in others. "I just . . ." He dabbed surreptitiously at his eyes, his heartstone throbbing sympathetically with his emotion. "This may be my only chance to be a wizard, Marja," he said, the words coming out with difficulty. "I'm here—the *first* one here, for a change. If I can rid Abron Mysti and Gyran Pass of this trouble—whatever it is"—he took a deep breath—"then maybe I'll be able to justify having wasted my possession of a heartstone for all these years."

"And what of the Wizard's Curse?" she asked quietly.

"I don't care," he said, and meant it. "Whatever the price, I'll pay it."

For a long minute the room was silent. "Nunisjan used to talk like that," Marja sighed at last. "Will you need a guide tomorrow to . . . where the trouble is?"

Saladar shook his head. "Thank you, but you'd better stay here. It's likely to be dangerous."

A ghost of a smile touched her lips. "So? What do I have to live for?"

"Marja—"

"I want to come, Saladar. I . . . want to see what this dream is that Nunisjan gave his life for."

Saladar bowed his head. "All right."

They left at sunrise the next morning, though the colors of the dawn were hidden by the mountains before them. Still, by the time they'd crossed to the other end of Abron Mysti and started up the slopes of the mountains, the sky above them was bright enough to see by.

And bright enough to show Wizardell in all its splendor.

"It was some wizard, several hundred years ago, who did this," Marja told him as they stepped into the straight-walled passage. "Gyran Pass doesn't quite extend all the way through to this side of the Bartop Mountains, and I suppose the wizard got tired of having to climb up along the side of Mount Mysti every time he came through from

Colinthe. So he just sliced a huge gap in the mountain and finished the pass properly."

Saladar nodded, raising his eyes briefly from the high walls of the gap to the still higher peaks of Mount Mysti towering above it. He'd heard the story of Wizardell, of course, but no story could match the sheer impact of seeing the place for himself. "Incredible," he murmured.

"Yes," Marja agreed, running her fingertips along the nearest wall as they walked. "I remember trying to gouge out a hole in one of the walls once when I was younger. I couldn't even make a good scratch in it."

"Yes, he would have had to permanently strengthen the rock, or the wind and snow would eventually have broken it down." *The things the right man can do with a heartstone,* Saladar thought, a touch of bitterness tainting the wonder in his heart. *Why can't I ever come up with ideas like this?* Resolutely, he shook the thought from his mind. "Where is this Lighttower that Cyng Borthnin mentioned?"

"At Wizardell's end, where the natural pass begins," Marja explained, pointing ahead. "There was a natural column of stone at that spot, and the wizard decided to leave it standing. But he rounded it and carved out a room in the top with a door and windows where men could run a light to help guide travelers at night."

"Does Abron Mysti do that?"

She shook her head. "There aren't enough nighttime travelers to make it worthwhile."

"So when whatever it was got into the Lighttower, no one was there to see it."

"Or to be killed by it," she countered stiffly.

He grimaced. "There's that, of course. How close are we?"

"About a tenth league from the Lighttower itself, but we'll be able to see it as soon as we round this bend."

Saladar nodded, drawing his heartstone out of his tunic and clutching it tightly in his hand. The straight walls bent slowly around . . . straightened out again . . . there was the Lighttower, fully as impressive as Wizardell itself—

And without warning a horrible wailing shriek exploded into the gap, filling Saladar's ears as it reverberated again and again from the stone walls.

Beside him Marja screamed, the sound utterly pale in contrast, as she flung herself cringing against the wall. Head ringing with terror,

Saladar was only dimly aware of grabbing her arm and dragging her back, squeezing his heartstone with manic strength—

The wailing cut off as suddenly as it had appeared, though for several seconds Saladar's ears seemed to echo with the memory of it. Beside him Marja clutched unashamedly at him, her whole body shaking. Saladar held her to him, working moisture back into his mouth, letting the heartstone's soothing power flow into them both.

Even so, it was several minutes before either of them could speak. "I see your problem," Saladar said at last.

Breathing deeply, Marja pulled back from him. But not too far. "Gods above and demons below," she whispered hoarsely. "I had no idea. No *idea*."

"Agreed." Saladar licked his lips. "I take it beasts simply refuse to pass the Lighttower?"

"Beasts and people both." She shuddered, violently.

Saladar glanced toward the Lighttower, now hidden again by the walls of Wizardell. "I can't say I blame them," he admitted. "Still . . . has anyone actually been attacked?"

"I doubt anyone's gotten that close," she retorted, a measure of spirit beginning to return.

He nodded. "Understandable. I suppose someone ought to find out for sure, though. You'd better wait here—"

"*Wait* a minute," she snapped, stepping into his path. "Gods and demons, Saladar—are you insane?"

He sighed. "Look, Marja, no hunting beast would warn its prey like that, at least not before it was close enough to attack. If there's something trapped or stuck in the Lighttower, it can't hurt me down here." He gestured toward the sheer walls rising above them. "By the same token, I can't do anything about it from down here . . . and it's pretty obvious I can't get up to the Lighttower from Wizardell."

For a long moment she gazed up at his face. Then she exhaled in a long, tired sigh. "All right," she said. "The way up to the Lighttower is only a short distance into Gyran Pass. I'll show you where."

Saladar had sensed her offer coming, but he was still impressed. "Thank you, Marja. But I could be wrong about what's in the Lighttower—"

"You'll never find the path by yourself," she cut him off angrily. "And I'd rather be with you than all alone here, anyway. Come on, let's get it over with."

"All right," he hesitated. "But perhaps I can make it easier for you. If you don't mind being deaf for the next half-hour or so."

"You can do that?" she asked, looking wary.

"I know the spell. I've never tested it, but it's supposed to be perfectly safe."

She grimaced. "I . . . all right."

Stepping close to her, Saladar placed the point of the heartstone against her forehead. Giving her what he hoped was a reassuring smile, he began to speak the spell.

The shrieking began again as they came around within view of the Lighttower, and for the first few steps Saladar didn't think he was going to make it. Unwilling to risk deafness for both of them—there might be other dangers in Gyran Pass besides the creature in the Lighttower—he had had to settle for protecting himself with a strong calming spell. But it didn't help nearly as much as he'd hoped it would. Gripping his heartstone, mentally ordering it to slow his heartbeat to a less frantic pace, he clutched Marja's hand and forced himself to keep going.

It was almost a shock when he abruptly noticed they were passing the smoothly rounded base of the Lighttower. *Half-done*, he told himself as they kept going. *The hard part's half-done. From here on it'll be easier.*

It wasn't really any easier, but it *did* turn out to be shorter. With the smooth walls of Wizardell giving way to the more natural contours of Gyran Pass, visibility around them changed dramatically, and without warning the wailing abruptly cut off as the Lighttower dropped out of sight behind a craggy hill.

Saladar stopped, his trembling knees refusing for a moment to continue. Marja gazed at him in silence, a mixture of concern and awe on her face. Giving her hand a reassuring squeeze, he got his feet moving again, and together they headed up into Gyran Pass.

They reached the path Marja had mentioned within a hundred paces, and Saladar had to admit that he probably *wouldn't* have found it on his own. From a totally ordinary cut between two boulders it stretched along an intermittent stream bed, twisting between scraggly trees and jutting layers of rock as it worked its way upward.

"We should be able to see the Lighttower from that rise ahead."

Concentrating on his climbing, Saladar jumped at the sound of Marja's voice. "You startled me," he muttered in vague embarrassment.

"Your hearing's back, then? I was starting to wonder if the spell had affected your voice, too."

She shook her head. "No. But it sounded strange when I tried talking without being able to hear—" She shivered.

"I'll have to remember that for next time." Saladar took a deep breath. "Well. I thank you for you help, Marja, but from this point on I'd better go alone."

"Why? Can't you protect me from whatever kind of beast is—?"

"It's not a beast. It's some sort of spiritual being."

She seemed to shrink slightly into her skin. "What?" she whispered. "Are you sure?"

He nodded. "It kept up that scream the whole time we were in sight of the Lighttower, without ever having to rest or even pause for breath. No physical creature can do that."

Marja licked her lips, her eyes staring past Saladar's shoulder. "But what would a spirit be doing in the Lighttower?"

"That's one of the things I'm going to have to find out," Saladar said grimly. "Maybe someone in Abron Mysti made an enemy of one of them—offended it somehow—and this is its way of taking revenge. Or maybe it was someone at the other end of Gyran Pass in Colinthe," he added as she started to object. "It may not have been your fault—shutting off the pass hurts both towns equally."

Marja shifted her gaze to his face. "Can you stop it? Destroy it, or send it back where it came from?"

He considered lying, but she deserved the whole truth. "I don't think I can destroy it. Spells of that power . . . well, if you don't do them exactly right, they can easily turn back against you."

Marja's lips pressed together into a bloodless line. "Perhaps that's what the Wizard's Curse is."

"Maybe part of it," Saladar said shortly. Reminders of dark curses weren't exactly what he needed just now. "As for sending the spirit back"—he shrugged—"that'll depend on what kind of being it is and why it's trying to close the pass. And maybe on whether I can reason or bargain with it."

Clenching her teeth, Marja straightened her shoulders. "Well, there's no point in standing here, then, is there? Let's go."

"Marja—"

"Saladar, I have to go with you." She looked up at him, her eyes pleading. "Nunisjan's dream, remember?"

He took a deep breath, exhaled it tiredly. He had no business taking her into danger like this, but he had to admit she'd earned the right to see what was trying to kill her town.

Besides which, deep down he knew he would welcome the company. The first time, he was quickly finding out, was harder on a man's courage than he'd expected it to be. "All right," he sighed at last. "Come on."

They topped the rise, and as Marja had guessed, the rounded top of the Lighttower was indeed visible through the grass and scrub. Saladar placed his heartstone between their two hands, hoping it would be able to keep both of them calm if the spirit started screaming again. Cautiously, they moved forward.

There were no windows on this side, but facing them from the rear of the Lighttower was the shaded opening of a doorway. The obvious direction for an attack to come from—though with spiritual beings that might not mean much—and Saladar kept his eyes on the black rectangle as they walked.

But the spirit didn't seem to be paying any attention to the approach behind it. No unearthly face appeared in the shadows; no ethereal form swooped down from the blue sky toward them . . . and as they continued on without even one of the well-remembered shrieks splitting the air, Saladar began to find the situation increasingly odd. And increasingly ominous.

Marja did too. "Do you think it's hiding?" she whispered nervously in Saladar's ear. "Waiting to ambush us?"

"I don't think so," he murmured back. "I'm beginning to think it's incapable of attacking anyone."

"That's good, right?"

"Maybe. Maybe not."

They reached the doorway, and there Saladar paused and took a deep breath. "Okay," he said, prying his fingers away from Marja's. "Wait here a second."

"Saladar—"

"Just for a minute," he assured her. "I've got an idea of what's going on, but I have to be sure."

Setting his teeth, he stepped under the low lintel into the Lighttower . . . to find the spirit waiting for him.

Not that it had much choice in the matter. Spread-eagled against a glinting star shape larger than a man, its red eyes turned toward Saladar from the window where its imprisoning pentagram had been propped up; it glared at him in an eloquent silence of rage.

For a moment Saladar gazed back. Then, with a grimace, he half-turned back toward the doorway. "It's all right, Marja," he called.

She came in quickly, a strangled gasp escaping her lips as she moved up behind him. "Gods above and demons below," she breathed. "What *is* that?"

"The source of your trouble. As you see, I was right about Abron Mysti or Colinthe offending someone. I was just a little off as to who the offended party was."

Marja stared at the spirit for a moment. "Whoever it was who was angry with us trapped that—whatever it is—on that pentagram?"

Saladar nodded. "I think it's called a Fury. Not a very intelligent type of spirit, from what I've heard, but relatively easy to trap. And perfectly adequate for terrifying people and beasts with."

Marja inhaled raggedly. "Why isn't is screaming at us now?"

Saladar shook his head. "I don't know. Perhaps whoever brought it in here set up a geas as part of the spell so that it would only scream at people coming through the pass. Or maybe the fact that we got past it means it won't try to terrify us anymore. Either way, be grateful for small favors."

Marja looked over her shoulder, frowning. "How *did* they get it in here? The doorway—look, it's not nearly big enough."

"I know. They must have assembled the pentagram in here and then said the trapping spell." He studied the pentagram. "That coating looks like tight windings of silver threads, probably wrapped around fresh oak branches."

"Silver?"

"Heartstone magic can't touch silver directly," he explained. "Whoever set this up certainly didn't believe in making things easy."

She looked at the Fury. "Is there anything you can do?"

"Oh, certainly." Saladar hesitated. "Basically, all I need to do to release the Fury is to break the pentagram."

"So what's the problem?"

"The problem is that a released spirit doesn't go back immediately," he said heavily. "It'll stay here for several seconds . . . and it'll use those seconds trying its best to kill us."

"It'll *what*? But we're trying to *help* it."

"Doesn't matter. As I said, Furies aren't very intelligent. They're driven by rage and hatred, and they don't much care who or what they attack."

Marja looked back at the doorway again. "Could we move it safely? I mean, just away from the windows, where it can't see the pass?"

"Won't do any good," Saladar shook his head. "Spirits don't see things the same way we do. If it was ordered to scream at passersby, it'll do that whether it's by the windows or not."

Marja hissed between her teeth. "So we can't leave the Fury here, and we can't release it. What *can* we do?"

"Move it outside, of course, where we've got more room. And for that"—he took a deep breath—"we're going to have to widen the doorway."

She stared at him. "How? The Lighttower is part of Wizardell, and I already told you how strong the walls are."

He nodded. "I remember. It just means I'll have to try to break that part of the spell."

"Wait a minute. You said that without the spell-strengthening the walls would collapse."

"Yes." Saladar pursed his lips. "But it should be possible to break the spell just around the doorway without harming the rest of Wizardell."

"Can *you* do it?"

"I think so, yes."

"You *think* so?" Her tongue darted across her lips. "That's not very reassuring. Maybe you ought to wait until you know for sure."

Saladar shook his head. "There's no point in waiting, Marja. I know as much as any other wizard—"

"Except you've never used that knowledge—"

"And anyway, now that we're here we might as well try," he cut her off sharply.

She stared at him, eyes hot with anger. "And besides which, if we take too much time thinking about it, some other wizard may come by and steal your thunder?"

"That's not fair."

"Isn't it?" she retorted. "Then why are you so eager to risk my town? Because you *are* risking it, you know. If Wizardell collapses, the trade routes will start up somewhere else and Abron Mysti will die."

"Abron Mysti is already dead!"

For a long moment they just glared at each other. Saladar squeezed his heartstone, willing it to calm him. Eventually, it did. "Marja, look," he sighed. "It's been two months since the Fury was trapped here. The trade routes are already changing—you know that. If you don't get them back this year, before winter closes the mountains, they'll never return. There isn't any choice; we *have* to take the risk."

"'We'?" she asked, voice dripping with irony.

"Yes, we," he told her. "Because I'll be in here when I speak the spell. If Wizardell collapses, I'll go with it."

He made her wait outside, as far away as she was willing to go, while he spoke the necessary spells.

It was straightforward enough, but that didn't make it any less nerve-racking. First he traced a large circle of shimmering red fire around the doorway with the tip of his heartstone. A long and convoluted spell, and the thin red line changed to blue and then to green and then to white. A second, equally long spell, and the section of rock within the circle began to look faintly hazy.

Saladar licked his lips, watching tensely for just the right moment. The haze began to coalesce, forming itself into a thousand thin lines across the stone. Almost . . . The lines drew in more and more of the haze, grew brighter and clearer—

Now! He shouted the last part of the spell, squeezing the heartstone between palm and thumb and pointing it at the circle. The heartstone flared in response—

And with a tremendous roar, the rock within the circle shattered.

Saladar staggered back, head throbbing with the echo of that thunderclap. Dimly, he was aware of the sound of running footsteps—

"Saladar!" Marja called, appearing in the freshly enlarged doorway and stepping hurriedly across the rubble with little heed for the treacherous footing.

"I'm all right," Saladar assured her. "Just . . . a little dizzy."

She caught his arms, an anxious expression on her face. "The Wizard's Curse?" she whispered.

"Will you forget the Wizard's Curse?" he growled. "Come on—I'll need your help to get that pentagram out of here."

She looked over at the Fury. "Will it . . . ?"

"It can't do anything to us while it's trapped there," he assured her. A strange tiredness seemed to be creeping over him. *The Wizard's Curse?* Angrily, he shook away the thought.

He looked over to find Marja's eyes on him. "But you said it would try to kill us when the pentagram was broken?" she asked carefully.

He nodded. "Yes, but don't worry. If I do this properly, neither of us will be anywhere near the Fury when it gets loose." Looking at the spirit, he braced himself. "Come on."

It was a long climb to the top of Mount Mysti, a climb made longer still by the need to drag his heartstone along the ground the entire distance. But at last they made it. Turning around, bracing himself against the icy wind, Saladar looked down.

They were indeed high up. Below, the top of the Lighttower was a foreshortened knob at the edge of Wizardell's straight-walled gap. To the Lighttower's right, at the very base of the mountain, was a toy star with a pebble beneath each corner, the pebbles being the boulders he and Marja had moved under each of the pentagram's five points. Even from this distance the setup looked strange, reminding Saladar of an oddly shaped table . . . or an oddly shaped altar.

"Is this going to be far enough away?" Marja asked into his thoughts, her teeth chattering in the cold.

"I hope so," Saladar said, breathing deeply of air that seemed somehow too thin. "There doesn't seem to be anywhere higher to go."

"Gods above and demons below," she muttered. "I wish this was over."

"It will be soon." Turning away from the edge of the mountain, Saladar studied the ground around them. A large jagged outcropping caught his eye, and he stepped over to it. Tapping it with his heartstone, he spoke a spell.

Imperceptibly at first, then with ever increasing amplitude, the boulder began to rock in place. Back and forth, back and forth, until, all at once, it broke free, thudding to the ground at Saladar's feet. Walking around to its far side, Saladar held his heartstone to it and pushed, rolling it over to the edge where Marja waited. "Right there," she told him, unfolding one of her arms and pointing to the ground.

"I see it," Saladar nodded, his eyes picking out the end of the thin red line his heartstone had left glowing on the ground. Shifting direction slightly, he maneuvered the boulder onto the line.

And all was ready. "Here we go," he muttered to Marja. Gripping the heartstone, he put his hand against the boulder and threw a last look below. Taking a deep breath, he called out one final spell and pushed the stone over the edge.

It rolled slowly at first . . . then faster, and faster, picking up speed as it tumbled down the mountainside. Once, it hit a hidden bump and bounced high in the air, eliciting a gasp from Marja. But it didn't matter; the boulder's path, traced so laboriously by the heartstone, wouldn't let it escape that easily. The stone hit the ground again, caught back onto the red line and continued down. Saladar squeezed the heartstone and held his breath—

And with a final bounce, the boulder smashed directly into the center of the pentagram.

The silver coating could protect the star from the power of a heartstone; against a falling rock, it was of no value whatsoever. Even from so far above, Saladar could imagine he heard the wrenching smash of wood and metal—

And with a shriek that seemed to freeze his blood in his veins the Fury rose from the wreckage.

Beside him, Marja screamed; but it was already all over. Even as the pale form arrowed upward toward them, red eyes flaming with mindless hatred, it was beginning to fade, its shriek taking on a strange, faraway quality. By the time it reached the mountaintop, it was nothing but pale red eyes and a blast of bitterly cold wind.

For a long moment they just stood there, listening to the shriek fade into the breeze. Then, slowly, as if in a dream, Marja turned to look at him. "You did it," she breathed. "You really did it."

"*We* did it," he corrected her. "I couldn't have done it without your help."

Carefully, almost shyly, Marja took his hand in hers. "Saladar—" She laughed suddenly, a short barking sound; and as he gazed at her, he saw two tears trickle down her cheeks. "Do you know that, for the first time since Nunisjan left . . . I think I understand why?"

Saladar put his arm around her shoulders, sympathetic tears blurring his own vision. Her eyes—there was a flicker of life again in those eyes, a flicker he'd not seen there before now. After three long years, he could sense that the healing of her soul had finally begun . . . and for that alone he would gladly have risked—

"What is it?" Marja asked, sensing the sudden tightness in his body.

"Nothing," he said, as casually as possible. "But we probably ought to get back."

Her face was suddenly stricken. "Gods and demons!" she whispered. "You mean . . . before . . . ?"

He nodded, a tight knot settling into his stomach. Now came the waiting . . . the waiting for the unknown. "I'd like to be back in Abron Mysti before the Wizard's Curse takes effect."

The night was full of strange dreams, but it was the faint noises outside that woke him the next morning. He was in bed, in Marja's cottage, and for a moment he just lay there, feeling oddly disoriented. Outside, the faint noises continued; easing out of bed, he went to the window to look.

Down in the center of town, the citizens of Abron Mysti had taken to the streets in obvious celebration. Beyond them, between the foothills leading into the mountains, he could see a line of travelers and their beasts heading into Wizardell.

Into Wizardell . . . and into Gyran Pass beyond.

For a long minute, he stood there, the bitterly familiar taste of defeat on his tongue. Then, closing his eyes against the sight, he turned back and began to dress.

Marja was still asleep by the time he was ready to go. For a moment he paused at the door to her room, gazing down at her face as shame warred against the requirements of courtesy. The shame won. Quietly, he turned away, crossing to the outer door and slipping outside. He had enough contempt for himself; he didn't need to feel hers as well.

The bridge was still in place and still untended, though the bridge keeper would undoubtedly be returning to his post very soon now. Crossing the river, Saladar headed away from the mountains. There was no need to look back, but as he topped the first rise in the road, he couldn't help doing so anyway.

Beyond the celebration, the line of travelers into Wizardell could still be seen, and Saladar felt his lip twist with impotent fury. So Gyran Pass had been reopened, and Abron Mysti saved . . . and once again, history had repeated itself. While he'd hesitated—while he'd wasted time with a woman not his own—someone else had beaten him to the goal.

Once again, he'd missed out on a chance to use his wizard's Power.

Tears welled up in his eyes, but even as he turned away from Abron Mysti, he knew it wasn't over yet. Not until he was dead would it be over. He'd spent years of his life becoming a wizard . . . and somehow, somewhere, he would find a way to use his hard-won Power to serve.

And when he did, he would gladly pay the price the Wizard's Curse demanded of him . . . because no matter what horror that price turned out to be, he would go to face it having finally achieved his life's goal.

And neither sickness nor frailty nor even death itself would ever be able to take that away from him.

HITMEN—SEE MURDERERS

●

It had been a long, slow, frustrating day, full of cranky machines, crankier creditors, and not nearly enough customers. In other words, a depressingly typical day. But even as Radley Grussing slogged up the last flight of stairs to his apartment he found himself whistling a little tune to himself. From the moment he'd passed the first landing—had looked down the first-floor hallway and seen the yellow plastic bag leaning up against each door—he'd known there was hope. Hope for his struggling little print shop; hope for his life, his future, and—with any luck at all—for his chances with Alison. Hope in double-ream lots, wrapped up in a fat yellow bag and delivered to his door.

The new phone books were out.

"Let your fingers do the walking through the Yellow Pages." He sang the old Bell Telephone jingle to himself as he scooped up the bag propped up against his own door and worked the key into the lock. Or, rather, that was what he *tried* to sing. After four flights of stairs, it came out more like, "Let your . . . fingers do the . . . walking through . . . the Yellow . . . Pages."

From off to the side came the sound of a door closing, and with a flush of embarrassment Radley realized that whoever it was had probably overheard his little song. "Shoot," he muttered to himself, his face feeling warm. Though maybe the heat was just from the exertion of climbing four flights of stairs. Alison had been bugging him lately about getting more exercise; maybe she was right.

He got the door open, and for a moment stood on the threshold carefully surveying his apartment. TV and VCR sitting on their wood-grain stand right where they were supposed to be. Check. The doors to kitchen and bedroom standing half-open at exactly the angles he'd put them before he'd left for work that morning. Check.

Through his panting Radley heaved a cautious sigh of relief. The existence of the TV showed no burglars had come and gone; the carefully positioned doors showed no one had come and was still there.

At least, no one *probably* was still there. . . .

As quietly as he could, he stepped into the apartment and closed the door, turning the doorknob lock but leaving the three deadbolts open in case he had to make a quick run for it. On a table beside the door stood an empty pewter vase. He picked it up by its slender neck, left the yellow plastic bag on the floor by the table and tiptoed to the bedroom door. Steeling himself, panting as quietly as was humanly possible, he nudged the door open and peered in. No one. Still on tiptoe, he repeated the check with the kitchen, with the same result.

He gave another sigh of relief. Alison thought he was a little on the paranoid side, and wasn't particularly hesitant about saying so. But he read the papers and he watched the news, and he knew that the quiet evil of the city was nothing to be ignored or scoffed at.

But once more, he'd braved the evil—braved it, and won, and had made it back to his own room and safety. Heading back to the door, he locked the deadbolts, returned the vase to its place on the table, and retrieved the yellow bag.

It was only as he was walking to the kitchen with it, his mind now freed from the preoccupations of survival in a hostile world, that his brain finally registered what his fingers had been trying to tell him all along.

The yellow bag was not, in fact, made of plastic.

"Huh," he said aloud, raising it up in front of his eyes for a closer look. It *looked* like plastic, certainly, like the same plastic they'd been delivering phone books in for he couldn't remember how many years. But the feel of the thing was totally wrong for plastic.

In fact, it was totally wrong for *any*thing.

"Well, that's funny," he said, continuing on into the kitchen. Laying the bag on the table, he pulled up one of the four more-or-less-matching chairs and sat down.

For a minute he just looked at the thing, rubbing his fingers slowly across its surface and digging back into his memory for how these bags had felt in the past. He couldn't remember, exactly; but it was for sure they hadn't felt like *this*. This wasn't like any plastic he'd ever felt before. Or like any cloth, or like any paper.

"It's something new, then," he told himself. "Maybe one of those new plastics they're making out of corn oil or something."

The words weren't much comfort. In his mind's eye, he saw the thriller that had been on cable last week, the one where the spy had been blown to bits by a shopping bag made out of plastic explosive. . . .

He gritted his teeth. "That's stupid," he said firmly. "Who in the world would go to that kind of trouble to kill *me*? Period; end of discussion," he added to forestall an argument. Alison had more or less accepted his habit of talking to himself, especially when he hadn't seen her for a couple of days. But even she drew the line at arguing aloud with himself. "End of discussion," he repeated. "So. Let's quit this nonsense and check out the ad."

He took a deep breath, exhaled it explosively like a shotputter about to go into his little loop-de-spin. Taking another deep breath, he reached into the bag and, carefully, pulled the phone book out.

Nothing happened.

"There—you see?" he chided himself, pushing the bag across the table and pulling the directory in front of him. "Alison's right; there's paranoia, and then there's para-*noi*-a. Gotta stop watching those late cable shows. Now, let's see here . . ."

He checked his white-pages listings first, both his apartment's and the print shop's. Both were correct. "Great," he muttered. "And now"— he hummed himself a little trumpet flourish as he turned to the Yellow Pages—"the pièce de résistance. Let your fingers do the walking through the Yellow Pages, dum dum de dum . . ." He reached the L's, turned past to the P's . . .

And there it was. Blazing out at him, in full three-color glory, the display ad for Grussing A-One-Excellent Printing And Copying.

"Now *that*," he told himself proudly, "is an *ad*. You just wait, Radley old boy—an ad like that'll get you more business than you know what to do with. You'll see—there's nowhere to go but *up* from now on."

He leafed through the pages, studying all the other print-shop ads and trying hard not to notice that six of his competitors had three-color displays fully as impressive as his own. That didn't matter. His ad—and the business it was going to bring in—would lift him up out of the hungry pack, bring him to the notice of important people with important printing needs. "You'll see," he told himself confidently. The *Printers* heading gave way to *Printers—Business Forms,* and then to *Printing Equipment* and *Printing Supplies.* "Huh; Steven's has moved," he noted with some surprise. He hadn't bought anything from Steven's for over a year—probably about time he checked out their prices again. Idly, he turned another page—

And stopped. Right after the short listing of *Prosthetic Devices* was a heading he'd never seen before.

Prostitutes.

"Well, I'll be D-double-darned," he muttered in amazement. "I didn't know they could advertise."

He let his eyes drift down the listings, turned the page. There were a *lot* of names there—almost as many, he thought, as the attorney list-ings at the other end of the Yellow Pages, except that unlike the lawyers, the prostitutes had no display ads. "Wonder when the phone company decided to let this go in." He shook his head. "Hoo, boy—the egg's gonna hit the fan for sure when the Baptists see *this.*"

He scanned down the listing. Names—both women's and a few men's—addresses, phone numbers—it was all there. Everything any-one so inclined would need to get themselves some late-night com-panionship.

He frowned. Addresses. Not just post office boxes. Real street addresses.

Home addresses.

"Wait just a minute, here," he muttered. "Just a D-double-darned minute." Nevada, he'd heard once, had legal prostitution; but *here*—"This is nuts," he decided. "The cops could just go right there and arrest them. Couldn't they? I mean, even those escort and massage places usu-ally just have phone numbers. Don't they?"

With the phone book sitting right in front of him, there was an obvious way to answer that question. Sticking a corner of the yellow bag in to mark his place, he turned backwards toward the E's. *Excavating Contractors, Elevators*—oops; too far—

He froze, finger and thumb suddenly stiff where they gripped a cor-ner of the page. A couple of headings down from *Elevators* was another list of names, shorter than the prostitutes listing but likewise distin-guished by the absence of display ads. And the heading here . . .

Embezzlers.

His lips, he suddenly noticed, were dry. He licked them, without noticeable effect. "This," he said, his words sounding eerie in his ears, "is nuts. Embezzlers don't advertise. I mean, come *on* now."

He willed the listing to vanish, to change to something more reasonable, like *Embalmers*. But that heading was there, too . . . and the *Embezzlers* heading didn't go away.

He took a deep breath and, resolutely, turned the page. "I've been working too hard," he informed himself loudly. "Way too hard. Now. Let's see, where was I going . . . right—escort services."

He found the heading and its page after page of garish and seductive display ads. Sure enough, none of them listed any addresses. Just for completeness, he flipped back to the M's, checking out the massage places. Some had addresses; others—the ones advertising out-calls only—had just phone numbers.

"Makes sense," he decided. "Otherwise the cops and self-appointed guardians of public morals could just sit there and scare all their business away. So what gives with *this*?" He started to turn back to the prostitute listing, his fingers losing their grip on the slippery pages and dropping the book open at the end of the M's—

And again he froze. There was another listing of names and addresses there, just in front of *Museums*. Shorter than either the prostitute or embezzler lists; but the heading more than made up for it.

Murderers.

He squeezed his eyes shut, shook his head. "This is crazy," he breathed. "I mean, *really crazy*." Carefully, he opened his eyes again. The *Murderers* listing was still there. Almost unwillingly, he reached out a finger and rubbed it across the ink. It didn't rub off, like cheap ink would, or fade away, like a hallucination ought to.

It was real.

He was still staring at the book, the sea of yellow dazzling his eyes, when the knock came at his front door.

He fairly jumped out of the chair, jamming his thigh against the underside of the table as he did so. "It's the FBI," he gasped under his breath. It was their book—their book of the city's criminals. It had been delivered here by mistake, and they were here to get it back.

Or else it was the *mob's* book—

"Radley?" A familiar voice came through the steel-cored wood panel. "You home?"

He felt a little surge of relief, knees going a little shaky. "There's paranoia," he chided himself, "and then there's para-*noi*-a." He raised his voice. "Coming, Alison," he called.

"Hi," she said with a smile as he opened the door, her face just visible over the large white bag in her arms. "Got the table all set?"

"Oh—right," he said, taking the bag from her. The warm scent of fried chicken rose from it; belatedly, he remembered he was supposed to have made a salad, too. "Uh—no, not yet. Hey, look, come in here—you've got to *see* this."

He led her to the kitchen, dropping the bag on the counter beside the sink and sitting her down in front of the phone book. The yellow bag still marked the page with the *Prostitutes* heading; turning there, he pointed. "Do you see what I see?" he asked, his mouth going dry. If she *didn't* see anything, it had suddenly occurred to him, it would mean his brain was in serious trouble. . . .

"Huh," she said. "Well, *that's* new. I thought prostitution was still illegal."

"Far as I know, it still is," he agreed, feeling another little surge of relief. So he wasn't going nuts. Or at least he wasn't going nuts alone. "Hang on, though—it gets worse."

She sat there silently as he flipped back to the *Embezzlers* section, and then forward again to point out the *Murderers* heading. "I don't know what else is here," he told her. "This is as far as I got."

She looked up, an odd expression on her face. "You *do* realize, I hope, that this is nothing but an overly elaborate practical joke. This stuff can't really be in a real phone book."

"Well . . . sure," he floundered. "I mean, I know that the phone company wouldn't—"

She was still giving him that look. "Radley," she said warningly. "Come on, now, let's not slide off reality into the cable end of the channel selector. No one makes lists of prostitutes and embezzlers and murderers. And even if someone did, they *certainly* wouldn't try to hide them inside a city directory."

"Yes, I know, Alison. But—well, look here." He pulled the yellow bag over and slid it into her hand. "Feel it. Does it feel like plastic to you? Or like anything else you've ever touched?"

Alison shrugged. "They make thousands of different kinds of plastics these days—"

"All right then, look here." He cut her off, lifting up the end of the phone book. "Here—at the binding. I'm a printer—I *know* how binding is done. These pages haven't just been slipped in somehow—they were bound in at the same time as all the others. How would someone have done *that*?"

"It's a joke, Radley," Alison insisted. "It has to be. All the phone books can't have— Well, look, it's easy enough to check. Let me go downstairs and get mine while you get the salad going."

Her apartment was just two floors down, and he'd barely gotten the vegetables out of the fridge and lined them up on the counter by the time she'd returned. "Okay, here we go," she said, sitting down at the table again and opening her copy of the phone book. "Prostitutes . . . nope, not here. Embezzlers . . . nope. Murderers . . . still nope." She offered it to him.

He took it and gave it a quick inspection of his own. She was right; none of the strange headings seemed to be there. "But how could anyone have gotten the extra pages bound in?" he demanded putting it down and gesturing to his copy. "I mean, all you have to do is just look at the binding."

"I know." Alison shook her head, running a finger thoughtfully across the lower edge of the binding. "Well . . . I *said* it was overly elaborate. Maybe someone who knows you works where they print these things, and he got hold of the orig—oh, my *God*!"

Radley jumped a foot backwards, about half the distance Alison and her chair traveled. "What?" he snapped, eyes darting all around.

She was panting, her breath coming in short, hyperventilating gasps. "The . . . the page. The listing . . ."

Radley dropped his eyes to the phone book. Nothing looked any different. "What? What'd you see?"

"The murderer listing," she whispered. "I was looking at it and . . . and it got longer."

He stared at the page, a cold hand working its way down his windpipe. "What do you mean, it got longer?" he asked carefully. "You mean like someone . . . just got added to the list?"

Allison didn't answer. Radley broke his gaze away from the page and looked at her. Her face was white, her breath coming slower but starting to shake now, her eyes wide on the book. "Alison?" he asked. "You okay?"

"It's from the devil," she hissed. Her right hand, gripping the table white-knuckled, suddenly let go its grip, darting up to trace a quick cross across her chest. "You've got to destroy it, Radley," she said. Abruptly, she looked up at him. "Right now. You've got to—" she twisted her head, looking all around the room—"you've got to burn it," she said, jabbing a finger toward the tiny fireplace in the living room. "Right now; right there in the fireplace." She turned back to the phone book, and with just a slight hesitation scooped it up. "Come on—"

"Wait a minute, Alison, wait a minute," Radley said, grabbing her hands and forcing them and the phone book back down onto the table. "Let's not do anything rash, huh? I mean—"

"Anything *rash*? This thing is a tool of the *devil*."

"That's what I mean," he said. "Going off half-cocked. Who says this is from the devil? Who says—"

"Who says it's from the *devil*?" She stared at him, wide-eyed. "Radley, just where do you think this thing came from, the phone company?"

"So who says it didn't come from the other direction?" Radley countered. "Maybe it was given to me by an angel—ever think of *that*?"

"Oh, sure," Alison snorted. "Right. An angel left you this—this—voyeur's delight."

Radley frowned at her. "What in the world are you talking about? These people are *criminals,* Alison. They've given up their right of privacy."

"Since when?" she shot back. "No one gives up any of their rights until they're convicted."

"But—" he floundered.

"And anyway," she added, "who says any of these people really *are* murderers?"

Radley looked down at the book. "But if they're not, why are they listed here?"

"Will you listen to yourself?" Alison demanded. "Five minutes ago you were wondering how this thing could exist; now you're treating what it says like it was gospel. You have no proof that any of these people have ever committed *any* crime, let alone killed anyone. For all you know, this whole thing could be nothing more than some devil's scheme to make you even more paranoid than you are already."

"I am *not* paranoid," Radley growled. "This city's dangerous—any big city is. That's not paranoia, it's just plain, simple truth." He pointed at the book. "All this does is confirm what the TV and papers already say."

For a long moment Alison just stared at him, her expression a mixture of anger and fear. "All right, Radley," she said at last. "I'll meet you halfway. Let's put it to the test. If there really was a murder tonight at"—she looked up at the kitchen wall clock—"about six-twenty, then it ought to be on the eleven o'clock news. Right?"

Radley considered. "Well . . . sometimes murders don't get noticed for a while. But, yeah, probably it'll be on tonight."

"All right." Alison took a deep breath. "If there *was* a murder, I'll concede that maybe there's something to all of this." She locked eyes with him. "But if there *wasn't* any murder . . . will you agree to burn the book?"

Radley swallowed. The possibilities were only just starting to occur to him, but already he'd seen enough to recognize the potential of this thing. The potential for criminal justice, for public service—

"Radley?" Alison prompted.

He looked at her, gritted his teeth. "We'll check the news," he told her. "But if the murder isn't there, we're not going to burn anything until tomorrow night, after we have a chance to check the papers."

Alison hesitated, then nodded. Reluctantly, Radley thought. "All right." Standing up, she picked up the book, closed it with her thumb marking the place. "You finish the salad. I'll be back in a couple of minutes."

"Where are you going?" Radley frowned, his eyes on the book as she tucked it under her arm.

"Down to the grocery on the corner—they've got a copy machine over by the ice chest."

"What do you need to copy it for?" Radley asked. "If the police release a suspect's name, we can just look it up—"

"We already know the book can change."

"Oh . . . Right."

He stood there, irresolute, as she headed for the door. Then, abruptly, the paralysis vanished, and in five quick strides he caught up with her. "I'll come with you," he said, gently but firmly taking the book from her hands. "The salad can wait."

It took several minutes, and a lot of quarters, for them to find out that the book wouldn't copy.

Not on any light/dark setting. Not on any reduction or enlargement setting. Not the white pages, not the Community Service pages, not the Yellow Pages, not the covers.

Not at all.

They returned to the apartment. The chicken was by now stone-cold, so while Radley threw together a passable salad, Alison ran the chicken, mashed potatoes, and gravy through the microwave. By unspoken but mutual consent they didn't mention the book during dinner.

Nor did they talk about it afterwards as they cleaned up the dishes and played a few hands of gin rummy. At eight, when prime time rolled around, they sat together on Radley's old couch and watched TV.

Radley wouldn't remember afterwards much about what they'd watched. Part of him waited eagerly for the show to be broken into by the announcement of what he was beginning to regard as "his" murder. The rest of him was preoccupied with Alison, and the abnormal way she sat beside him the whole time. Not snuggled up against him like she usually was when they watched TV, but sitting straight and stiff and not quite touching him.

Maybe, he thought, she was waiting for the show to be broken into, too.

But it wasn't, and the 'tween-show local newsbreak didn't mention any murders, and by the time the eleven o'clock news came on Radley had almost begun to give up.

The lead story was about an international plane crash. The second story was his murder.

"Authorities are looking for this man for questioning in connection with the crime," the well-scrubbed newswoman with the intense eyes said as the film of the murder scene was replaced by a mug shot of a thin, mean-looking man. "Marvin Lake worked at the same firm with the victim before he was fired last week, and had threatened Mr. Cordler several times in the past few months. Police are asking anyone with information about his whereabouts to contact them."

The picture shifted again, and her co-anchor took over with a story about a looming transit strike. Bracing himself, Radley turned to Alison.

To find her already gazing at him, her eyes looking haunted. "I suppose," he said, "we'd better go check the book."

She didn't reply. Getting up, Radley went into the kitchen and returned with the phone book. He had marked the *Murderers* listing with the yellow non-plastic bag. . . . "He's here," Radley said, his voice sounding distant in his ears. "Marvin Lake." He leaned over to offer Alison a look.

She shrank back from the book. "I don't want to see it," she said, her voice as tight as her face.

Radley sighed, eyes searching out the entry again. Address, phone number . . .

"Wait a minute," he muttered to himself, flipping back to the white pages. L, La, Lak . . . there it was: Marvin Lake. Address . . . "It's not the same address," he said, feeling an odd excitement seeping through the sense of unreality. "Not even close."

"So?" Alison said.

"Well, don't you see?" he asked, looking up at her. "The white pages must be his home address; *this* one"—he jabbed at the Yellow Pages listing—"must be where he is right now."

Alison looked at him. "Radley . . . if you're thinking what I think you're thinking . . . please don't."

"Why not?" he demanded. "The guy's a murderer."

"That hasn't been proved yet."

"The police think he's guilty."

"That's not what the report said," she insisted. "All they said was that they wanted to question him."

"Then why is he *here*?" Radley held out the open phone book.

"Maybe because you *want* him to be there," Allison shot back. "You ever think of *that*? Maybe that thing is just somehow creating the listings you want to see there."

Radley glared at her. "Well, there's one way to find out, isn't there?"

"Radley—"

Turning his back on her, he stepped back into the kitchen, turning to the front of the phone book. The police non-emergency number . . . there it was. Picking up the phone, he punched in the digits.

The voice answered on the seventh ring. "Police."

"Ah—yes, I just heard the news about the Cordler murder," Radley said, feeling suddenly tongue-tied. "I think I may have an idea where Marvin Lake is."

"One moment."

The phone went dead, and Radley took a deep breath. Several deep breaths, in fact, before the phone clicked again. "This is Detective Abrams," a new voice said. "Can I help you?"

"Ah—yes, sir. I think I know where Marvin Lake is."

"And that is . . . ?"

"Uh—" Radley flipped back to where his thumb marked the place. A sudden fear twisted his stomach, that the whole *Murderers* listing might have simply vanished, leaving him looking like a fool.

But it hadn't. "Forty-seven thirty West Fifty-second," he said, reading off the address.

"Uh-huh," Abrams grunted. "Would you mind telling me your name?"

"Ah—I'd rather not. I don't really want any of the spotlight."

"Yeah," Abrams said. "Did you actually see Lake at this address?"

This was starting to get awkward. "No, I didn't," Radley said, searching desperately for something that would sound convincing. "But I heard it from a—well, a pretty reliable source," he ended lamely.

"Yeah," Abrams said again. He didn't sound especially convinced. "Thanks for the information."

"You're—" The phone clicked again. "Welcome," Radley finished with a sigh. Hanging up, he closed the phone book onto his thumb again and turned back to face Alison.

She was still sitting on the couch, staring at him over the back. "Well?"

He shrugged. "I don't know. Maybe they won't bother to check it out."

She stared into his face a moment longer. Then, dropping her gaze, she got to her feet. "It's getting late," she said over her shoulder as she started for the door. "I'll talk to you tomorrow."

He took a step toward her. "Alison—"

"Good night, Radley," she called, undoing the locks. A minute later, she was gone.

For a long moment he just stood there, staring at the door, an unpleasant mixture of conflicting emotions swirling through his brain and stomach. "Come on, Alison," he said quietly to the empty room. "If this works, think of what it'll mean for cleaning up this city."

The empty room didn't answer. Sighing, he walked to the door and refastened the deadbolts. She was right, after all; it *was* late, and he needed to be at work by seven.

He looked down at the phone book still clutched in his hands. On the other hand, Pete would be in by seven, too, and it didn't hardly take two of them to get the place ready for business.

And he really ought to take the time to sit down with the book and find out just exactly what this miracle was that had been dropped on his doorstep.

It was nearly one-thirty before he went to bed . . . but by the time he did, he'd made lists of every murderer, arsonist, and rapist in the book.

The next time one of those listings changed, he wouldn't have to wait for the news reports to find out who was guilty.

He got to the shop just before the seven-thirty opening time, feeling groggy but strangely exhilarated.

"Morning, Mr. Grussing." Pete Barnabee nodded solemnly from up at the counter as Radley closed the back door behind him. "How you doing?"

"I'm fine, Pete," Radley told him. "Yourself?"

"Pretty tolerable, thank you."

It was the same set of greetings, with only minor variations, that they'd exchanged every morning since Radley had first hired Pete two months ago. "So. The place ready for business?" he asked the other.

"All set," Pete confirmed. "You seen the new phone book yet?"

"Yeah—mine came yesterday," Radley nodded, resisting the urge to tell Pete about the strange Yellow Pages that had come with his. "The new ad looks pretty good, doesn't it?"

"Best of the bunch," Pete said. "Oughta bring in whole stacks of new business."

"Let's hope so." Radley looked at his watch. "Well, time to let the crowds in," he said, walking around the counter and unlocking the front door. "Incidentally, you didn't happen to catch any news this morning, did you?" he added as he turned the "Closed" sign around.

"Yeah, I did," Pete answered. "They didn't mention our ad, though."

"Very funny. I was just wondering if the cops found that guy they were looking for in the Cordler murder."

"Oh, yeah, they did," Pete nodded. "Marvin Lake or something, right? Yeah, they found him holed up somewhere on West Fifty-second last night."

Radley felt a tight smile crease his cheeks. "Did they, now?" he murmured, half to himself. "Well, well, *well.*"

Pete cocked an eyebrow at him. "You know the guy?"

"Me? No. Why do you ask?"

Pete shrugged. "I dunno. You just seem . . ." He shrugged again.

Again, Radley was tempted. But he really didn't know Pete well enough to trust him with a secret like this. "I'm just happy that scum like that is off the street," he said instead. "That's all."

"Oh, he's still on the street," Pete said, squatting down to fuss with the loading tray on one of the presses. "Made bail and walked right out."

Radley made a face. That figured. The stupid leaky criminal justice system. "They'll get him again."

"Maybe. Maybe not. You don't get many volunteer stoolies after the first one bites it."

Radley stared at him, his throat tightening. "What are you talking about?"

"Oh, it's just that an hour after Lake walked out of the police station the guy who lent him that apartment turned up dead. Shot twice in the face." Pete straightened up, brushed off his hands briskly. "Ready for me to start on the Hammerstein job?"

Somehow, Radley made it through the morning. At lunchtime he rushed home.

"Detective Abrams," he told the person who answered the phone. "Tell him it's the guy who gave him Marvin Lake's address last night."

"One moment." The line went on hold.

Wedging the phone between shoulder and ear, Radley hauled the phone book onto the table and opened it to the Yellow Pages. The M's . . . there. Mo, Mu—

"This is Abrams." The other man sounded tired.

"This is Ra—the guy who told you where Marvin Lake was last night," Radley said. He had the *Murderers* listing now. Running a finger down it . . .

"Yeah, I recognize the voice," Abrams grunted. "You know where he's gone?"

Radley opened his mouth . . . and froze. The Marvin Lake listing was gone.

"You still there?" Abrams prompted.

"Uh . . . yeah. Yeah. Uh . . ." Frantically, Radley scanned the listing, wondering if he'd somehow been looking at the wrong place. But the name wasn't under the L's, or under the M's, or anywhere else.

It was just gone.

"Look, you got something to say or don't you?" Abrams growled. "If you do, spit it out. If you don't, quit wasting everyone's time and get off the phone, okay?"

"I'm sorry . . ." Radley managed, staring at the spot where the Marvin Lake listing should have been. "I thought—well, I'm sorry, that's all."

"Yeah. We're all sorry for something." Abrams sounded slightly disgusted. "Next time just write me a postcard okay?" Without waiting for an answer, he hung up.

Blindly, Radley groped for the hook and hung up the handset, his eyes still on the page. "This," he announced to himself, "is crazy. It's *crazy*. How can it be here one day and gone the—"

And right in mid-sentence, it hit him. "Oh, real smart, Radley," he muttered. "What are you using for brains, anyway, oatmeal? Of *course* Marvin Lake's not here anymore—if *he* had any brains he'll have left town hours ago. And soon as he leaves town . . ."

He sighed and closed the book, the all-too familiar tastes of embarrassment and frustration souring his mouth. "Doesn't matter," he told himself firmly. "Okay. So this one got away. Fine. But the next one won't. There's still gotta be a way to use this thing. All you have to do is find it."

He returned to the shop and got back to work.

If the new display ad had helped at all, it wasn't obvious from the business load. For Radley the day turned out to be an offset copy of the previous one, with the added secret frustration of knowing that a double murderer had slipped through his fingers.

And then he got home, to find Alison waiting for him.

"Did you see this?" she asked when they were safe behind the triple-locked door. The article the newspaper was folded to . . .

"I heard about it, yeah," he said. "Tried to call in Marvin Lake's new address to the police on my lunch hour, but the listing's gone. Best guess is he skipped town."

"So it didn't really do any good, did it?"

"It did a lot of good," he countered. "It showed that what the book says is true."

"Not really. We still don't *know* that Marvin Lake killed anybody."

"We don't? What about that guy?" He jabbed a finger at her newspaper. "If he didn't kill Cordler, why would he kill the guy who hid him from the cops?"

"We don't know he did *that,* either," she retorted. "Face it Radley—all you have there is hearsay. And not very good hearsay, either."

"It's good enough for me," he said doggedly. "Half the time people get away with crimes because the police don't know who to concentrate their investigations on. Well, this is just what we need to change that."

"And all thanks to Radley Grussing, Super Stoolie."

"Sneer all you like," Radley growled. "This is *truth,* Alison—you know it as well as I do."

"It's not truth," she snapped back. "It may be *true,* but it's not *truth.*"

"Oh, well, *that* makes sense," he said, with more sarcasm than he'd really intended. "I can hardly wait to hear what the difference is."

She sighed, all the tension seeming to drain out of her. "I don't know," she said, her voice sounding suddenly tired. "All I know is that that book is wrong. Somehow, it's *wrong.*" She took a deep breath. "This isn't good for you, Radley. Isn't good for us. People like you and me weren't meant to know things like this. Please, *please* destroy it."

He looked at her . . . and slowly it dawned on him that his whole relationship with Alison was squatting square on the line here. "Alison, I can't just throw this away," he said gently. "Can't you see what we've got here? We've got the chance to clean away some of the filth that's clogging the streets of this city."

"And to fluff up Radley Grussing's ego in the process?"

He winced. "That's not fair," he said stiffly. "I'm not trying to make a name for myself here."

"But you like the power." She stared him straight in the eye. "Admit it, Radley—you *like* knowing these people's darkest secrets."

Radley clenched his teeth. "I don't think this discussion is getting us anywhere." He turned away.

"Will you destroy the book?" she asked bluntly from behind him.

He couldn't face her. "I can't," he said over his shoulder. "I'm sorry, Alison . . . but I just *can't.*"

For a long moment she was silent. Then, without a word, she moved away from him, and he turned back around in time to see her collect her purse and jacket from the couch and head for the door. "Let me walk you downstairs," Radley called after her as she unlocked the deadbolts.

"I don't think I'll get lost," she said shortly.

"Yes, but—" He stopped.

She frowned over her shoulder at him. "But *what?*"

"I just thought that . . . I mean, there are a lot of rapists running loose in this city. . . ."

She gazed at him, something like pain or pity or fear in her eyes. "You see?" she said softly. "It's started already." Opening the door, she left.

Radley exhaled noisily between his teeth. "Nothing's started," he told the closed door. "I'm just being cautious. That's hardly a crime."

The words sounded hollow in his ears, and for a minute he just stood there, wondering if maybe she was right. "No," he told himself firmly. "I can handle this. I *can*."

Turning back to the kitchen, he pulled a frozen dinner out of the refrigerator and popped it into the microwave. Then, pulling a notebook from the phone shelf, he flipped it open and got out a pen. Time to compare the Book's listings of murderers, arsonists, and rapists against the lists he'd made last night. See who, if anyone, had sold their souls to the devil in the past fourteen hours.

According to the papers, there had been two gang killings in the city that day, both of them drive-by shootings. Both apparently by repeaters, unfortunately, because no new names had appeared in the *Murderers* listing. The *Arsonists* listing hadn't changed since last night, either.

On the *Rapists* list, though, he hit paydirt.

The phone rang six times. Then: "Hello?"

A woman's voice. Radley gripped the phone a little tighter. He'd hoped the man lived alone. "James Whittington, please," he said.

"May I ask who's calling?"

A secretary, then, not a wife? A thin straw, but Radley found himself clutching it hard. "Tell him I'd like to discuss this afternoon's activities with him," he instructed her. "He'll understand."

There was a short silence. "Just a minute." Then came the sound of a hand covering the mouthpiece, and a brief and heavily muffled conversation. A moment later, the hand was removed. Radley waited, and after nearly ten seconds a man's voice came on. "Hello?"

"Is this James Whittington?"

"Yes. Who is this?"

"Someone who knows what you did this afternoon," Radley told him. "You raped a woman."

There was just the briefest pause. "If this is supposed to be a joke, it's not especially funny."

"It's no joke," Radley said, letting his voice harden. "You know it and I know it, so let's cut the innocent act."

"Oh, the tough type, huh?" Whittington sneered. "Making anonymous calls and vague accusations—that's *real* tough. I don't suppose you've got anything more concrete. A name, for instance?"

"I don't know her name," Radley admitted, feeling sweat beading up on his forehead. This wasn't going at all the way he'd expected. "But

I'm sure the police won't have too much trouble rooting out little details like that."

"I have no idea what the hell you're talking about," Whittington growled.

"No?" Radley asked. "Then why are you still listening?"

"Why are *you* still talking?" Whittington countered. "You think you can shake me down or something?"

"I don't want any money," Radley said, feeling like a blue-ribbon idiot. Somehow, he'd thought that a flat-out accusation like this would make Whittington crumble and blurt out a confession. He should have just called the police in the first place. "I just wanted to talk to you," he added uncomfortably. "I suppose I wanted to see what kind of man would rape a woman—"

"*I didn't rape anyone.*"

"Yeah. Right. I guess there's nothing to do now but just go ahead and tell the cops what I know. Sorry to have ruined your evening." He started to hang up.

"Wait a second," Whittington's voice came faintly from the receiver.

Radley hesitated, then put the handset back to his ear. "What?"

There was a long, painful pause. "Look," the other man said at last. "I don't know what she told you, but it wasn't rape. It *wasn't*. Hell, *she* was the one who hit on *me*. What was I supposed to do, turn her down?"

Radley frowned, a sudden surge of misgiving churning through his stomach. Could the Book have been wrong? He opened his mouth—

"*Damn* you."

He jumped. It was a woman's voice—the same voice that had originally answered the phone. Listening in on an extension.

Whittington swore under his breath. "Mave, get the hell off the phone."

"No!" the woman said, her voice suddenly hard and ugly. "No. Enough is enough—damn it all, can't you even drive to the airport and back without screwing someone? Oh, God . . . *Traci*?"

"Mave, shut the hell up—"

"Your own *niece*?" the woman snarled. "God, you make me *sick*."

"I said *shut up*!" Whittington snarled back. "She hit on *me*, damn it—"

"She's *sixteen years old*!" the woman screamed. "What the hell does she know about bastards like you?"

Radley didn't wait to hear any more. Quickly, quietly, he hung up on the rage boiling out of his phone.

For a minute he just sat there at his table, his whole body shaking with reaction. Then, almost reluctantly, he reached for the Book, still open to the *Rapists* listings, and turned to the end. And sure enough, there it was:

Rapists, Statutory—See Rapists.

Slowly, he closed the Book. "It was still a crime," he reminded himself. "Even if she really *did* consent. It was still a crime."

But not nearly the crime he'd thought it was.

He took a deep breath, exhaled it slowly. The tight sensation in his chest refused to go away. A marriage obviously on the brink, one that probably would have gone over the edge eventually anyway. But if his call hadn't given it this particular push . . .

He swallowed hard, staring at the Book. The solitude of his apartment suddenly had become loneliness. "I wish Alison was here," he murmured. He reached for the phone—

And stopped. Because when she'd finished sympathizing with him, she would once again tell him to burn the Book.

"I can't do that," he told himself firmly. "She can play with words all she wants to. The stuff in the Book is *true*; and if it's true then it's *truth*. Period."

A flicker of righteousness briefly colored his thoughts. But it faded quickly, and when it was gone, the loneliness was still there.

He sat there for a long time, staring at nothing in particular. Then, with another sigh, he hitched his chair closer to the kitchen table and pulled the Book and notebook over to him. There were a lot of criminals whose names he hadn't yet copied down. With the whole evening now stretching out before him, he ought to be able to make a sizeable dent in that number before bedtime.

He arrived at the shop a few minutes before eight the next morning, his eyelids heavy with too little sleep and too many nightmares. Never before had he realized just how many types of crime there were in the world. Nor had he realized how many people were out there committing them.

Business was noticeably better than it had been the previous few weeks, but Radley hardly noticed. With the evil of the city roiling in his mind's eye like a huge black thundercloud, the petty details of print-ing letterhead paper and business cards seemed absurdly unimportant. Time and again he had to drag his thoughts away from the blackness of the thundercloud back to what he was doing—more often than not, finding a bemused-looking customer standing there peering at him.

Fortunately, most of them accepted his excuse that he hadn't been sleeping well lately. Even more fortunately, Pete knew his way around well enough to take up the slack.

Partly from guilt, partly because he wanted to give his attention over to the Book when he went home, Radley stayed for an hour after the shop closed, getting some of the next day's work set up. By the time he left, rush hour was over, leaving the streets and sidewalks about as empty as they ever got.

It was a quiet walk home. Quiet, but hardly peaceful. Perhaps it was merely the relative lack of traffic, the fact that Radley wasn't used to walking down these streets without having to change his direction every five steps to avoid another person. Or perhaps it was merely his own fatigue, magnifying the caution he'd always felt about life here.

Or perhaps Alison had been right. Perhaps it *was* the Book that was bothering him. The Book, and the page after page of *Muggers* he'd leafed through that first night.

It was an unnerving experience, and by the time he reached his building he was seriously considering whether to start carrying a gun to work with him. But as soon as he left the public sidewalk, the sense of imminent danger began to lift; and by the time he was safely behind his deadbolts he could almost laugh at how strongly a runaway imagination could make him feel.

Still, he waited until he'd finished dinner and had a beer in his hand before hauling out the Book, the newspaper, and his notebook and beginning the evening's perusal.

There had been two more murders—again, apparently by repeat-ers, since there were no new names under the appropriate listing in the Book. Ditto with rapists and armed robbers. The *Muggers* listing had increased by eleven names, but after wasting half an hour com-paring lists it finally dawned on him that isolating the new names wouldn't do anything to let him link a particular person to a par-ticular crime. The *Burglars* listing, increased by three, presented the same problem.

"Growing like a weed," he muttered to himself, flipping back and forth through the Book. "Just like a weed. How in blazes are we ever going to stop it?"

It was nearly nine o'clock when he finally went back to the *Embezzlers* listing . . . and found what he was looking for.

A single new name.

And what was more, a name Radley couldn't find mentioned anywhere in the newspaper. Which made sense; a crime like embezzlement could go unnoticed for weeks or even months.

Radley had tried informing on a murderer, and had wound up making matters worse. He'd tried wangling information out of a rapist, with similar results.

Perhaps he could become a conscience.

The phone was picked up on the third ring. "Hello?" a cool, MBA-type voice answered.

"Harry Farandell, please," Radley said.

"Speaking," the other man acknowledged. "Who's this?"

"Someone who wants to help you get off the path you're on before it's too late," Radley told him. "You see, I know that you embezzled some money today."

There was a long silence. "I don't know what you're talking about," Farandell said at last.

Almost the same words, Radley remembered, that James Whittington had used in denying his rape. "I'm not a policeman, Mr. Farandell," Radley told him. "I'm not with your company, either. I could call both of them, of course, but I'd really rather not."

"Oh, I'm sure," Farandell responded bitterly. "And how much, may I ask, is all this altruism going to cost me?"

"Nothing at all," Radley assured him. "I don't want any of the money you stole. I want you to put it back."

"What?"

"You heard me. Chances are no one knows yet what you've done. You replace the money now and no one ever will."

Another long silence. "I can't," Farandell said at last.

"Why not? You already spent it or something?"

"You don't understand," Farandell sighed.

"Look, do you still have the money, or don't you?" Radley asked.

"Yes. Yes, I've still got it. But—look, we can work something out. I'll make a deal with you; any deal you want."

"No deals, Mr. Farandell," Radley said firmly. "I'm trying to stop crime, not add to it. Return the money, or else I go to the police. You've got forty-eight hours to decide which it'll be."

He hung up. For a moment he wondered if he should have given Farandell such a lenient deadline. If the guy skipped town . . . but no. It wasn't like he was facing a murder charge or something equally serious. And anyway, it could easily take a day or two for him to slip the money back without anyone noticing.

And when he had done so, it would be as if the crime had never happened.

"You see?" Radley told himself as he turned to a fresh page in the notebook. "There *is* a way to use this. Tool of the devil, my foot."

The warm feeling lasted the rest of the evening, even through the writer's cramp he got from tallying yet more names in his notebook. It lasted, in fact, until the next morning.

When the TV news announced that financier Harry Farandell had committed suicide.

Business was even better that day than it had been the day before. But again Radley hardly noticed. He worked mechanically, letting Pete take most of the load, coming out of his own dark thoughts only to listen to the periodic updates on the Farandell suicide that the radio newscasts sprinkled through the day. By late afternoon it was apparent that Farandell's financial empire, far from being in serious trouble, had merely had a short-term cash-flow problem. In such cases, the commentators said, the standard practice was to take funds from a healthy institution to prop up the ailing one. Such transfers, though decidedly illegal, were seldom caught by the regulators, and the commentators couldn't understand why Farandell hadn't simply done that instead.

Twice during the long day Radley almost picked up the phone to call Alison. But both times he put the handset down undialed. He knew, after all, what she would say.

He made sure to leave on time that evening, to get home during rush hour when there were lots of people on the streets. All the way up the stairs he swore he would leave the Book where it was for the rest of the night, and for the first hour he held firmly to that resolution. But with dinner eaten, the dishes washed, and the newspaper read, the evening seemed to stretch out endlessly before him.

Besides, there had been another murder in the city. Taking a quick look at his list wouldn't hurt.

There were no new names on the listing, which meant either that the murderer was again a repeater or else that he'd already left town. The paper had also reported a mysterious fire over on the east side that the police suspected was arson; but the *Arsonists* listing was also no longer than it had been the night before.

"You ought to close it now," he told himself. But even as he agreed that he ought to, he found himself leafing through the pages. All the various crimes; all the ways people had found throughout the ages of inflicting pain and suffering on each other. He'd spent he didn't know how many hours looking through the Book and writing down names, and yet he could see that he'd hardly scratched the surface. The city was dying, being eaten away from beneath by its own inhabitants.

He'd reached the T's now, and the eight pages under the *Thieves* heading. Compared to some of the others in the Book it was a fairly minor crime, and he'd never gotten around to making a list of the names there. "And even if I did," he reminded himself, "it wouldn't do any good. I bet we get twenty new thieves every day around here." He started to turn the page, eyes glancing idly across the listings—

And stopped. There, at the top of the second column, was a very familiar name. A familiar name, with a familiar address and phone number accompanying it.

Pete Barnabee.

Radley stared at it, heart thudding in his chest. No. No, it couldn't be. Not Pete. Not the man—

Whom he'd hired only a couple of months ago. Without really knowing all that much about him . . .

"No wonder we've been losing money," he murmured to himself. Abruptly, he got to his feet. "Wait a minute," he cautioned himself even as he grabbed for his coat. "Don't jump to any conclusions here, all right? Maybe he stole something from someone else, a long time ago."

"Fine," he answered tartly, unlocking the deadbolts with quick flicks of his wrist. "Maybe he did. There's still only one way to find out for sure."

There were more people on the streets now than there had been on his walk through the dinnertime calm the night before: people coming home from early-evening entertainment or just heading out for later-night versions. Radley hardly noticed them as he strode back to the print shop, running the inventory lists through his mind as best he could while he walked. There were any number of small items—pens and paper and such—that he wouldn't particularly miss even if Pete had been pilfering them ever since starting work there. Unfortunately, there were also some very expensive tools and machines that he could ill afford to lose.

And he'd already discovered that *Thieves, Petty* and *Thieves, Grand* were both included under the *Thieves* heading.

He reached the shop and let himself in the back door. The first part of the check was easy, and it took only a few minutes to confirm that the major machines were still there and still intact. The next part would be far more tedious. Digging the latest inventory list out of the files, he got to work.

It was after midnight when he finally put up the list with a sigh—a sigh that hissed both relief and annoyance into his ears. "See?" he told himself as he trudged back to the door. "Whatever Pete did, he did it somewhere else. Unless," he amended, "he's just been stealing pencils and label stickers."

But checking all of those would take hours . . . and for now, at least, he was far too tired to bother. "But I *will* check them out eventually," he decided. "I mean, I don't really care about stuff like that, but if he'll steal pencils, who's to say he won't back a truck up here someday and take all the copiers?"

It was a question that sent a shiver up his back. If that happened, he would be out of business. Period.

He headed toward home, the awful thought of it churning through his mind . . . and, preoccupied with the defense of his property, he never even heard the mugger coming.

He just barely felt the crushing blow on the back of his head.

He came to gradually, through a haze of throbbing pain, to find himself staring up at a soft pastel ceiling. The forcibly clean smell he'd always associated with hospitals curled his nostrils. . . . "Hello?" he called tentatively.

There was a moment of silence. Then, suddenly, there was a young woman leaning over him. "Ah—you're back with us," she said, peering into each of his eyes in turn. "I'm Doctor Sanderson. How do you feel?"

"My head hurts," Radley told her. "Otherwise . . . okay, I guess. What happened?"

"Best guess is that you were mugged," she told him. "Apparently by someone who doesn't like long conversations with his victims. You were lucky, as these things go: no concussion, no bone or nerve damage, only minor bleeding. You didn't even crack your chin when you fell."

Reflexively, Radley reached up to rub his chin. Bristly, but otherwise undamaged. "Can I go home?"

Sanderson nodded. "Sure. You'll have to call someone to get you, though—your friend didn't wait."

"Friend?" Radley frowned. The crinkling of forehead skin gave an extra throb to his headache.

"Fellow who brought you in. Black man—medium build, slightly balding. Carried you about five blocks to get you here—sweating pretty hard by that time, I'll tell you." She frowned in turn. "He told the E/R people you needed help—we just assumed he was a friend or neighbor or something."

Radley started to shake his head, thought better of it. "Doesn't sound like anyone I know," he said. "I certainly wasn't with anyone when it happened."

Sanderson shrugged slightly. "Good Samaritan, then. A vanishing breed, but you still get them sometimes. Anyway. Your shoes are under the gurney there; come on down to the nurses' station when you're ready and we'll run you through the paperwork."

He thought about calling Alison to come get him, but decided he didn't really want to wake her up at this time of night. Especially not when he'd have to explain why he'd been out so late.

With his wallet gone, he had no money for a cab, but a tired-eyed policeman who had brought in a pair of prostitutes gave him a lift home. What the blow on the head had started, the long trek up the steps to his apartment finished, and he barely made it to his bed before collapsing.

His headache was mostly gone when he awoke. Along with most of the day.

"Yeah, I figured you were sick or something when you didn't show up this morning," Pete said when he called the print shop. "Didn't expect it was something like *this*, though. You okay?"

"Yeah, I'm fine," Radley assured him, a wave of renewed shame warming his face. How could he ever have thought someone with Pete's loyalty would betray him? "Let me shower and change and I'll come on down."

"You don't need to do that," Pete said. "Not hardly worth coming in now, anyway. If I may say so, it don't sound to me like you oughta be running 'round yet, and I can handle things here okay." There was a faintly audible sniff/snort, and Radley could visualize the other man smiling. "And I really don't wanna have to carry you all the way home if you fall apart on me."

"There's that," Radley conceded. "I guess you're right. Well . . . I'll see you in the morning, then."

"Only if you feel like it. Really—I can handle things until you're well. Oops—gotta go. A customer just came in."

"Okay. Bye."

He hung up and gingerly felt the lump on the back of his head. Yes, Pete might have had to carry him home, at that. *That* little outing had sure gone sour.

As had his attempt to catch a murderer. And his attempt to solve a rape. And his attempt to stop an embezzlement.

In fact, everything the Book had given him had gone bad. One way or another, it had all gone bad.

"But it's truth," he gritted. "I mean, it *is*. How can truth be bad?"

He had no answer. With a sigh, he stood up from the kitchen chair. The sudden movement made his head throb, and he sat down again quickly. Yes, Pete might indeed have wound up carrying him.

Like someone else had already had to do.

Radley flushed with shame. In his mind's eye, he saw a medium-build black man, probably staggering under Radley's weight by the time he reached the hospital. Quietly helping to clean up the mess Radley had made of himself.

"I wish they'd gotten his name," he muttered to himself. "I'll never get a chance to thank him."

He looked down at the Book . . . and a sudden thought struck him. If the Book contained the names of all the criminals in town, why not the names of all the Good Samaritans, too?

He opened to the Yellow Pages, feeling a renewed sense of excitement. Perhaps this, he realized suddenly, was what the Book was really for. Not a tool for tracking down and punishing the guilty, but a means of finding and rewarding the good. The G's . . . there they were. Ge, Gl, Go . . .

There was no *Good Samaritans* listing.

Nor was there an *Altruists* listing. Nor were there listings for bene-factor, philanthropist, hero, or patriot. Or for good example, salt of the earth, angel, or saint.

There was nothing.

He thought about it for a long time. Then, with only a slight hesitation, he picked up the phone.

Alison answered on the fourth ring. "Hello?"

"It's me," Radley told her. "Listen." He took a careful breath. "I know the difference now. You know—the difference between *true* and *truth*?"

"Yes?" she said, her voice wary.

"Yeah. *True* is a group of facts—any facts, in any combination. *Truth* is *all* the facts. Both sides of the story. The bad *and* the good."

She seemed to digest that. "Yes, I think you're right. So what does that mean?"

He bit at his lip. She'd been right, he could admit now; he *had* enjoyed the knowledge and power the Book had given him. "So," he said, "I was wondering if you'd like to come up. It's . . . well, you know, it's kind of a chilly night."

The Book burned with an eerie blue flame, and its non-plastic bag burned green. Together, they were quite spectacular.

PROTOCOL

"I was thinking," Aimee Shondar said casually as she set the last of the breakfast dishes in the drainer, "that I might go to the market this morning."

Her husband Ted lifted his eyes up over the facplate with the look on his face that she'd known would be there. "I was going to fix the garden today," he said, his tone mildly reproving, as if she should have remembered that. "We had a second Stryder come through last night, you know."

"No, I didn't," Aimee said, frowning. Usually she was the first one awake when a Stryder came lumbering across their land in the middle of the night. "What did he hit?"

"Mostly the tomokado area," Ted said, sounding disgusted. "I swear sometimes they deliberately take whatever route will let those size-twenty feet of theirs do the most damage. A lot of it should be salvage-able, but it'll take most of the day to replant the vines. I really don't have the time to go to market with you."

"I wasn't asking you to," Aimee said, fighting to keep her voice steady. "I can go by myself."

The look in Ted's face deepened. "We've been through this, Aimee," he reminded her in the patient tone of an adult explaining a difficult concept to a young child. "I don't want you going to the village alone."

"I know that," Aimee said, feeling a quaver trying to nudge its way into her voice. She hated confrontations, hated them with a passion.

"But I'm twenty-four years old. It's high time I started learning how to do things on my own."

"So take up knitting," Ted suggested. "Or hydroponics, or supportable architecture. Better yet, come help me in the garden today and we can both go to the market tomorrow."

"But the shoreline traders are coming in today," Aimee protested. "All the best fish will be gone by tomorrow."

With a sigh, Ted laid aside the facplate. "Okay, fine," he said. "I guess I can do the garden tomorrow."

"I already said you don't have to go with me," Aimee said, feeling familiar stirrings of annoyance and frustration. He was patronizing her again. She hated when he patronized her. "I'm perfectly capable of dealing with the Stryders all by myself."

"Really?" he countered, the patient tone starting to fray about the edges. "There's only been one time *I* know about when you were actually alone with them."

Aimee had known the conversation would eventually end up here. All conversations about going into the village alone ended up here. But even knowing that, and expecting it, the comment still hit her in the gut like a Stryder's razordisk. "That's not fair," she insisted, the quaver in her voice into full shake mode now. "Aunt Ruth sneezed during the protocol. It wasn't my fault."

"I never said it was," Ted said calmly. "Look, kiddo, I don't blame you a single scrappy seed. Matter of fact, I've always been rather impressed by the fact that a kid your age didn't panic at what happened, and even managed to get all the way back home by yourself. And past, what, two more Stryders, too?"

Aimee shivered at the memory. After twelve years, she still shivered at the memory. "Three," she corrected him quietly.

"Three," he repeated. "My point is that you can't go through an experience like that without it affecting you. I feel you tense up every time a Stryder lumbers into view, like a rabbit facing a doggerelle. I'm just afraid that—well, look, I'm just afraid, that's all. Okay?"

Aimee sighed deep within her. "I know," she said. "But someday I'm going to have to grow up."

He smiled. "You're already grown up just fine, Aimee," he assured her. "Maybe it's just me who's still feeling traumatized by the past."

"And so I should humor you?"

"Something like that." He stood up, brushing the breakfast crumbs off his coveralls. "Give me a couple of minutes to change and we'll go."

The road leading toward the village was more crowded than usual this morning, Aimee thought as they headed out, with both pedestrians and pull carts wending their way between the ruts. Apparently, everyone in the district had fresh fish on their mind. It made her glad she hadn't let Ted talk her into waiting until tomorrow.

"Nice day for a walk, anyway," Ted commented as he steered her around a cart rattling noisily over the rough road. One of the wheels seemed on the verge of falling off, she noticed as they passed it. Too bad, too—the cart itself looked almost new.

But then, what little they had in the way of heavy machinery never seemed to last very long these days. As a girl, Aimee remembered her grandmother spinning grand stories about machines from the colony ship that could create perfectly round, perfectly smooth wheels, as well as other incredible devices that could last for years and years.

But no one had seen anything like that for a long time, and it was unlikely anyone ever would. The Stryders had long since plowed their random Juggernaut paths across and through all the colonists' major manufacturing areas, leaving nothing but rubble behind. Only in the more small-scale areas of electronics manufacture had the colonists been able to maintain anything of the technology they'd brought from Earth.

And it was just as well they'd been able to keep that. Without the language translators and the protocol programs coded into their fac-plates, the entire colony would long ago have been slaughtered.

"Did you check the list before we left?" Ted asked.

Aimee nodded. "At last report there were four Stryders in the square, with two more—"

"Stryder!" someone ahead of them called.

The knot of people jerked to a halt, a sudden eerie silence ringing in Aimee's ears as the rattle of the carts abruptly ceased. She slid her fac-plate from its belt pouch, feeling her pulse throbbing at the base of her throat. Somewhere up ahead, Death Incarnate was coming. Coming to snatch the unwary, or the careless, or the foolish. . . .

And then, there he was, just rounding one of the trees ahead to the left of the road: three meters of tall, golden-skinned being, like a mythological Greek god impossibly come to life. He was walking more or less toward the group of humans, his path cutting diagonally across the road ahead of them.

Beside her, Ted lifted his plate chest high. "Fifty meters ahead, angling inward thirty degrees left to right," he murmured rapidly toward the plate. All around them, Aimee could hear others muttering into their own plates.

And even with her stomach trying to do gymnastic maneuvers around her spleen, she found herself smiling tightly to herself. This one, at least, was a no-brainer. She'd done this protocol so many times she could practically quote it. *Stand still, head bowed to look one meter in front of you, hands folded in front of your chest—*

"Stand still, head bowed to look at the ground one meter in front of your feet, with your hands folded in front of your chest," she heard Ted's plate give the protocol for this kind of encounter. "Holding objects in your folded hands is acceptable. If he changes direction to approach at less than ten degrees, drop to your knees as soon as he comes within your peripheral vision, head still bowed. Resume activities when you can no longer see him. If he continues or increases his angle, maintain position. Resume activities when you can no longer hear his footsteps."

All around her, Aimee could hear the protocol message being repeated from another thirty plates. For her part, she had already bowed her head, folding her hands around her plate at her chest. Straining against the tops of her eyelids so that she could see if the Stryder changed direction toward her, she tried to ignore the tension quivering through her muscles.

Did all the people around her have that same quivering, she wondered? Certainly they all had cause to. The Stryders had killed over a quarter of the colonists in their first two months on the ground, and had probably killed one a week in the thirty years since then. Everyone knew someone who had died suddenly and violently at the edge of a razordisk for making some mistake in the protocol. She was hardly alone on that score.

And yet somehow, all the rest of them managed to get through the day just fine. Maybe Ted was right, she thought distantly. Maybe she just didn't have the emotional strength to face the Stryders alone.

The thudding footsteps were getting closer. Aimee tensed a little harder; and then the footsteps were past and heading back into the forest to the right. She took a deep breath, let it out slowly. The footsteps faded into the forest sounds—

"All clear," someone on that edge called softly.

There was a general rustling as everyone relaxed, coming out of their stiff bows and taking a few deep breaths of their own. A murmur of conversation rippled through the crowd, and here and there Aimee heard a nervous giggle or a mother calming her frightened children. With a multitonal group squeak, the carts started up again, and the crowd shambled back on its way.

"Why didn't you check the protocol?" Ted asked, his voice tight.

"I didn't need to," Aimee told him. "Most contacts are in that ninety-to-ten-degree approach angle. I know that one by heart."

"I don't care if you've got it tattooed on your retinas," Ted growled. "You don't play like that with Stryders. Ever."

"I'm not a child, Ted," Aimee shot back in a low voice, feeling heat rising into her cheeks. To be lectured that way in the privacy of her own home was bad enough; but have it thrown into her face in public was humiliating in the extreme. "I can take care of myself."

"Then prove it," he countered, not bothering to lower his voice. "And you can start by calling up the protocol yourself instead of relying on someone else to do it for you."

Clenching her teeth, Aimee kept her eyes on the back of the woman walking ahead of them. "Whatever you say."

The rest of the trip—aside from the creaking of the carts, the buzz of conversation from the rest of the crowd, and the rustlings of the forest—was very quiet.

The settlement of Venture had once been envisioned as the first and possibly greatest city of the new colony, a sprawling metropolis filling the land between the forest and the ocean shore thirty miles to the east, with the mysterious Great White Pyramid as the center of a huge park within its borders. But with the discovery of the Stryders, all such grandiose plans had long ago faded into dust. Small villages were about as extensive as human habitation got here, and even that was sometimes pushing their luck. The more decentralized the populace, the better.

Still, even a small village was a treat after the isolation of the forest. Aimee took deep breaths as they passed the outer rings of houses and shops and continued inward, drinking in the aromas of cooking and baking and commerce and people. It was like waking from a dream, she always thought at this point. A reminder of what it was to be human.

"Two more have come in," Ted grunted from beside her, studying his plate. "We'll probably run into at least one of them."

"That's okay," Aimee said, looking around at the various merchants opening up their shops and trying to ignore the butterflies testing their wings in her stomach. "I'm ready."

"And if and when it happens, you check the protocol," he said tartly. "I don't see any fish here. The dealers must be somewhere on the other side of the Sanctuary."

"Yes, they're probably on the east side, near the butchers," Aimee agreed as they started to angle off to the right. "Most of the other people seem to be heading that direction—"

"Stryder!" the call drifted back.

Everyone stopped dead in their tracks. "Where?" Aimee heard a man growl. "I don't see anything."

"That way!" a young girl answered, pointing to the left, her voice a mixture of excitement and dread. "I can hear him!"

Just about twelve years old, Aimee noted with a quiet shudder as she gazed at the girl's profile. The same age she herself had been when that Stryder had cut down Aunt Ruth beside her.

At her side now, Ted was nudging her urgently with his elbow. Pushing back the memories, she pulled out her plate.

And then, from the direction the girl was pointing, the Stryder appeared from behind a tree. He pushed past the side of one of the booths, his bulk bending back the memory plastic and eliciting a soft crunch from something inside, and headed straight toward them.

The butterflies in Aimee's stomach took flight as she lifted the plate to her lips. "Fifty meters to the left, coming straight toward me," she said, her lips feeling cold and dry. "He just pushed past a booth, probably breaking something inside."

"Go down on your right knee, continuing to face forward, leaving your left knee bent at a ninety-degree angle," the plate instructed her. "Put your left hand on your left knee, palm resting on the kneecap, fingers pointed down along the shin. Set your plate down on the ground and then put your right hand across the back of your left, elbow pointing forward and bent at a ninety-degree angle, fingers pointed straight out toward the Stryder. Lower your head to look at your crossed hands."

She did as instructed. Her right arm wasn't quite long enough to make a precise ninety-degree angle, and she had to lean her shoulder forward a little to compensate. Peripherally, she could see everyone nearby following suit as she gazed at her hands. Those farther away, of course, would be doing the protocol for a ten-to-ninety-degree sideways approach.

What did it all mean? After thirty years, no one still had an answer to that question. The Stryders didn't even seem to notice the humans scurrying around their feet, at least as long as they obeyed the strange rules of the protocol. They couldn't be communicated or reasoned with; they couldn't be deflected or lured or frightened away from the complex paths they wove through human-occupied land; and they couldn't be killed, at least not with any weapon the colonists had ever been able to bring against them.

They were like berserkers or Juggernauts, living in a secret self-contained world within their own minds, creating their secret rules for others to follow. Only when the protocol was broken did they come out of those shells, and then only to kill with instant and emotionless efficiency. No one knew where they lived, if they indeed lived in any particular place or society. The colony ship's sensors hadn't spotted any such groupings on its way in, and the handful of brave or rash souls who had tried to track the Stryders back through the forest had never been heard from again.

Every possible approach to communication had been attempted, to no avail. The colonists had tried human speech, both at normal pitch and as shifted to other segments of the auditory spectrum. Lights had been tried, and mathematical and geometric symbols, and odors and tastes and Morse and Jartrac codes. Kla'ka Four, the nearest thing to a general trade language that the archaeologists had ever found in this region of space, had had no more impact with the Stryders than any of the Earth languages had.

Someone had even talked the colony's governors into letting her try an interpretive dance. That had garnered the same nonresults as everything else, except that the dancers had died even faster.

The Stryder was coming closer now, his slow, steady footsteps shaking the ground and sending shivers through Aimee's knee. She kept her eyes down, double-checking the angle of her elbow and wondering if the crowd was too tightly packed for the Stryder to get through without stepping on someone. As far as she knew, that had never happened, but there was always a first time. Out of the corner of her eye, she could see the man directly in front of her fidget slightly, possibly wondering the same thing. *Hold still*, she pleaded silently with him as he fidgeted again.

The approaching Stryder was well within razordisk range, and she had no desire to see the man fidget his way to a bloody death. The footsteps were practically on top of her—

And suddenly, the air filled with a sound that froze her blood and wrenched her back a dozen years to that horrible day with Aunt Ruth. A sound like the moan of a wounded wolfbat.

The Stryder had activated his razordisk.

A scream bubbled up in Aimee's throat; desperately, viciously, she forced it down. Screaming wasn't part of the protocol.

The nervous man in front of her apparently wasn't as strong or as self-controlled as she was. He gave another twitch at the sound, the worst one yet.

Aimee's breath was coming in short, painful bursts now. No doubt; the razordisk was for him. She wanted to squeeze her eyes shut, to block out her view of his back before the silvery death cut through his heart and lungs and spine and left him broken on the roadway.

But shutting her eyes wasn't part of the protocol, either. Instead, she focused her attention on the back of her own hand, counting the veins and praying that for once a Stryder would change his mind and go away without killing someone—

The wolfbat moan changed pitch; and with a flash of reflected sunlight the razordisk shot past her forehead, snapping back in its return flight half a racing heartbeat later. A burst of bright red erupted across her vision, obscenely brilliant in the morning sunlight.

And without even a last gasp, Ted toppled over and collapsed into a spreading pool of his own blood.

The footsteps resumed their plodding, and the Stryder passed through the rest of the crowd, without so much as stepping on an outstretched toe.

The Sanctuary was a slightly irregular circle, perhaps ten meters across, in the center of the village square and bordered by a hedge of meter-high bushes dotted with delicate orange-colored flowers. For some unknown reason, the Stryders always avoided the ring, as well as ignoring everything that went on inside it. Anyone who wanted to relax and not have to think about Stryders for a few minutes could step through one of the three narrow gaps into the circle and sit down on one of the benches set around the inside.

The time limit for most people was ten minutes before they had to give up their place to someone else and move on. For someone like Aimee, there was no such restriction.

She was sitting in the shady side of the circle, staring down at the ground, when a pair of booted feet suddenly intruded. "Here," a man's voice said, sounding like it was coming from far away.

She looked up, the haze of unreality glazed across her eyes parting just far enough to show an earnest young face gazing down at her from above a stiff uniform collar. "What?" she asked. Her voice sounded as distant as his.

"I brought you something to drink," he said. "It'll help you feel better."

She lowered her eyes from his face, down past the policeman's badge pinned to his uniform jacket, and focused at last on the cup in his hand. "No, thank you," she murmured.

He seemed to hesitate, then moved to the bench and sat down beside her. "I'm sorry for your loss, Mrs. Shondar," he said quietly. "I wish there was something I could say or do to help."

"Thank you," she said mechanically, still staring at the cup in his hand. "I don't . . . what did he do wrong?"

"I don't know," the patrolman said. "Did you happen to notice anything?"

Aimee shook her head, tearing her eyes away from the cup to look across at the far side of the hedge and the orange flowers. Once, she knew, there had been a plan to plant this species of hedge around the whole colony, giving them permanent protection against the Stryders. But everywhere else that it was planted, the flowers came out yellow, and the Stryders trampled them into the ground as uncaringly as they did tomokado vines. "I saw the man in front of me twitching," she said. "I wasn't facing toward Ted."

"No, of course not," the patrolman agreed. "Well, Sergeant Royce is running the facplates' records now. We'll know soon enough what happened."

"But how could he have done anything wrong?" Aimee protested. "It was all right there. He knew how to follow the protocol."

"I know," the policeman said. "But sometimes it's such a small and subtle mistake that you don't even notice it until it's too late. You're sure you didn't see anything?"

"No," Aimee said, frowning up at him. Granted that it had been twelve years since the last time she'd gone through this, the questions weren't going at all the way she remembered them. "I'm sorry. What was your name again?"

"Patrolman Ricardo Clay," he told her, not taking offense even though she had the vague feeling he'd given her his name at least twice already. "The reason I ask, Mrs. Shondar, is that we've already talked to most of the people who were closest to you. None of them has any recollection of your husband breaking protocol, either."

"But that's impossible," Aimee said. "If he follows protocol, they have to let him live. Don't they?"

Clay's lip twitched. "As far as we can tell, they don't actually *have* to do anything," he reminded her soberly. "But up to now, yes, as long as a person stayed within protocol, he was okay."

"What do you mean, 'up to now'?" Aimee asked. "Has something changed?"

"I don't know." Clay's eyes shifted over her shoulder. "Maybe we're about to find out."

Aimee looked behind her. An older patrolman was coming toward them, sergeant's braid glittering on his shoulder, her facplate gripped in his right hand. "Mrs. Shondar," he greeted her as he stepped up beside Clay. "I'm Sergeant Royce. We've just done a complete analysis of yours and your husband's plate records."

His eyebrows lifted slightly. "And we'll be damned if we can find anything he did to break protocol."

Aimee's skin began to prickle. There'd been just the slightest emphasis on the word *he*. "What are you suggesting?" she asked. "If he didn't break protocol, why is he dead?"

"As I said, we really don't know," Royce said, an odd glint in his eye. "Though it's possible we might have missed something. Your plate doesn't have a very clear view of the event; we're still analyzing your husband's."

"But if you didn't miss anything?"

Royce was still eyeing her strangely. "Then we may have something new cropping up," he said. "Maybe some little nuance we haven't gleaned from the Pyramid record yet."

Automatically, Aimee's eyes drifted over his shoulder to the slivers of white that could be seen through the surrounding trees. The Great White Pyramid, with its detailed listing of the protocol set out in five languages—Kla'ka Four among them—had been the colony's salvation after all the attempts to communicate with or destroy the Stryders had failed. "But that's impossible," she said. "Isn't it? The archaeologists and linguists have been over it a thousand times. How could they possibly have missed anything?"

"I don't know," Royce said evenly. "But I'm sure you agree that anything's possible." He paused, just a fraction of a second too long. "By the way, have you ever gone out and looked at the Pyramid yourself?"

"My aunt took me to see it once when I was ten," she told him slowly. "I haven't been there since."

"Uh-huh," Royce said. "That was your Aunt Lydia, wasn't it? The one who was pretty good at reading Kla'ka Four?"

Aimee looked at Patrolman Clay, who was in turn peering up at Sergeant Royce. The younger man looked as confused as she felt. "She read me a few lines," she acknowledged. "Mostly parts of the protocol I already knew."

"'Mostly'?" Royce echoed.

"All right, it was *all* parts of the protocol I already knew," Aimee said, anger beginning to seep into the numbness. What was he trying to say, anyway? "Is that better?"

"If it's the truth," Royce said, his expression not changing in the slightest. "Tell me, Mrs. Shondar: how have you been getting along with your husband?"

The wisps of anger vanished into something very cold. "What do you mean?" she asked carefully.

"What I mean is that several of the people we interviewed mentioned that the two of you had an argument on the way to Venture this morning," Royce said. "What was it about?"

Aimee swallowed. "That was a private matter between me and my husband."

"Maybe," Royce said, his eyes hardening. "Maybe not. This is a death investigation; and in death investigations we have a lot of latitude as to what gets to stay private and what doesn't."

Clay cleared his throat. "Excuse me, sir, but I'm a little confused. This is a simple Stryder death, not a homicide."

"Is it?" Royce countered. "Again, maybe or maybe not. You haven't answered my question, Mrs. Shondar."

It took Aimee a moment to even remember what the question was. "Ted was angry because I did the protocol from memory instead of calling it up on the plate," she said. "I told him I knew that particular one by heart; he didn't think it was a good idea to do it that way."

"He was right about that, actually," Clay murmured. "Two-thirds of all Stryder killings are a result of people getting complacent or careless."

"I wasn't getting complacent," Aimee snapped. "If anyone out there this morning knew what messing up the protocol would mean, it was me."

"Yes, of course," Clay said hastily. "I didn't mean to suggest you were taking it lightly."

"Still, as long as we're on the subject," Royce put in, "how about telling us what your relationship was like with your Aunt Ruth?"

Aimee felt the memory of that day tearing through her stomach. "What kind of a question is that?" she snarled, her voice starting to shake. "I loved my aunt."

"Just like you loved your husband?" Royce asked pointedly. "Tell me: did you have a similar argument with her that morning? Possibly on the same subject of being treated like a child?"

Royce's face was beginning to swim in front of her eyes. "I don't know what you're talking about," she said, her voice sounding like it was coming out of a deep well. The whole world was starting to swim now. . . .

She awoke with a start, to find herself lying on the bench where she'd been sitting. Directly above her, the sky had turned a dark shade of purple with tinges of red and yellow in it.

What in the *world* . . . ?

She started to lift her head, instantly regretting the decision as her neck abruptly screamed from a dozen locales at the hasty movement. Carefully, stifling a moan, she eased it back down again.

"Ah—you're awake," a voice came from behind her.

More carefully this time, Aimee lifted her head and turned it around. Patrolman Clay was walking across the Sanctuary ring toward her, his shirt sleeves rippling in the evening breeze.

The *evening* breeze?

She looked around again. It was evening, all right, with the brilliant colors of sunset peeking through the trees to the west. "What happened?" she asked.

"You fainted," Clay explained, coming to her side and helping her sit up. "We called Dr. Bhahatya, who said it would be best to let you sleep, so we had him give you an injection."

"Was that your idea?" Aimee asked, carefully stretching stiff arms. "Calling the doctor, I mean."

Clay shrugged slightly. "Mostly."

"Sergeant Royce won't be very happy about that," she warned bitterly. "Interrupting his interrogation that way."

Clay waved a hand casually. "He'll get over it."

"I don't think so." Aimee closed her eyes briefly. "He thinks I murdered my husband, doesn't he?"

She opened her eyes in time to see Clay purse his lips. "You have to admit it's an intriguing idea," he said. "If you could somehow find a way to make someone break protocol—without also doing it yourself, of course—you'd have a way to commit the perfect murder. In front of witnesses, too."

A lump rose into Aimee's throat. "I loved my husband, Patrolman Clay," she said. "I really did. I didn't want him dead. I didn't want Aunt Ruth dead, either. Doesn't anyone believe me?"

"I believe you," Clay said quietly. "But I don't believe what happened today is just an unexplained accident, either. *Something* happened to cause that Stryder to attack."

"But what?" Aimee asked. "I didn't do anything. I *know* I didn't."

"Maybe it was something subtle," Clay suggested. "Something so small that you didn't even notice it. Or maybe it's something else, some new layer in the protocol that we haven't figured out yet."

"Like what?" she asked.

"I don't know," Clay said. "Maybe it's something having to do with you personally. You were, what, twelve years old when your aunt was killed?"

"That's right."

"And it's been another twelve years since then," Clay continued. "Maybe the Stryders are celebrating an anniversary or something."

Aimee winced. "That's a horrible thought."

"I agree," Clay said. "And personally, I don't believe it for a second. But until we figure out what happened, we can't afford to dismiss any of the possibilities."

"Including the possibility that I deliberately murdered them?"

Clay started to speak, but apparently thought better of it. "Look, it's going to be dark soon. Why don't you stay in the Sanctuary tonight where you'll be safe, and we can talk more in the morning."

Aimee's first reaction was to insist that she wasn't afraid of the dark, and that she was perfectly capable of traveling. But the reaction was pure pride, and her pride had already caused enough damage for one day. Besides, she really didn't feel like a walk all alone in the dark. "All right," she said.

"Good." Almost shyly, he smiled at her. "I've got to get back to work—I'm on evening patrol tonight. I'll leave you my coat, though, in case you get cold."

She looked down, noticing for the first time that his jacket was neatly folded right where her head had been lying on the bench. Apparently, it had already served duty as her pillow. "Thank you," she said.

"No problem," he said, moving toward one of the gaps in the hedge. "I'll look in on you a little later." He paused at the gap, glanced around for any signs of Stryders, then strode out into the gathering dusk.

For a long time, Aimee sat on the bench, watching the sky fade into purple and then into starlit black. The businesses around the square were long since closed, but there were enough lights from nearby residences to throw a faint glow over the area.

And with the ghostly light washing over her, she gazed at the stars and listened to the night breezes whispering through the trees.

And tried to think.

What had she done? Because she *had* done something. Everyone agreed on that, even those like Patrolman Clay who didn't think she'd done anything on purpose. Somehow, something she'd done had caused a Stryder to kill her husband.

But how? And why? Could she have been angrier at him than she'd realized? Some kind of deep or lingering anger that she didn't even know was there?

No. She'd loved her husband. Hadn't she? Of course she had. And she'd loved Aunt Ruth, too. The older woman had irritated her sometimes, but *everyone* had irritated her sometimes back then. Part of being twelve, she supposed.

But if somehow her subconscious had latched onto that irritation and figured out a way to break protocol for someone else . . .

She shook her head decisively. No. Aunt Ruth had sneezed. That sneeze, and the resulting rearrangement of head and torso and arms, was what had broken protocol and gotten her killed. These were two entirely different cases, despite Sergeant Royce's efforts to link them.

What about Patrolman Clay's theory? Could it be a matter of who she was, rather than something she'd done? Had the Stryders somehow gotten it into their heads that every twelve years someone standing or kneeling or crouching beside her should die?

But no. That didn't make any sense.

But then, what sense did the protocol make in the first place? Why impose such arbitrary rules of conduct on helpless people, with death as the punishment for every single infraction?

And not just on human beings. Whoever had set up the Pyramid with its five languages had clearly been trying to make sure that at least five different species would be able to learn and follow the protocol. Apparently, the Stryders played this same vicious game with everyone who happened by.

Except that this particular group of playmates weren't going to simply play the Stryders' game for awhile and then move on. If Earth hadn't sent a follow-up ship by now, they never would. The colonists were trapped here. Trapped on this otherwise lovely and bountiful world with the Stryders and their protocol.

And if there was something new happening with that protocol, they weren't going to be living here much longer.

So what in heaven's name had she *done*?

Her plate was lying on the bench near Patrolman Clay's folded jacket. Slowly, reluctantly, she reached over and picked it up. The record of Ted's death was in there, recorded in all its horrifying detail. The thought of watching it . . .

It's been another twelve years since then, Patrolman Clay had suggested. *Maybe the Stryders are celebrating an anniversary.*

She took a deep breath. The thought of living through Ted's death again made her feel violently ill. But she had to know. Bracing herself, she keyed for the record.

It was as bad as she'd expected. Worse. With the position the plate had been in, she could only see Ted's left side, but that was enough to send her stomach into a fresh knot. She watched and listened as she and Ted went into the protocol positions; watched and listened as the Stryder clumped toward them; watched and listened at that horrible moment when the razordisk whipped past overhead, cutting into Ted's side with a splash of red and then returning like a deadly yo-yo to its owner. She heard herself give a strangled gasp as Ted fell to the ground; saw the image turn half red as a stray drop of blood landed on the recording lens, partially obscuring it.

And she saw the Stryder pass by, looming overhead like a giant tree as he made his unconcerned way past his victim. The footsteps faded into the distance, and she heard herself begin to moan . . .

With a stabbing jerk of her finger, she shut off the record, squeezing her eyes tightly shut as if cutting off the images would somehow destroy the memory.

But at the same time, she knew she couldn't afford to lose any bit of that memory. Not yet. Sergeant Royce had said Ted's plate didn't show exactly what had happened, either. If they were going to figure out how he had broken protocol, it was going to be up to her to figure it out.

Slowly, tiredly, she opened her eyes.

To find a Stryder standing directly across the Sanctuary ring, just outside the hedge.

Staring at her.

Her heart seemed to freeze in her chest. No one knew how exactly the hedge protected them against the Stryders. One theory was that they liked the orange flowers so much they didn't want to risk damaging them. Another was that the delicate aroma somehow obscured their vision, so that they literally couldn't see what was happening inside the hedge.

But all anyone really knew was that, up to now, the hedge had kept the Stryders away from you.

But then, up to now, following the protocol had done the same thing.

Up to now.

The Stryder was still standing there. Still staring at her. Aimee stared back, holding as still as she could, Ted's image of a rabbit facing a dog-gerelle flashing through her mind. No Stryder had ever stared at her that way before. For that matter, she couldn't recall ever seeing a Stryder even standing still before. Even when they killed, they never so much as broke stride.

And yet, this one was standing. *And* staring.

Was it the same Stryder who had killed Ted? There were supposed to be subtle differences between them, but Aimee had never been able to tell one Stryder from another. Could Sergeant Royce have been right about her somehow instigating the attack? Had the Stryder later realized that, and decided that Aimee deserved to die, too?

She realized she had stopped breathing. Slowly, carefully, she inhaled, feeling terribly alone. If only someone was here with her; Patrolman Clay, or even Sergeant Royce. If the Stryder wanted her, of course, there was nothing either of them could do. But suddenly she was terrified at the thought of dying without another human present to say good-bye to.

The Stryder still hadn't moved, and she found herself wondering bleakly what he was waiting for. The hedge itself was certainly no physical barrier, and his razordisk probably had enough range to get her here at the far side anyway. What was he waiting for?

And then, suddenly, something inside her snapped. If this was her night to die, she wasn't going to take it hiding beneath the flowers in a corner like a frightened rabbit. Standing up, stuffing her facplate back into its pouch, she started across the Sanctuary ring toward the Stryder.

With every step, she expected him to raise his right arm and send the razordisk nestled beneath it flashing toward her, to cut through her heart and lungs and to quiet forever the agonizing memory of Ted's death. But still he stood there, unmoving, as she approached.

Until finally she stood just inside the hedge from him.

For a long moment she gazed silently at him, staring up into his face. Every variation of the protocol she'd ever heard made you bow down before a Stryder ever got this close; and though she'd seen plenty of telephoto pictures of them, she realized suddenly that no picture or video had ever really done them justice.

It was an old face. A face that had seen many things; a face that somehow reflected deep wanderings in secret thoughts and paths. Even in the darkness his eyes were bright as he stared down at her, and Aimee could feel a sense of eminence and mystery and serenity hovering around him. Like a Greek god, she'd often thought, or the wise mentor to humanity that so many people had longed for over the centuries.

Only these mentors killed on a whim.

She took a deep breath. If this was indeed her night to die, then nothing she could do could stop it. But perhaps she could at least voice her objections to this insanity before that happened. "Why?" she asked, her voice sounding harsh and crowlike against the Stryder's innate grandeur. "Why did you kill him?"

The Stryder seemed to consider that. Or maybe he was just ignoring her. The first colonists had tried to talk to the Stryders too, she remembered. All it had gotten them was killed.

And then, abruptly yet smoothly, he lifted his arm.

Aimee flinched back, her eyes dropping to the razordisk against his forearm. But the arm stopped, and there was no wolfbat moan, and the weapon didn't move. Slowly, she let her gaze travel down the arm to the huge hand reaching over the hedge toward her. The hand was cupped, palm up, as if he wanted something.

Aimee swallowed. What did he want? In another human, the gesture might have indicated that she was to take his hand, as if he was preparing to lead her somewhere. But somehow, she sensed that wasn't it.

And then she noticed that not all the fingers were cupped. One of them was stretched out straight—almost curved under, in fact—pointing at her belt pouch.

At her facplate.

"My plate?" she asked, reaching carefully toward it. "Is that what you want?"

The Stryder didn't move or speak. Carefully, wondering if she was in fact reading him correctly, she began working the plate free. Was he trying to tell her there was a protocol for this kind of face-to-face meeting? She couldn't imagine there being such a thing; and even if there was, no Stryder ever gave out hints like that, even in mime. Their entire range of responses was either to ignore or to kill.

Still, this one was already doing things she'd never heard of from a Stryder. Maybe, for once, one was actually giving a human the benefit of the doubt. She got the plate out and lifted it to her lips—

And with a smooth motion, the Stryder turned his cupped hand over and plucked it from her grasp. Turning, he strode away across the square and disappeared around a shop.

Aimee watched him go, her body seeming to sag inside her skin. So that was it. No benefit of the doubt; no communication; no nothing. The Stryder had indeed realized he'd made a mistake earlier, and this was his way of rectifying it.

Because without a plate, she was as good as dead. Her mind flicked back to that day with Aunt Ruth, and how she'd had to use her plate to pull up the protocol three more times before she was able to make it home. By taking her plate, the Stryder was effectively condemning her to death the minute she left the safety of the Sanctuary.

Slowly, she turned and headed back across the circle. *Relax,* she tried to tell herself. *Just stay here until Patrolman Clay gets back, and he'll get you a new plate.*

But that would be at best a temporary fix. If the Stryders could take one plate away from her, they could take the next one away, and the next one, and the next, until at some point she would be caught out in the open with a Stryder and no idea what the protocol was to keep him away.

And even in her despair, she could see the irony in it. Sergeant

Royce had all but accused her of getting a Stryder to kill her husband for her. Now, by taking her plate, this Stryder was doing that exact same thing to her.

She reached the bench where Patrolman Clay's jacket lay and sat down beside it. All sorts of desperate plans and ideas had chased each other through her mind on the short walk across the circle, but she knew there was no point in trying any of them tonight. In the morning, perhaps, she would be able to think more clearly.

Assuming, of course, the Stryders didn't come for her before then.

But if they did, there was still nothing she could do tonight. And at the moment she was too drained of emotion to even worry about it. Stretching out on the bench, pillowing her head on the folded jacket, she drifted off to sleep.

"Mrs. Shondar? Aimee?"

She woke with a start, muscles jerking with sudden terror. But it wasn't one of the Stryders who had haunted her dreams crouching over her, just Patrolman Clay. In the pink predawn light she could see the lines of tension were back in his face. "Yes, I'm awake," she said, her mouth feeling dry. "What is it?"

"Come on," he said, taking her hand and urging her upward. "You need to see this."

Abruptly, the memories of the night flooded back. "I can't," she protested, even as she swung her legs over the side of the bench. "He took my plate."

"Who, Sergeant Royce?" Clay asked, frowning.

Aimee shook her head. "One of the Stryders."

Clay's eyes widened. "One of the *Stryders?* But . . ."

He inhaled sharply, his face abruptly changing. "Oh, my God," he said softly. "So *that's* it. Come on, you *definitely* need to see this."

There was something in his voice that stifled all further protest. Standing up, she let him lead her across the Sanctuary circle.

There, lying on his back in the square a few meters outside the hedge, was a Stryder.

Dead.

Aimee caught her breath. "What—"

"He was there when I got back a few minutes ago," Clay told her. "We can check your husband's plate record, but I'm betting he's the one who killed him."

He gestured toward the Stryder. "Which must be why the other Stryder took your plate. So he could figure out who he was, too."

"I don't understand," Aimee said, unable to take her eyes off the body. She was so accustomed to thinking of the Stryders as messengers of death that it was a shock to see one lying there dead himself. "What's he doing here?"

"Don't you see?" Clay said quietly. "He killed your husband. Only he shouldn't have, because your husband hadn't done anything wrong."

Aimee turned to him, sudden understanding twisting through her heart. "Are you saying . . . ?"

"Your husband didn't break protocol, Aimee," Clay said. "Neither did you. It was the *Stryder* who broke it."

His lips compressed briefly. "And even for Stryders, I guess, the penalty for breaking protocol is death."

Aimee looked out at the body again, a dark and depressing confusion tugging at her emotions. "They're trapped by it too," she said quietly. "For all their cold-blooded killing, they're as trapped by the protocol as we are."

"So it seems," Clay agreed. "Well. Come on, let's get you a new plate, and I'll escort you home."

"It's not that easy," Aimee said, looking at him again. "What about him?"

Clay frowned. "What do you mean? What about him?"

"What do we do with the body?" Aimee asked. "Do we leave it there for the Stryders to collect? Or do we bury it, or build a funeral pyre, or walk in a circle around it with our heads bowed, or what? What's the protocol for this?"

The tension lines were back in Clay's face. "Oh, my God," he breathed. "We'd better get someone out to the Pyramid. And fast."

OLD-BOY NETWORK

●

The sunlight was glowing softly through Rey's eyelids when he woke up that last morning. For a few minutes he just lay there, luxuriating under the warm weight of the blankets and comforter, happy to be alive.

She had smiled at him again.

He smiled himself at the thought. The left side of his mouth didn't join in the smile, of course, but for once he almost didn't even care. At first the half-paralyzed face had bothered him terribly, even more than having been made a cripple. But today, none of it seemed to matter.

Because it hadn't seemed to matter to her. And if it didn't matter to her, it certainly shouldn't matter to him.

She had smiled at him. For the fifth time in the past four weeks—he'd been keeping count—she had smiled at him.

He yawned deeply. "Curtains: open," he called.

From across the room came a soft hum as the filmy curtains were pulled aside. He pried open his eyelids—rather literally in the case of his left eyelid, which had a tendency to glue itself shut overnight—and looked outside.

The sun was high up over the stark Martian landscape. He'd slept in unusually late this morning.

But that was all right. Unless and until Mr. Quillan called for him, his time was his own.

And if that call held off, and if he was lucky, he might see *her* again.

His chair was waiting beside his bed where he'd left it. Throwing back the blankets, he maneuvered himself to the edge of the bed and got himself into it. "Chair: bathroom," he ordered.

Obediently, the chair rolled across the room and through the wide door of his bathroom. He took care of the usual morning business; and then it was time for a quick shower. The breakfast he'd ordered last night should be waiting by the time he was done.

Idly, he wondered what the meal would consist of. Mr. Quillan had been talking with the other men and women on the Network quite a lot lately, and that much TabRasa sometimes played funny games with his memory in general. Still, surprises could be pleasant, too.

By the time Rey was dressed and back in his chair the tantalizing aroma of Belgian waffles was wafting through the bathroom door. He rather hoped he'd asked for bacon with it, but it turned out he'd ordered a side of sausage instead.

No problem. He liked sausage too. He would just order bacon tomorrow.

Maneuvering his chair up to the table, wondering what *she* liked for breakfast, he began to eat.

"So this is Mars," Hendrik Thorwald commented, gently swirling his coffee cup as he gazed out the floor-to-ceiling windows at the landscape and the cluster of domes that made up Makaris City. "Not nearly as claustrophobic as the Ganymede Domes."

"That's because here you can at least walk around outside without a full vacuum suit," Archer Quillan pointed out, sipping at his own spiced coffee as he watched the circling motion of the other's cup. It was almost as if Thorwald thought he was holding a brandy snifter.

A simple nervous habit? Or did it imply that the man drank too much?

Neither added up to much of a recommendation, in Quillan's book. But in this case, Quillan's book didn't matter. Thorwald's net worth had reached the magic trillion-dollar mark, and McCade wanted him in, and that was that. His wealth had made him an Old Boy, as McCade sardonically called them, and he would be offered a spot in the Old-Boy Network.

"Of course, you need an air supply and parka," Thorwald said. "Still, it's not as cold as the travel books make it sound."

"Hardly worse than a typical Swedish winter, I imagine," Quillan said politely.

"Hardly at all." Turning away from the window, Thorwald resettled himself in his chair to face Quillan again. "But you didn't ask me all the way to Mars to compare weather. We've had our breakfast; we've had our coffee. Let's talk business."

"Indeed," Quillan agreed. Straight and direct, with neither belligerence nor apology. Much better. "Actually, it's not so much business as it is an invitation. You've reached the magic trillion-dollar mark, and the thirty or so of us already in that rather exclusive club would like to congratulate you on your achievement."

Thorwald inclined his head slightly. "Thank you."

"But as you'll soon realize, if you haven't already, making a trillion dollars is only the first step," Quillan continued. "The challenge now is to hold onto it. Currently, you're Target Number One for every con man, minor competitor, and ambitious young Turk in Northern Europe, all of whom hope to pry some of that money away from you."

"Joined by every governmental taxing agency from Earth to the Jovian Moons and back again," Thorwald added sourly.

"Absolutely," Quillan said. "And with all of them nipping at your heels, I would venture to guess that your biggest headache these days is that of secure communications."

"Hardly an insightful guess," Thorwald pointed out. "That's *everyone's* biggest headache. Even the best encryption methods I can get my hands on can't keep up with the government snoops and industrial spies."

"Indeed," Quillan said. "And of course, there's also that awkward time-lag whenever you're transmitting across the Solar System. It would be nice to eliminate that, wouldn't it?"

The gentle swirling of the coffee cup came to a halt. "I seem to remember from school that that's a basic limitation of the universe," he said, his eyes searching Quillan's face.

"That's what they taught in my school, too," Quillan said. "Tell me, Hendrik: what would you give to have an absolutely secure information and transmission channel? I mean *absolutely* secure?"

Thorwald snorted gently. "Half my fortune. Cash."

Quillan smiled. "Then you're looking at a real bargain," he said. "All it will cost you is a mere eight hundred million dollars. Paid to the right people, of course."

Carefully, Thorwald set his cup on the polished crystal coffee table. "Tell me more."

"I'll do better," Quillan said, getting to his feet. "I'll show you."

"Downstairs?" the broad-shouldered man repeated, his thick forehead wrinkling. "You were just downstairs yesterday."

"Because downstairs is where the piano is," Rey said, the frozen left half of his mouth slurring the words slightly. Grond was one of Rey's caretakers, which meant he was on call whenever Rey needed something his chair or automated suite couldn't handle.

He was also, Rey had long ago decided, something of a private watchdog.

"Yeah, but so what?" Grond grunted. "You've got a perfectly good keyboard in your room."

"That's a keyboard," Rey explained patiently. "The piano downstairs is a baby grand. There's a big difference in how it sounds."

The wrinkles deepened. Obviously, that was something Grond had never noticed. Possibly music itself was something Grond had never noticed. "Mr. Quillan isn't going to like you going downstairs all the time."

"He's never said I couldn't," Rey countered. "Just that he didn't want me talking to anyone."

"Yeah, but every *day*?" Grond objected. "You're up and down those stairs like a yo-yo."

"Would you rather get a couple of guys and move the piano upstairs?" Rey suggested helpfully.

Grond exhaled disgustedly. "Fine. Whatever you want."

"Thank you," Rey said. "Chair: library."

He felt his heart starting to pound as the chair passed the second floor landing and began climbing down the wide staircase. Down here, on the mansion's first floor, was where *she* worked. *Let her be working in the library today*, he pleaded silently with the universe. *Please. Let her be in the library.*

There were three women in traditional black-and-white maid's outfits working on the brass and wrought iron when Rey reached the bottom of the stairs. None of them was her.

As usual, none of the maids even looked up as the chair rolled along the hallway toward the library. It was as if Rey didn't even exist. Maybe they all had orders to treat him that way.

Or maybe they just didn't like him. No one here really liked him. *Except.*

There were two other maids dusting the old-style books lining the shelves as he rolled through the library door. Again, *she* wasn't among them.

Rey's heartbeat slowed back to a quiet ache as he made his way across to the baby grand piano, trying hard not to let the disappointment drag him down. All right, so two days in a row had been too much to expect. He would see her again. Maybe tomorrow.

"You got half an hour," Grond warned, crossing the room ahead of him and moving the piano bench out of the way. "Then it's back upstairs."

Rey nodded, not trusting himself to speak. He settled his chair in place in front of the keyboard and punched in Beethoven's Moonlight Sonata on the music desk. Tentatively, he began to play.

He wasn't very good at it. In fact, he rather hated playing the baby grand. There was no way to play it quietly, and every mistake and hesitation seemed to echo accusingly back across the room at him. Grond's glowering presence a few steps away didn't help, either.

But he had to pretend he was enjoying himself. This piano was his best excuse for coming downstairs, and he didn't dare let Grond know the truth.

He had finished playing what he could of the Beethoven and had shifted to some easier Stephen Foster when a movement across the room caught the corner of his eye. He turned his head to look—

And felt his heart leap like an excited child.

It was *her.*

His breath felt suddenly on fire in his chest as he watched her walk alongside the shelves, a brass-polishing kit in her hand. So far she hadn't looked his direction; but her path was bringing her ever closer to the piano. Eventually, he knew, she would have to notice him.

And when that happened, would she smile again?

He kept playing, his suddenly stiff fingers feeling as wooden as xylophone keys. She was coming closer, and closer . . .

And then, just before it seemed impossible that she could avoid seeing him, she looked over at the piano. Her large brown eyes met his—

And she smiled.

It was like the first drink of water splashing down a throat of a weary desert traveler. This was no ordinary smile, not just the kind a proper servant would politely offer one of the master's other employees. This was a real, genuine smile. The kind of smile a person saved for a good friend.

He had no illusions as to what she could see in him, not in this wheelchair and all. But between Mr. Quillan, the unsmiling caretakers, and the rest of the oblivious household staff, he longed for someone who he could just talk to. Someone who could care for him solely for who he was. Someone who could be his friend.

Maybe, just maybe, she could be that friend.

"Susan?" someone called from the doorway.

Her eyes and smile lingered on Rey's face for another second, lighting his heart and soul. Then, almost reluctantly, he thought, she turned back toward the door. "Yes?" she called.

Susan. So now he had a name to go with the face and the smile. *Susan.*

"You haven't finished out here yet," a woman's voice said, an undertone of disapproval to it. "Come do this first."

"Yes, ma'am," Susan said. "I'm coming."

Her eyes flicked back to Rey, and she smiled again. Not the same wide smile as the first, but a smaller, private one. The kind of smile shared by friends who are both in on the same private secret.

The kind of smile that promised she would be back later.

She turned and walked across the room. Rey watched her go, the image of that smile dancing in front of his eyes.

He was sure of it now. She would be his friend.

There was a heavy tap on Rey's shoulder. "You going to play, or what?" Grond rumbled.

With a mild surprise, Rey realized his fingers had come to a halt. "Of course I'm going to play," he said, shifting back to the Beethoven with new vigor. Susan would be back, just as soon as she'd finished out there. She would be back, and she would smile at him again. Beneath his fingers the piano was singing now—

And then, from his chair, came a soft trilling sound.

He could have cried. *No,* he begged the universe. *No. Not now. Not when she'll be coming back any minute.*

But the universe didn't care. With a tired sigh, he let his fingers come to a halt again on the keys. "Chair: Mr. Quillan's office," he ordered sadly.

The master had called, and it was time to go to work.

. . .

"The basic neurological theories are obscure, but there for the taking," Quillan said as he gestured Thorwald to a chair in his private, ultra-secure third-floor office. "The genius of our associate in Ghana was in pulling it all together. And, of course, having the will to act on it."

"Telepathy." Thorwald shook his head, as if not sure he approved of the word. "Frankly, I wouldn't have believed it."

Quillan smiled. "Frankly, you still don't," he said. "That's why you're here. McCade thought you'd find the demonstration more effective if you were a few million kilometers away from him at the time."

Across the room, the door chimed. Quillan keyed the remote, and the panel slid open to reveal Rey in his chair. "Come in, Rey," he invited. "Hendrik, this is Rey, my personal terminal of the Old-Boy Network. Seventeen years old, in case you're wondering. The younger they are when we get them, the better they react to the procedure."

"A cripple?" Thorwald said, frowning.

"An unavoidable side effect of the process," Quillan explained as Rey rolled into the room, the door sealing shut behind him. "It turns out the human brain hasn't got enough spare neurological capacity to handle telepathy. Some creative clearing and retasking is needed."

He stood up as Rey rolled to a stop beside the desk. "You basically need two clear areas to work with," he said, circling around behind the boy. "The first is the section that operates the legs. No big loss; a programmed wheelchair can let him get around just fine."

He touched Rey's left cheek. "The other is the lower left side of the face. Smile for Hendrik, Rey."

The skin around Thorwald's eyes and lips crinkled with revulsion as Rey gave him that broken half-smile of his. "I see," he said.

"Disgusting, isn't it?" Quillan agreed. "All completely reversible." It wasn't, of course, and he and all the rest of the Old Boys knew it. Sometimes he toyed with the idea of telling Rey the truth, just to see what the boy's reaction would be.

So far he'd resisted that temptation. Maybe someday when he was particularly bored he'd give it a shot.

"Has he actually performed any reversals?" Thorwald asked.

"At another eight hundred million a shot?" Quillan said pointedly. "Besides, in the fifteen years the Network has been running all the telepaths have worn out well before the ten years they signed on for. Easier and cheaper at that point just to replace them."

Thorwald sent an almost furtive look at Rey. "Should we be talking this way . . . ?"

"Not a problem." Quillan patted Rey's shoulder. "Rey is an excellent telepath. I'm sure he'll go the distance."

"Besides," he added, gesturing to the flesh-colored band around Rey's neck as he sat back down again, "standard procedure is to give our telepaths a dose of TabRasa-33 after every session. Memory scrambler; wipes out all short-term memories for the preceding twenty to thirty minutes. I could tell him I'm going to kill him tomorrow and he wouldn't remember a thing about it an hour from now. Well; let's get started."

Reaching into his desk, Quillan pulled out a stack of photos and a small picture stand. "Pictures of each of the others' terminals," he explained, showing Thorwald the stack as he set up the stand in front of Rey. "All Rey has to do is visualize the face, and the other telepath will pick up on the signal."

"And then?" Thorwald asked.

"Then we're in," Quillan said, selecting the photo of McCade's current telepath and putting it on the stand. "Go ahead, Rey."

For a moment Rey gazed at the photo, as if trying to memorize it. Then, that familiar but still creepy look settled over his face. His eyes seemed to glaze over, his half-functional mouth went a little slack, and he let out a huffing sigh. "He's in contact," Quillan murmured. "Now it's just a matter of the other telepath sending for McCade."

"By phone?"

Quillan shook his head. "Single-tone, single-duration signal button on the wheelchair," he said. "You never, ever want to have anything near your telepath that can record or transmit."

"Including other people?" Thorwald asked.

"Especially other people," Quillan agreed grimly. "Except for his caretakers, no one in this house is allowed to talk to Rey or even get within three meters of him."

"Why don't you just lock him up?" Thorwald asked.

"Counterproductive," Quillan said. "You let your telepath get too bored or in too much of a rut and he burns out faster. It's cheaper in the long run to let them roam around a little. You just have to make sure there's no way to pass information back and forth. He's not allowed any writing instruments, obviously."

Abruptly, Rey seemed to straighten up. "Hello?" he said.

"McCade?" Quillan asked.

There was a brief pause. "Yes," Rey said. "Quillan, I presume?"

"Correct," Quillan said. "I have an acquaintance of yours here with me. Would you care to say hello?"

"Hello, Hendrik," Rey said. "I trust Archer is treating you well?"

"Quite well, thank you," Thorwald said. His eyes, Quillan noted, had the suspicious look of a small child watching his first magician. "What's new at the ranch?"

"Well, we've got six new lambs," Rey said. "Looks like we may get another twenty before the season runs its course. Has Archer invited you to drive up Ascraeus Mons yet?"

"He has, and I've turned him down," Thorwald said. "Barbaric place, this. The next time we meet, I think we'll do it at *my* house."

"Now, be honest, Hendrik," Rey said. "Is it Mars you find barbaric, or Archer's lack of a proper wine cellar? When you visit him, Archer, you'll have to talk him out of a bottle of the '67 Bordeaux Sanjai. I understand he bought up the entire year's vintage, except for a few bottles that went to some New York hotel by mistake. Which one was it again, Hendrik?"

"The Ritz-Aberdon," Thorwald said, shaking his head. "I don't believe this."

"Neither did I, at first," Rey said. "But as you see, it does work."

"So it would appear," Thorwald said. "So aside from allowing me to safely tell rude jokes about the President, Secretary-General, and Chairman of the Financial Reserve, what exactly is this good for?"

Rey made an odd snorting noise. "Shall we give him the standard example, Archer?" he invited.

"Certainly," Quillan said, smiling. "At the moment, Hendrik, Mars is nine light-minutes from Earth. That means that information traveling by radio or laser takes nine minutes to get from there to here. Jonathan, what's the Unified European Market doing at the moment?"

"Odd that you should ask," Rey said. "As it happens, Bavarian General Transport hit a peak price of eighty-nine point three exactly four minutes ago. Two minutes later, the profit-hunters moved in, and it's been on its way down ever since. Eighteen points so far, with no signs of a turnaround. I believe, Hendrik, that you have some minor investments in BGT?"

It was as if someone had touched a match to Thorwald's lower lip. His whole body jerked, his eyes lighting up as the true reality of the situation suddenly caught up with him. "God," he bit out, twisting his wrist up to look at his watch. "But—"

"Exactly," Quillan said, reaching to his desk computer and punching up his InstaTrade connection. "The news of that eighty-nine high won't hit the Martian Repeater Lists for another five minutes, and the downturn won't start for seven. Would you care to place a sell order? Effective, say, six minutes from now?"

"God," Thorwald muttered again, swiveling the computer around and starting to punch in his personal codes. "The possibilities—"

"Are endless," Quillan agreed. "Stock manipulation, advance warnings of news events that could affect your holdings or your businesses, tips to share back and forth without all those ambitious young Turks listening in. The sky's the limit."

"Or rather, the sky is no longer the limit," Rey put in dryly. "You can do conference calls, too, by setting out two or more photos for your telepath. *That* one can have uses all its own. As we all found out in that Estevez matter a few months back."

"Indeed," Quillan said. "The Securities Enforcement people got suspicious of Sergei Bondonavich and planted a spy on him. When Mr. Estevez suddenly disappeared—down an abandoned salt mine near Berchtesgaden, I believe—the rest of his group descended on Sergei like middle-management attacking the company Christmas buffet. He spun them a complete frosted sugar cookie, then hot-footed it onto the Network with a conference call and clued the rest of us in on the story he told. By the time their associates came knocking on our own doors ten minutes later, we were able to corroborate every detail."

"All without a single indication that there'd been any communication between us," Rey added. "As far as I know, they still haven't even located Estevez's body."

"All right, I'm convinced," Thorwald said. "What's the catch?"

"There isn't any," Rey assured him. "Each of us in the Old-Boy Network has basically arrived. Each of us is powerful enough to be largely immune to attacks from the others, even if one of us was foolish enough to try. No, at this point our main focus is to bite off the heads of the smaller fish nipping at our tail fins."

"And to deal with the self-appointed guardians of all that is right and good," Quillan said contemptuously. "The solar system is our private pond now, to borrow Jonathan's fish metaphor. Why not swim together?"

"I presume Archer's already quoted you the price," Rey said. "The only other requirement is that you share secrets and information with the others in fair value for what you receive. And, of course, that you maintain complete airtight security on the whole operation. If you'd like, we'll give you a week to think about it."

"No need," Thorwald said, straightening up from the computer. "I'm in."

"Excellent," Rey said. "Then enjoy the rest of your stay, and call me when you get back to Earth. I'll have things set up, and we'll go from there. Oh, and do try to get up Ascraeus Mons at least once. No trip to Mars is complete without it."

"I'll think about it," Thorwald said. "Good-bye, Jonathan."

He looked at Quillan. "Is that right? Do I say good-bye?"

"You can," Quillan said. "Rey, break contact. How was it?"

He watched as Rey gave the little shudder he always did as he cleared the connection. "Pretty clear," the boy said, rubbing at his lips. "The other . . . he didn't seem completely on track today."

"What does that mean?" Thorwald asked, frowning.

"The contact wasn't as sharp as it should have been," Quillan explained. "At least, in Rey's estimation."

"What could cause that?"

"The other telepath might have been distracted." Quillan looked at the clock. "Or tired—it is only four a.m. at McCade's ranch. Any misfires, Rey?"

"No," Rey said hesitantly. "I don't think so."

"Misfires?" Thorwald asked.

"As Rey listens to what I'm saying, the other telepath hears it through his ears and brain," Quillan explained. "Rather like hearing an echo, I expect. The other telepath then repeats the message back to McCade, and it's Rey's turn to hear the echo as he speaks."

"That's why there was that pause before the other end answers," Thorwald said, nodding. "McCade had to get the message relayed, and then answer."

"Correct," Quillan said. "Misfires are when the other telepath doesn't repeat the message exactly the way it was sent. Usually it's only a dropped word here or there, and usually it's just carelessness or a case of someone using sentences too long or complicated for the telepath to handle."

"But if it's not?"

"Then it could be the first sign of a burned-out telepath," Quillan said bluntly. "At which point, that particular Old Boy is advised that it may soon be time to upgrade his equipment."

He patted Rey on the shoulder. "Fortunately for McCade's wallet, it sounds like his mouthpiece is holding up just fine." He shifted his hand, squeezing the collar around Rey's neck in the proper place. "That'll be all, Rey."

"Yes, sir," Rey murmured, his eyes starting to glaze over as the TabRasa trickled into his bloodstream.

"Go take a nap," Quillan added. "Chair: Rey's bedroom."

The chair turned and rolled across the room. "Trouble?" Thorwald asked as the door opened and passed the chair and its dozing passenger out of the office.

"I don't know," Quillan said slowly. "It occurs to me that there's another possibility for that sub-par connection just now. That it may not be *McCade's* telepath who's tired or distracted.

Quillan got up from his chair. "Help yourself to my cigars, or anything else you want. I'll be back soon."

Rey woke abruptly, with the disorientation that always came after a dose of TabRasa. After three years he was used to it, but it was never entirely comfortable.

Still, there were worse things in life. Much worse things. He could certainly put up with it for the remaining seven years of his contract.

And when he had finished, Mr. Quillan would give him back his legs and his face, and he would get the bonus money he'd been promised.

And his parents and siblings would finally be able to get off that dirt-scrabble Central American farm and have the kind of financial security that had never been more than an impossible dream for anyone in his village.

For a minute he let himself enjoy that thought. Then, bidding his family a silent goodbye, he began searching for the edge where memory ended and this most recent gap began.

Yes; the library. The piano. Beethoven.

Susan.

He let her image hover in front of his closed eyes, tracing every line and curve in his memory. Making sure that, no matter how much TabRasa Mr. Quillan gave him, he would never, ever forget that face. That face, or that smile.

That smile that had promised she would be back . . .

With a start he opened his eyes and looked over at his clock, then grabbed for the arm of his chair. Less than an hour had gone by since the library, which meant she was probably still cleaning somewhere in the house. If he could figure out where, he could at least explain to her that he hadn't just casually run out on her.

He wasn't supposed to talk to anyone except his caretakers, he knew. But surely Mr. Quillan would understand this one time. Surely he would.

"That's her," Grond said, nodding across the solarium at one of the three maids polishing the brasswork around the flower pots. "Name's Susan Baker; came on about three months ago. A little standoffish, the house-keeper says, but she has no complaints about her work."

"What about her attention to Rey?"

"Probably the last month or so," Grond said. "That's when he started acting strange. Making excuses all the time to go downstairs."

Quillan nodded, studying the girl. About eighteen years old, thin, dark hair, plain mousy face. Not at all attractive, to his way of thinking. "But she's never talked to him?"

"No, sir." Grond was positive. "At least, not on my watch. Hasn't even gotten within four meters. All she's done is smile."

Mentally, Quillan shook his head. Such a lot of fuss and bother over so very little.

If it was, indeed, a lot of fuss and bother. "Go get her," he ordered, stepping to one of the chairs beside the curved windows and sitting down.

A minute later she was standing in front of him. "Yes, sir?" she asked tentatively.

For a moment Quillan just gazed up at her. Sometimes letting an underling squirm under a direct glare could squeeze out a glimpse of a guilty conscience.

But she just stood there, looking puzzled. "I understand you've been trying to meet my nephew," he said.

She frowned a bit harder. "Your nephew, sir?"

"The boy in the wheelchair," Quillan amplified. "Recovering from a serious accident. Weren't you told when you arrived here that if you saw him you weren't to speak to him?"

"Yes, sir, I was," she said. "But I haven't spoken to him."

"You've smiled at him," Quillan said, making the words an accusation.

Again, nothing but more puzzlement. "I smile at everyone," she protested, her face looking more mouse-like than ever. "I was just trying to be friendly."

"I don't want you to be friendly," Quillan said firmly. "Not to him. The psychological aspects of the accident have been far more severe than even the physical damage. He needs time to work it all through."

"I understand, sir," she said. "But . . ."

"But?" Quillan echoed, making the word a challenge.

"Wouldn't it be better for him to mix with other people?" she asked, the words coming out in a rush. "To see that he can be accepted just like he is?"

Quillan raised his eyebrows. "Are you telling me that my thousand-dollar-an-hour psychologists don't know what they're talking about?" he asked pointedly.

She actually winced. "No, sir," she said in a low voice.

"Good," Quillan said. "I would hate to think I'd been wasting all that money when an unschooled cleaning woman had better advice to give. You're to stay away from him. You're not to talk to him, or look at him. You're especially not to smile at him. Is that clear?"

"Yes, sir," she said, bobbing her head.

"Good," Quillan said. "Then get back to work."

"Yes, sir," she said again. In that peculiar gait people have when they're trying not to look like they're hurrying, she hurried away.

Grond stepped to his side. "Sir?"

"I don't know," Quillan said thoughtfully. "She seems such a pathetic specimen to be distracting our terminal."

Abruptly, he came to a decision. "Give her a month's severance and get her out of the house," he said, standing up. "Right now. Tell her we'll collect her things from her room and send them on to her at the Ares Hiltonia—set up a room there for her. You pack her bags yourself, and make sure to look everything over carefully while you do."

"Yes, sir," Grond said. "What exactly am I looking for?"

"Anything that might suggest she's more than the waste of skin she appears," Quillan said. "A camera, perhaps. Nothing electronic gets into this house that I don't know about, but it's possible to make a purely mechanical camera."

"If there's anything there, I'll find it," Grond promised. "You want her *just* out of the house?"

Quillan rubbed his lower lip as he gazed across at the girl's back. Grond was right. She was almost certainly harmless; but on the other hand, Rey was a multi-million-dollar investment. There was no point in taking the risk. "You just give her that month's severance," he said. "I'll call Bondonavich and have him get whoever handled Estevez to take care of her more permanently."

Grond's lumpy forehead wrinkled. "You're going to have *Rey* send the order for her to disappear?"

"TabRasa is a wonderful invention," Quillan reminded him. "You just get her out of my house."

"Yes, sir."

Hunching his shoulders once, Grond headed across the solarium. Giving the girl one last look, Quillan headed for the door.

No, Rey wouldn't like it. Not at all. But by the time he realized what was going on, the call would be in progress and there would be nothing he could do about it.

And the boy would certainly get over it. TabRasa was indeed a wonderful invention.

She wasn't in the library. She wasn't in the main hallway, either, or the kitchen, or the dining room.

Where could she be?

Sitting in the middle of the hallway, Rey looked around him at the various directions he could go, his heart pounding uncomfortably. He wasn't even supposed to be down here alone, never mind giving himself a tour of the house this way. So far the only servants he'd seen were all at a distance, and as usual none of them had given him a second glance. But sooner or later, if he kept at this, he was bound to bump squarely into someone.

And then what? Would he compound his disobedience by asking where Susan was?

At this point he didn't really know what he would do. All he knew was that he needed to find her. Turning the chair around, he headed down the main hallway. Somewhere back here, he had heard, was a stairway that led down to the servants' quarters.

He had just rounded a corner off the main hallway when an older man emerged from the theater room. "Rey!" he said with surprise. "What are you doing here?"

Rey froze. *Someone* was talking to *him*! And not just someone, but a man he'd never seen before in his life. Some guest of Mr. Quillan's?

But whether or not Rey knew who he was, it was clear he knew who Rey was. "You're not supposed to down here alone," the man growled, striding toward him. "Where's your caretaker?"

"I—I don't know," Rey managed. "He's not—"

"Get yourself upstairs," the man snapped. "Right now."

"Yes, sir," Rey said automatically. "Chair—"

He stopped short as a face suddenly seemed to appear before his eyes, pushing aside his mental picture of Susan. "Yes, I'll get him," he murmured in response to the silent call, pressing the signal button underneath his chair's armrest.

"What is it, a call?" the man asked, glancing around. "Come on, we'd better get you to his office."

"He says it's very important," Rey murmured. "Vitally important."

"What's vitally important?" Mr. Quillan's voice came from somewhere behind him.

The man looked up over Rey's shoulder. "He's got a call from someone," he said. "I thought you said he's not supposed to be down here alone."

"He's not," Mr. Quillan said grimly, coming around the chair into Rey's line of sight and glaring down at him. "Rey, what are you doing here?"

"Vitally important," Rey repeated. "Must talk to you. Now."

"Damn," Mr. Quillan muttered. He glanced around, gestured toward the door across from the theater room. "Chair: Conference Room One. It's secure enough," he added to the other man as the chair started rolling, "and faster than getting him upstairs to the office. This just better be *damn* urgent."

A minute later they were in the conference room. Mr. Quillan checked the monitors built into the table, then dropped into one of the chairs. "All right, we're secure," he said. "This is Quillan. Who is this?"

As if it were being carried down a long hollow tube, Rey heard a man's voice in the distance. *This is McCade.*

"This is McCade," he repeated.

We've got a problem.

"We've got a problem," Rey echoed.

*Or rather, you do. I've just learned Enforcement has planted a spy
on you—*

"Or rather, you do," Rey said. "I've just learned Enforcement has
planted a spy on you—"

Named Susan Baker.

"Named Susan Ba—"

Abruptly, Rey faltered, her face springing into sharp new focus in
front of his eyes. Susan Baker? *Susan?*

"What?" Mr. Quillan snapped, bounding up out of his chair. "Susan
what?"

"Baker," Rey stammered. "I—Mr. Quillan—"

But the other wasn't even listening. "Grond!" he shouted into his
remote as he sprinted toward the door. "Stop her! Don't let her get out
of the house!"

He slammed the door open and was gone. *What's happening?* the
voice echoed through Rey's mind.

Rey didn't answer. Swiveling his chair around, he started toward
the door.

A hand grabbed at his shoulder. "No you don't," the other man bit
out. "Where do you think you're—?"

The last word came out in a strangled gasp as Rey slammed his
elbow with all the strength he could manage into the man's abdomen.
Maneuvering the chair around the table and potted trees, he rolled out
the door.

They were all there, down by the bend in the hallway: Quillan,
Grond, and Susan. Grond had a grip on Susan's arm, holding it bent
behind her back. Her face—that wonderful, kind face—was twisted
almost beyond recognition with pain and fear.

"Stop!" Rey shouted. Or at least, he tried to shout. Instead, the words
came out as barely a squeak. Susan's eyes flicked to Rey's face, a wordless
plea there . . .

And with a sudden blaze of anger, Rey sent the chair rolling toward
the trio at full speed. Words weren't going to stop Grond now, he knew.
From somewhere in the distance he could hear the warbling of some
kind of alarm—

And then, to his astonishment, five men charged into view around
the corner of the hallway. Grond barely had time to snap a warning
before three of them leaped at him, wrenching Susan's arm out of his
grip and wrestling him to the floor. One of the others pushed warningly

at Quillan's chest, while the last hurriedly pulled Susan away from the confusion. "You all right?" Rey heard him ask.

"I'm fine," she breathed, looking over at Rey again. "There's Rey," she added.

"Right," the man said briskly, beckoning Rey toward him. "Rey? Come on over."

Rey let the chair coast to a halt where he was, staring at them in confusion. Did Susan know these people? What were they doing here? Who were they? "It's all right, Rey," Susan called, smiling weakly as she rubbed her arm. "Don't worry. These are the good guys."

Quillan snorted loudly. "And they'd better enjoy themselves while they can," he said. "You've leaned way over the mark with this one, Winslow. *Way* over. By this time tomorrow you'll be on suspension, pending charges of gross misconduct."

"No, I don't think so," the man beside Susan—Winslow—said calmly. A dozen more men appeared around the corner, all of them dressed in police uniforms, and strode purposefully past Rey. Glancing over his shoulder, he saw them start checking the rooms. "Come on, Rey, join the party," Winslow added. "It's all over. Really."

Hesitantly, Rey nudged the chair forward. "Let's run through the formalities, shall we?" Winslow said, turning his attention back to Quillan. "Archer Quillan, you're under arrest for stock manipulation, illegal business practices—"

He paused dramatically. "*And* obstruction of justice and accessory after the fact in the murder of Securities Enforcement agent Juan Estevez."

Quillan snorted again. "And you'll be awaiting a full psychiatric examination on top of it," he said scornfully. "You couldn't make charges like that stick to the floor."

Winslow smiled. "You might be surprised," he said. "You see, we finally have a witness to all this sludge-water manipulation you and your trillionaire buddies have been indulging in. Someone who can quote your words exactly. Yours, *and* Jonathan McCade's, *and* Sergei Bondonavich's. Everything you've said on your cozy little Old-Boy Network for the past month, in fact."

"You *are* insane," Quillan insisted, looking at Susan and then Rey. "There's not a thing either of them can tell you. I've made sure of that."

"Who said I was talking about either of them?" Winslow countered, shifting his eyes toward the corner. "Julia?" he called, raising his voice. "It's safe—come on in."

He looked back at Quillan. "We knew we couldn't get anything from the inside," he said. "Between TabRasa and electronic countermeasures, you had all those bases covered.

"And so we arranged for you to deliver the information *outside* the house. To us."

"You're bluffing," Quillan said flatly. "Nothing has left this house."

"Ah, but it has," Winslow said. "We figured that with all this paranoid secrecy, you'd probably have Rey locked away someplace where he would be starved for human contact. So we provided him with a friendly face. A face that, hopefully, he would always have hovering at the edges of his mind."

"A pathetic face," Quillan said contemptuously, looking at Susan.

"In your opinion," Winslow said. "But obviously not in Rey's. Tell me, Quillan; have you ever heard of a carbon copy?"

Quillan frowned. "A what?"

"A carbon copy," Winslow repeated. "That's an out-of-date term for a duplicate you make of a communication to send elsewhere. That's basically what we were getting."

Quillan was looking at the man as if he were crazy. "What in the System are you talking about?" he demanded. "There aren't any copies."

"That's where you're wrong." Winslow gestured at Susan. "Meet Enforcement Agent Trainee Susan Converse."

And then, from around the corner, rolled another wheelchair. A wheelchair just like Rey's. A wheelchair holding a young woman.

A woman with a very familiar face . . .

Quillan inhaled sharply. "And," Winslow added quietly, "meet Susan's identical twin sister Julia. As you can see, your associate in Ghana was willing to cut himself a deal."

"We'll want you to stay on Mars another couple of weeks," Susan said, setting a mug of hot tea on the table in front of Rey as she slid into the seat across from him. "Just in case we need you to add to your deposition."

"So what Mr. Quillan said was true?" Rey asked, looking down at his tea, afraid to look directly at her. Her, or her sister. "When they took him away? That you were just using me?"

"They needed to be stopped, Rey," she said gently. "They didn't believe any of the rules applied to them anymore. Juan Estevez was just one example of the sort of thing they were getting away with every day.

Quillan would have killed you, too, once you were of no more use to him. Just as he killed the telepath he had before you."

She reached across the table and touched his hand. "But that said, no, we weren't just using you. Any more than we were just using Julia. Or me."

"You and Julia volunteered," Rey said bitterly. "I didn't have any choice in the matter."

"How could we have asked you?" Susan pointed out. "Quillan had you totally isolated."

"From everybody except Julia," Rey countered, his voice coming out harsher than he'd expected. "You ever think of that? *She* could have asked me."

"Winslow suggested that," Julia's slightly slurred voice said softly from Rey's left. "But I was afraid to."

The sheer surprise of the comment got Rey's gaze up out of his tea. She'd been *afraid* to? "Why?

To his surprise, he saw tears gathering at the corners of her eyes. "Because there was no proof I could give you," she said softly. "I was afraid you'd think I was just trying to stir you up against Quillan. I thought you'd never want to see me or talk to me . . ."

She looked away. "There's no reversal, Rey. We're going to be like this for the rest of our lives. We're never going to fit in anymore, not with anyone. I was afraid if you started hating me . . ."

Rey looked at Susan. There were no smiles there now, on that face whose every line he'd memorized. Nothing but love and heartache and sadness as she gazed at her sister.

He looked back at Julia. Then, hesitantly, he reached over and took her hand. "It's okay," he said. "Really. I've never hated anyone in my life. I'm sure not going to start with you."

She looked back at him, blinking away the tears. Then, almost as if afraid to believe it, she gave him a tentative smile.

A half smile, with the left part of her lips frozen in place. A nervous, almost frightened smile.

Rey smiled back. With the enormity of the sacrifice she'd made now crashing in on her, what Julia really needed was someone who could understand her. Someone who could care for her solely for who she was. Someone who could be her friend.

He would be that friend.

PROOF

●

"*There was a little girl, she had a little curl right
in the middle of her forehead;
And when she was good, she was very, very good,
and when she was bad, she was horrid.*"
—Henry Wadsworth Longfellow

Breakfast had been oatmeal again, that god-awful freeze-dried pap that
Angel Morris could never quite get to come out right, no matter how
much or how little of the dispenser's hot water she used. The coffee was
worse than usual, too, tingling her tongue and leaving a strange after-
taste behind. Probably someone new had made the low bid for food
services, and the new contract had started.

She finished eating and put the bowl and cup down the disposal
chute to be dissolved, cleaned, and reassembled in time for lunch. Then
she dressed herself in the most presentable of her light gray jumpsuits,
and sat on the edge of her cot, watching one of the interchangeable sit-
coms playing on the tiny screen set into the wall and wondering why the
hell they even bothered with the TV in the first place. They ought to be
able to feed the programs directly through the tiny CURL disk that had
been implanted into the center of her forehead. Skipping the TVs might
even save them enough money to buy some better shows.

It seemed like forever, but finally the warning buzzer came. The
door snicked open, and she stepped out into the long corridor, join-

ing the other women with their identical gray jumpsuits and identical bland faces heading out to the yard for the day's brief taste of fresh air. Another wonderful day in the paradise-on-Earth that was Oregon's Hillcrest Prison.

The last day she planned on ever spending in here.

"You all know how it all started," Mr. Jacobs said, his voice quiet and earnest and eminently reasonable. "The citizens wanted violent criminals locked securely away, but at the same time balked at paying the high costs involved. The state was heading for yet another fiscal crisis when Dr. Alan Cartier came up with his breakthrough Cognitive Universal Reality Linkage system.

"I'm sure you're all at least somewhat familiar with the CURL system, but let me just run through some of the highlights and perhaps dispel a few of the myths that have sprung up about it. First, the system only affects the prisoner's visual perception; that is, touch and taste and hearing are all quite normal and unaffected. Second, there are no direct psychological or mental effects involved, though I understand that researchers are working on such areas for future penal applications.

"Finally, civil libertarian hysteria and accusations to the contrary, there is absolutely nothing cruel or unusual about the system. The prisoners are not fed frightening or malicious images in order to keep them in line, nor are they shown alluring mirages to taunt or torture them. They're merely shown a few things that aren't there, and kept from seeing a few other things that are. With the prisoners preparing their own freeze-dried meals in their cells, and with automated fiber-reformable dishware and uniforms eliminating the need for food-service and laundry facilities, this has brought prison staffing costs down to a bare minimum, while still protecting both the citizens and the handful of actual guards on the site."

The midday sun was shining brightly as the prisoners filed out into the exercise yard that encircled the prison building like a wide, grassy moat. Of course, with the CURL in place, all that sunlight could be just an illusion. Still, Angel could feel the warmth on her face, so it probably was real.

She took a deep breath, then another, savoring the clean, crisp scent of the outdoor air. It wasn't until she was outside that she ever realized how genuinely bad the air inside really smelled, that sickening mixture of sweat and smoke and toilets and, occasionally, vomit. It always made going back inside that much harder.

That, at least, she wouldn't have to worry about today.

She gazed out at the barriers standing between her and freedom as she and the other women began dispersing across the yard, heading to the various pieces of exercise equipment or to just walk around and savor the sunshine. The first of those barriers was the waist-high wire-mesh warning fence that ringed the edge of the yard. Beyond that was a twenty-yard open area patrolled by dozens of guards with tasers, fighting batons, and compact shoulder-slung Uzi machine guns at the ready. Beyond that, should a prisoner somehow make it that far, was the outer wall itself, thirty feet of forbidding stone topped by coils of razor wire, with guard towers rising from each corner.

Only it wasn't real. None of it was. Or at least, very little.

One of the other prisoners bumped into her, and she spun around. "Watch it, skank," she growled.

"Sorry," the other woman said, her bland, featureless face not changing in the slightest as she moved hastily away. Angel watched her go, her skin crawling as she silently cursed the vicious bastard who'd thought this one up. Every single face, every single body in this place looked exactly the same. It was like being locked up with a bunch of faceless robot zombie clones, making the view inside the wall as bland and tasteless as the morning oatmeal.

"The CURL also provides what's known as 'shrouding,' overwriting all the inmates' features and body type with a single uniform pattern as seen by all the other prisoners," Mr. Jacobs continued. "The purpose, of course, is not to eliminate potential friendships, but to defuse potential arguments and fights. After all, it's impossible to instigate a feud with someone if you can't pick that person out of a crowd. And you'd have to be a fool or completely psychotic to start a random fight when you can't tell whether the other person is smaller and weaker or bigger and nastier than you yourself are."

A wide walking path had been worn into the ground just inside the warning fence, the grass there beaten down by a thousand restless feet with nothing else to do. A dozen other prisoners were already striding along it as Angel arrived and worked herself into the pattern.

She gazed out at the guards as she walked. There were at least fifty of them out there today, looking back at her with expressionless faces, and she noted once again with a deep and vicious anger that *they* had been allowed to keep real faces and bodies.

But then, they had to . . . because the deep dark secret of Hillcrest Prison was that most of them weren't there at all.

Most of the prisoners didn't know that, of course. Most of them were gullible enough, or stupid enough, to take all this at face value.

But then, most of them hadn't made a point of sleeping with anyone who actually worked in the prison system the way she had while she was still on the outside. His name had been Carl, one of the few men she'd ever slept with whose name she'd bothered to learn.

"Angel Morris is a perfect case in point," Mr. Jacobs said. "Though convicted for only two murders, she's the probable perpetrator of at least seven more over a fifteen-year period. And unlike most of those incarcerated at Hillcrest, she *has* shown herself willing to pick fights with her fellow inmates, even with the shrouding in place. Guards have had to taser her twice in the past week just to calm her down. Apparently, she's not only violent and vicious, but stupid as well."

With one final grunt Carl rolled off her onto his side of the bed. "Whew!" he breathed. "You sure are something, Angelface. You know that?"

"I've been told," Angel said, forcing herself to snuggle up against his side. He'd gotten what he wanted. Now it was her turn. "So. It must be fun to work at Hillcrest, huh?"

"Naw," he said, fumbling at the bedside table and coming up with a cigarette. "It *is* pretty funny, though."

"Funny?"

"To see all those stupid sheep wandering around inside a wall that's not there," he said. "Mostly not there, anyway—the bottom seven feet are real enough. But the rest of it, plus the guard towers and razor wire—" He shook his head as he lit the cigarette, the light from the match throwing strange shadows across his face. It was one of those Turkish cigarettes she absolutely hated, and she crinkled her nose in disgust at the smell. "Sometimes you just want to tell them how stupid they are, just so you could see the looks on their faces."

"But you'd get fired if you did that, wouldn't you?"

He snorted. "Fired, hell. We'd probably get stampeded. There are only five of us out there on any shift, you know. Five guards, for a hundred prisoners or more outside at a time! You believe that?"

"It's the CURL that makes it work, right?" she asked, probing delicately. "It makes them see what isn't there?"

"That, and makes them *not* see some of the stuff that *is* there," he said smugly. "Gotta admit it's kind of cool."

"And there's nothing that can stop it, huh?"

"Oh, sure, lots of things," he said, tapping the cigarette off into an ashtray. "The computer feeding the images could crash. Not going to happen, though. A good shock nearby might scramble it, too, at least for a second or two. Or someone could get some long needle-nose pliers and pull it out of her forehead. 'Course, that would hurt. A lot."

"A shock, you say," she said, latching onto the interesting part. "You mean an electrical shock, like a taser or something?"

"Yeah." He stretched, the movement sending a few ashes drifting into the air. "Hey, be a good girl and go get me a beer, would you, Babe?"

She stiffened, her breath catching in her throat, a blood-red haze dropping like a curtain across her vision. *Babe* . . . "What did you mean, the CURL makes them not see things that are there?" she asked, forcing her voice to stay calm.

"Enough shop talk, huh?" he said tiredly. "Damn, but you've got a weird idea of what to chat about afterward. Just go get that beer, huh?"

"Don't you mean, go get that beer, *Babe*?" she countered.

"Whatever," he said off-handedly.

Her right hand groped for the sheets, got a good grip on them and squeezed, fighting against the terrible ache to do him right here and now. *Not yet*, she warned herself urgently. *Not yet. Not until he tells you everything.* "Okay," she said, prying her fingers loose from the sheets and slipping out from under them. "Then will you tell me what's there the prisoners can't see?"

He grunted. "Sure," he said tiredly. "Whatever."

She padded barefoot to the kitchen and got two beers out of the refrigerator. Then, crossing to the butcher block, she pulled out the biggest knife there.

Later, after it was all over, she made sure to carefully wash the blood off her hands as she finished off the last of her beer.

. . .

She was approaching one of the guards now, standing a half dozen feet inside the mesh fence, his eyes flitting alertly back and forth across the yard. "Nice day," she called, smiling at him as she passed.

There was just the barest of pauses before his eyes shifted to focus on her. But it was enough. "Yeah," he grunted back.

Angel continued walking, still smiling as she marked the man's face in her mind. She'd never managed to get Carl to tell her how to tell the real guards from the phantom ones, but since being put in here she'd figured it out for herself. The real ones could respond to her questions and comments right away, but the computer running the CURL system had to take a moment to process the input and come up with an answer for the fake ones.

She glanced back over her shoulder at the phantom guard. There was something odd about their shadows, too, she'd noted, something that didn't look quite real against the genuine grass beneath their feet.

But she didn't just have Carl's word and her own speculation to go on. She'd seen the reality for herself, twice, just before those taser shots had knocked her out. She'd seen the shortened wall, and the faces of her fellow prisoners, and the empty spaces that up to that moment had been filled by threatening guards.

Unless that had all been yet another trick, this one a trick of the taser and her looming unconsciousness and her own desire to believe there was indeed a way out of here. Certainly as she gazed out now across the prison yard it was hard to believe that her eyes could lie to her so effectively and persistently.

But whether those taser images had been the proof she craved or not, today was the day she had to make her move. There'd been some technical glitch with her sentencing hearing, she knew, but it was back on track now. And if it went badly and they transferred her to death row, she might never get another chance at this.

Facing forward again, being careful not to bump into any of the slower walkers on the track, she continued around the track.

"The system has been up and running for five years," Mr. Jacobs said. "And in that time, it's shown itself to provide better prison security at a fraction of traditional costs.

"But despite all these precautions—despite all our technology and planning and preparation—things can and do sometimes go terribly wrong."

She had to make six circuits of the track, but when she was finished she had all five of the real guards pinpointed.

Not surprisingly, all these months of herding human cattle had made them sloppy. Instead of spacing themselves more or less evenly around the yard, they'd clumped themselves together on one side, probably so that they could relieve the boredom by chatting together. Being a prison guard, after all, was probably nearly as bad as being one of the prisoners.

The problem—for them—was that the prison buildings rose a good two stories up from the center of the ground. That meant that, from where they all stood, there was a whole chunk of the exercise yard they couldn't see.

There would be cameras, of course, watching those blind spots. But Hillcrest's touted budget savings had cut into that aspect of prison life, too, and she doubted there would be more than a single man on duty in the monitor room. He certainly wouldn't be expecting anyone to make a run for it.

And he certainly would have no way of stopping her.

She continued on around the track, keeping an eye on the guards in their little discussion group until they disappeared out of sight behind the corner of the building. She gave it another ten paces, just to be sure. Then, taking a deep breath, she put a hand on the mesh fence, vaulted over it, and ran for the wall.

The phantom guards reacted, of course, swinging their guns toward her and shouting for her to halt. But even here they reacted with the slight hesitation that showed her guess and her gamble had been right. Even as they continued to threaten her they could do nothing but stand impotently in place as she blew past them. The wall loomed ahead; bracing herself, she crouched down and leaped.

She slammed chest-first into the stone, sending a shock straight through to her spine. But Carl's pillow talk and her own brief glimpses proved to be correct. Her fingertips slipped through the supposedly solid rock and caught onto the edge of the genuine wall. Weeks of fingertip pushups and bicep isometrics now proved their worth as she pulled herself up and got a leg onto the top. Rolling herself up and over, she caught a glimpse of the other prisoners staring at her in astonishment and chagrin as she slipped through the wall and out onto the far side. With her fingers still gripping the top, she managed to turn herself upright again as she dropped the short distance to the ground, landing on her feet.

The landscape surrounding the prison was about as bleak as anything she could imagine: flat, dusty ground as far as she could see, with clumps of grass and small brown bushes the only vegetation. Miles and miles of nothing, with hunger and thirst the only promise for anyone foolhardy enough to make the effort.

But she wasn't fooled. There was no wilderness here, only the lying CURL feeding hopelessness to her eyes. There was a town out there somewhere, a town she could disappear into if only she could get to it.

But the prison still had one trick left up its sleeve. Instead of heading straight away from the wall, she turned and ran parallel to it, keeping as close to the stone as possible. Carl had insisted that the invisible moat wouldn't be fatal, but would merely send the unwary escapee sliding helplessly down a gentle slope to a deep containment pit where she could be retrieved at the guards' leisure.

Unfortunately, with this particular illusion her shadow trick wouldn't be of any use. But she didn't need tricks anymore. She knew human nature, and she understood how the real world operated, and she knew there had to be a road somewhere across the moat to let in the midnight truckloads of supplies used to restock the prisoners' food bins. And the logical place for the five real guards to have clustered was the spot where that road came in, where they would be going out again when their shift was over.

From inside she could hear the alarms blaring the news of her escape. But once again the state's stinginess was going to work in her favor. Half the prisoners in the yard had seen her go through the imaginary wall, and the guards' absolute first priority would be to bully or bluff or batter them back into their cells before they realized that their prison was a tissue of lies and made their own mass break for freedom.

Once again, she was right. She reached the spot where the guards had been clustered and slowed to a walk, easing herself away from the wall now as she carefully probed at the ground with her foot. It was just as well she'd stayed close to the wall: barely four feet away from it the toe of her shoe dipped beneath supposedly solid ground as she found the moat. She continued on, one foot sliding along the moat's edge, until a half dozen steps later she hit solid ground again.

With the alarms still blaring, a few more tentative taps were all she dared take time for. But she had no doubt she'd found the road. Taking a couple of deep breaths to replenish her lungs, she headed away from the prison. Her eyes told her she was running on dusty, uneven ground, but her feet felt the smooth hardness of pavement beneath them. She kept going, wondering how far she would have to get before the feed to the CURL was cut off . . .

And then, as if she'd broken through a curtain she hadn't even known was there, the world around her suddenly changed.

The wilderness vanished, leaving her pounding along a new black-topped road amid a field of lush green grass. A hundred yards ahead another blacktopped road encircled the prison grounds, and beyond that were the modest homes of a small town stretching toward the green Oregon hills beyond.

The sheer shock of it caught her feet in a stumble, nearly toppling her flat onto her face. It was one thing to know on an intellectual level that what she'd been seeing in the prison wasn't real. It was something else entirely to get clear of the CURL's influence and actually see the reality for herself.

There were no cars moving along any of the streets within her view, but the first house past the circular road had a small blue Ford parked in the driveway. Smiling grimly to herself, she picked up her pace. Where there was a car, there was probably someone home.

"Because, you see, unless you physically lock a person away in something the size of a coffin, it's simply impossible to give a one-hundred-percent guarantee that he or she won't ever get out," Mr. Jacobs said. "Unfortunate, and potentially disastrous. But that is the way of the human spirit."

The man who answered the door barely had time for his eyes to go wide before Angel gut-punched him with every ounce of her weight and strength. He gave an agonized cough and staggered backward as she came in, kicking the door closed again behind her. "Car keys," she snapped. "Where are they?"

"Here," he managed, fumbling in his pocket with one hand as he clutched at his stomach with the other. His shaking fingers misfired, dropping the key ring on the rug with a muted tinkle.

"Money?" she asked, giving him a shove backward and retrieving the keys.

"Wallet," he said, nodding toward the kitchen table. Already his breath was coming a little easier, she noted as she crossed to the table. She might need to hit him again.

And then, even as she picked up the wallet, she spotted the real jackpot lying on the counter beside the sink. A jackpot in the form of a nice shiny Colt 9mm autoloader.

"Well, well," she said, dropping the wallet into the top of her jumpsuit as she stepped over and picked it up. The weight felt good in her hand. "What have we here?"

"It's not loaded," the man wheezed carefully.

"No?" She worked the slide halfway, glancing down long enough to confirm there was a round in the chamber, then looked up again. "Looks loaded to me."

"Okay, look," he said, trying to cajole through his gasping. "You got what you need, right? How about just going away now. How about it, Babe?"

She stiffened, the old familiar pain and rage stirring inside her. "What did you call me?" she asked softly.

"What?" he asked. "Oh. You mean 'Babe'?"

"Yeah. That," she said, taking a step toward him. "You know what happens to men who call me that?"

He shook his head. "No."

"This," she said, and squeezed the trigger.

The blast was deafening in the small room. The man toppled backward, twisting over to land heavily on his face on the rug. If he'd screamed, the sound of the shot had covered it up.

Pity. The screaming was usually the most satisfying part.

Stuffing the gun inside her jumpsuit beside the wallet, she slipped out the front door. That shot would certainly have been heard, but small-town people were always slow to react, and she would be well on her way long before any of them thought to call 911. Jogging across the lawn to the driveway, she circled around the car to the driver's side and jabbed the key into the keyhole.

Or rather, jabbed it straight *through* the keyhole.

And straight through the entire car.

For a horrible second she froze; and then, swearing viciously, she dug her hand into her jumpsuit and hauled out the gun.

But it was too late. Even as she tried to bring it around, invisible hands closed around her wrists.

There was no chance—she knew that from the start. But she fought them anyway, lashing out with all her strength as the fury and hatred and frustration came boiling out of her. She fired round after round from the gun, knowing full well that she was merely shooting into the air but unable to stop herself. More invisible hands grabbed at her arms as invisible bodies pressed against her, trying to force her to the ground. Still she fought, spitting curses at the cowardly attackers who didn't even have the guts to show themselves.

The bodies pressing against her chest seemed to part slightly, as if allowing someone or something through. Before she could take advantage of the lull, she heard a familiar crackle, and smelled the familiar stink of ozone, and the strength suddenly evaporated from her muscles as the high-voltage jolt from a taser arced through her.

And as she collapsed into her attackers' arms, the CURL in her forehead sputtered . . . and for a single fraction of a second she saw the genuine reality around her.

There was no town here, no roads leading off to green hills and freedom. The single road she'd run along from the prison wall continued ahead of her to a pair of tall, chain-link fences with rolls of razor wire between them. What she'd seen as nice little suburban houses were instead storage buildings, the house she'd invaded nothing but a large guard post.

And then her eyes closed, and the darkness took her.

The darkness, too, was reality.

"And so, thanks to our brave volunteer, the CURL itself, and the fact that Angel Morris didn't think to confirm that the bullets in her gun were real instead of blanks, we have now had a unique opportunity to see exactly what this vicious serial killer would do if she ever genuinely escaped from prison," Mr. Jacobs concluded his presentation. "According to Oregon law, as you know, a jury must answer three questions in the affirmative if it is to impose the death penalty: first, whether the death of the deceased was committed deliberately and with the reasonable expectation that death of the deceased or another would result; second, whether the conduct of the defendant in killing the deceased was unreasonable in response to the provocation, if any, by the deceased; and third, whether there is a probability that the defendant would commit criminal acts of violence that would constitute a continuing threat to society.

"The first two you have already answered in the affirmative. The third has now, I believe, been definitively proved.

"The People rest. We, and this court, await your sentencing verdict."

THE RING

●

It had been the fifth freefall day in a row on Wall Street, the kind of day that grinds all the anger and frustration out of an investor and leaves him feeling nothing at all, unless it's a weary desire for rest or death and either would be fine with him.

Which was why Nick Powell, department store floor manager and formerly-hopeful stock market investor, walked completely past the small curio shop on his way home from work before the exotic gold ring sitting on its black velvet pad in the window finally registered.

Even then, he almost didn't stop. His modest and carefully nurtured portfolio had been nearly wiped out in the bloodletting, and there was no place for impulse purchases in a budget that included food and clothing and a Manhattan rent.

But his girlfriend Lydia loved odd jewelry, and a week's worth of preoccupation with the markets had turned their permanent simmering disagreement about money first into a shouting argument and then into a cold and deadly silence. A suitable peace offering might help patch things up.

And who knew? In a little shop like this the ring might even be reasonably priced. Retracing his steps, Nick went inside.

"Afternoon," the shopkeeper greeted him. He was an old man, tall and thin, with wrinkled skin and a few gray hairs still holding tenaciously to his pale skull. But his blue eyes were sharp enough, and there was a sardonic twist to the corners of his mouth. "What can I do for you?"

"That ring in the window," Nick said. "I wonder if I might look at it."

The old man's eyes seemed to flash. "Very discerning," he said as he left the counter and crossed to the window. Nick winced as he passed, something about the air that brushed across his face sending a tingle up his back. "Antique German," the shopkeeper went on as he turned around again, the ring nestled in the palm of his hand. "Here—don't be afraid. Come and see."

Don't be afraid? Frowning at the odd comment, Nick leaned over to look.

Sitting behind a dusty window in the fading sunlight, the ring had been impressive. Pressed against human flesh in a bright, clean light, it was dazzling.

It was gold, of course, but somehow it seemed like a brighter, clearer, more vibrant gold than anything Nick had ever seen before. The design itself was equally striking: a meshed filigree of long, thin leaves intertwined with six slender human arms, each complete with a tiny but delicately shaped hand. "It's beautiful," he managed, the words catching oddly in his throat. "German, you say?"

"Very old German," the shopkeeper said. "Tell me, are you rich?"

Nick grimaced. So much for any peace offering to Lydia. It probably would just have earned him a lecture on extravagance anyway. "Hardly," he said, taking a step toward the door. "Thanks for—"

"Would you *like* to be rich?"

Nick frowned. There was an unpleasant gleam in the old man's eyes. "Of course," Nick said. "Who doesn't?"

"How badly?"

The standing disagreement with Lydia flashed through his mind. "Badly enough, I'm told," he muttered.

"Good." The old man thrust his hand toward Nick. "Here. Take it. Put it on."

Slowly, Nick reached over and took the ring. The old man's skin, where he touched it, felt cold and scaly. "What?"

"Put it on," the old man repeated.

"No, it's not for me—it's for a lady friend," Nick said.

"It doesn't want her," the old man said flatly, an edge to his voice. "Put it on."

Nick shook his head. "There's no way it'll fit," he warned, slipping the filigreed gold onto his right ring finger. Sure enough, it stopped at the second knuckle. "See? It—"

And broke off as the ring somehow suddenly slid the rest of the way to the base of the finger.

"It likes you," the old man said approvingly. "It knows you can do it."

"It knows I can do what?" Nick demanded, pulling on the ring. But whatever trick of flexible sizing had allowed it to get over the knuckle, the trick was apparently gone. "What the hell *is* this?"

"It's the Ring of the Nibelungs," the old man said solemnly.

"The *what*?"

"The Ring of the Nibelungs," the old man repeated, the somber tone replaced by irritation. "Crafted hundreds of years ago by the dwarf Alberich from the magic gold of the Rhinemaidens. It carries the power to create wealth for whoever possesses it." His lip twisted. "Don't you ever listen to Wagner's operas?"

"I don't get to the Met very often," Nick growled, twisting some more at the Ring. "Come on, get this thing off me."

"It won't come off," the old man said. "As I said, it likes you."

"Well, I don't like it," Nick shot back. "Come on, give me a hand."

"Just take it," the old man said. "There's no charge."

Nick paused, frowning. "No charge?"

"Not until later," the other said. "Shall we say ten percent of your earnings?"

Nick snorted. The way things were going, a deal like that would soon have the old man owing *him* money. "Deal," he said sarcastically. "I'll just back up the armored car to your door, okay?"

The other smiled, his eyes glittering all the more. "Good-bye, Mr. Powell," he said softly. "I'll be seeing you."

Nick was two blocks away, still trying to get the Ring off, when it suddenly occurred to him that he'd never told the old man his name.

There weren't any messages from Lydia waiting on his machine. He thought about calling her, decided that it wouldn't accomplish anything, and ate his dinner alone. Afterwards, for the same reason people tune into the eleven o'clock news to see a repeat of the same multicar crash they've already seen on the six o'clock news, he turned on his computer and pulled up the data on the international stock markets.

Only to find that, to his astonishment, the six o'clock crash wasn't being repeated.

He stared at the screen, punching in his trader passcode again and again. The overall Nikkei average was down by nearly the same percentage as the Dow. But somehow, impossibly, Nick's stocks had not only survived the drop but had actually increased in value.

All of his stocks had.

He was up until after four in the morning, checking first the Nikkei, then the Hang Seng, then the Sensex 30, then the DJ Stoxx 600. It was the same pattern in all of them: the overall numbers bounced up and down like fishing boats in a rough sea, but Nick's own stocks stubbornly defied the trends, rising like small hot-air balloons over the violent waters.

He fell asleep on his desk about the time the London exchanges were opening . . . and when he awoke, stiff and groggy, the NYSE had been open for nearly an hour, he was two hours late for work, and already he'd made up nearly everything he'd lost in the past two days. By the time the market closed that afternoon, his portfolio's value had made it back to where it had been before the freefall started.

By the end of the next week, he was a millionaire.

He broke the news to Lydia over their salads that Saturday at Sardi's. To his annoyed surprise, she wasn't happy for him.

In fact, just the opposite. "I don't like it, Nick," she said, her face somber and serious in the candlelight. "It isn't right."

"What's not right about it?" Nick countered, trying to keep his voice low. "Why shouldn't one of the little people get some of Wall Street's money for a change?"

"Because this was way too fast," Lydia said. "It's not good to get rich so quickly."

Nick shook his head in exasperation. "This is one of those things I can't win, isn't it?" he growled. "I head into the dumpster and you don't like it. I turn around and bounce into the ionosphere, and you *still* don't like it. Can you give me a hint of what income level you *would* like me to have?"

"You still don't get it, do you?" Lydia said, her eyes flashing with some exasperation of her own. "It's not about the money. It's about your obsession with it."

"Could you keep your voice down?" Nick ground out, glancing furtively around the dining room.

"Because you're just as focused on money now as you were a week ago," Lydia said, ignoring his request. "Maybe even more so."

"Only because I've got more to be focused on," Nick muttered.

Heads were starting to turn, he noted with embarrassment, as nearby diners began to tune in on the conversation.

"Exactly," Lydia said. "And I'm sorry, but I can't believe someone can make a million dollars in two weeks without some serious obsessing going on."

Heads were definitely turning now. "Half the people in this room do it all the time," Nick said, wishing that he'd waited until dessert to bring this up. Now they were going to have to endure the sideways glances through the whole meal.

Still, part of him rather liked the fact he was being noticed by people like this. After all, he was on his way to being one of them.

"I'm just worried about money getting its claws into you, that's all," Lydia persisted.

Out of sight beneath the table, Nick brushed his fingers across the filigreed surface of the Ring that, despite every effort, still wouldn't come off. "It won't," he promised.

"Then prove it," Lydia challenged. "If money's not your master, give some of it away."

The old shopkeeper's face superimposed itself across Lydia's. *Ten percent of your profits, Mr. Powell.* "I can do that," Nick said, suppressing a shiver. "No problem."

"And I don't mean give it to the IRS," Lydia said archly. "I mean give some of it to charity or the community."

"No problem," Nick repeated.

Lydia still didn't look convinced. But just then a pair of waiters appeared at their table, one sweeping their salad plates deftly out of their way as the other uncovered freshly steaming plates, and for the moment at least that conversation was over.

Despite the rocky start, the meal turned out to be a very pleasant time. Lydia might like to claim the high ground in her opinions about money, a small cynical part of Nick noted, but she had no problem enjoying the benefits that money could bring.

They were halfway through crème brulee for two when a silver-haired man in an expensive suit left his table and his dark-haired female companion and came over. "Good evening," he said, laying a gold-embossed business card beside Nick's wine glass. "I couldn't help over-hearing some of your conversation earlier. My congratulations on your recent achievement."

"Thank you," Nick said, his heartbeat picking up as the name on the card jumped out at him. This was none other than David Sonnerfeld, CEO of one of the biggest investment firms in the city. "I was just lucky."

"That kind of luck is a much sought-after commodity on Wall Street," Sonnerfeld said, smiling at Lydia. "Would you by any chance be interested in exploring a position with Sonnerfeld Thompkins?"

"He already has a job," Lydia put in.

"Actually, I don't," Nick corrected her. "I quit this afternoon."

Lydia's eyes widened. "You *quit*?"

"Why not?" Nick demanded, feeling the heat rising to his cheeks. Was she *never* going to let up? "It's not like I need it anymore."

"Quite right," Sonnerfeld put in smoothly. "A man with the talent for making money hardly needs a normal job. On the other hand, the right position with the right people can certainly enhance both your career and your life." He gestured down at the card. "Why don't you come by the office Monday morning. Say, around eleven?"

"That would be—yes, thank you," Nick managed.

"Excellent," Sonnerfeld said, reaching out his hand. "Mr.—?"

"Powell," Nick said, reaching out and taking the proffered hand. "Nick Powell."

"Mr. Powell," Sonnerfeld said, giving his hand a quick, firm shake. "That's an interesting ring. Oh, and do bring your portfolio and trading record with you." With a polite smile at Lydia, he returned to his waiting companion and they headed toward the exit.

"I take it he's someone important?" Lydia murmured.

"One of the biggest brokerage men in the city," Nick told her, his hands starting to shake with reaction. "And he's interested in *me*."

"Or he's just interested in your money." Lydia dropped her gaze to his hand. "So you're still wearing that thing?"

"I happen to like it," Nick said, hearing the defensiveness in his voice. He'd been too embarrassed at first to tell her he couldn't get it off, and now he was stuck with the lie that he actually liked the damn thing.

"It's grotesque," she insisted, peering at the Ring like it was a diseased animal. "Those leaves look half drowned. And the hands all look like they're grabbing desperately for something."

Nick held the Ring up for a closer look. Now that she mentioned it, there *did* seem to be a sense of hopelessness in the arms and hands. "It's old German," he said. "Styles change over the centuries, you know."

"I don't like it," Lydia said, a quick shiver running through her.

"I'm not asking *you* to wear it," Nick growled, scooping up a bite of the crème brulee.

But the flavor had gone out of the delicate dessert. "Come on, let's get out of here," he said, laying down his spoon. "You coming back to my place?"

"That depends," she said, gazing evenly at him. "Will you promise not to check on your money every ten minutes?"

"What, you mean go into the vault and count it?" he scoffed.

"I mean will you leave the computer off?"

He sighed theatrically. "Fine," he said. "I promise."

But later, an hour after she'd fallen asleep, he stole out of the bedroom and went online to check the foreign market predictions. What she didn't know wouldn't hurt her; and besides, his finger underneath the Ring was suddenly hurting too much for him to sleep.

An hour later, his curiosity satisfied and the pain gone as inexplicably as it had appeared, he crept back into bed.

And in his dreams he was the master of the world.

The Monday meeting at Sonnerfeld Thompkins was every bit as impressive as Nick had expected it to be. Sonnerfeld pulled out all the stops, introducing him to the rest of the firm's top people and studying Nick's portfolio with amazement and praise.

Midway through lunch, under Sonnerfeld's polite but steady pressure, Nick agreed to join Sonnerfeld Thompkins on a trial basis.

The first month was like a chapter from a financial success book. Nick's Midas touch continued, with every stock or bond or commodity he picked turning to gold with a perfect sense of timing. There were a few false starts, but every time he tried to buy a property that he would later find was irretrievably on its way down, his finger started hurting so badly he could hardly type. Eventually, he learned how to read the telltale twinges that came before the actual pain started.

Pain or not, though, his purchases made money for himself and the firm and its clients, and that was the important thing. By the end of the month Sonnerfeld was talking—just theoretically, of course—of putting Nick on the fast track to full partner, and wondering aloud about the flow of the name Sonnerfeld Thompkins Powell. Everything was going perfectly.

Everything, that is, except Lydia. In the midst of all the success she continued her self-appointed role as rainmaker to Nick's private parade. Before the Ring had come to him Nick had been ready to ask her to marry him, his lack of proper finances the only thing holding him back. But now, just when he was gaining the sort of wealth and power that would attract most women, Lydia was instead growing more distant. While she still permitted him to spend money on her for dinners and modest gifts, her disapproval of what she called his obsession was never far below the surface. He couldn't pause in the middle of an evening to check the international funds without getting a lecture, and she went nearly ballistic when he tried to give her a simple little thirty-thousand-dollar necklace.

Nothing he did seemed to make any difference. He set up a charity distribution trust fund with direct access from one of his accounts to fulfill his promise to share the wealth; she applauded it as a good first step but thought the five percent he routinely sent to it was far too small for a man of his means. He bought a new cell phone with internet trading capabilities programmed in so that he could make any last-minute trades on the way home from work. He put Sonnerfeld and the rest of his staff on a special vibration mode on his cell phone and a special flashing-light code on his home phone so that he could let any late-night calls go to voice mail if Lydia was around to disapprove.

None of it helped. Lydia seemed bound and determined to make him feel guilty about his success.

And finally, midway through the last weekend of that otherwise glorious first month Nick decided he'd had enough of her complaining.

He was still brooding over it Monday morning when the runaway bus slammed into a line of pedestrians twenty feet in front of him.

"I'm surprised you even came in," Sonnerfeld said, sitting on the corner of his desk as he handed Nick a cup of coffee. Or rather, tried to hand it to him. Nick's hands were shaking so much that he couldn't even hold it. Eventually Sonnerfeld gave up and instead set it down on the desk. "Why don't you just go home?"

"I'm okay," Nick said, gazing out Sonnerfeld's floor-to-ceiling windows at the brooding clouds hanging over the New York cityscape. "It was just a freak accident."

"Still had to be pretty unnerving," Sonnerfeld said. "But if you think you're okay . . . ?"

"I'm fine," Nick said, getting up and heading for the door. "Time and tide, and all that."

Sonnerfeld gave him a thumb's up. "Good man."

It was mid-afternoon, and Nick had finally managed to put the bus crash mostly out of his mind when he heard that one of the firm's up-and-coming young brokers had been mugged and beaten while returning from lunch. Returning, in fact, from the very restaurant Nick had been planning to go to until he'd been pulled into a last-minute emergency meeting.

Ten minutes later Nick was in a cab, heading for the bank. Ten minutes after that, he was on his way to the shop where he'd gotten the Ring.

The old shopkeeper was waiting. "I've been expecting you," he said gravely. "How are you enjoying your new success?"

"I've got your money," Nick said, pulling out a certified check. "You said ten percent—I've made it twenty."

"Very generous of you," the old man said approvingly, his hand darting out like a striking rattlesnake to pluck the check from Nick's fingers.

"So we're square, right?" Nick said, wincing again at the unpleasant touch of the other's skin. "So call them off."

"Call who off?"

"Whoever it was tried to run me down with a bus this morning and then mugged Caprizano at lunch," Nick said. "I got the message, and you've got your money. Okay?"

The other shook his head. "I had nothing to do with any of that, Mr. Powell," he said. "It's the curse working."

"No, but look, I got you the—" Nick broke off. "The *what*?"

"The curse," the old man said softly. "You didn't think all that money was just going to fall into your lap without any consequences, did you?"

Nick's skin began tingling. The whole idea of a curse was absurd . . . but then, so was a Ring that could make you rich. "What kind of curse are we talking about?" he asked carefully.

"Death and destruction, of course," the old man said, his eyes taking on a faraway look. "The Rhinemaidens laid it on the gold when Alberich stole it from them." His eyes came back and he smiled tightly. "That's the one part Wagner got wrong. He said it was *Alberich* who cursed it."

"Never mind who cursed it," Nick snapped. "Are you saying it's coming after *me*?"

"Of course," the old man said, sounding surprised that Nick would even have to ask. "You have the Ring."

"So that's why you let me have the damn thing instead of using it yourself," Nick bit out, twisting at the Ring.

The old man shook his head. "It won't come off, Mr. Powell," he said. "It likes you. More than that, it likes the money you're making." He cocked his head to the side. "I don't suppose you'd consider turning your assets into gold? It especially likes gold."

"In a minute I'm going to get on the phone and convert it to Rwanda francs," Nick growled. "Now tell me how I get it off."

"You don't," the old man said softly. "Not while you're alive."

Nick stared at him. "How do you know so much about this?"

"Because I was there from the beginning." The old man lifted his hand to the side of his head and tugged at something.

And abruptly shrank into a short, wide, bearded man holding a sort of metal cap in his hand. "I *am* Alberich," he said.

Nick looked at the metal cap. "The Tarnhelm," Alberich answered his unspoken question, wiggling the cap between his fingers. "It gives its owner the power to change shape at will." He smiled. "Wagner *did* get that one right."

And with that, the reality of magic Rings and their curses suddenly came sharply into focus. "This curse," Nick said between dry lips. "If it's coming after me, why did Caprizano and those people just walking down the street get hurt?"

"The Ring's trying to protect you," Alberich said. "It will succeed, too, for awhile. And I can also help."

"For a price, I suppose?"

"Of course," Alberich said.

"Why am I not surprised?" Nick growled. "And if I refuse, or you miss one? The curse nails me, I die, and the Ring moves on to someone else?"

"Basically," Alberich said casually. "But at least your heirs will still have your money." He shrugged. "If any of them are still alive."

And right on cue, Nick's cell phone vibrated.

He snatched it from his pocket, his heart suddenly pounding. "Powell."

"Nick, it's Amy," the choked voice of Sonnerfeld's assistant said. "There's been a terrible accident. Mr. Sonnerfeld's fallen down an elevator shaft."

Nick looked at Alberich. How many times, he wondered, had the dwarf watched this same scenario play itself out, losing victim after victim to the Ring's curse while he grew rich on his ten percent?

Amy was still talking. "I'm sorry—what was that?" Nick asked.

"I said you need to get back here right away," she said. "The whole board's coming in for emergency session—oh, *God*—"

"I understand," Nick cut in. "I'll be right there."

"Your boss?" Alberich asked as he closed the phone. "Yes, that's the usual pattern. From the edges of your life inward—strangers, co-workers, boss. Fortunately, you don't have a wife or children, or they'd be next."

Nick's stomach twisted into a hard knot. *Lydia.* . . . "I've got to go," he said, his voice sounding hollow in his ears as he headed for the door.

"Remember what I said," Alberich called after him. "For an extra forty percent I can help protect you from the curse."

"I'll think about it," Nick called over his shoulder.

To his relief, Lydia was sitting safe and sound at her desk when he barged into her office. "Come on," he said, without preamble, grabbing her wrist and all but hauling her out of her chair. "We're going on a trip."

"Nick, what in the world do you think you're doing?" she demanded as she tried to pull from his grip.

"I've got a cab waiting," he said, ignoring her struggles as he pulled her across the room under the astonished stares of her colleagues. "You've got ten minutes to pack, and you'll need your passport. We've got just three hours until the next flight to Frankfort."

"To Frankfort?" she echoed as he got her out the door. "You mean . . . *Germany*?"

"I don't mean Kentucky," Nick said. "Come on."

A moment later they were in the cab, weaving their way through the city's streets. Nick could feel Lydia's puzzled and hostile glare on him, but he ignored it. As long as he kept her close, maybe the Ring's protection would extend to her, too.

Meanwhile, he had to find a permanent solution to the problem. It was these damn Rhinemaidens who had put the damn curse on the damn Ring. Maybe they could take it off.

The sky had been clouding over as they landed at Frankfort International Airport. The commuter flight to Stuttgart had run into some more serious weather, and as Nick got them on the road in their rental car, the rain was starting in earnest.

By the time he pulled off the road beside the slope leading down to the Rhine river the full fury of the storm had broken.

"This is the place?" Lydia shouted over the wind as they picked their way carefully through the trees and rocks toward the surging water below.

"Assuming Wagner knew what he was talking about," Nick called back. "This is definitely the place he described for the scenery in the first Bayreuth production of Götterdämmerung. We'll just have to see if he got it right."

They fell silent, concentrating on the climb, and Nick found himself marveling once again at the remarkable woman beside him. He'd told her the whole story on the way to the airport from her apartment, fully expecting her to order the cabby to forget LaGuardia and take them straight to Bellevue. But to his surprise, she'd not only taken it calmly, but had actually believed the story.

Or at least, she'd pretended to believe it. Still, that was more than he would have gotten from anyone else he knew.

The rain had moderated a little by the time they reached the bottom of the slope, but the winds had become more turbulent. Carefully, Nick moved to the edge of the river, wiping at the sheet of water streaming down his face as he peered across the roiling whitecaps spilling over the treacherous rocks. "Rhinemaidens!" he shouted. "I've brought you your Ring. Come and get it."

There was no answer but the whistling of the wind. "What if they're not here?" Lydia asked.

Nick shook his head wordlessly, looking back and forth down the shoreline.

And frowned. There, about fifty yards downriver, he could see a squat figure standing with the stillness of a rock, facing their direction.

It was Alberich.

"I knew you'd come," the dwarf said as Nick and Lydia slogged through the wet grass to him. "They all do, sooner or later. Hoping to bribe or beg or threaten their way out of the curse."

"News flash—I'm not here to beg," Nick told him. "I'm here to give them back their Ring."

Alberich snorted in disgust. "Fool. You really think you're the first one to think of *that*?"

"They won't take it back?" Lydia asked.

Alberich looked her up and down. "You must be the one he was going to buy the Ring for." He snorted. "Waste of effort. You're not nearly ambitious enough."

"You mean I'm not greedy enough," Lydia shot back. "Why won't they take it back?"

"Of course they'll take it back," the dwarf said maliciously. "The problem is, the Ring won't leave him. That means the Rhinemaidens will have to take a bit more than just the gold."

Lydia inhaled sharply. "You mean . . . his *finger*?"

"Or his hand," Alberich said. "Possibly his whole arm."

Lydia looked at Nick in horror. "No! They *can't*."

"They will." Alberich pointed to a jagged rock in the middle of the river, barely visible above the surging water. "That's their rock, and they're already on their way. But there *is* an alternative."

"What is it?" Lydia asked.

"Forget it," Nick snarled. "He's just playing another angle."

"I'm as strong as they are," Alberich told her. "For another twenty percent I can keep them away from him."

"I said forget it," Nick said again. He could see something in the water now, moving toward him just below the surface. "Even if it costs my whole arm, it'll be worth it."

"Nick, that's insane," Lydia said urgently. "We're in the middle of nowhere, with our car fifty feet up a hill. You'll bleed to death before we can get you to a hospital."

And then, abruptly, three slender bodies surged out of the water onto the shore, and six hands grabbed at his clothing.

"Back!" Alberich snapped, leaping to Nick's side and pulling his right arm away from the grasping hands.

"The Ring!" the Rhinemaidens called in unison, their voices thin and ancient and terrifying. One of them shoved her way beneath Alberich's grip; and suddenly there was a tug-of-war going on for Nick's right arm.

"Give us the Ring," one of the Maidens said, her hand wrapping like a vice around Nick's ankle and tugging him toward the river. "You retain it at your peril."

"I know," Nick said. "I want to give it to you—really I do."

"Only the waters of the Rhine can wash away the curse," the third Maiden said, her hands on Nick's jacket, her face up close to his. Over the smell of fish he caught a glimpse of sharp barracuda teeth.

"It won't let go," Nick pleaded.

"It likes him," Alberich said, pushing the first Maiden's hands off Nick's arm. "Don't be a fool, Nick. I can still save you."

Nick blinked. *It likes you.* Alberich had said the same thing the first time Nick had set eyes on the Ring.

Only the Ring didn't like Nick. All it liked was his money.

His money. "Lydia!" he shouted, shaking his left arm free long enough to dig his phone from his pocket. "Here," he said, tossing it awkwardly toward her.

For a second she fumbled, then caught it in a solid grip. "Who do I call?" she shouted back, flipping it open.

"Phone list one—second entry," Nick said, stumbling as the third Maiden got a fresh grip on his left arm and pulled him another step closer to the river. The one who'd been tugging on his ankle abandoned that approach and moved instead to Nick's right arm, and now Alberich had two sets of hands and teeth to fight off. "Input trader passcode 352627."

Lydia nodded and leaned over the phone. The Maiden on Nick's left arm shifted one hand to his belt. He kicked at her legs; it was like kicking a pair of oak saplings. "I'm in," Lydia called.

"There are five funds listed." On Nick's right arm, one of the two Maidens opened her mouth and lowered the pointed teeth toward the Ring. Nick cringed, but Alberich slapped the creature's cheek and shoved her back again. "Transfer everything in the first four into the fifth."

"What are you doing?" Alberich demanded, frowning at Nick in sudden suspicion.

"The Ring doesn't like *me*," Nick said. "It just likes my money."

"What?" The dwarf spun toward Lydia. "No!" Abandoning Nick's arm, he charged toward Lydia.

And suddenly Nick was fighting all three Maidens by himself. "Alberich!" he shouted as they dragged him toward the river. "Help me!"

"For what?" the dwarf spat, lunging for the phone. But Lydia was faster, twisting and turning and keeping it out of his reach even as she continued punching in numbers. "Seventy percent of nothing? She's throwing it all away, isn't she?"

"She's transferring it into my charity distribution account," Nick said. His feet were in the icy water now, the Maiden on his left arm already in up to her knees. "All the Ring cares about is money. And as of right now—"

"You're broke!" Lydia shouted in triumph. "You hear me, Ring? He's broke."

Spinning away from Lydia, Alberich threw himself back at the Ring. "Get away from the Ring!" he shouted.

"The Ring is ours," the Maidens chorused in their eerie unison.

"It's mine!" Alberich snarled, grabbing Nick's wrist.

Something cold ran up Nick's back, something having nothing to do with the water swirling around his feet. Lydia was right—with all his money now in the irrevocable trust fund, he had nothing left in the world.

But the Ring still wasn't letting go.

"Is this how you want to die?" Alberich demanded, pulling at Nick's arm with one hand as he shoved at the Maidens with the other. "Drowned in the Rhine by ancient creatures who have nothing left but hate and greed? There's still time for us to make a deal."

"I don't want a deal," Nick said. He was knee deep in the river now, the numbingly cold water threatening to cramp his calf muscles. Out of the corner of his eye, he could see Lydia doing something with the phone. "I don't want money. All I want—"

And without any warning at all, the Ring came loose.

Nick's arms were still pinioned, but for the moment no one was gripping his hand. With a desperate flick of his wrist, he sent the Ring arcing into the air toward the center of the river and the Rhinemaidens' rock. "No!" Alberich screeched, diving toward it.

But the Maidens were ready. Two of them twisted their arms around the dwarf's neck and dragged him into the river, swimming backwards toward their rock. The third Maiden dived into and then out of the water like a dolphin, reaching up and catching the Ring in midair as it fell. For a moment she held it triumphantly aloft, then turned and disappeared with her sisters beneath the waves.

And then Lydia was at Nick's side, pulling at his now aching arms, helping him back to the shore. "What did you do?" Nick asked, shivering violently. The storm, he noticed, was starting to abate. "How did you get it to let go?"

"You had no money," she told him, wrapping her arm around his waist and leading him toward the cliff where their car waited. "But you still had the potential to earn it all back."

He nodded in understanding. "So you fired me."

"I text-messaged your resignation to Sonnerfeld Thompkins," she confirmed. "I guess it'll never be Sonnerfeld Thompkins Powell now. I'm sorry."

Nick blinked a few lingering drops of water from his eyes. "I'm not. Thank you."

"I'm glad it worked." She paused. "Nick . . . your phone list. Number two was your on-line investment number, three and four and five were Sonnerfeld and your office. Number one . . ."

"Is you," Nick confirmed with a tired sigh. "You've always been number one. I just forgot that for awhile."

She squeezed his hand. His aching, ringless, *free* hand. "Come on," she said softly. "Let's go home."

TROLLBRIDGE

Traffic seemed lighter than usual tonight, Kersh thought from his toll booth as he watched the lines of cars and trucks streaming through the George Washington Bridge's toll plaza.

Or maybe it was that the traffic the past two nights had been unusually heavy. Kersh could never tell about those things. All he knew was that the lines of headlights and tail lights stretched all the way to the horizon, the headlights streaming in from New Jersey, the tail lights returning again from Manhattan.

In the old days, he thought wistfully, every one of those incoming vehicles would have had had to stop at booths like his. An endless stream of people giving Kersh money to cross his bridge.

But those days were long gone. First had come the automated bins where the drivers simply tossed in their coins. Far worse was the abomination called the E-Z Pass. Those drivers still paid, of course, but they paid from their homes, without Kersh or anyone else in the plaza ever seeing or handling that money.

Which meant that sitting as he did in the booth marked E-Z Pass/Cash, Kersh had to endure the frustration of sitting idly while most of the cars drove through without even slowing down.

Sometimes the drivers waved cheerily as they passed. That just made it worse.

A movement at the corner of Kersh's eye snapped him out of his gloomy reverie. A late-model Chevy was slowing down as it approached his booth. An E-Z Pass user being extra cautious? Or someone with actual, real cash?

Kersh focused on the car. The driver had two hundred and eighty dollars on him, he saw, plus another four hundred in traveler's checks. The woman beside him had seventy dollars cash and two hundred in traveler's checks. Tourists, then, on their way to a grand adventure in New York City.

And tourists almost never had E-Z Passes.

Sure enough, the car slowed to a stop, the driver's window sliding down as it did so. "Evening, sir," Kersh said politely, his heart pounding with anticipation. "Six dollars, please."

They were a young couple, tired but still showing that spark of anticipation as they thought of the museums and plays and nightlife awaiting them. The driver's expression slipped at bit as he caught full sight of Kersh's wide face and shaggy brown hair, but the Midwestern courtesy that came with the Wisconsin tags quickly asserted itself. "Good evening," he said politely to Kersh as he handed over a ten dollar bill.

"Thank you," Kersh said, handing over the four singles he'd pulled from his cash drawer as soon as he'd sensed the ten in the other's hand. "Enjoy your visit."

"Thanks," the young man said, and drove off.

Kersh gripped the ten-dollar bill, savoring the feel of it between his thick fingers. Then, carefully, he slid it into the proper slot in the drawer. Watching the Wisconsin car as it climbed the long stretch of the bridge, he silently wished the young couple a pleasant trip to the Big Apple.

And wished them safety, as well. Not all the people in New York were friendly to strangers.

Not all the people in New York were even people.

He turned back to the lines of cars streaming across the toll plaza, feeling a sudden surge of loneliness for central Europe and the old wooden bridges where he'd grown up so many centuries ago. Did his fellow trolls still live beneath any of those bridges, he wondered?

Probably not. The deep places of the world had been vanishing for centuries, and with them the beings who had once lived and thrived there. As far as he knew, he was the last troll in this part of the country. Possibly in the entire United States.

Possibly even in the entire world. Someday, he would be gone, too.

But until then, at least he still had a job that allowed him to cling to the old ways.

Another car was slowing down as it approached his booth. The driver was alone, with sixty-eight dollars in his wallet and a twenty ready in his hand. Feeling his heartbeat again speeding up, Kersh pulled a ten and four ones from his cash drawer and waited.

Seventeen more cars stopped and gave Kersh money before his shift ended five hours later. The day-shifter took over the booth, and Kersh headed toward the lot where the toll plaza employees parked their cars. From the lot it was only a short walk down to the Palisades Interstate Park stretching along the Hudson River where he made his home. The park was closed at this hour, of course, but over the years Kersh had found lots of ways to get in and out.

As he walked through the darkness, savoring the smell of trees and dirt and water, he found himself gazing up at the underside of the bridge. For all his trollish tendencies toward self-pity, he *did* realize know how lucky he was to have a bridge he could call his own. Even if he could only work it for a third of each day.

And not just any bridge, but a magnificent bridge, spanning a magnificent river. Kersh smiled, his eyes tracing the familiar lines and angles—

His large, flat feet stumbled to a halt. He knew every inch of that bridge, and there was something different up there tonight. Two somethings, in fact: a pair of cylinders about half the size of the orange barrels the Port Authority used when they needed to block off a lane for repairs.

But these barrels weren't orange, and they were fastened to horizontal girders where no orange barrel had any business being. Had the workers begin some maintenance on his bridge that he hadn't heard about?

And then the wind shifted slightly, and he caught a faint whiff of something he'd smelled once before. It had been two years ago, when the Department of Homeland Security had run a nighttime test on the bridge. A test that had included anti-terrorist agents, bomb-sniffing dogs . . . and bombs.

For a long minute he stared upward at the barrels. Then, squaring his massive shoulders, he turned and retraced his steps back toward the toll plaza.

The man seated behind the supervisor's desk was middle-aged, with the slightly greasy hair and unshaven cheeks of a man who'd been hauled out of bed at five-thirty in the morning. But for all that, his eyes were bright and alert. "Mr. Kersh," he said politely as Kersh entered the room. "Please sit down."

"Thank you," Kersh said, lowering his bulk cautiously onto the office's single guest chair. It wasn't nearly strong enough to support his weight, but over the years he'd learned how to keep his legs angled backward so that he wasn't so much sitting on the chair as he was squatting over it.

"I'm Special Agent McBride," the man went on. "I'm investigating the bombs we removed from the bridge an hour ago."

Kersh felt a lump form in his throat. So they *had* been real bombs. He'd asked several people over the past couple of hours, trying to find out for sure. But no one had been willing or able to tell him. "Is the bridge all right?" he asked.

"It's fine," McBride assured him. "The bombs weren't very big, and they weren't positioned with any expertise. They would have made a couple of very big bangs, and scared the hell out of a lot of people, but the damage would have been minor." He raised his eyebrows. "Of course, that's only *relatively* minor," he amended. "You say you spotted the bombs after your shift?"

"Yes, that's right," Kersh said, feeling a flow of relief wash through his tension. His beloved bridge was safe.

"May I ask how?" McBride asked.

"What do you mean?"

"You left your booth at five this morning, supposedly heading home," McBride said, his eyes steady on Kersh's face. "Yet ten minutes later, you were back with the news that you'd seen something under the bridge." He paused. "In pitch darkness. From a spot you shouldn't have been in if you were actually on your way home."

Kersh swallowed, his tension suddenly back. "It wasn't really *pitch* dark," he pointed out carefully. "There are a lot of lights from the bridge and the city. And I've got good eyes."

"Good enough to pick out two small anomalies among all those girders and braces?"

"I know the bridge," Kersh said, forcing his voice to stay calm. He wasn't very smart, but it was abundantly clear where Agent McBride was going with this. "I spend a lot of time in the park just looking up at it."

"Really," McBride said. "You like bridges, do you?"

"I like them a lot," Kersh said. "They're kind of in my blood."

"Mm," McBride murmured. "Why were you there when you were supposed to be going home?"

Behind his bushy beard, Kersh grimaced. What could he say? That the address he'd given the Port Authority was only a mail drop, and that he actually lived in a hole below the bridge, the way trolls had for centuries? "I like to take a walk along the edge of the park before I head home," he improvised desperately. "It helps me unwind."

"Your job requires a lot of unwinding time, then?" McBride asked, not quite sarcastically.

"I just like looking at the bridge," Kersh said. Even to his own ears, it sounded pretty lame.

"Mm," McBride said again. "Well, I think that's all I need right now. Thank you for your time."

"You're welcome," Kersh said, standing up and backing toward the door. "Will you be finished in time for me to work my shift tonight?"

"You'll need to call in later this afternoon," McBride told him. "We should know by then when we'll be reopening the bridge." He hesitated. "And thank you for your warning."

"You're welcome," Kersh muttered again, and escaped.

He headed down toward the park, barely even noticing all the Federal agents and Port Authority people milling around, his mood and eyes darkened with grief and loss.

Because it was over. All his years with the bridge. McBride would dig into his background and find out that he didn't live where he said he did. Someone else would notice that the age on his old employment record was all screwy. Someone else would find out that he didn't have a birth certificate or immigration papers, just the Social Security card he'd been issued when the program first began in 1935.

They would probably blame him for the bombs and put him in prison. They might even figure out that he wasn't really human.

But if it was over, it wasn't over quite yet. Maybe there was still time for him to find out who had put those bombs on his beloved bridge.

And he had a pretty good idea where to start looking.

Kersh spent the day wandering through town, visiting shops, historic sites, and parks. He had a big lunch, considered going to a movie so he could get a little sleep, decided instead to continue his walk.

He had company, of a sort, throughout most of the day. McBride had apparently assigned someone to follow him and report on his activities. The man was pretty good at his job, with a bagful of tricks that included a roll-up hat, sunglasses, a reversible jacket, and even a false mustache that he could quickly put on or take off.

Not that any of it helped him any. The man had exactly forty-four dollars in his wallet, which made him very easy for Kersh to pick out of the crowd.

At two o'clock he called his supervisor and was told not to come in, that the bridge wouldn't be opening until the start of morning rush hour. Kersh thanked him, and continuing his wanderings.

An hour after sunset, he slipped away from McBride's agent and returned to his bridge.

Normally, Kersh spent most of his time at the south end of the park, in the hole he'd dug beneath his bridge. Tonight, though, he had another destination in mind. Somewhere along the river, he knew, lived a group of water goblins.

He was nearly to the north end of the park when he finally found their nest, hidden among the stones and grasses at the edge of the water. "Goblins!" he called softly but firmly. "Goblins! I would speak with you."

For a long minute the only sounds were the soft lapping of the river against its banks and the distant whooshing of the city traffic. Then, with a sudden rippling of the water, a small wizened figure pulled itself up onto the shore. "What do you want, Troll?" he demanded in a grating voice.

"I want to know what you did to my bridge," Kersh growled back.

"*Your* bridge?" the goblin sneered.

"Yes, *my* bridge," Kersh said. "You set two bombs to try to destroy it."

Three more goblins popped up out of the water beside the first. "And if we did?" the first goblin challenged. "What are you going to do about it?"

The four of them took a menacing step toward Kersh. "I don't want any trouble," Kersh protested, taking a long step backwards. There were more goblins gathering back there, he knew—he'd heard them leave the water, and he could smell their dank odor on the light breeze. If the four in front of him would take just one more step . . .

"Go away, Troll," the first goblin demanded as they moved in unison toward Kersh. "Leave us or you will die, wrapped in waterweeds like a newborn."

"I don't want any trouble," Kersh said again. He took another step backward.

And threw out an arm behind him to grab the nearest lurking goblin squarely around his thin throat.

The goblin gave a startled gurgle, which changed to a high-pitched squeak as Kersh hauled him off his feet and swung his body across the half dozen other goblins who had thought they were sneaking up on the big intruder. There was a flurry of squeaks, gasps, and curses as bodies went flying into the reeds or rocks or back into the river itself.

Kersh spun back around just as the four original goblins charged. Three of them managed to stop in time; the fourth went flying into the river as Kersh swung his makeshift club across his torso. "But if *you* want trouble," he added, lowering the squirming goblin to his side, "I can do that, too."

"Enough," a new voice rumbled from somewhere inland.

Kersh turned to see a much larger goblin emerge from concealment in the grasses. "You're their king?" Kersh asked as he spotted the crown of water plants entwined around the other's hairless head.

"I am," the Goblin King confirmed. "Release him, and ask what you will."

Kersh hesitated. Technically, a Goblin King only had to tell the truth if he himself was a prisoner. But the old rules had slackened somewhat over the years. It was probably worth showing a little good faith.

Besides, if the creature lied to him, Kersh could always come back later and wring his scrawny little neck.

"I want to know why you put those bombs on my bridge," Kersh said, letting go of his prisoner's neck. The creature scurried away, wheezing out curses as he went.

"We had nothing to do with any bombs," the Goblin King said without hesitation. "Or with your precious bridge. Why would we?"

"Because the bridge allows humans to bypass your domain," Kersh said. "Without bridges, many more would travel by boat, bringing fresh victims into your reach."

The Goblin King hissed out a watery laugh. "And we waited more than seventy years after the bridge was built to decide to do this?"

That was a good point, Kersh had to admit. "You might only now have gotten fed up about it," he suggested hesitantly.

"What we have *gotten* is resigned to it," the Goblin King growled. "Besides, even if we were somehow able to destroy all the bridges, the humans would merely use the tunnels. Then the bridges would be rebuilt, and we would be no better off than we are now."

Another good point, Kersh decided regretfully. Besides, how would the goblins have gotten the bombs up there in the first place? They were strong enough, but they couldn't climb worth anything. "I suppose not," he conceded.

The Goblin King hissed something bitter-sounding in the goblin language. "Then go," he ordered. "Seek elsewhere for your enemy, and leave us at what peace we still have."

"I will," Kersh said. "I'm sorry to have bothered you."

The Goblin King pointed a bony finger at Kersh's chest. "But if I were you, I would look in only one direction for the creatures who threaten your bridge." He tilted the finger up to point at the sky. "Look to the air, Troll. Look to those creatures who have always hated the intrusions of human metal and stone into their domain."

Kersh frowned. Intrusions of metal and stone? "You mean the air sprites?"

The Goblin King snorted. "The legendary brilliance of trollish minds," he said contemptuously. "*Yes*, I mean the air sprites. Seek them out, and take your vengeance there."

"Perhaps I will," Kersh said. "Farewell."

He turned and made his way back along the riverbank, the anger that had been directed toward the water goblins now shifting to the air sprites. Those little pests, at least, would have no problem getting to the underside of his bridge.

The question was, how was he going to catch one of them and confirm they were the guilty parties? Most of the time they wafted through the air like living ghosts, only rarely coming in reach of earthbound creatures like himself.

They *could* be caught, he remembered, if he could lure one of them into a spider web. But the days were long gone when there were spiders who could be hired or bribed for such a purpose.

But with a little of that trollish brilliance the Goblin King had mentioned, maybe he could come up with another way.

It was after midnight when Kersh finally heard the faint whispering sound that announced that an air sprite was near.

He sat up a little straighter, peering out from behind the bushes where he was hiding. He could see the sprite now, a nearly transparent shape whose edges billowed leisurely like curling smoke on a nearly windless day. There was a faint bluish tint to the image, which meant this particular sprite was female. She was hovering about six feet above the wooden bowl of sugar water that Kersh had set out in the center of a stand of outward-bent ferns, her head moving back and forth as she searched for danger. A moment later, apparently satisfied, she began drifting downward.

Silently, stealthily, Kersh got a grip on the vine he'd rigged up as a trigger and waited. The sprite floated the rest of the way to the bowl, her flowing edges fluttering with ecstasy as she sipped at the sweet liquid. Gently, Kersh pulled the vine.

The fronds snapped upward and inward, closing on the sprite like the jaws of a Venus flytrap. The sprite twitched and tried to duck away, but as she dodged one group of fronds she backed into one of the others.

And suddenly the whole group of ferns was churning back and forth as the sprite fought furiously to free herself from the trap.

Lunging to his feet, Kersh shoved his way through the concealing bushes. "Don't struggle," he warned the sprite. "It'll only make it worse."

The sprite's only answer was to redouble her efforts against the mysterious force that had trapped her against the fern. Kersh walked toward her, shaking his head. Sprites were not the brightest creatures around. Something seemed to tingle past his head, like a screech or call too high-pitched for troll ears to hear. He reached the sprite and leaned over to get a grip on her.

And bellowed as a hundred needles suddenly jabbed into his skin.

He leaped backward, his corkscrewing arms sending blue- and red-tinged sprites flying in all directions. But each one that he managed to throw off was replaced by two more, digging their tiny insubstantial teeth into his hide as hard as they could.

Kersh's skin was thick and tough, as many a would-be adventurer had learned to his sorrow over the years. But even trollish hide could take only so much. The air around him was thick with hazy bluish and reddish creatures, swarming around like the wasps from a hundred hives. He hadn't realized there were even this many in the New York area, let alone within range of his trapped sprite's distress call. Clenching his teeth, he swung his arms even harder, trying to shake them off.

"We will strip the flesh from your bones, Troll," a tiny voice said in Kersh's ear, and dug his teeth into Kersh's earlobe.

"Not a chance!" Kersh shouted back, batting him away.

"Release her!" a different voice demanded. "Release your prey!"

"Then leave my bridge alone!" Kersh snarled. "You hear me? You touch my bridge again and I'll kill you all." Through the growing pain, he again heard the tingling of the not-quite-audible voice.

And abruptly, the biting stopped.

Slowly, disbelievingly, Kersh came to a halt, breathing heavily, his whole body burning from the bites. The hills and trees of the park, the river and the city lights beyond the river—everything was still colored with swirling hints of red and blue. The sprites were still there, more than ready to resume their attack.

So why had they stopped?

"Your bridge has been harmed?"

It was the first sprite again. Only this time, the voice was calm and controlled, without the fury that Kersh had heard there earlier. It might even have held a little concern. "Someone tried to destroy it," Kersh said, still panting.

"We're sorry to hear that," the sprite said. "We know what bridges mean to trolls." He paused. "Yet the bridge appears to be as always."

"The harm was stopped before it could happen," Kersh said. "Are you saying it wasn't you?"

"Of course not," the sprite said. "Who would think we would do such a thing?"

Kersh grimaced. "It was the Water Goblin King."

"Of course." It was hard to put disgust into such a tiny voice, Kersh reflected, but the sprite had no difficulty whatsoever in pulling it off. "Goblins enjoy pitting peoples against each other, while they sit back and watch the blood and destruction. Never trust what a goblin says, Troll."

"No," Kersh said, thoroughly confused now. Clearly, someone was lying to him. But who? "So you *didn't* try to hurt my bridge?" he asked, just to make sure.

"We do not destroy," the sprite said firmly. "That is not our purpose. Besides, why would we want to hurt any bridge?"

"Because you don't like the structures humans build into your air," Kersh said. "That's what the—that's what I've heard."

"Most of the time that's true," the sprite conceded. "But bridges are different. Especially now that most of the humans' horseless carts pass over without stopping."

Kersh felt his eyes narrow. "What do you mean by that?" he demanded.

"Not because it robs you of your purpose," the sprite hastened to explain. "But because the thrill of the ride is better this way."

"You ride the *cars*?" Kersh asked, wondering if he'd heard that right. "But I thought you couldn't touch metal."

"Oh, no, we don't actually touch them," the sprite explained. "We fly along close behind them, riding in the calm among the winds."

"Ah," Kersh said as he finally understood. "It's called drafting."

"Drafting," the sprite said. "An interesting word. I shall remember it. I simply meant that when the carts stop to pay you for crossing your bridge, we must stop with them."

"So it's better when they don't," Kersh said with a sigh. Everyone, it seemed, benefited from the stupid E-Z Passes. Everyone except him. "So you really don't dislike bridges?"

"Traveling—drafting—behind carts on a bridge takes us higher in the air than when they travel their usual pathways of hardened earth," the sprite said. "It's a pleasure we never had in the old days."

"I understand," Kersh said. "I'm sorry I accused you." He looked down, suddenly remembering the sprite in his trap. "Here, let me help you."

He knelt beside the sprite and carefully pulled her free of the ferns he'd tricked out. "What *is* that?" the other sprite asked, moving cautiously in for a closer look. "It doesn't look like spider web."

"No, it's something the humans create," Kersh told him as the trapped sprite came free and flew quickly away. "It's called duct tape. Very strong."

"Interesting," the sprite said. "Is it made from actual ducks?"

"Artificial ones," Kersh assured him. It seemed the simplest thing to say. "I'm sorry for the trouble I've caused you."

"We and the trolls have never been friends," the sprite said gravely. "But we've never truly been enemies, either. We understand you, and your need to have a bridge of your own."

"Thank you for your patience," Kersh said, bowing to the floating figure. "If there's ever anything I can ever do for you, please don't hesitate to ask."

"Perhaps it is we who can help *you*," the sprite said. "Tell us how exactly your bridge was threatened."

Kersh told him about the bombs. "I see," the sprite said thoughtfully when he'd finished. "So you are seeking someone who is both a good climber, and who can climb while carrying a load."

"*And* who doesn't know much about bridges," Kersh added, remembering what McBride had said about the bombs not being in the right places to cause much damage.

"Yes," the sprite said. "In that case—"

"Lord Albho!" a new voice cut in. "There is someone climbing beneath the bridge!"

Kersh tilted his head back, his eyes searching the span overhead. "Where?"

"Here," the sprite said, moving between Kersh and the bridge.

And through the sprite's faint reddish image, Kersh saw it: a smallish figure, laboriously crawling along the underside of the bridge roadway, heading toward the New Jersey end.

"I see him," Lord Albho said. "A long way for him to have climbed from the far end."

"Or else he climbed up the tower," Kersh said. The figure was nearly to the same place the other bombs had been. No way Kersh could swim out to the tower, climb up to the span, and catch up with him in time.

Which left him only one other option. "I'll have to climb up the anchorage," he said, heading west across the park. "Thanks for your help."

The sprite's answer, if he gave one, was lost in the wind whistling past Kersh's ears.

He reached the edge of the park and continued on, running full speed toward the mass of concrete and steel that formed his bridge's western anchorage. The city's nighttime traffic had long since faded to a trickle, and as far as he could tell no one spotted him. He reached the anchorage and started up, climbing hand over hand as fast as he could. He could only hope it would be fast enough.

The small figure, another barrel strapped across his back, was still toiling his way along the support members when Kersh reached him. And now, close up, Kersh could see that the creature was a gnome.

Which made no sense at all. What in the world was an underground creature like a gnome doing on Kersh's bridge?

But that question could wait. "Stop!" he ordered, putting the full weight of trollish anger into his voice.

The gnome jumped like he'd been bitten by a swarm of air sprites, his thin body jerking around toward his unexpected visitor.

Jerked around too far, in fact. He lurched sideways, the load on his back pulling him off-balance. His hands scrambled frantically at the supports as he tried to regain his grip, but it was too little too late. With a mournful screech, he lost his grip and fell toward the ground below.

And gave another startled screech as Kersh lunged forward, darting one hand downward and snatching the other's bony wrist.

The gnome gave another screech. "Don't drop me," he pleaded in a gravelly voice. "Please. Don't drop me."

"Who are you?" Kersh demanded. "Why are you trying to destroy my bridge?"

"Please," the gnome pleaded. "I was only doing it for her. Just for her. She's dying—she needs this."

"What does she need?" Kersh bit out, feeling his arm muscles starting to tremble with fatigue. Gnomes weren't particularly heavy, but a gnome plus a barrel of explosives definitely was. And the long climb had burned through Kersh's reserves of strength. "To see my bridge destroyed?"

"No, not that," the gnome said. "Please pull me up—I'll explain everything."

"You'd better," Kersh warned. Clenching his teeth, he started to pull.

Only to discover to his horror that he couldn't. His strength—his massive, trollish strength—was gone. All of it. "You have to drop that barrel," he said. "Do it—there's no one below who'll get hurt."

"I can't," the gnome said. "It's looped around the arm you're holding. Please, just pull me up."

Kersh tried again, but it was no use. "I can't," he gritted. "You're too heavy."

"Don't drop me," the gnome pleaded. "Please."

"Don't worry," Kersh said. But the words were hollow . . . because if anyone had cause to worry, it was the gnome.

Because Kersh's own last chance now was to let the other fall to his death. Only then might he have enough strength to pull himself back up onto the safety of the bridge.

The gnome deserved to die, anyway. Hadn't he tried to destroy Kersh's bridge, and perhaps hundreds of humans along with it?

"Please," the gnome begged.

Kersh clenched his teeth, looking around desperately. But there was nothing. Nowhere for his feet to get a purchase; no one and nothing that could help them. The shallows of the river rippled along far below, the water glittering tantalizingly in the city lights.

But Kersh knew the water's promise was an empty one. The depth they would need to survive a fall of this distance was much too far away for him to reach.

The trembling in his muscles was getting worse. Another few minutes and his grip would give way. This was, he knew, his very last chance to save himself.

And then, over the rippling water, he heard a voice.

It was an ethereal voice, a haunting voice, rich with the lure of things bright and wonderful as it sang a wordless song of invitation and love. The music filled Kersh's ears, banishing his anger and even his fear.

He closed his eyes, savoring the music like he'd never savored anything before. The agony in his arms, the danger to his bridge, even his own imminent death—none of it mattered anymore. All that mattered was the song.

The song, and a sudden overwhelming desire to seek out the singer. To hear the music up close, the way it was meant to be heard.

The thought wasn't even fully formed in his mind when he suddenly found himself swinging by his arm from the bridge, drawing on deep sources of strength he hadn't even known he had. Higher and higher he swung, back and forth, ignoring the pain in his arms and the little bleatings of the gnome still hanging below him. The song was calling to him, rising on the wind, stretching out to his heart as it beckoned him to the deep, open water.

The song reached its climax; and as Kersh reached the top of his arc, he shoved himself off the bridge with his last ounce of strength, hurling himself and the gnome in a long, high arc toward the river. The wind whistled past, chilling his sweat-soaked face and arms as the two of them fell toward the dark river below—

They hit with a tremendous splash, and as the water closed over Kersh he braced himself for the bone-breaking impact that would come as he slammed into the riverbed.

But he didn't. His momentum eased, and then stopped, still with only water beneath his feet. That last powerful push had somehow sent them flying far enough outward to reach the safety of deep water. Kicking with his feet, digging into the water with his free hand, he started to claw his way toward the surface far above.

And then, a hand appeared from nowhere, grabbing onto the back of his collar. A second later, he found himself being pulled upward far faster than he could have managed even with both hands free. The weight of the gnome he was still gripping suddenly eased, and he realized that the little creature had finally been able to rid himself of his deadly burden. The water above Kersh grew lighter . . .

With another violent splash, his head broke through the surface. Gasping for breath, he let go of the gnome's arm and stretched out both hands to keep himself afloat. He spotted the gnome a few feet away, his thin face and large eyes showing a fading panic as he also gulped in great lungfuls of air. Holding him tightly, keeping his face well above the water, was a young woman.

Or rather, something that looked like a young woman. "Thank you for not dropping him," she said quietly to Kersh.

"Thank you for saving our lives," Kersh replied. "You're a siren?"

She nodded, and Kersh could see now that the eyes in that young face looked old. Old, and tired, and sad. "What happens now?" she asked.

Kersh took a couple of deep breaths. With her song no longer filling his mind, his arms suddenly felt like lead weights. "You can start by helping us back to shore," he said. "And then," he added, eyeing her as sternly as he could manage under the circumstances, "we need to talk."

"You have to understand," Grizzal said, his voice pleading, his thin gnome body shivering in the chilly night air. "Without purpose to her life, Serina was wasting away. Dying. I'd tried everything else. This was the only other thing I could think of."

"What, destroying my bridge?" Kersh countered.

"She needed to see people plunging into the water around her," Grizzal said, clutching the hand of the ancient-eyed woman sitting on the ground beside him. "I know it wouldn't have been the same as if she'd sung them in. I know that. But I thought it might at least keep her alive until I could come up with something else."

"I told him not to," Serina said, her voice as tired as her eyes. "I know that my purpose is gone. That those who demanded such service from me are gone, as well."

"And it was an evil purpose besides," Kersh said.

"Robbing travelers who only wanted to cross a river in peace was any less evil?" Grizzal countered.

Kersh grimaced. "I know," he conceded. "But—"

"But it was your purpose," Serina said. "We are what we are."

"I never killed people, anyway," Kersh muttered. But he could nevertheless felt some sympathy for this creature of the old world, trapped hopelessly and without purpose here in the new.

"The people I sang to didn't always die, either," Serina said. "I always kept singing after they went into the water, hoping the extra strength I could give them would let them reach the shore."

"It's not death she needs anyway," Grizzal insisted. "It's sailors coming to her song. That's all she wants. That's all she needs."

Kersh shook his head. "You should have picked a smaller bridge."

Grizzal clutched his thin knees with his arms. "Or picked one without a troll."

"We won't bother you again," Serina said quietly. "You, or your bridge. Thank you again for saving Grizzal."

She stood up, helping the still shivering gnome to his feet. Turning, they headed south along the river.

Kersh looked up at the span arching over his head, a sudden ache in his heart. *Your bridge*, she'd said. Only he had no bridge. Not anymore. In fact, at this point he would be lucky if there weren't already an arrest warrant out for him.

He looked back at the two figures walking slowly down the shoreline. "Hey!" he called, hauling himself to his feet.

They turned. "Yes?" Serina asked.

"This is ridiculous," Kersh declared as he joined them. "We've lived on this world for hundreds of years. We can't just give up. *You* can't just give up."

"You have an idea?" Grizzal asked hopefully.

"Not yet," Kersh admitted. "But we've got brains, and we've got experience."

"Right," Grizzal muttered.

"It'll be enough," Kersh said firmly.

"If it's not," Serina offered, "we also have a chest full of gold and gems."

Kersh blinked. "We do?"

"*We* do," Grizzal said, giving the siren a quick frown. "Gnomes guard treasures. You didn't know that?"

"Nope," Kersh assured him. "But that's great. It means we've got brains, experience, *and* money. So let's put our heads together and see what we can come up with."

The faint screams of a hundred children were drifting through the midmorning breezes when Kersh heard a soft, nearly-forgotten voice in his ear. "Greetings to you, Troll."

"And to you, Lord Albho," Kersh said, squinting out of the corner of his eye. The air sprite was even harder to see in the bright sunlight than he was at night, especially hovering against the bright colors of Kersh's new home. "I trust you and your people are well?"

"We are," Lord Albho said, and Kersh could hear the puzzlement in his voice. "What is this place? I have never seen its like."

"This is where I now live and work," Kersh told him. "My job with the other bridge came to an end."

"Yes, we noticed your absence," Lord Albho said. "We were mourning your passing until one of my people chanced upon you here." The faint figure started suddenly as distant music joined the children's screams. "That voice!" he breathed. "Is that a *siren*?"

"Indeed it is," Kersh confirmed. "She sings all day long, watching with immense satisfaction as lines of people come to her and then hurl themselves into the depths of the water."

"And *drown*?" Lord Albho asked, sounding shocked. "And you stand by and do nothing to stop it?"

"I not only don't stop it, I help her do it," Kersh said with a grin. "And, no, they don't actually drown. On the contrary, they enjoy the experience. Of course, she's not using anywhere near the full power of her song. That would probably cause trouble." He pointed up at the sign arching over them. "You see that sign? In the words of the humans, it says *Siren's Cove*."

"Yes, I see it," the sprite said, sounding more confused than ever. "Then they even know a siren is here?"

"Well, of course they don't know she's a *real* siren," Kersh said. "They just think it's a clever name for the newest section of the Crusoe Island amusement park."

Lord Albho flittered a little higher to look past Kersh's shoulder. "An *amusement* park?"

"That's right," Kersh said. "Our little corner of the park has three pools, two surf runs, a coral reef, and twelve of the best water slides in the business. And there's something about that song of Serina's that people say adds an extra touch of excitement to the experience."

"I see," Lord Albho murmured. "Very clever."

"Thank you," Kersh said modestly. "Actually the three of us came up with the idea together."

"The three of you?"

"Me, Serina, and Serina's husband Grizzal," Kersh said. "He handles maintenance on our pumps and filters. Turns out gnomes are really good at hauling gremlins out of machinery."

"So I've heard," Lord Albho said, his voice suddenly thoughtful. "So the humans slide downward inside those curved tubes?"

"That's right," Kersh said. "And you know, I'll bet drafting along behind them would be a really interesting experience."

"I was just thinking the same," the sprite said. "May I?"

"We would be honored by your presence," Kersh said. Around the curve of the entrance walkway, a pair of adults and two young boys appeared, each carrying a swim bag. "I have to go back to work now," he murmured. "But please come by later and tell me how it was."

"I will," the sprite promised, and flitted away.

Kersh drew himself up to his full height. "I am the troll of the bridge," he called in a deep voice. "Who approaches?"

The father nudged the older of the two sons. The boy looked up, a little anxiously, but reassured by his parents' smiles he turned back to Kersh and squared his shoulders. "I am Adam," he said, pitching his own voice as low as he could. "I seek to cross your bridge."

"Step forward, Adam," Kersh said. The parents, he saw, had brought plenty of cash. It would be a full, rich day for them all. "The toll for you and your companions is fifty-four dollars."

Solemnly, the boy handed over the money. "You have paid," Kersh intoned. "Cross in peace."

"Thank you, troll," the boy said solemnly. He glanced at his parents again, and then he and his brother dashed across the short arch of the decorative entryway bridge.

The parents followed, and as they passed the father winked at Kersh. "Nice makeup job," he murmured.

"Thank you, sir," Kersh said, bowing his head. "Have a wonderful visit."

He smiled as he watched the family head into the park. It would indeed be a full and rich day.

For them all.

CHEM LAB 301

"Hello, everyone," Gerald Kleindst called from his desk at the front of the room. "My name is Gerald Kleindst, and I'll be your teaching assistant for the semester. Welcome to Chem Lab 301."

It took the group of twenty students another few seconds to settle down: disentangling from final phone calls, punching up the proper course heading with their tap-tips, and ending their first-day conversations with their fellow classmates. But that was all right with Gerald. He'd been here for six years as he slogged his way toward his doctorate, had taught various chem labs for four of those years, and had found that those first few settling-down moments were often the best indicators as to how that particular class was going to go.

Because while it wasn't mentioned in the catalog, the chemistry professors and TAs knew full well that 301 was in fact the make-or-break class. This was where the students started getting their hands on the advanced equipment: the splicers, assemblers, fragmenters, and analyzers. This was where they would prove they could visualize how complex molecules went together, not just show their competence at slathering stuff from bottles into beakers and getting what the text said they should.

From all indications, this class looked to be a middle-roader. Possibly upper-middle. The students for the most part got themselves together quickly and were now facing him, ready to listen. Gerald hadn't checked their GPAs or other vitals—the administration frowned on such enquiries, especially this early in the semester when it might prejudice the instructor's attitude toward the students—but they all had the kind of attentive, eager expressions that said they were here to learn and not just fulfil some science-class requirement.

All except one. One of the young men near the center of the room was still gazing intently out the window. Gerald tapped up the class roster, keyed for the ID photos, and found the day-dreamer: Winston DeVries. "Mr. DeVries?" he called mildly.

With a start, Winston jerked his head back around. "Yes?"

"Just making sure you were with us," Gerald said. "Once again, welcome to Chem Lab 301. As you may know, this is the class where you'll finally leave the Middle Ages of science, with the same test tubes and bottled powders you probably had in your Junior Chemistry Sets when you were nine years old. This is where you'll enter the mid-twenty-first century and real, cutting-edge science. By the time Professor Ross and I are finished with you, you'll be designing and creating chemicals from scratch for specific, targeted purposes. You'll have had experience with the Flixdane Molecule Slicer—" he pointed to one of the machines lined up along the side wall "—the Champion Resonant Spin Analyzer, and—" he lifted the pointing finger in a cautionary gesture "—if you *really* impress me, I may even let you use my personal favorite—" he leveled the finger again "—the Sakuta NanoSembler. *The* machine of choice for building new worlds from individual atoms." He glanced around the room, noting that the students seemed suitably and properly impressed.

As well they should be. NanoSemblers were normally reserved for senior- and graduate-level labs, and it was only through the grace and cash of some anonymous alumnus that the 301 labs had been equipped with them at all. It was an opportunity most college juniors never had a shot at.

Though not everyone seemed to appreciate that. Winston was once again looking toward the side of the room—surreptitiously, but still looking. Frowning, Gerald flicked a glance that direction, wondering what on the quad was so fascinating today.

Only then did he realize that Winston wasn't looking out the window at all. He was gazing moon-eyed toward the young woman in seat Five-Two.

To be honest, Gerald couldn't blame him. The woman was a beauty, with high cheekbones, raven-black hair, big eyes, and perfect lips, the kind of woman who one would normally expect to have gone into acting, modeling, or politics instead of chemistry.

She was going to be a distraction, Gerald knew. And not just to the students.

But he was the instructor, and he would make sure he acted professionally. And while these men and women were in his classroom, they would do likewise.

Fortunately, this particular semester he was going to have an unusual and, for the students, unexpected diversion to help keep the focus on their classwork.

"And as an added bonus," he continued, surreptitiously tapping his fingers to pull up the woman's name, "we're going to have an unofficial observer who'll be vetting both the class and your performance." Putting his tongue to his upper teeth, he blew a short whistle.

And from the back of the room, where she'd been lying unseen under one of the tables, came Rosie.

She was an impressive sight: seventy-five pounds of the sleek coat, panting tongue, and wagging tail of a perfect chocolate Labrador retriever. Personally, Gerald had always preferred the black variety, but the chocolate was his second favorite. "This is Rosie," he announced as she trotted up to the desk and sat down on her haunches. Sherrie Nolan, he noted, and her ID picture didn't nearly do her justice. With a twinge of guilt he tapped back out of the roster. "She's a sniffer dog on loan from the Justice and Legal Studies Department. We're going to be helping her learn how to find and identify various chemicals and drugs."

A hand went up. "Does that mean we're going to be making illegal substances?" one of the men asked.

"Are you asking hopefully, or apprehensively?" Gerald countered.

"Neither," the student said hastily. "Just asking."

"Ah," Gerald said. "Well, either way, the answer is no. Justice and Legal Studies, remember? However, we *will* be dealing with some of the fragments and chemical markers all dangerous drugs and chemicals have in common. Smugglers sometimes bring in their contraband in fragments, planning to put the pieces back together with the aid of one of the NanoSembler's baby brothers. We'll be helping Rosie learn how to spot those fragments."

He tapped up the first page of the class curriculum. "And since she may start chewing the furniture if she gets bored," he added, "let's head back to the tables and get ready to do some *science*."

. . .

The class, as Gerald had tentatively concluded on that first day, turned out indeed to be one of the middle-road ones.

Most of the students were competent, though not brilliant. A couple were near-brilliant, and there were a couple of slightly-laggard ones in the mix to balance them out. All in all, it made for a very credible Gaussian curve in his gradetext.

Sherrie turned out to be not as much of a distraction as he'd feared. None of the males in the class was ever quite able to forget she was there, but she'd clearly learned a few tricks over the years for making it clear, in a nice and non-down-putting way, that she was there for the class work and the class work only. Most of the men figured it out within the first two weeks and accepted it with varying degrees of grace or regret.

All except Winston. His eyes simply wouldn't let the woman go, whether she was sitting at her desk during the instruction and recap sessions, or bent over her lab table juggling beakers and burners.

He was also one of the laggards, and Gerald had to wonder how much of that relative slowness was the unalterable limitations of talent and ability and how much was the perfectly alterable limitation of unfocused attention.

Still, whenever he judged Winston's eyes and mind had lingered too long, he could always send in Rosie.

Everyone in the class loved her. Even those who'd clearly had reservations about having her underfoot quickly became comfortable with the arrangement. It even added an extra layer to the friendly competition, as each lab pair tried to be first to create that session's chemical mix and earn themselves Rosie's first bark of approval.

It got to be so normal, in fact, that the one day Gerald accidentally gave Rosie the wrong sample to sniff, resulting in a class with no approving barks at all, an outside observer would have thought everyone's favorite uncle had just died. The relief in the room when he discovered and owned up to his error had been palpable, but he'd had to send Rosie to each table for a sniff and bark in order to fully restore the class's spirits.

She had become a part of the class. It wasn't until the day before Winter Break, though, that Gerald found out just how vital a part she was.

. . .

The lab session was over, the see-you-in-Januarys had been said, and the last students had trickled out. Gerald sat at his desk, tapping up the last comments and keeping half an eye on the clock. If he hurried, he might still be able to miss some of the mad rush as the campus turned itself inside out and scattered students and professors alike all across the Eastern Seaboard and beyond.

He'd finished the last report and was checking the grammar and format when he suddenly noticed that Rosie was across the room, sitting on her haunches and staring up at the NanoSembler. "Rosie?" he called.

There was no response. Frowning, Gerald got up and walked over to her.

Only then did he spot the softly-glowing indicator lights on the NanoSembler's control panel.

"What the hell?" he muttered under his breath. He'd demonstrated the machine for the class two weeks ago, just to show them a little of what it could do. But he'd been careful to shut it off, and no one else in the class was DNA-coded to the device.

Or were they?

He hurried back to his desk as a sudden horrible thought struck him. The only way this could happen was if two errors happened to line up just right . . .

They did. The TA who'd had this room and class last semester had failed to properly clear his students' access codes.

And Winston DeVries had taken, and failed, that same class.

Winston was able to access the NanoSembler, and even having failed 301 once had probably learned enough to know how to operate the machine.

The question was, what exactly had he used it to create?

Clearly, Gerald's first call needed to be to Campus Security. He grabbed his phone, keyed it on—

And hesitated. He had no proof that Winston had done anything wrong. For that matter, he had no proof that the young man had done anything more than simply turn on the machine.

Actually, he couldn't even prove *that*.

Winston had already failed a mid-level class. Calling Security down on him would add a second black mark to his record.

Gerald couldn't do that to the kid. Not unless it was really justified.

The NanoSembler had an activity log, of course. But given the machine's primary function of creating patentable chemicals, that log came from the factory heavily protected, seriously encrypted, and wrapped in a double layer of legal thorn hedges. Getting a clear readout could take weeks.

Gerald couldn't afford to wait that long. If Winston had created something dangerous or illegal he needed to be stopped before he could use it, and only Security could find him in time.

Security . . . or maybe Rosie.

She was still sitting by the NanoSembler. "Rosie, come," Gerald ordered, going over to the desk where Winston had been sitting half an hour ago. It was a long shot, but Rosie should be capable of what he had in mind. "Winston DeVries," he said, pointing to the chair. "Come on—Winston DeVries."

For a moment those big brown eyes just gazed at him. Then, leaning forward, she gave the chair a sniff. "Got it?" Gerald asked. "Good. Let's go find him."

A minute later they were out in the cold afternoon air.

Gerald kept his hands jammed into his pockets as he walked, wishing he'd brought his heavier coat this morning. Of course, he hadn't known when he left his apartment that he would be going anywhere except the short walk between his car and the chem building.

At least there wasn't any snow on the ground. He had no idea how Rosie would have handled that, or if human scent even stuck to ice crystals.

As it was, she seemed to have no doubts at all about where she was going.

They had left the campus proper, crossing the busy boundary street into town, when he spotted Winston. He was in one of the neighborhood's most popular soup-and-sandwich diners, sitting at a two-person table one row back from the big front window.

And he wasn't alone. Sherrie Nolan was with him.

Gerald puzzled over that as he hurried across the last fifty yards separating him from the diner. As far as he'd noticed, there had never been sparks of any kind flying between Winston and Sherrie. Certainly no sparks had come from Sherrie's direction.

But on second, closer study he realized it wasn't what he'd first thought. Sherrie's body language was completely proper, almost to the point of being prim, the posture of a woman just having a simple, Platonic drink or snack with a fellow classmate. If Winston thought his invitation was going to end differently, Gerald reflected, he was looking down the barrel of a big disappointment.

Having his chem lab TA crash the party wasn't going to make that final letdown any easier. But Gerald had no choice. He had to find out what the young man had been up to.

He was nearly to the diner, and was working out what exactly he was going to say, when Sherrie turned around in her seat to look at something over her shoulder.

And as Gerald watched, Winston reached over the table and surreptitiously sprinkled something into her soup bowl.

He nearly ran down the girl handing out menus at the reception station as he barreled his way into the diner, Rosie trotting along right behind him. He bumped past a couple of frat-type guys, nearly flattened an oblivious tap-texting girl, and reached the table just in time to flick Sherrie's spoon out of her fingers as she started to dip it into her chowder. "What in—?" she demanded, twisting around. "Oh—Mr. Kleindst. I didn't realize—"

"What was it?" Gerald snapped, glaring at Winston. "The stuff you put in her soup. What was it?"

Winston's face had gone white. "What are—I don't know what you're talking about," he managed.

"You got into the NanoSembler," Gerald said, distantly aware that the whole diner had gone suddenly quiet. "You made up something, and you just now put it in Sherrie's soup. What was it?"

In a tri-vi thriller, Gerald reflected bitterly, the villain either blurted out a confession or else made some desperate move that confirmed his guilt. Real life, unfortunately, didn't play by such easy rules. Winston had had a moment to collect himself, he'd done so, and he wasn't about to go down easily. "I have no idea what you're talking about," he insisted. "I picked up the salt—that's all. Anyway, how could I have fiddled with the NanoSembler? I'm not even coded for it."

"You had coding left over from last semester," Gerald said. But the moment had passed, and he knew it.

Worse, so did Winston. He might have been caught, but there was no way Gerald could prove anything. In fact, he couldn't even prove enough to get Security interested or a court order for the NanoSembler's log. Whatever Winston had done, whatever he'd created in Gerald's chem lab, he was going to get away with it.

Unless . . .

It was a long shot. A dangerous long shot. But it was all Gerald had left.

"Fine," he said between clenched teeth. "So there's nothing wrong with this soup?" Before Winston could answer, Gerald picked up the bowl—

And set it on the floor beside the table.

"Rosie?" he invited, gesturing to the bowl and mentally crossing his fingers. "Here. Eat."

Winston's eyes widened as Rosie dropped her head obediently to the bowl. "Wait a second," he protested. "You can't—"

"Eat," Gerald repeated.

And with a gurgling that sounded remarkably like the noise from a half-stopped drain, Rosie did.

Winston's face had recovered from the earlier shock of Gerald's unexpected entrance and accusation. Now, as he watched Rosie gobbling down Sherrie's soup, the process reversed, again draining his skin of color. Gerald watched in silence, noting out of the corner of his eye that Sherrie was doing the same.

A minute later, the slobbering sounds faded away. "Fine," Gerald said into the fresh silence. "Whatever you put in the soup is now inside a dog. A dog who, incidentally, weighs only half as much as Sherrie. We can all sit here and see what it does to her, or you can tell me—right now—whether I need to get her to the vet for emergency treatment. Which is it going to be?"

Winston was still staring at Rosie. He opened his mouth, but no words came out.

"Winston?" Sherrie said. To Gerald's surprise, there was no anger or outrage in her voice, but only softness and compassion. Compassion for Rosie, certainly, but also compassion for Winston.

Maybe it was her tone, and the implied forgiveness, that finally made the difference. Or maybe it was Winston's own compassion and fears for what he'd done to the beloved class pet. "GHB," he whispered, almost too softly for Gerald to hear. "Gamma-hydroxybutyric acid."

Gerald felt his stomach tighten. He should have guessed. Winston, mooning unrequitedly after the most beautiful, most desirable woman he'd probably ever known . . . "I see," he said. "In that case, I guess I'd better find a vet. Come on, Rosie."

He looked at Sherrie, watching as the compassion in her face turned to a quiet horror. She, too, knew what GHB was, and what had almost happened to her.

She also wasted no time with conversation or accusations. Even as Gerald and Rosie walked back out into the cold air she was already in her coat and heading at a fast walk for the exit. It was, Gerald knew, the last time she would ever have a friendly snack with Winston.

In fact, given the number of witnesses in the diner, it was possibly the last time any woman on campus would do so.

The NanoSembler had been designed to facilitate the building of disease-ending drugs, hunger-curing plant variants, and revolutionary fabrication materials.

Not so desperate and depraved college students could create their own supply of date-rape drugs.

Clem Chee's eyes stopped moving as the news article came to an end, and he shook his head as he tapped it away. "Whoa," he said. "That was *not* what I was expecting when I suggested this little trial."

"Well, that's science for you," Gerald said philosophically. "Was Galileo looking for new wonders in the heavens? Was Einstein trying to unify time and space?"

"Actually, yes, they were," Clem said dryly. "On the other hand, a lot of *your* field's discoveries came from trying to turn lead into gold."

"I suppose," Gerald said. "The point is that in science you should always expect the unexpected." He braced himself. "I just hope you're pleased enough at the results that you're willing to overlook whatever problems came from me making Rosie eat that soup."

"Oh, there weren't any problems," Clem said casually. "Actually, she was designed so that she could follow up olfactory data with taste samples. Eating is fine—I just haven't put the sensors in there yet."

"Oh, wonderful," Gerald growled. Two days of worrying, for nothing. "That would have been nice to know. I was afraid she would short out and collapse halfway to the door."

"Not at all," Clem said. "But after this, I'm definitely putting those sensors on the fast track."

"They could be useful," Gerald agreed. "So will you be changing her name?"

"What, from Rosie?" Clem asked. "No way. Besides, what would I change it to?"

"Rotsie, of course," Gerald said. "Robotic Olfactory *and Taste* Sensor and Integrator, Experimental."

"That only makes sense if I build her into a Rottweiler design," Clem pointed out. "Besides, the technical term for sense of taste is gustation. Rogsie? Ugh."

"I suppose you're right," Gerald said. "Anyway, congratulations. Chemical Labrador Model 301 was a resounding success."

He smiled. "I can hardly wait to see what you've got planned for Chem Lab 302."

PAWN'S GAMBIT

●

To: *Office of Director Rodau 248700, Alien Research Bureau, Clars*
From: *Office of Director Eftis 379214, Games Studies, Var-4*
Subject: *30th annual report, submitted 12 Tai 3829.*
Date: *4 Mras 3829*

Dear Rodau,

I know how you hate getting addenda after a report has been
processed, but I hope you will make an exception in this
case. Our most recently discovered race—the Humans—
was mentioned only briefly in our last annual report, but
I feel that the data we have since obtained is important
enough to bring to your attention right away.

The complete results are given in the enclosed film,
but the crux of the problem is a disturbing lack of consistency with standard patterns. In many ways they are
unsophisticated, even primitive; most of the subjects
reacted with terror and even hysteria when first brought
here via Transphere. And yet, unlike most primitives,
there is a mental and emotional resilience to the species
which frankly surprises me. Nearly all of them recovered
from their fear and went on to play the Stage-I game
against their fellows. And the imagination, skill, and sheer
aggressiveness used in the playing have been inordinately
high for such a young species, prompting more than one

off-the-record comparison between Humans and the Chanis. I suppose it's that, more than anything else, that made
me unwilling to let this data ride until our next report.
Confined as they are to their home planet, the Humans
are certainly no threat now; but if they prove to be even
a twelfth as dangerous as the Chanis they will need to be
dealt with swiftly.

Accordingly, I am asking permission to take the
extraordinary step of moving immediately to Phase
III (the complete proposal is attached to my report). I
know this is generally forbidden with non-spacing races,
but I feel it is vital that we test Humans against races of
established ability. Please give me a decision on this as
soon as possible.

Regards,
Eftis

To: *Office of Director Eftis 379214, Game Studies, Var-4*
From: *Office of Director Rodau 248700, A.R.B., Clars*
Subject: *Addendum to 30th annual report.*
Date: *34 Forma 3829*

Dear Eftis,

Thank you for your recent addenda. You were quite right to
bring these Humans to our attention; that is, after all, what
you're out there for.

I find myself, as do you, both interested and alarmed by
this race, and I agree totally with your proposal to initiate
Phase III. As usual, the authorization tapes will be a few
more weeks in coming, but—unofficially—I'm giving you
the go-ahead to start your preparations. I also agree with
your suggestion that a star-going race be pitted against your
Human: an Olyt or Fiwalic, perhaps. I see by your reports
that the Olyts are beginning to resent our testing, but don't
let that bother you; your results clearly show they are no
threat to us.

Do keep us informed, especially if you uncover more
evidence of Chani-like qualities in these aliens.

Sincerely,
Rodau

The glowing, impenetrable sphere of white mist that had surrounded
him for the last five minutes dissolved as suddenly as it had formed, and
Kelly McClain found himself in a room he had never seen in his life.

Slowly, carefully, he looked around him, heart pounding painfully
in his ears. He'd screamed most of the panic out of his system within
the first three minutes of his imprisonment, but he could feel the terror
welling up into his throat again. He forced it down as best he could. He
was clearly no longer in his office at the university's reactor lab, but losing his head wasn't going to get him back again.

He was sitting in a semicircular alcove facing into a small room, his
chair and about three-quarters of his desk having made the trip with
him. The room's walls, ceiling, and floor were made of a bronze-colored
metal and were devoid of any ornamentation. At the right and left ends
of the room he could see panels that looked like sliding doors.

There didn't seem to be a lot to be gained by sitting quietly and hoping everything out there would go away. His legs felt like they might
be ready to hold him up again, so he stood up and squeezed his way
through the six-inch gap between his desk and the alcove wall. The
desk, he noted, had been sheared smoothly, presumably by the white
mist or something in it. He went first to the panel in the right-hand
wall; but if it *was,* in fact, a door, he could find no way to open it. The
left-hand panel yielded identical results. "Hello?" he called tentatively
into the air around him. "Can anyone hear me?"

The flat voice came back at him so suddenly it made him jump.
"Good day to you, Human," it said. "Welcome to the Stryfkar Game
Studies Center on Var-4. I trust you suffered no ill effects from your
journey?"

A *game* studies center?

Memories flashed across Kelly's mind, bits of articles he'd seen in
various magazines and tabloids over the past few months telling of people kidnapped to a game center by extraterrestrial beings. He'd skimmed
some of them for amusement, and had noted the similarity between the

stories; humans taken two at a time and made to play a strange board game against one another before being sent home. Typical tabloid tripe, Kelly had thought at the time.

Which made this an elaborate practical joke, obviously.

So how had they made that white mist?

For the moment, it seemed best to play along. "Oh, the trip was fine. A little boring, though."

"You have adjusted to your situation very quickly," the voice said, and Kelly thought he could detect a touch of surprise in it. "My name is Slaich; what is yours?"

"Kelly McClain. You speak English pretty well for an alien—what kind are you, again?"

"I am a Stryf. Our computer-translator is very efficient, and we have had data from several of your fellow Humans."

"Yes, I've heard about them. How come you drag them all the way out here—wherever *here* is—just to play games? Or is it a state secret?"

"Not really. We wish to learn about your race. Games are one of the psychological tools we use."

"Why can't you just talk to us? Or, better still, why not drop in for a visit?" Much as he still wanted to believe this was a practical joke, Kelly was finding that theory harder and harder to support. That voice—like no computer speech he'd ever heard, but nothing like a human voice, either—had an uncomfortable ring of casual truth to it. He could feel sweat gathering on his forehead.

"Talking is inefficient for the factors we wish to study," Slaich explained offhandedly. "As to visiting Earth, the Transphere has only limited capacity and we have no long-range ships at our disposal. I would not like to go to Earth alone."

"Why not?" The tension had risen within Kelly to the breaking point, generating a reckless courage. "You can't look *that* bad. Show yourself to me—*right now*."

There was no hesitation. "Very well, the voice said, and a section of the shiny wall in front of Kelly faded to black. Abruptly, a three-dimensional image appeared in front of it—an image of a two-legged, two-armed nightmare. Kelly gasped, head spinning, as the misshapen head turned to face him. An x-shaped opening began to move. "What do you think, Kelly? Would I pass as a Human?"

"I—I—I—" Kelly was stuttering, but he couldn't help it; all his strength was going to control his suddenly rebellious stomach. The creature before him was *real*—no make-up job in the world could turn a man into *that*. And multicolor hologram movies of such size and clarity were years or decades away . . . on Earth.

"I am sorry; I seem to have startled you," Slaich said, reaching for a small control panel Kelly hadn't noticed. The muscles moved visibly under his six-fingered hand as he touched a button. The image vanished and the wall regained its color. "Perhaps you would like to rest and eat," the flat voice went on. The door at Kelly's left slid open, revealing a furnished room about the size of an efficiency apartment. "It will be several hours before we will be ready to begin. You will be called."

Kelly nodded, not trusting his voice, and walked into the room. The door closed behind him. A normal-looking bed sat next to the wall halfway across the room, and Kelly managed to get there before his knees gave out.

He lay face-downward for a long time, his whole body trembling as he cried silently into his pillow. The emotional outburst was embarrassing—he'd always tried to be the strong, unflappable type—but efforts to choke off the display only made it worse. Eventually, he gave up and let it run its course.

By and by, the sobs stopped coming and he found himself more or less rational once more. Rolling onto his side, unconsciously curling into a fetal position, he stared at the bronze wall and tried to think.

For the moment, at least, he seemed to be in no immediate physical danger. From what he remembered of the tabloid articles, the aliens here seemed truly intent on simply doing their psychological study and then sending the participants home. Everything they'd done so far could certainly be seen in that light; no doubt they had monitored his reactions to both their words and Slaich's abrupt appearance. He shuddered at the memory of that alien face, feeling a touch of anger. Psychological test or not, he wasn't going to forgive Slaich very quickly for not giving him some kind of warning before showing himself like that.

The important thing, then, was for him to stay calm and be a good little test subject so he could get home with a minimum of trouble. And if he could do it with a little dignity, so much the better.

He didn't realize he'd dozed off until a soft tone startled him awake. "Yes?"

"It is time," the computerized voice told him. "Please leave your rest chamber and proceed to the test chamber."

Kelly sat up, glancing around him. The room's only door was the one he'd entered by; the test chamber must be out the other door of the room with the alcove. "Where's the other player from?" he asked, swinging his feet onto the floor and heading for the exit. "Or do you just snatch people from Earth at random?"

"We generally set the Transphere to take from the vicinity of concentrated energy sources, preferably fission or fusion reactors when such exist," Slaich said. "However, you have made one false assumption. Your opponent is not a Human."

Kelly's feet froze halfway through the door, and he had to grab the jamb to keep his balance. This was a new twist. "I see. Thanks for the warning, anyway. Uh . . . what *is* he?"

"An Olyt. His race is somewhat more advanced than yours; the Olyts have already built an empire of eight planets in seven stellar systems. They have been studied extensively by us, though their closest world is nearly thirty light-years from here."

Kelly forced his legs to start walking again. "Does that make us neighbors? You never said how far Earth is from here."

"You are approximately forty-eight light-years from here and thirty-six from the Olyt home world. Not very far, as distances go."

The door on the far side of the room opened as Kelly approached. Getting a firm grip on his nerves, he stepped through.

The game room was small and relatively dark, the only illumination coming from a set of dimly glowing red panels. In the center of the room, and taking up a good deal of its floor space, was a complex-looking gameboard on a table. Two chairs—one strangely contoured—completed the furnishings. Across the room was another door, and standing in front of it was an alien.

Kelly was better prepared for the shock this time, and as he stepped toward the table he found his predominant feeling was curiosity. The Olyt was half a head shorter than he, his slender body covered by what looked like large white scales. He was bipedal with two arms, each of his limbs ending in four clawed digits. His snout was long and seemed to have lots of teeth; his eyes were black and set back in a bettle-browed skull. Picture a tailless albino alligator wearing a wide sporran, Sam Browne belt, and a beret. . . .

Kelly and the Olyt reached their respective sides of the game table at about the same time. The board was smaller than it had first looked; the alien was little more than a double arm-length away. Carefully, Kelly raised his open hand, hoping the gesture would be properly interpreted. "Hello. I'm Kelly McClain; human."

The alien didn't flinch or dive down Kelly's throat. He extended both arms, crossed at the wrists, and Kelly discovered the claws were retractable. His mouth moved, generating strange noises; seconds later the computer's translation came over an invisible speaker. "I greet you. I am Tlaymasy of the Olyt race."

"Please sit down," Slaich's disembodied voice instructed. "You may begin when you have decided on the rules."

Kelly blinked. "How's that?"

"This game has no fixed rules. You must decide between you as to the objective and method of play before you begin."

Tlaymasy was speaking again. "What is the purpose of this?"

"The purpose is to study an interaction between Olyt and Human," Slaich said. "Surely you have heard of this experiment from others of your race."

Kelly frowned across the table. "You've been through this before?"

"Over one hundred twenty-eight members of my race have been temporarily taken over the last sixteen years," the Olyt said. Kelly wished he could read the alien's expression. The computer's tone was neutral, but the words themselves sounded a little resentful. "Some have spoken of this game with no rules. However, my question referred to the stakes."

"Oh. They are as usual for this study: the winner is allowed to return home."

Kelly's heart skipped a beat. "*Wait* a minute. Where did *that* rule come from?"

"The rules and stakes are chosen by us," Slaich said flatly.

"Yes, but . . . What happens to the loser?"

"He remains to play against a new opponent."

"What if I refuse to play at all?"

"That is equivalent to losing."

Kelly snorted, but there wasn't much he could do about it. *With dignity,* he thought dryly, and began to study the game board.

It looked like it had been designed to handle at least a dozen widely differing games. It was square, with two five-color bands of squares running along its edge; one with a repeating pattern, the other apparently random. Inside this was a checkerboard-type design with sets of concentric circles and radial lines superimposed on it. To one side of the board itself sat a stack of transparent plates, similarly marked, and a set of supporting legs for them; to the other side were various sizes, shapes, and colors of playing pieces, plus cards, multisided dice, and a gadget with a small display screen. "Looks like we're well equipped," he remarked to the Olyt, who seemed also to be studying their equipment. "I guess we could start by choosing which set of spaces to use. I suggest the red and—is that color blue?—the square ones. He indicated the checkerboard.

"Very well," Tlaymasy said. "Now we must decide on a game. Are you familiar with *Four-Ply*?"

"I doubt it, but my people may have something similar. Describe the rules."

Tlaymasy proceeded to do so. It sounded a little like go, but with the added feature of limited mobility for the pieces once on the board. "Sounds like something I'd have a shot at," Kelly said after the alien had demonstrated some of the moves with a butterfly-shaped playing piece. "Of course, you've got a big advantage, since you've played it before. I'll go along on two conditions: first, that a third-level or fourth-level attack must be announced one move before the attack is actually launched."

"That eliminates the possibility of surprise attacks," Tlaymasy objected.

"Exactly. Come on, now, you know the game well enough to let me have that, don't you?"

"Very well. Your second condition?"

"That we play a practice game first. In other words, the *second* game we play will determine who gets to go home. Is that permissible?" he added, looking up at one of the room's corners.

"Whatever is decided between you is binding," Slaich replied.

Kelly cocked an eyebrow at his opponent. "Tlaymasy?"

"Very well. Let us begin."

It wasn't such a hard game to learn, Kelly decided, though he got off to a bad start and spent most of their practice game on the defensive. The strategy Tlaymasy was using was not hard to pick up, and by the time they finished he found he could often anticipate the Olyt's next move.

"An interesting game," Kelly commented as they retrieved their playing pieces from the board and prepared to play again. "Is it popular on your world?"

"Somewhat. The ancients used it for training in logic. Are you ready to begin?"

"I guess so," Kelly said. His mouth felt dry.

This time Kelly avoided the errors he'd made at the beginning of the practice game, and as the board filled up with pieces he found himself in a position nearly as strong as Tlaymasy's. Hunching over the board, agonizing over each move, he fought to maintain his strength.

And then Tlaymasy made a major mistake, exposing an arm of his force to a twin attack. Kelly pounced, and when the dust of the next four moves settled he had taken six of his opponent's pieces—a devastating blow.

A sudden, loud hiss made Kelly jump. He looked up, triumphant grin vanishing. The Olyt was staring at him, mouth open just enough to show rows of sharp teeth. Both hands were on the table, and Kelly could see the claws sliding in and out of their sheaths. "Uh . . . anything wrong?" he asked cautiously, muscles tensing for emergency action.

For a moment there was silence. Then Tlaymasy closed his mouth and his claws retracted completely. "I was upset by the stupidity of my play. It has passed. Let us continue."

Kelly nodded and returned his gaze to the board, but in a far more subdued state of mind. In the heat of the game, he had almost forgotten he was playing for a ticket home. Now, suddenly, it looked as if he might be playing for his life as well. Tlaymasy's outburst had carried a not-so-subtle message: the Olyt did not intend to accept defeat graciously.

The play continued. Kelly did the best he could, but his concentration was shot all to hell. Within ten moves Tlaymasy had made up his earlier loss. Kelly sneaked glances at the alien as they played, wondering if that had been Tlaymasy's plan all along. Surely he wouldn't physically attack Kelly while he himself was a prisoner on an unknown world . . . would he? Suppose, for example, that honor was more important to him than even his own life, and that honor precluded losing to an alien?

A trickle of sweat ran down the middle of Kelly's back. He had no evidence that Tlaymasy thought that way . . . but on the other hand he couldn't come up with any reasons why it shouldn't be possible. And that reaction had looked *very* unfriendly.

The decision was not difficult. Discretion being the better part and all that—and a few extra days here wouldn't hurt him. Deliberately, he launched a bold assault against Tlaymasy's forces, an attack which would require dumb luck to succeed.

Dumb luck, as usual, wasn't with him. Seven moves later, Tlaymasy had won.

"The game is over," Slaich's voice boomed. "Tlaymasy, return to your Transphere chamber and prepare to leave. Kelly McClain, return to your rest chamber."

The Olyt stood and again gave Kelly his crossed-wrists salute before turning and disappearing through his sliding door. Kelly sighed with relief and emotional fatigue and headed back toward his room. "You played well for a learner," Slaich's voice followed him.

"Thanks," Kelly grunted. Now, with Tlaymasy's teeth and claws no longer a few feet in front of him, he was starting to wonder if maybe he shouldn't have thrown the game. "When do I play next?"

"In approximately twenty hours. The Transphere must be reset after the Olyt is returned to his world."

Kelly had been about to step into his rest chamber. "Twenty hours?" he echoed, stopping. "Just a second." He turned toward the alcove where his desk was sitting—but had barely taken two steps when a flash of red light burst in front of him. "Hey! he yelped, jumping backwards as heat from the blast washed over him. "What was *that* for?"

"You may not approach the Transphere apparatus." Slaich's voice had abruptly taken on a whiplash bite.

"Nuts! If I'm being left to twiddle my thumbs for a day I want the books that are in my desk."

There was a momentary silence, and when Slaich spoke again his tone had moderated. "I see. I suppose that is all right. You may proceed."

Kelly snorted and walked forward warily. No more bursts of light came. Squeezing around to the front of his desk, he opened the bottom drawer and extracted three paperbacks, normally kept there for idle moments. From another drawer came a half-dozen journals that he'd been meaning to read; and finally, as an afterthought, he scooped up a couple of pens and a yellow legal pad. Stepping back to the center of the room, he held out his booty. "See? Perfectly harmless. Not a single neutron bomb in the lot."

"Return to your rest chamber." Slaich did not sound amused.

With the concentration needed during the game, Kelly had temporarily forgotten he'd missed both lunch and dinner. Now, though, his growling stomach was demanding attention. Following Slaich's instructions, he requested and obtained a meal from the automat-type slots in one wall of his cubicle. The food was bland but comfortably filling, and Kelly felt his spirits rising as he ate. Afterwards, he chose one of his paperbacks and stretched out on the bed. But instead of immediately beginning to read, he stared at the ceiling and thought.

Obviously, there could be no further question that what was happening to him was real. Similarly, there was no reasonable hope that he could escape his captors. There were no apparent exits from the small complex of rooms except via the Transphere, whose machinery was hidden behind metal walls and was probably incomprehensible anyway. He had only Slaich's word that the Stryfkar intended to send him home, but since they apparently had made—and kept—similar promises to other humans, he had no real reason to doubt them. True, the game rules this time seemed to be different, but Tlaymasy had implied the Stryfkar had pulled this on several of his own race and had released them on schedule. So the big question, then, was whether or not Kelly could win the next game he would have to play.

He frowned. He'd never been any great shakes as a games player, winning frequently at chess but only occasionally at the other games in his limited repertoire. And yet, he'd come surprisingly close today to beating an alien in his own game. An alien, be it noted, whose race held an empire of eight worlds. The near-victory could be meaningless, of course—Tlaymasy might have been the equivalent of a fourth-grader playing chess, for instance. But the Olyt would have had to be a complete idiot to suggest a game he wasn't good at. And there was also Slaich's reaction after the game; it was pretty clear the Stryf hadn't expected Kelly to do that well. Did that mean that Kelly, average strategist that he was, was still better than the run-of-the-mill alien?

If that was true, his problems were essentially over. Whoever his next opponent was, it should be relatively easy to beat him, especially if they picked a game neither player had had much experience with. Four-Ply might be a good choice if the new tester wasn't another Olyt; the game was an interesting one and easy enough to learn, at least superficially. As a matter of fact, it might be worth his while to try marketing it when he got home. The game market was booming these days, and while Four-Ply wasn't likely to make him rich, it could conceivably bring in a little pocket change.

On the other hand . . . what was his hurry?

Kelly squirmed slightly on the bed as a rather audacious idea struck him. If he really *was* better than most other aliens, then it followed that he could go home most any time he wanted, simply by winning whichever game he was on at the moment. And if *that* were true, why not stick around for another week or so and learn a few more alien games?

The more he thought about it, the more he liked the idea. True, there was an element of risk involved, but that was true of any money-making scheme. And it couldn't be *that* risky—this was a *psychology* experiment, for crying out loud! "Slaich?" he called at the metallic ceiling.

"Yes?"

"If I lose my next game, what happens?"

"You will remain here until you have won or until the test is over."

So it didn't sound like he got punished or anything if he kept losing. The Stryfkar had set up a pretty simple-minded experiment here, to his way or thinking. Human psychologists would probably have put together something more complicated. Did that imply humans were better strategists than even the Stryfkar?

An interesting question, but for the moment Kelly didn't care. He'd found a tiny bit of maneuvering space in the controlled environment they'd set up, and it felt very satisfying. Rules like these, in his book, were made to be bent.

And speaking of rules . . . Putting aside his paperback, Kelly rolled off the bed and went over to the cubicle's folding table. Business before pleasure, he told himself firmly. Picking up a pen and his legal pad, he began to sketch the Four-Ply playing board and to list the game's rules.

To: *Office of Director Rodau 248700, A.R.B., Clars*
From: *Office of Director Eftis 379214, Game Studies, Var-4*
Subject: *Studies of Humans*
Date: *3 Lysmo 3829*

Dear Rodau,

The Human problem is taking on some frightening aspects, and we are increasingly convinced that we have stumbled upon another race of Chanis. Details will be transmitted when all analyses are complete, but I wanted to send you this note first to give you as much time as possible to recommend an assault force, should you deem this necessary.

As authorized, we initiated a Phase III study eight days ago. Our Human has played games against members of four races: an Olyt, a Fiwalic, a Spromsa, and a Thim-fra-chee. In each case the game agreed upon has been one from the non-Human player's world, with slight modifications suggested by the Human. As would be expected, the Human has consistently lost—but in each case he has clearly been winning until the last few moves. Our contact specialist, Slaich 898661, suggested early on that the Human might be *deliberately* losing; but with both his honor and his freedom at stake Slaich could offer no motive for such behavior. However, in a conversation of 1 Lysmo (tape enclosed) the Human freely confirmed our suspicions and indicated the motive was material gain. He is using the testing sessions to study his opponents' games, expecting to introduce them for profit on returning to his world.

I'm sure you will notice the similarities to Chani psychology: the desire for profit, even at the casual risk of his safety, and the implicit belief that his skills are adequate to bring release whenever he wishes. History shows us that, along with their basic tactical skills, it was just these characteristics that drove the Chanis in their most unlikely conquests. It must also be emphasized that the Human shows no signs of military or other tactical training and must therefore be considered representative of his race.

Unless further study uncovers flaws in their character which would preclude an eventual Chani-like expansion, I personally feel we must consider annihilation for this race as soon as possible. Since we obviously need to discover the race's full strategic capabilities—and since our subject refuses to cooperate—we are being forced to provide a stronger incentive. The results should be enlightening, and will be sent as soon as they are available.

Regards,
Eftis

The door slid back and Kelly stepped into the test chamber, looking across the room eagerly to see what sort of creature he'd be competing against this time. The dim red lights were back on in the room, indicating someone from a world with a red sun, and as Kelly's eyes adjusted to the relative darkness he saw another of the alligator-like Olyts approaching the table. "I greet you," Kelly said, making the crossed-wrist gesture he'd seen at his first game here. "I am Kelly McClain of the human race."

The Olyt repeated the salute. "I am *ulur* Achranae of the Olyt race."

"Pleased to meet you. What does *ulur* mean?"

"It is a title of respect for my position. I command a war-force of seven spacecraft."

Kelly swallowed. A trained military man. Good thing he wasn't in a hurry to win and go home. "Interesting. Well, shall we begin?"

Achranae sat down. "Let us make an end to this charade quickly."

"What do you mean, 'charade'?" Kelly asked cautiously as he took his seat. He was by no means an expert on Olyt expressions and emotions, but he could swear this one was angry.

"Do not deny your part," the alien snapped. "I recognize your name from the reports, and know how you played this game for the Stryfkar against another of my people, studying him like a laboratory specimen before allowing him to win and depart. We do not appreciate the way you take our people like this—"

"Whoa! Wait a second; I'm not with them. They've been taking *my* people, too. It's some sort of psychology experiment, I guess."

The Olyt glared at him in silence for a long moment. "If you truly believe that, you are a fool," he said at last, sounding calmer. "Very well; let us begin."

"Before you do so we must inform you of an important change in the rules," Slaich's voice cut in. "You shall play *three* different games, instead of one, agreeing on the rules before beginning each. The one who wins two or more shall be returned home. The other will lose his life."

It took a second for that to sink in. "*What*?" Kelly yelped. "You can't do that!" Across the table Achranae gave a soft, untranslatable hiss. His claws, fully extended, scratched lightly on the game board.

"It is done," Slaich said flatly. "You will proceed now."

Kelly shot a frustrated glance at Achranae, looked up again. "We will not play for our lives. That sort of thing is barbarous, and we are both civilized beings."

"Civilized." Slaich's voice was thick with sudden contempt. "You, who can barely send craft outside your own atmosphere; you consider yourself *civilized*? And your opponent is little better."

We govern a sphere fifteen light-years across," Achranae reminded Slaich calmly, his outburst of temper apparently over. For all their short fuses, Kelly decided, Olyts didn't seem to stay mad long.

"Your eight worlds are nothing against our forty."

"It is said the Chanis had only five when they challenged you."

The silence from the speaker was impressively ominous. "What are the Chanis?" Kelly asked, fighting the urge to whisper.

"It is rumored they were a numerically small but brutally aggressive race who nearly conquered the Stryfkar many generations ago. We have heard these stories from traders, but do not know how true they are."

"True or not, you sure hit a nerve," Kelly commented. "How about it, Slaich? Is he right?"

"You will proceed now," Slaich ordered, ignoring Kelly's question.

Kelly glanced at Achranae, wishing he could read the other's face. Did Olyts understand the art of bluffing? "I said we wouldn't play for our lives."

In answer a well-remembered flash of red light exploded inches from his face. Instinctively, he pushed hard on the table, toppling himself and his chair backwards. He hit hard enough to see stars, somersaulted out of the chair, and wound up lying on his stomach on the floor. Raising his head cautiously, he saw the red fireball wink out and, after a moment, got warily to his feet. Achranae, he noted, was also several feet back from the table, crouching in what Kelly decided was probably a fighting stance of some kind.

"If you do not play, both of you will lose your lives." Slaich's voice was mild, almost emotionless, but it sent a shiver down Kelly's spine. Achranae had been right: this was no simple psychology experiment. The Stryfkar were searching for potential enemies—and somehow both humans and Olyts had made it onto their list. And there was *still* no way to escape. Looking across at Achranae, Kelly shrugged helplessly. "Doesn't look like we have much choice, does it?"

The Olyt straightened up slowly. "For the moment, no."

"Since this contest is so important to both of us," Kelly said when they were seated again, "I suggest that you choose the first game, allowing me to offer changes that will take away some of your advantage— changes we both have to agree on, of course. I'll choose the second game; you'll suggest changes on that one."

"That seems honorable. And the third?"

"I don't know. Let's discuss that one when we get there, okay?"

It took nearly an hour for the first game, plus amendments, to be agreed upon. Achranae used three of the extra transparencies and their supports to create a three-dimensional playing area; the game itself was a sort of 3-D "Battleship," but with elements of chess, Monopoly, and even poker mixed in. Surprisingly enough, the mixture worked, and if the stakes hadn't been so high Kelly thought he would have enjoyed playing it. His own contributions to the rules were a slight adjustment to the shape of the playing region—which Kelly guessed would change the usual positional strategies—and the introduction of a "wild card" concept to the play. "I also suggest a practice game before we play for keeps," he told Achranae.

The Olyt's dark eyes bored into his. "Why?"

"Why not? I've never played this before, and you've never played with these rules. It would make the actual game fairer. More honorable. We'll do the same with the second and third games."

"Ah—it is a point of honor?" The alien cocked his head to the right. A nod? "Very well. Let us begin."

Even with the changes, the game—Skymarch, Achranae called it—was still very much an Olyt one, and Achranae won the practice game handily. Kelly strongly suspected Skymarch was a required course of the aliens' space academy; it looked too much like space warfare to be anything else.

"Did the Stryf speak the truth when he said you were not starfarers?" Achranae asked as they set up the board again.

"Hm? Oh, yes." Kelly replied distractedly, his mind on strategy for the coming game. "We've hardly even got simple spacecraft yet."

"Surprising, since you learn space warfare tactics so quickly." He waved his sheathed claws over the board. "A pity, too, since you will *not* be able to resist if the Stryfkar decide to destroy you."

"I suppose not, but why would they want to? We can't be any threat to them."

Again Achranae indicated the playing board. "If you are representative, your race is unusually gifted with both tactical skill and aggressiveness. Such abilities would make you valuable allies or dangerous adversaries to my starfaring race."

Kelly shrugged. "You'd think they'd try to recruit us, then."

"Unlikely. The Stryfkar are reputed to be a proud race who have little use for allies. This harassment of both our peoples should indicate their attitude toward other races."

The Olyt seemed to be on the verge of getting angry again, Kelly noted uneasily. A change in subject seemed in order. "Uh, yes. Shall we begin our game?"

Achranae let out a long hiss. "Very well."

From the very beginning it was no contest. Kelly did his best, but it was clear that the Olyt was able to *think* three-dimensionally better than he could. Several times he lost a piece simply because he missed some perfectly obvious move it could have made. Sweating, he tried to make himself slow down, to spend more time on each move. But it did no good. Inexorably, Achranae tightened the noose; and, too quickly, it was all over.

Kelly leaned back in his chair, expelling a long breath. It was all right, he told himself—he had to expect to lose a game where the alien had all the advantages. The next game would be different, though; Kelly would be on his own turf, with *his* choice of weapons—

"Have you chosen the game we shall play next?" Achranae asked, interrupting Kelly's thoughts.

"Idle down, will you?" Kelly snapped, glaring at the alien. "Give me a minute to think."

It wasn't an easy question. Chess was far and away Kelly's best game, but Achranae had already showed himself a skilled strategist, at least with warfare-type games. That probably made chess a somewhat risky bet. Card games involved too much in the way of chance, for this second game Kelly needed as much advantage as he could get. Word games like Scrabble were obviously out. Checkers or Dots were too simple. Backgammon? That was a pretty nonmilitary game, but Kelly was a virtual novice at it himself. How about—

How about a *physical* game?

"Slaich? Could I get some extra equipment in here? I'd like a longer table, a couple of paddles, a sort of light, bouncy ball—"

"Games requiring specific physical talents are by their nature unfair for such a competition as this," Slaich said. "They are not permitted."

"I do not object," Achranae spoke up unexpectedly, and Kelly looked at him in surprise. "You stated we could choose the games and the rules, and it is Kelly McClain's choice this time."

"We are concerned with psychological studies," Slaich said. "We are not interested in the relative abilities of your joints and muscles. You will choose a game that can be played with the equipment provided."

"It is dishonorable—"

"No, it's okay, Achranae," Kelly interrupted, ashamed at himself for even suggesting such a thing. "Slaich is right; it would've been completely unfair. It was dishonorable for me to suggest it. Please accept my apology."

"You are blameless," the Olyt said. "The dishonor is in those who brought us here."

"Yes," Kelly agreed, glancing balefully at the ceiling. The point was well taken. Achranae wasn't Kelly's enemy; merely his opponent. The Stryfkar were the real enemy.

For all the good that knowledge did him.

He cleared his throat. "Okay, Achranae, I guess I'm ready. This game's called *chess. . . .*"

The Olyt picked up the rules and movements quickly, enough so that Kelly wondered if the aliens had a similar game on their own world. Fortunately, the knight's move seemed to be a new one on him, and Kelly hoped it would offset the other's tactical training. As his contribution, Achranae suggested the pawns be allowed to move backwards as well as forwards. Kelly agreed, and they settled into their practice game.

It was far harder than Kelly had expected. The "reversible pawn" rule caused him tremendous trouble, mainly because his logic center kept editing it out of his strategy. Within fifteen moves he'd lost both bishops and one of his precious knights, and Achranae's queen was breathing down his neck.

"An interesting game," the Olyt commented a few moves later, after Kelly had managed to get out from under a powerful attack. "Have you had training in its technique?"

"Not really," Kelly said, glad to take a breather. "I just play for enjoyment with my friends. Why?"

"The test of skill at a game is the ability to escape what appears to be certain defeat. By that criterion you have a great deal of skill."

Kelly shrugged. "Just native ability, I guess."

"Interesting. On my world such skills must be learned over a long period of time." Achranae indicated the board. "We have a game similar in some ways to this one; if I had not studied it I would have lost to you within a few moves."

"Yeah," Kelly muttered. He'd been pretty sure Achranae wasn't running on beginner's luck, but he'd sort of hoped he was wrong. "Let's get back to the game, huh?"

In the end Kelly won, but only because Achranae lost his queen to Kelly's remaining knight and Kelly managed to take advantage of the error without any major goofs of his own.

"Are you ready to begin the actual game?" Achranae asked when the board had been cleared.

Kelly nodded, feeling a tightness in his throat. This was for all the marbles. "I suppose so. Let's get it over with."

Using one of the multifaced dice they determined the Olyt would have the white pieces. Achranae opened with his king's pawn, and Kelly responded with something he dimly remembered being called a Sicilian defense. Both played cautiously and defensively; only two pawns were taken in the first twenty moves. Sweating even in the air-conditioned room, Kelly watched his opponent gradually bring his pieces into attacking positions as he himself set his defense as best he could.

When the assault came it was devastating in its slaughter. By the time the captures and recaptures were done, eight more pieces were gone . . . and Kelly was a rook down.

Brushing a strand of hair out of his eyes with a trembling hand, Kelly swallowed hard as he studied the board. Without a doubt, he was in trouble. Achranae controlled the center of the board now and his king was better defended than Kelly's. Worse yet, he seemed to have mastered the knights move, while Kelly was still having trouble with his pawns. And if the Olyt won this one . . .

"Are you distressed?"

Kelly started, looked up at his opponent. "Just a—" His voice cracked and he tried again. "Just nervous."

"Perhaps we should cease play for a time, until you are better able to concentrate," Achranae suggested.

The last thing Kelly wanted at the moment was the alien's charity. "I'm all right," he said irritably.

Achranae's eyes were unblinking. "In that case, I would like to take a few minutes of rest myself. Is this permissible?"

Kelly stared back as understanding slowly came. Clearly, Achranae didn't need a break; he was a game and a half toward going home. Besides which, Kelly *knew* what an upset Olyt looked like, and Achranae showed none of the symptoms. No, giving Kelly the chance to calm down could only benefit the human . . . and as he gazed at the alien's face, Kelly knew the Olyt was perfectly aware of that.

"Yes," Kelly said at last. "Let's take a break. How about returning in a half-hour or so?"

"Acceptable." Achranae stood and crossed his wrists. "I shall be ready whenever you also are."

The ceiling over Kelly's bed was perfectly flat, without even so much as a ripple to mar it. Nonetheless, it reflected images far more poorly than Kelly would have expected. He wondered about it, but not very hard. There were more important things to worry about.

Pulling his left arm from behind his head; he checked the time. Five more minutes and Slaich would sound the little bell that would call them back to the arena. Kelly sighed.

What was he going to *do*?

Strangely enough, the chess game was no longer his major concern. True, he was still in trouble there, but the rest period had done wonders for his composure, and he had already come up with two or three promising lines of attack. As long as he kept his wits around him, he had a fair chance of pulling a win out of his current position. And that was Kelly's real problem . . . because if he did, in fact, win, there, would have to be a third game. A game either he or Achranae would have to lose.

Kelly didn't want to die. He had lots of high-sounding reasons why he ought to stay alive—at least one of which, the fact that no one else on Earth knew of the threat lurking behind these "games," was actually valid—but the plain fact was that he simply didn't *want* to die. Whatever the third game was chosen to be, he knew he would play just as hard and as well as he possibly could.

And yet . . .

Kelly squirmed uncomfortably. Achranae didn't deserve to die, either. Not only was he also an unwilling participant in this crazy arena, but he had deliberately thrown away his best chance to win the contest. Perhaps it was less a spirit of fairness than one of obedience to a rigid code of honor that had kept him from capitalizing on his opponent's momentary panic; Kelly would probably never know one way or the other. But it really didn't matter. If Kelly went on to win the chess game he would owe his victory to Achranae.

The third game . . .

What would be the fairest way to do it? Invent a game together that neither had played before? That would pit Kelly's natural tactical abilities against Achranae's trained ones and would probably be pretty fair.

On the other hand, it would give the Stryfkar another chance to study them in action, and Kelly was in no mood to cooperate with his captors any more than necessary. Achranae, Kelly had already decided, seemed to feel the same way. He wondered fleetingly how long the Stryfkar had been snatching Achranae's people, and why they hadn't retaliated. Probably had no idea where this game studies center was, he decided; the Transphere's operations would, by design, be difficult to trace. But if he and Achranae didn't want to give the Stryfkar any more data, their only alternative was to make the rubber game one of pure chance, and Kelly rebelled against staking his life on the toss of a coin.

The tone, expected though it was, startled him. "It is time," Slaich's flat voice announced. "You will return to the test chamber."

Grimacing, Kelly got to his feet and headed for the door. Maybe Achranae would have some ideas.

"Are you better prepared to play now?" the Olyt asked when they again faced each other over the board.

"Yes," Kelly nodded. "Thanks for suggesting a break. I really *did* need it."

"I sensed that your honor did not permit you to make the request." The alien gestured at the board. "I believe it is your move."

Sure enough, now that his nerves were under control, Kelly began to chip away at Achranae's position, gradually making up his losses and taking the offensive once more. Gambling on the excessive value the Olyt seemed to place in his queen, Kelly laid a trap, with his own queen as the bait. Achranae bit . . . and five moves later Kelly had won.

"Excellent play," the Olyt said, with what Kelly took to be admiration. "I was completely unprepared for that attack. I was not wrong; you have an uncanny tactical ability. Your race will indeed be glorious starfarers someday."

"Assuming we ever get off our own world, of course," Kelly said as he cleared the board. "At the moment we're more like pawns ourselves in this game."

"You have each won once," Slaich spoke up. "It is time now to choose the rules for the final game."

Kelly swallowed and looked up to find Achranae looking back at him. "Any idea?" he asked.

"None that is useful. A game of chance would perhaps be fastest. Beyond that, I have not determined what my duty requires."

"What are the possibilities?"

"That I should survive in order to return to my people, or that I should not, to allow you that privilege."

"A pity we can't individually challenge the Stryfkar to duels," Kelly said wryly.

"That would be satisfying," Achranae agreed. "But I do not expect they would accept."

There was a long silence . . . and an idea popped into Kelly's mind, practically full-blown. A risky idea—one that could conceivably get them *both* killed. But it might just work . . . and otherwise one of them would certainly die. Gritting his teeth, Kelly took the plunge. "Achranae," he said carefully, "I believe I have a game we can play. Will you trust me enough to accept it *now,* before I explain the rules, and to play it without a practice game?"

The Olyt's snout quivered slightly as he stared across the table in silence. For a long moment the only sound Kelly could hear was his own heartbeat. Then, slowly, Achranae cocked his head to the right. "Very well. I believe you to be honorable. I will agree to your conditions."

"Slaich? You still holding to the rules you set up?" Kelly called.

"Of course."

"Okay." Kelly took a deep breath. "This game involves two rival kingdoms and a fire-breathing creature who harasses them both. Here's the creature's underground chamber." He placed a black marker on the playing board, then picked up three of the transparent plates and their supports and set them up. "The two kingdoms are called the Mountain Kingdom and the Land City. The Mountain Kingdom is bigger; here's its center and edge." He placed a large red marker on the top plate and added a ring of six smaller ones around it, two squares away. Moving the black marker slightly so that it was directly under one edge of the ring, he picked up a large yellow marker. "This is the Land City," he identified it, moving it slowly over the middle transparency as his eyes flickered over the board. Ten centimeters between levels, approximately; four per square . . . he put the yellow marker eight squares from the red one and four squares to one side. It wasn't perfect, but it was close and would have to do. "Finally, here are our forces." He scattered a dozen each red and yellow butterfly-shaped pieces in the space between the two kingdoms. "The conditions for victory are twofold: the creature must be dead, and there can be no forces from the opposing side threatening your kingdom. Okay?"

"Very well," Achranae said slowly, studying the board carefully.

Once again Kelly wished he had a better grasp of Olyt expressions. "How are combat results decided?"

"By the number of forces involved plus a throw of the die." Making up the rules as he went along, Kelly set up a system that allowed combat between any two of the three sides—and that would require nearly all of both kingdoms' forces combined to defeat the creature with any certainty. "Movement is two squares or one level per turn, and you can move all your forces each turn," he concluded. "Any questions?"

Achranae's eyes bored unblinkingly into his, as if trying to read Kelly's mind. "No. Which of us moves first?"

"I will, if you don't mind." Starting with the pieces closest to the Olyt's kingdom, Kelly began moving them away from the red marker and toward the black one. Achranae hesitated somewhat when it was his turn, but he followed Kelly's example in moving his forces downward. Two of them landed within striking range of some of Kelly's; but the human ignored them, continuing onward instead. Within a few more moves the yellow and red pieces had formed a single mass converging on the black marker.

The fire-breathing creature never had a chance.

"And now . . . ?" Achranae sat stiffly in his chair, his claws about halfway out of their sheaths. The creature had been eliminated on the Olyt's turn, making it Kelly's move . . . and Achranae's forces were still intermixed with the human's. A more vulnerable position was hard to imagine, and Achranae clearly knew it.

Kelly gave him a tight smile and leaned back in his seat. "Well, the creature's dead—and in their present positions none of your forces can threaten my kingdom. So I guess I've won."

There was a soft hiss from the other side of the table, and Achranae's claws slid all the way out. Kelly held his breath and tensed himself to leap. Surely Achranae was smart enough to see it . . . and, abruptly, the claws disappeared. "But my kingdom is *also* not threatened," the Olyt said. "Therefore I, too, have won."

"Really?" Kelly pretended great amazement. "I'll be darned. You're *right*. Congratulations." He looked at the ceiling. "Slaich? By a remarkable coincidence we've both won the third game, so I guess we both get to go home. Ready any time you are."

"No." The Stryf's flat voice was firm.

A golfball-sized lump rose into Kelly's throat. "Why not? You said anyone who won two games would be sent home. You set up that rule yourself?"

"Then the rule is changed. Only one of you can be allowed to leave. You will choose a new game."

Slaich's words seemed to hang in the air like a death sentence . . . and Kelly felt his fingernails digging into his palms. He really hadn't expected the aliens to let him twist their rules to his advantage—he already knew this was no game to them. But he'd still hoped . . . and now he had no choice but to gamble his last card. "I won't play any more games," he said bluntly. "I'm sick of being a pawn in this boogeyman hunt of yours. You can all just take a flying leap at yourselves."

"If you do not play you will lose by forfeit," Slaich reminded him.

"Big deal," Kelly snorted. "You're going to wipe out earth eventually anyway, aren't you? What the hell difference does it make where I die?"

There was a short pause. "Very well. You yourself have chosen. Achranae, return to your Transphere chamber."

Slowly, the alien rose to his feet. Kelly half expected him to speak up in protest, or to otherwise plead for the human's life. But he remained silent. For a moment he regarded Kelly through the transparent game boards, as Kelly held his breath. Then, still without a word, the alien crossed his wrists in salute and vanished behind the sliding door. "You will return to your rest chamber now," Slaich ordered.

Letting out his breath in a long sigh, Kelly stood up and disassembled the playing board, storing the pieces and plates away in their proper places. So it had indeed come down to a toss of a coin, he thought, suddenly very tired. The coin was in the air, and there was nothing to do now but wait . . . and hope that Achranae had understood.

To: *Office of Director Rodau 248700, A.R.B.: Clars*
From: *Office of Director Eftis 379214, Games Studies, Var-4*
Date: *21 Lysmo 3829*

XXXXX URGENT XXXXX

Dear Rodau,

It is even worse than we expected and I hereby make formal recommendation that the Humans be completely obliterated. The enclosed records should be studied carefully, particularly those concerning the third game that was played. By using his tactical skills to create a game he and his opponent could jointly win, the Human clearly demonstrated both the ability to cooperate with others, and also the rare trait of mercy. Although these characteristics gained him nothing in this particular instance—and, in fact, can be argued to have been liabilities—we cannot assume this will always be the case. The danger that their cooperative nature will lead the Humans into a successful alliance instead of betraying them to their destruction cannot be ignored. If the Chanis had been capable of building alliances they might well have never been stopped.

It is anticipated that a full psycho-physiological dissection of our Human subject will be necessary to facilitate the assault fleet's strategy. We request that the proper experts and equipment be sent as soon as they become available. Please do not delay overlong; I cannot guarantee our Human can be kept alive more than a year at the most.

Eftis

Kelly's first indication that the long wait had ended was a faint grinding sound transmitted through the metal walls of his rest chamber. It startled him from a deep sleep—but he hardly even had time to wonder about it before the room's door suddenly flashed white and collapsed outward. Instantly, there was a minor hurricane in the room, and Kelly's ears popped as the air pressure dropped drastically. But even as he tumbled off the bed three figures in long-snouted spacesuits fought their way in through the gale, and before he knew it he'd been stuffed in a giant ribbed balloon with a hissing tank at the bottom. "Kelly McClain?" a tinny, static-distorted voice came from a box by the air tank as the balloon inflated. "Are you safe?"

Kelly's ears popped again as his three rescuers tipped him onto his back and carried him carefully toward the ruined door. "I'm fine," he said toward the box. "Is that you, Achranae?"

It was almost fifteen seconds before the voice spoke again; clearly, the Olyt's translator wasn't as good as the Stryfkar's. "Yes. I am pleased you are still alive."

Kelly's grin was wide enough to hurt, and was probably even visible through his beard. "Me too. *Damn*, but I'm glad you got my message. I wasn't at all sure you'd caught it."

They were out in the Transphere chamber before the response came, and Kelly had a chance to look around. In the ceiling, stretching upwards through at least two stories' worth of rock, was a jagged hole. Moving purposefully through the chamber itself were a dozen more Olyts in the white, armor-like suits. "It was ingenious. I feared that I would not be allowed to leave, though, once I had seen the board."

"Me too—but it looks like we had nothing to worry about." Kelly grinned again—it was so good to talk to a friend again! "I'll lay you any odds that the Stryfkar haven't *yet* noticed what I did. It's the old can't-see-the-forest-for-the-trees problem; they'd seen that four-tiered board used for so many different games that it never occurred to them that you and I would automatically associate it with Skymarch, the only game we'd ever played on it. So while they took my kingdoms-and-dragon setup at face value, you were able to see the markers as a group of objects in space. I gambled that you'd realize they represented our home worlds and this one, and that you'd take note of the relative distances I'd laid out. I guess the gamble paid off."

Kelly was beneath the ceiling hole now, and a pair of dangling cables were being attached to his balloon's upper handholds. "We shall hope that winning such risks is characteristic of your race," Achranae said. "We have destroyed the Stryfkar base and have captured records that show a large force will soon be coming here. We have opened communication with your race, but they have not yet agreed to a tactical alliance. Perhaps your testimony will help persuade them. It is hoped that you, at least, will agree to aid us in our tactical planning."

The ropes pulled taut and Kelly began moving upward. "I'm almost certain we can find some extra help on Earth," Kelly told the Olyt grimly. "And as for me, it'll be a pleasure. The Stryfkar have a lot to learn about us pawns."

ABOUT THE AUTHOR

Timothy Zahn is a *New York Times* bestselling science fiction author of more than forty novels, as well as many novellas and short stories. Best known for his contributions to the expanded Star Wars universe of books, including the Thrawn trilogy, Zahn won a 1984 Hugo Award for his novella "Cascade Point." He also wrote the Cobra series, the Blackcollar series, the Quadrail series, and the young adult Dragonback series, whose first novel, *Dragon and Thief*, was an ALA Best Book for Young Adults. Zahn currently resides in Oregon with his family.

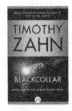
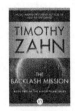

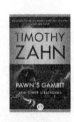

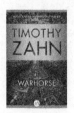

OPEN ROAD

INTEGRATED MEDIA

Open Road Integrated Media is a digital publisher and multimedia content company. Open Road creates connections between authors and their audiences by marketing its ebooks through a new proprietary online platform, which uses premium video content and social media.